THE SINEWS OF LOVE

Pei Sha is fifteen when the story opens. Her
father has just sold her sixteen-year-old sister
Orla to a dealer in women "for marriage of the
bed", for the cash he needs to buy a part share
in Po Shan's fishing junk. Such sales, illegal now
just a few miles away in Communist China, are
still the custom in Hong Kong, and Orla goes
willingly, glad to escape from the family's
poverty into a rich man's home; but the wind of
change is blowing in Hong Kong, and to Pei Sha
the transaction is an insult. Nor does her father
live to enjoy its benefits: within a day or two he
and her mother are lost in a great tidal wave, and
the bride price is lost with them. The
surviving members of the Ming family are taken
in by Po Shan. Life is precarious, but they get
by . . .
So begins a novel that sweeps the reader from
one dramatic scene to another. Ardent, lyrical,
tender, explosive, this is a novel that will remain
in the mind.

The Sinews of Love

Alexander Cordell

Money is the sinews of love as of war
George Farquhar (1678-1707)

CORONET BOOKS
Hodder Paperbacks Ltd., London

Copyright © Alexander Cordell, 1965
First published 1965 by Victor Gollancz Ltd.
Coronet edition 1972

Printed and bound in Great Britain for
Coronet Books,
Hodder Paperbacks Ltd,
St. Paul's House, Warwick Lane,
London, EC4P 4AH
by Hazell Watson & Viney Ltd,
Aylesbury, Bucks

ISBN 0 340 15476 4

For
Constance Helena

1

HONG KONG HELD its breath at the end of the Great Heat.

For in the month of September, in the year I was fifteen, there came a big wind from the sea, a sea-bitch that built a wave twenty feet high in the estuary of Shatin, and the wave came roaring in from Tolo and swept people away to die. Many of these were Tan-gar, the fisher-folk of my clan. Yet I remember this September not because of the great typhoon, not even for my birthday. I remember it because Orla, my sister, whom we called Gold Sister because of her beauty, was sold by my father to a dealer in women for a marriage of the bed.

This, the old ones say, is the sinews of love.

The baked earth flung up strange smells after a month of summer flame, and the curved tile roofs of Fo Tan, my village, flared red under a typhoon sky of bronze. The distant peaks of Tai Mo Shan were shrouded with swansdown clouds, the sea waving green and crested, spuming with joy at the thought of the coming slaughter.

'Pei Sha,' said Orla, my sister, 'a big wind is coming,' and she took pins from her mouth and put them in her hair, turning her head this way and that in the big Ming family mirror which once belonged to my grandfather in Kwangtung. Next she said, spitting on her fingers and tying her hair into a top-knot, 'The storm signal is up in the Navy Yard on Hong Kong island. This morning your Big Nose Ginger missionary man do say a typhoon is coming.'

This rudeness angered me. Turning over in bed, I replied, 'Do not worry. Suelen will see to it when she wakes.'

'This wind will see to Suelen,' she said. 'Hei Ho Fat Woman do say that come night it will be standing on the tails of ten thousand cats.'

With eyes narrowed in pretended sleep, I watched her, and Orla was beautiful. At sixteen she was a woman with all the curves belonging to a woman. Preening, grimacing, she lifted her cheongsam skirt in the mirror, looking over her shoulder.

'How's that for a leg, Little Sister?'

7

'I have seen better on Butcher Lai's meat stall.'

'That is because you are only a sister,' and she pulled her skirt to the thigh. 'A leg like that can send the boys raving.'

'You hush, lest Suelen do hear you,' I said, fearful. In a dream Orla replied:

'You know, Pei Sha, if I slit this old skirt up to the waist they wouldn't know sixteen from twenty.'

"*Whisht!* You will waken Suelen!"

Orla groaned. '*Ai-yah!* It is always hush for old Suelen. Soon she will not bother me for I will be in Tai Po – and if she had legs like mine I expect she'd be showing them.' Then she went to the wash corner, slopped water into a basin, peeled off her dress and drawers and there was nothing on her. Bare as an egg she bent over the cot of our baby brother Tuk Un, sweeting and kissing the air above him in love, then she was head first into the bowl, splashing and bubbling.

I watched her. With my hands on my tiny breasts, I watched, for I would have had them as large and beautiful as Orla's. Often I had seen the city girls washing behind the windows of slum Kowloon, the lamp-light gleaming on their sun-black bodies, all as slim as boys, being Cantonese. But Orla's body was as white as an English girl's – unusual for a Tan-gar – with the same curves and roundness. This is the body of a concubine, my father used to say, and it should be treasured with oil and perfumes. And it will bring us trouble – we who have had no child born out of wedlock for generations; better she gives joy in a rich man's bed than roam the alleys like a bitch-dog and bring me home a litter of pups.

Then Suelen, my big sister, would look over her chopsticks with lights in her eyes and stare at my father with disdain. This, my wonderful Suelen!

Now, trying to forget Orla, I sat up in bed and got out a book for studying, but I heard a shout from the fields and above the stumps I saw Hui, my young brother, running in the window and he shouted wildly, his voice a reed above the summer music.

'Orla, get dressed,' I cried, 'Hui is coming!'

'And welcome. There is nothing on me he has not seen before.'

'But boys are with him!'

'That makes them lucky. There is nothing like education,' which was one for me.

8

And as she said it the door went back on its hinges. 'Aha, got her!' cried Hui. 'Fat old Orla bare again, look boys!'

He was ten years old, a man before his time – chasing the village girls already, stalking the English boys for fighting, and I loved him enough to eat him. Hands on hips he stood in the doorway, grinning, muddy from the Shatin fishing, and his horrible friends were peeping round his legs.

'Hui!' I gasped, shocked.

'In boys, in,' he cried. 'Ten cents a time. Fat old Orla, *in!*'

'Bitch-dogs, running dogs!' cried Orla, snatching at a towel and swiping.

And then Hui stared past me at Suelen's straw bed, his expression changing, and ducked and ran, followed by his friends. For Suelen was rising on her elbows. Pushing her black hair from her face, she stared, her great eyes moving darkly under her heavy brows. Orla froze too, gripping her hands.

'How dare you,' whispered Suelen, 'cover yourself decent.'

Suelen was not my true sister, but a Hakka – one of the guest-people brought into service centuries back by rich Cantonese. My parents had adopted her after finding her wandering homeless in a Kwangtung famine when she was six years old, and they had taken her in for free labour with the idea of selling her later, but there was no beauty in her. Now aged twenty-four, Suelen was as big and broad as a northern man. She rose from the bed, shaking out her glorious, black hair, her eyes shining with disgust and anger.

'There is no shame in you, Orla – naked before a pack of boys.'

Orla did not reply, but her eyes were flashing threats at Hui, and him sitting on the step now, whittling at a new fishing prong, all grins and wickedness.

'Nor shame in you either,' cried Suelen, lifting him with her foot. 'Away outside while your sister dresses, or I flay you!'

Hui floundered and ran and she watched him go with smiling eyes, for Hui was the make-believe son of her womb she had fashioned without the help of a man, since none desired her. Faintly came Hui's cries to his friends on the heated air, and the wind came down from the mountains and whimpered over the sea, breathing typhoon. Suelen said to me:

'You better, child?'

9

'Ah.'

'Did the American missionary man come today?'

Orla said, with one leg in her drawers, 'He came, but Pei was sleeping. He left the cholera medicine for her, and more books.'

'Books?' Suelen swung to me. 'You did not tell me this. Show me.'

I protested, 'Suelen, they are only come this morning!'

Her face was wonderful to see, for she loved learning. 'Show me now, Pei Sha!'

She was always pestering me about the studying. Because my brain was sharp, she and the missionary kept me at it night and day – even now, on the eighteenth day of my cholera, she was at me about the books. While the other girls were out in the night markets with their boys, I was studying. But although I was top of my form in Fo Tan village school, my father turned his face from me, for I was a girl, not a son. Now, drearily, I brought the books from under the blanket, saying, 'The missionary brought two books. That one is silly old English. This one is a part of the lovely *Dream of the Red Chamber*, and is in Chinese.'

'You have finished it?'

'*Tin Hau!* It is a hundred pages and I have only just got it, woman.'

'Do not blaspheme, do you hear me?' She clasped my hands. 'Read every word, little precious – every word – hear me?'

'And where will reading get her?' asked Orla. 'Papa is right for once. Reading is for men, and education is lies.'

Suelen said softly, 'Read, read, Pei Sha. To read is life – do not the great scholars say this – even Ku Yen-wu, of whom you speak?'

Orla said at the mirror, 'Well, this one cannot read a damned word, but she has better things to speak for her. And I will be back from Tai Po in silk long before Pei Sha's study buys a cloth jacket.'

'O, aye?' Suelen turned. 'What is good enough for you is bad for Pei Sha, for she is brilliant in the head. And one day when she travels on the Star Ferry to work in the Bank of China she will thank God for me.'

'And when will all this happen?' asked Orla wearily.

Suelen rose. 'She will not labour in the fields or in a rich man's bed like you, for I can buy an earth coolie for a few dollars a day and a rich man's joy almost as cheaply.'

'This is a pity,' said Orla, preening in the mirror. 'The rates should be higher.'

In the afternoon the sky grew dark and the wind rose to a higher note of anger. Tuk Un, my Second Brother, awoke and reached for Suelen, as always, and she was having him on her knee for cooing when my mama came in with the breast milk which sent him crowing delighted, for he was ten months old and a nipple hunter. Mama came in laughing, as always, wiping away rain. Little and fat was my mother on the stool, all sunlight and chatters, her savings bright gold in her smiles as Tuk Un hammered her and sucked. '*Wheeah*,' she said, 'that is a wind indeed! You are safest nursing the old cholera, Pei, for they are tying things down all over town. Even the kidneys are flying kites on Butcher Lai's meat stall and Hei Ho Fat Woman's is flat on its face already, with pots and pans bowling, and serve her right.' She kissed Tuk Un, smelled him deep, gasped with joy, and shifted him on to the other one. 'No sign of Papa?'

'Time he was back from Shatin or I will not be going to Tai Po tonight,' said Orla.

Mama nodded, her eyes sad. 'I know that road. If Shatin floods neither Papa nor the merchant man will arrive tonight.'

'Best place for the pair of them,' said Suelen, 'stuck in Shatin.'

Mama frowned. 'Soon the ferries will stop.'

'All the aeroplanes are flat on the ground at Kai Tak airport,' whispered Hui, now in bed with me. 'Force Seven—what does it mean?'

Suelen said at nothing, 'If Shatin floods and Papa does not come tonight this will show Tin Hau's displeasure at the sale of a daughter – do you realise?' And my mama's eyes went wide at this, for she and Papa were Tan-gar, and Tin Hau, the Queen of Heaven, was their god above all gods. Mama said softly, 'Suelen, Orla will obey her father. Let that be the end of it. Finish now.'

Suelen straightened. 'I am not started. I will start when Papa and the dealer in women arrive,' and she made a fist of her hand and went round the room like a caged tiger, thumping her palm. My mother said:

'Suelen, you are adopted, not a natural daughter. Keep your place!'

My sister lowered her face. Softly now, 'Yes, Mama.'

'Then remember. Orla is of this family. You are Hakka. You are not even of our blood – though we love you, you are not of the clan. Leave this to Papa.'

I pitied Suelen. She worked on the building sites seven days a week, like all earth coolies, for just over a dollar an hour. Often I had seen her under the poles, her buttocks twisting expertly to the loads – a trick of the earth coolies, for a load is time, not weight. Now Orla said joyfully, 'Do not look so evil, Suelen. Soon I will be home with big money. No longer will you labour equal with men or Hui shine shoes along the Praya, and Papa can buy his big junk and sail to Shanghai and Amoy!'

'With the money he gets for selling his child,' said Suelen bitterly.

'Listen!' commanded Hui, his finger up, and the silence screamed. In a lull of the sighing wind we heard it again; footsteps.

'They come,' said Hui. 'Papa and the dealer in women.'

I sat up in the bed. Suelen grew tense. Mama gave Tuk Un to Hui and fought to get them away, and Orla rose to her feet by the mirror, her head back, smiling, drawing her hands down her fine, curved body.

My father came first, bowing the dealer in, subservient as always. The merchant came, severe in his black mandarin gown, and I saw a face arrogant with wealth; pouched eyes as lazy-lidded as a rice crow's. How strange is life that I should later know this man Wing Sui so well. Stranger, as if I had called to him he fixed his eyes on me.

'Three daughters, eh, Ming? Lucky man.'

'Better – I have also two sons,' said Papa, 'but only one daughter is for sale. You will not want the biggest, and the youngest is just out of the cholera. Orla, come!'

Orla swaggered to him, copying the actresses, but she was like beef at market, hips wiggling. Nodding approval, the dealer walked slowly round her, and said, 'She is a bag of hay. She stands like a slattern and walks like a hoyden, but we will mend her. Yes, Ming, four thousand dollars.'

'And two hundred,' said my father, screwing at his hands.

Shocked, Wing Sui swung to him. 'You twist the bargain we made in Shatin. Four thousand, not a cent more.'

'And two hundred. Four thousand two hundred dollars I need to buy a share in a junk and take my family back to the sea.'

'I shall not break the bargain! Four thousand – two thousand now, two thousand when she completes her apprenticeship.' The dealer folded his arms. Suelen said, 'Papa, you bargain for the body of your child as if she were a common whore.'

'Four thousand two hundred now or I raise the price higher,' cried my father, and the dealer shrugged and turned towards the door, saying:

'Keep her. I can buy European women near that figure.'

'Then buy them, whoremonger,' said Suelen, but my father ran and slammed the door and flung out his hands in supplication. The dealer sighed, smiling, and said:

'That is better. Four thousand, and half paid now.' His smile faded and he turned to Suelen. 'And keep a knife near that woman's tongue for she doesn't know the length of it.'

My father snatched the money from his hand, and counted it. Sickened, I turned away. In moments Orla was bending over me.

'Goodbye, Pei Sha,' she said.

I heard brief chatter, the merchant's barked goodbyes. When I looked again all were gone save Mama, who was putting Tuk Un to bed, and Suelen standing against the wall by the Ming mirror. She was weeping. This was strange since I had never seen Suelen weep before.

2

IN THE MORNING I watched my father dress and this he did with great care lest he be uncovered. Buttoning his jacket he came to my bed and stood there with the money for Orla in his hands, and said:

'Pei Sha, do you see this money? Had you earned your keep instead of mooning your life away with school and books, your sister might not have been sold.'

'Yes, Papa.'

He added, 'I prefer brilliance in sons, and I thank God for Hui and Tuk Un for I have had my fill of women.'

'And we our fill of men,' said Suelen, coming in from the yard. Dull anger was stirring on her mouth. There was a fine grace in her as she stood there defiant to my father, this coming from the head loads of her childhood. Her cheeks were broad and flat, her nostrils wide and her teeth large and shining, and with her great, slanted eyes she watched my father with a smouldering calm as he spread the bank notes on the floor before the altar of Tin Hau our goddess, the Queen of Heaven: lighting two joss sticks, he kowtowed, and said over his shoulder, 'Today we travel to Sai Kung, back to the sea-life. Only those who walk will get there since I will not wait for laggards.'

Hui came in fighting the door, for the wind was rising to a fury in the fields. Hearing this, he said, 'Never mind, Papa. If old Pei cannot walk I will carry her – on my back I will carry her like a donkey.'

'She walks like the rest of us,' said Papa.

'She rides,' said Suelen, staring down at him. My father scrambled to his feet, defiant, then turned away. Hui said joyfully, 'She rides! What Suelen says do go for me, eh, Papa?'

A word about First Brother while on the subject.

He was thick in the shoulders and dark handsome, for he had fed while the rest of us starved. His teeth were white in his wide Tan-gar smile and there was a great joy in him, for life itself was a wand of magic to be bent to his will. For his living he shoe-shined along the Kowloon pavements and the Hong Kong Praya, and sometimes I went with him, for I loved the water-front. It is strange and wonderful sitting there with Hui watching the people pass. Here, with the harbour tide slamming along the old stone quays go the big American sailors like great, white Peking ducks, some with shrill Chinese street-women hanging on their arms.

'Two more dead by dawn,' Hui would say and the boys would giggle and roll on the pavements, which I thought disgusting.

But oh, I do love the Hong Kong Praya! Here is a honk honk of geese and the quack quack of ducks and the roar of the traffic thunders and crashes when the ferries barge in from Yaumati and drop their jaws to the surge of cars. There the uniformed policemen with their graceful dances and accusing fingers stand, unheeding of the hatreds; now pass the cheongsam ladies, up-swept at the bosom, undone at the knees, their radiant faces bright in sunlight; now cat-women, those with purrs, says Hui, their whiskers deep in the cream of life, a sigh a dollar: all this and more you see along the Praya which will be alive when the world is dead, says Suelen.

'*Phstt!*' I put my fingers to my lips now and Hui sauntered across to me. We waited until my father gathered up the bank notes and went out with a glare at Suelen. And the moment he was gone Suelen got Hui's ear and held him.

'Listen, you – Pei Sha needs to go to see her American missionary man, and you will take her.'

'Down to Shatin? Two miles?' he protested. 'I am not an elephant!'

'There was big talk just now!'

Suelen said, 'You will take her in Papa's old rickshaw.'

'You are as addled as ten-year eggs, the pair of you.'

'Hui,' I said, 'if you take me to the American missionary man I will give you a Bank of Hell note for a hundred and fifty thousand dollars.'

'That is money,' said Suelen drily.

'For the Festival of Ghosts?' He grimaced as boys do. 'But that is just finished!'

'Next year will come,' I answered. 'The money can be pledged in the meantime.'

'I will take you. Money now!'

'Money afterwards,' said Suelen, 'you are worse than your father.'

'Quick then – on my back and away before Papa comes back!'

Out of the bed with me and on to Hui's back and he ran down the alley slum to the hole where the rickshaw stood, and into the back I went and into the shafts went Hui, and down to Shatin he raced to the mission of the American doctor, to the one who had taught me and nursed me through this illness. I could not leave Fo Tan village without this goodbye, for this one, like the men and women of the World Lutheran Service, and scores of other societies, were giving back to Hong Kong what the money-bags were taking out of it.

After this sad goodbye to a saint, Hui and I came back to Fo Tan to be one with our own people, for that afternoon we were leaving our village.

What is there in an unnumbered shanty hut on a hillside

that clutches at the heart? Shielding my eyes from the fierce sun, I looked at my village. Below me the tin roofs criss-crossed the bright green of the valley; beyond was a maze of alleys where children played noisily, the big, yellow house of Head Man Leung, the stall shops, the place of the compradore. And farther still lay the quicksilver sheen of Tolo Harbour and bright islands swarming to a glaring horizon. The threatened wind has dropped and some say this is the eye of the typhoon, its lull, but we do not believe it; we are still travelling to Sai Kung. *Look!* Below are the green swamps of the paddy fields, the terraced hills of the market gardeners whose red-roofed hovels splash the green with blood, a torn battlefield of flowing rice where the black-hatted Hakka work. What is there in this bit of ancient China that grips the heart?

Every inch of this black earth floor I know, for I have watched it through illness after illness, hunger after hunger: every stain on the faded walls is a demon king or dragon. From every corner comes the smell of incense, of sweet and sour pork when times were good and the bitter bite of black bread when times were bad – and oh! – the crunched sugar-cane and sweet mooncakes on the mid-autumn festivals! *Ai-yah!* And when the New Year came blazing in on his firecrackers and feasting, the rat-holes of that hut danced with joy. There, behind the curtain, came the hot, sweet smell of blood and a gasping and faint cries when Mama brought forth Tuk Un, though she made no sound, for Suelen was off shift and sleeping, she said.

'*Wheeah!*' cried Hui, 'Mama, Suelen – look, Pei Sha is crying!'

'I am not,' I said, indignant.

For we were outside the hut now and the villagers were crowding about us, and then there were prayers and a clattering of shoulder-poles and who had got the Ming mirror for God's sake and who the devil suggested travelling to Sai Kung on market day never mind typhoon, for the crowds will be packed like herrings in ice-cubes.

The village was shouting, throwing out its arms to us, Head Man Leung was bowing deep, for we were leaving with a fair name and all debts paid.

'Kiss your village,' said Suelen, 'in your heart, Ming Pei Sha.'

'Goodbye, Fo Tan,' I said.

16

The family, led by my father, got moving. Papa first, bowed under his bamboo shoulder-pole, him with pots and cans and bedding, then came me in the rickshaw – what you could see of me, for you know what it is like when you move – with Hui in the shafts again, then Suelen, her big rush baskets bouncing on her pole, next Mama with Tuk Un on her back blowing bubbles and shouting with excitement, and away we went at speed to impress the neighbours. Now, at the junction with the Shatin road we stopped and looked back and saw a forest of hands and heard the cheering, and were proud. And we were filled with a new and tremendous joy, for we were going back to the craft of the sea, which had been the birthright of the Mings for centuries. After four stagnant years of being anchored to the land by the typhoon that had smashed our big junk, we were running for the oceans again, for the shimmering snapper fish and garoupa, the big crab-snares, the lobster-cages for the float-ing restaurants of Shatin and Aberdeen, and there was an excitement gripping me at the very thought of it, a joy of adventure that does not lie in books.

'Faster!' cried Papa.

Now, with afternoon closing upon us the sun shone with a sudden and terrifying splendour, and the estuary became jewelled and glittering with heat. A mile above the crag which the English call Amah Rock a cloud was gathering, great, black, like a bag of fury, its base fire-shot, its billows crowned with copper hue, its edges with a glaring whiteness. All that morning the wind had been blustering and crying and sweeping up the sea now the day was quiet. Suelen, now leading, stopped by the roadside and lowered her burdens.

'The typhoon is coming,' she said, pointing.

'The typhoon is gone,' said Papa.

'But the big winds sometimes turn,' protested Mama. My father buttoned his coat.

'Forget the wind, come or go. Before its first gust we will be safe in Sai Kung.' He got under his shoulder-pole and straight-ened. 'We go.'

'Pray to your gods,' Suelen whispered, and I heard her and said nothing.

It was two o'clock when we reached Shatin.

Stand reverently aside to the passing funeral, everybody in white; wince to the clash of cymbals, the brazen blasts of trumpets, for somebody important has died. We did not guess, as we waited for a path, that death would visit many more in Shatin before the night was out. Now came the mourners supported by relatives, then the professional mourners, their six-inch nosedrips telling the grief of those left, their cries heart-rending in the heated air. Papa was impatient of life, never mind death. On he went, his load barging people aside.

'Hey-ho, hey-hoaah! Watch your legs there, here is a live family on the move! *Heyaah!*' and he plunged into the stall crowds of Shatin with my poor little Hui straining in the shafts and Mama and Suelen following, all sweating tigers. Now to the sea-front, to the jam-packed spars of Tan-gar and Hoklo, the boat-people, for here the sea-children mate with the land. And the stalls of the vendors were filled to overflowing – for those with the money to buy – sugar-coated lotus seeds, roasted cock-roaches, golden wheat and black beans, chicken giblets fried crisp and red and a hundred miles of fat pork sausages that brings the spit to the mouth. Pig slices and steam-rollered duck starts rumbles in empty bellies, soya beans spilled over great dried fish whose sightless eyes held the dull complaint that life should treat them so: beset with flies, whole hogs hung crucified on doors, their pinioned vitals sweating in the heat, the blistered fat of their entrails flinging off their reek of dying. Sadly for me, for I love the crowds and commotion, the stalls die away behind us. Again the wind threatens, says Suelen. Near Tai Wai, in the shade of a frangipani tree we rested, and there was peace away from the dust of the road and the sweating agony of the poles. Outstretched like vagrants, we slept, and while we slept the wind rose, and when we awoke the sea was going mad in the estuary and was building a great wall of water out beyond Tolo, the junk men said.

For the first time I was afraid.

We boiled rice over a wood fire, I remember, and Suelen said, 'Papa, the tide in the estuary is higher, I can smell brine in the wind.'

For there is no nose in this world like the nose on a Hakka.

18

My father did not reply.

'Ming Ho,' said Mama, 'listen to that wind. There is no sense in camping on low ground in Shatin. We should be travelling on the track to the hills.'

And even Hui, returning from a squatting, said, 'I did speak to a village girl and she did tell me that the Big Nose Gingers have put up Force Nine in the Navy Yard, and that the typhoon has turned again and is coming for Hong Kong. I called to her, but she began to cry, and ran.'

My father said, 'Would you believe the stupid Navy before the word of a Tan-gar fisherman? My grandfather sailed the Hankow bore and the secrets of typhoons he handed on to me.'

Suelen said at nothing, 'Rest his bones in peace. He knows a typhoon best who died in one,' and she settled herself back in the thick, lush grass with all the time in the world. Such was my father's mood that nobody protested again, but I saw Mama watching the sky. With her rice-bowl in one hand and sticks in the other she supped the rice through her strong white teeth, gasping and swallowing. And miles above her in the copper sky there began a low sighing and rumbling. Mist began to swirl among the peaks of Ma On Shan, wreathing in billows across the canyons of the sky as if in haste to deluge the brittle land.

Rising, my father said, 'Suelen, Pei Sha, Hui, follow me,' and we did so until we came to a little glade where, on a mossy bank, stood two urns of burial. Papa said:

'Look well on these urns for they contain the bones of my parents long since dead. With my own hands I drew these bones from the tomb and washed and cleaned them and placed them here. These two were children of the sea. I buried them with jade in the nine orifices of their bodies, and upon their bones you will swear. Pei Sha, hear me. No female in this family will expose herself in sight of strangers. The collar of every samfoo jacket will be worn high, the trousers will not show the ankle. Swear to obey this rule.'

'I swear,' I said, and he turned to Hui, saying:

'Cricket fighting will cease at Sai Kung – indeed, gambling of any kind will stop – especially the mahjong, which is a game for men, not boys.'

And my poor Hui bowed his head, he being a terror for gambling.

'Foul words and rough jokes also.' Papa glared at him. 'Fighting English boys and chasing girls. At your age boys are keen to learn the secrets beneath a woman's garments. . . .'

Suelen said, 'Papa, he is a child, a child!'

'Swear that you shall put such things from you, Hui!'

'I swear,' said Hui. And my father turned to Suelen and said:

'Nor are you guiltless, Ming Suelen. I know all things, even of the labouring man who followed you home from the building sites. Any such followers appearing in Sai Kung I will cool in the sea myself.' But he did not ask her to swear, because he knew Suelen.

Often I had seen a little Hakka man lay wild flowers on our window sill. Inches shorter than Suelen, he was nevertheless a man in miniature, and most handsome. And Suelen would pretend not to notice him but the moment he had gone she would sneak out and put the flowers in water.

'The temple in Joss House Bay will be visited regularly. A shrine to Tin Hau, our queen, will be kept in the aft cabin of the *Cormorant*, the junk we are sharing. None shall do personal things before her. The man with whom we are sharing this junk is called Chu Po Shan. He and his missus are great fishermen. Treat them with the greatest respect or account to me.'

'Yes, Papa,' we all said, for this was reasonable.

He patted his pocket. 'With this two thousand dollars I will buy a share in this junk, but the other two thousand dollars payable after Orla's apprenticeship will also become Po Shan's, this has been agreed. Do you swear obedience to this man Po Shan, our partner on the sea?'

We did so, and my father drew himself up to his full height and looked at the sky, and said, 'The typhoon is upon us. The storm is coming and it will be terrible. But if we can survive its anger on the land – how better we will ride it in the middle of the ocean? Tin Hau, our god, is with us!'

'Run!' cried Hui, and we did so, for the rain was sheeting down and the wind was howling in the trees. Hui bundled me into the rickshaw, Mama tied Tuk Un on to her back, and Suelen and my father got under their loads. We ran along the roadside and I saw, over my shoulder, the rollers of the estuary climbing up upon each other – three, four, five layers of water being built by the pressure of the wind. The sea bellied and slopped against the sea-wall, drenching us, and the rain fell in bucketing tub-washes that raced across the sheeted road before us, building up into a flood. I stared through the rain down the road to Shatin. We were the only humans in sight. Then came real wind, in howls.

'Run!' shrieked Suelen.

It was a new design of storm, a sea-bitch with waves.

The Shatin estuary was spraying white arms upwards. Dominated until now by the fury of the wind, flattened against the ocean bed by ungovernable pressures, the sea broke loose in monster fury. It bucked, it leaped in foaming pinnacles, each higher than the next and mating with its neighbour until, in freedom, it rose to maniacal peaks of water: and the peaks became waterspouts that merged into a single wall of green, wave-topped and crested, all in minutes. And even as I watched in the bucking rickshaw the great wave grew, hesitating in a mad-horse uncertainty, wondering where to charge.

'Faster!' cried Suelen, and she caught Mama by the hand and heaved her on towards the high ground. I saw Hui's streaming face and his terror as he splashed on, now knee-deep in the rising sea. My father had flung away his burdens and was running free, gaining from us with every yard in his madness. My mother was already failing and as we overtook her I reached out and snatched Tuk Un from her back and heaved him into the rickshaw. It was all in seconds. One moment we were safe, the next nearly covered in the tidal wave from Shatin. I shrieked to Hui to stop, for Suelen and my mother were fifty yards behind us, but my voice was drowned in the roar and I snatched a look at the estuary. The wall of water had now grown to an appalling height, towering from the base. And even as I watched the foam broomed off its pinnacles by the syphon of the wind, which now was shrieking. The wave charged, struck the sea-wall a hundred yards behind us and slopped back; then, as if infuriated by this challenge to its immensity, it mounded to a new height and rushed again, and I saw behind it the driving force – a gigantic wave rolling in from Tolo. Now the flood was growing about us. With a roar the sea-wall was breached. The typhoon wind rose to a note of sirens – a hundred and seventy miles an hour, they said later, and the flood came roaring over Shatin. Hui stumbled and fell. The rickshaw leaped, spilling me out with Tuk Un in my arms, then cartwheeled past me as I fought myself free of it. I slipped, and Tuk Un shrieked as we went under water. I lost him, then snatched at his shimmering face. Upright again, gripping him, I staggered on, but a fresh gush of water propelled us full length. A tree trunk came down and I flung my arm across it, letting myself wallow along in the flood and fighting to keep Tuk Un's face above water. Then the trunk struck a bank, shaking me off and I lay on the edge of the bank, in mud. New waves came down, flushing over us so I rolled away, clawing at grass and undergrowth for a hold, found one and heaved myself up. I vomited. With Tuk Un hard against me I got to my knees, shrieking for Suelen.

And Suelen came with Hui by the hair; dragging herself from the mud and branches, floundering to safety. For me the world was growing dark, the old cholera sweeping across my mind.

'Higher, Pei!! Get higher!'

Dimly I heard Suelen's command and dragged Tuk Un up, clear of another spate of roaring water. Wallowing in mud, Suelen and Hui came to me, and with Tuk Un screaming above the roar of the wind we watched the wave slowly drown Shatin. The flood surged past us, and with it came the tragic refuse of Lok Lo Ha and To Fung, Ma Liu Shui and even Tai Po: the shattered planks of sampans, great masts splintering like spears from the tapestry of weave baskets and rattan, the bedding of the Hoklo and Tan-gar, my own people. The crushed poop of a junk I saw, overturning and diving like a mammal, now a string of bright washing, a child's doll, a group of rice-bowls miraculously tinkling in circles. And in the filth, the black tracery of branches came the dead and dying, mouths gaping for air, hands clawing. In groups they came down the Shatin Road as the tidal wave had flushed them out – singly, as from a deck or doorway, or whole families spewed through windows into a roaring sea. Tumbling in the foam, somersaulting through the breached sea-wall they came, carried joyously on the crest of the wave, plunging alive in the deeper pools, these, the children of Tolo.

Later we searched the dead, though I do not remember this. Suelen and Hui saw over seventy dead in Shatin, but they did not find Mama or Papa. Later, we slept, in mud.

The moon was fatal white in a dreary sky when we crossed the mountain next day – still bound for Sai Kung; Fo Tan village, they told us along the road, was desolate.

Every yard of that walk to Sai Kung stands clearly in my mind, and we entered it in darkness, having slept in the mountains, and begged food from the stalls. In the village the tiny houses crouched like animals for the spring, hostility for the destitute, for this is part of the China law. Nothing stirred save the dying wind whimpering in the eaves and gables. As if the typhoon had sucked it in with a breath and spat it out, Sai Kung village, like us, lay exhausted under the garish moon.

3

IN A BACKWATER where the wind had scarcely laid a finger, a man was sitting. Seeing us coming, he rose from his hunkers and he was good to see, being handsome, and of the Hoklo fisher-folk.

'Good morning,' said Suelen, and bowed. 'We seek the junk of Chu Po Shan, the Tan-gar.'

'There are three Chu Po Shans.' This double bass.

'This one late of Fukien and the fisheries near Amoy – him and his missus.' She looked around the desolate harbour. 'Is he wrecked?'

'As wrecked as us all, woman,' answered the man, 'but not by typhoon, for we are sailors. What the typhoons leave the business-men take.' He hoicked from the back of his throat and spat past us. 'Aye, the soft-bellied money-bags with their fancy airs and fancy women – engines on credit, sails on credit, kerosene, too, and a fat old interest paid monthly, or *finish!*' He groaned. 'Give me private enterprise and I'll show you public criminals.' Gripping Hui's shoulder, he pointed. 'Fourth junk from starboard on the middle flow – come on, lad – shiver up the herring roes, whistle up a sampan,' and Hui grinned and put his fingers in his mouth and shrilled to deafen us.

'Aye, good for a lubber,' said the man and cupped his hands to his mouth, shouting, 'Chen Fu Wei!'

23

A little sampan nosed a path from the festooned craft of the harbour. It came, its prow rocking madly to a woman plying a stern oar sweep. We waited.

I looked around us. Here in soaked agony squatted the Boat-People, the old and very young, for the men and strong women were recovering their swamped boats from the sea and already there was a foreman's song going as they got the levers under the big ones. The sampan came waddling up to the quay and we climbed down into it.

'I am seeing double,' exclaimed Suelen, and stared at the girl in the boat.

And the girl in the boat stared back – at me. Suelen said, 'See Hui, here are twins – here is another Pei Sha sister for you, have you ever seen such a likeness?'

'One is enough,' grumbled Hui.

Before me was this Chen Fu Wei, and she was fiercely beautiful with her sun-hat tipped over her eyes, her face sun-black with her Hoklo life of the sea, her smile like a bright spring morning.

'Two peas in the pod,' said the man on the quay. 'Two like that one – I would never have believed it,' and for his cheek he got a tirade of vulgar back-gabble from the sampan girl, disdainful waves and a nose up air. Suelen said:

'Take us to Chu Po Shan of Canton, child, and while you are at it explain your likeness to my little sister.'

'There can be no likeness,' replied the girl. 'I am Chen Fu Wei, a Hoklo, and she is silly old Tan-gar by her eyes.'

'Talk of Po Shan, then,' said Suelen. 'He may please you better,' for there is not much love lost between Hoklo and Tan-gar, and Suelen was in business she did not understand.

'Ah, Po Shan!' said Chen. 'There is a man and a half! But now he is a midwife. His missus has been at it through the typhoon, and by the fuss she is making she sounds like triplets.'

'His wife is in labour?'

'These three days, and the women say she will lose it again. Poor Tai Tai – her first in three years, and the likes of me have to hide from children.' She jerked her thumb at Hui. 'What is he snivelling for?'

'Our parents were lost in the typhoon.'

'God help you,' said Chen. 'God help us all in this forsaken

24

place.' She drove the sampan expertly with great indolent sweeps of the stern oar, nodding towards the jetty. 'Some have lost loved ones, some junks have not yet returned.'

'Are you wed?' I asked, for she carried no ring.

'And delivered of a son,' she answered, 'my little Yin Yin, though I lost my man in storm.'

'Rest his bones,' said Suelen and Chen Fu Wei made a face, replying:

'Rest my bones now he is gone. The one I lost hasn't been missed – I am sick of men.'

Now we were in the midst of the big junks and there was a clanging of pails as they bailed out bilge-water and the shouted commands of the Old Men, the captains. Blankets were out to dry, poop-covers being hammered down, sun-hatches stitched up. Chen drove the sampan to the newest, largest junk of all, crying:

'Po Shan of Canton coming up, and watch him for he is a devil with women.' Tipping back her sun-hat she yelled up to the rail, 'Po Shan, visitors!'

'Ah!' A roar came back, deep bass, flat as a growl.

Excitement filled me as the *Cormorant* towered above us. Of China teak, she had young and arrogant lines, with a great snapper fish on her prow, its mouth pinioned by a hook, beautifully carved, and along her thwarts was a rail for children, always proof of quality: her sheets and sails were of the best, too, all ropes being spliced, not knotted, the hallmark of the sea-man captain, and topping her great middle mast was the red and starred pennant of China.

'Communist,' said Suelen, and Chen shrugged.

'He sails as he thinks fit and under any flag – last week he was hauling the Union Jack because the Governor was in Sai Kung. He has a fine war on him, they say, and the marks of whips and thumb screws, for he sailed the freedom fighters out of Sai Kung to the mainland.' Glaring up, she bellowed, 'Po Shan!'

A man came to the rail. Stripped to the waist he gripped it with huge hands, and the sun flashed on his bulging arms. His chest was massive, and to my astonishment it was covered with hair, this being unusual in our men, the Tan-gar.

'Land visitors,' shouted Chen. 'How is old Tai Tai?'

'The woman's twisted up.'

'Is the midwife with her?'

His voice rose. 'Would I be shouting for women if the midwife was with her, silly bitch? The midwife's in labour, too, and twins expected.'

'Are you needing help?' asked Suelen.

'Ah, but not from strangers.' Then he looked away and wiped his sweating face. 'Can you deliver, woman?'

'Not down here,' said Suelen.

He nodded at me. 'Bring Chen, too, she will help.'

'This is not Chen,' replied Suelen. 'You'd better get used to it, man, there are doubles round here.'

He stared from Chen Fu Wei to me. 'By the gods! Another she-devil in Sai Kung? The fates are breeding them. Would you be the Mings?'

'Aye.'

'Where are your parents?' He threw a rope ladder and Chen caught and steadied it and Suelen, climbing it, said, 'One thing at a time, Po Shan. Here, give me a hand,' and he reached down, took her under the arms and swung her over the rail like a baby.

'Me, too,' said Hui, and leaped at the ladder, scrambling up, and I sat with Tuk Un in my arms with Chen Fu Wei lounging on the prow, her eyes drifting over me, weighing me up. She smiled and I smiled back. She winked, and I knew that she was all wickedness, that life was gay and made for Chen Fe Wei of Sai Kung. Tuk Un awakened in my arms then, squalling with the wind, for he had not drunk since yesterday, and I kissed and rocked him while he clawed at the front of me, smelling for my mother: finding nothing, his world was empty, and he was terrified.

'That boy needs feeding,' said Chen Fu Wei, and she crossed her legs and put one foot in the air, the sandal dangling. The difference between us was clear. She was the fierce, pirate Hoklo, I was Tan-gar. She was sampan, and I was junk, deep sea. Way up the China coast go the Tan-gar, and there are not better fishermen between Hong Kong and Hiroshima, and she knew it.

And Tuk Un, understanding nothing of such pride, bawled on.

Chen Fu Wei squinted at the sun, saying, 'It do happen that I am feeding my Yin Yin, and I carry enough for six. If he would like a bit of old Hoklo then he is welcome, even if the tribe is wrong.'

I did not reply. It would need Suelen's permission for such a great decision. And just then Suelen put her face over the rail and shouted:

'Hoklo girl, Po Shan says you're milking. Can you spare some? The little one hasn't fed for hours,' and her face disappeared.

Chen Fu Wei opened her arms to me, smiling, and I gave her Tuk Un and he smelled of her and went quiet, watching with great eyes as she unbuttoned her jacket, then he fought her and drank deep of her with great gasps of joy.

'It is not poisoned,' she said, and I knew then that there was little difference between Hoklo or Tan-gar: this the sea was teaching me, that the size of the boat makes no difference to the mother. And while I thought these things, and learned, Chen Fu Wei held Tuk Un against her great brown breast, and winked, and smiled. Around us the harbour burned and glittered as the morning caught fire. Presently there came from the cabin of the junk above us a strange cry, and Tuk Un stopped his drinking to listen. Holding him, Chen rose in the sampan, calling:

'Tan-gar, Tan-gar!'

I said, 'You call the man Po Shan?'

'I call your sister the big one.'

'My sister is Hakka,' I replied. 'There are many tribes.'

'In Sai Kung we have no need of tribes, but the use of the tribe name is a compliment. What is her name?'

'Her name is Suelen,' and I cried up, 'Suelen, Suelen!'

And Suelen appeared again. Chen Fu Wei said:

'We heard a cry, woman. Has Po Shan breeched a son at last?'

'That was the cry of Po Shan himself,' replied Suelen. 'His son is dead.'

Later, when Tuk Un was all floppy and drowsy with milk, I climbed the rope ladder with him and stood on the deck of the *Cormorant* for the first time, and the blood of generations leaped within me. Chen Fu Wei and Suelen spoke in whispers, for women whisper at a time like this.

Leaning on the aft rail Po Shan was sobbing.

'*Ai-yah*,' this Chu Po Shan!

27

The very sight of him spun me.

If there is a better-looking man in Kwangtung Province I would like to meet him, and there was a great and sinewy strength in him that came out and struck me. His was a massive calm, his face noble, his nose unflattened, as if the ancient blood of the lords of Macau had enriched him. Striped in brown welts across his great back were the scars of the Japanese lash, but he did not speak, they tell me, although they were at him for hours. He possessed a watch, another shock, a band of silver on his thick wrist where the black hairs curled. His hands were calloused with his life of ropes and chains, the thumbs splayed with the torture of the thumbscrew. Sitting in the cabin of the junk with Tuk Un in my lap, I watched him eat, shovelling in the rice with noisy gulps, and when he had finished he pushed away his bowl, belched deep and rose, moving with the strange grace of a man handy with decks and oceans. At the cabin window, he said:

'The amount agreed was four thousand dollars – this for a quarter share in the junk. Now I am offered two thousand in six months' time.'

Suelen said, 'You would have had two thousand today, but the money was drowned with my father. Give me two years and I will pay you every dollar.'

'Two years!' He waved her down. 'God, woman, I owe five thousand now!'

'It is all I can offer, but I am not begging.'

There was no sound but wave-lap and distant voices on the jetty, also a sigh. For behind the curtain of the aft cabin Po Shan's missus lay, sheet-white, unmoving while she grieved for her lost boy. Earlier I had visited her, this being my father's friend. Beside her, on a table set low amid all the jumble of nets, bob-floats, landing scoops, and lanterns, was the tiny red altar of Tin Hau, her god, in front of whom two joss-sticks burned. Po Shan said now:

'You know this dealer in women?'

'Wing Sui of Shatin.'

'There is a Wing Sui in Shatin I would not sell a wonk-dog.' He turned from the window. 'Where is the copy of the contract?'

Suelen said softly, 'This, too, was drowned with my father,' and Chu Po Shan threw up his hands in despair, shouting:

'Hakka, see my position. How can I do business with you and yours? I am in debt to the finance company that drinks my life-blood – am I to fish a sea-junk or open a home for fatherless children?'

'You who have no children should show compassion to children who have no fathers,' came the voice of his wife, and the shock of it turned us to the curtain. Po Shan said:

'Tai Tai, would you break me?'

The curtain went back and she glared at him. 'If I had the strength to rise from this bed. The children of your friend are homeless and you stand there arguing like a Hong Kong banker, for profit.'

'Eh,' whispered Po Shan, 'I am plagued with women.'

Tai Tai rose up in the bed. 'We cannot birth a son and we are being offered two free.' She turned to Suelen. 'See to him, Ming Suelen – it is we who should be paying, not the Mings.'

'If you feed us we will labour free,' cried Hui.

Po Shan elbowed him aside, booming, 'I keep no slaves!' Towering above Suelen, he said, 'Are you Tan-gar? Your face, your speech is Hakka – how can you be of the Mings?'

Suelen told him.

'Then your belly will sicken on the sea, woman, it was built for toil on land.'

'I was built to mother this family,' retorted Suelen, 'I go where they go.'

So deep he groaned, his hand to his head, and then pointed. 'How old is he?'

'Ten, sir,' said Hui, his face alive. 'And I have always wanted for a sea-man with gold-thread and parrot-fish on the lines and see them all silver on the tubs when the junks come home.'

Po Shan grinned and wiped his sweating face. 'And you?' He nodded at me.

'She is a scholar,' Suelen answered. 'She can read and write in Chinese and English and knows the songs of the great Taoists – she can even tell a chapter from Su Tung-po, the poet.'

He weighed this, his dark eyes moving over to me, and I knew his mind, for he was born for women. He said, 'She is ill.'

'The cholera. She is better now, but still weak.'

'She is much like Chen Fu Wei. Explain this, child,' he said to me.

29

'They both have great beauty,' replied Suelen, 'that is the explanation. But Pei Sha also has talent. She can play on the pi pa and sing like Hoy Tui, the actress.'

'Excellent,' he replied. 'But can she also cook and scrub – can she stitch sail canvas with bare fingers and know the course by the stars or a sea-route by the swing of the lead? See my position.'

'I see it,' cried Tai Tai from the bed. 'Such things are for oafs like you, Po Shan – have you no respect for the classics, you lumbering bull of a man?'

'God help me,' he muttered, his face low.

'Ah, God help you when I am from this bed,' she said. 'Slip your cables and away out of it. Take to sea with honour. God! We have starved together and you have made less noise.'

'We will starve again with these leeches about!'

Suelen drew herself up. 'We will go. We shall not come between husband and wife!'

'Stay!' Po Shan roared, 'or I will never hear the end of it.' He wagged his finger in Suelen's face: 'But four thousand dollars from you within two years or every Ming is ashore – women, boys – *all!*'

Later, next day with shadows of dusk fingering the aft cabin walls, Po Shan drew us about him, saying, 'Listen. We sail on the midnight tide. Suelen and I have searched the Shatin estuary but much of the flood is still there. Together we have enquired, we have also examined the dead, but there is no sign of your parents. Perhaps they are in the estuary mud, this the Head Man told me. The soldiers are digging. But one thing is sure – I cannot delay here until they are found. The way out of debt is to fish. To laze in harbour awaiting the return of the dead to die also. Is this agreed?'

'It is sense,' said Suelen, and wept.

He went on, 'I am bound for Bias Bay north to the Kwangtung coast for there is talk of snapper shoals moving there, seeking shelter from the big winds. This will be bad weather sailing. Do we go?' He looked at me. 'Answer, Pei Sha, for you are weakest!'

'We go, sir.'

'But first to Joss House Bay and the temple of Tin Hau. We

have been spared the flood, through the mercy of our queen, whom we worship.' From his pocket he pulled a tiny strap and silver bell and tossed it to Hui. 'This was for my son who was never born. On a junk it tells a child's whereabouts. Strap it to the ankle of your brother Tuk Un – see it never comes off, lest he falls overboard.'

'Aye, sir,' said Hui, his eyes large in his man's face.

'Now come closer, for here are some rules of the sea,' and he lifted his great arms over us. 'There are rules, there are laws. Break the rules and look out for me. Break the laws and the sea will kill you. First, when eating fish aboard this junk, never turn the fish in the rice-bowl lest the junk itself tries to overturn, believing itself commanded.'

At this point we nodded, and he said, 'Women listen! This junk has eyes that can see through darkness – a sea-pinnacle, a wreck beyond the human eye. This junk, being alive, links its destiny with its crew. Often then, it will steer itself with skill when its crew is blind in fog or darkness. So when drying nets never drape them over the prow of this junk or you will blind it, and all might die. Ming Suelen, do you hear me?'

'I hear you.'

He grunted deep, the sweat lining his face as he fought for intelligence. 'Next – eating again. When laying down chopsticks at the end of a meal never place them across the rice-bowl, or the junk will run aground, thinking it is the Old Man's wish. This, of course, is the work of devils, the whisperers. Many devils will sail with us, eager to get from one port to another, so watch the tiller lest they alter course.'

This was the greatest danger, as Hui said later, telling me of the time in a neighbouring village when the compradore's daughter married her man. This was a scandal. For when the couple took to bed there was a red devil sitting up between them and little Fu Tai took one look and was head first through the window and half way up the mountain with the village behind her, imploring, and it took the grandparents and Head Man himself to coax her back to bed.

Now Po Shan said, 'Rainbows next. Listen, Hui, and later instruct Tuk Un. However rainbows at sea may delight you children – do not point at them or you will break a finger.' He pointed at the Ming mirror which that very day Suelen had found in Shatin. 'Guard that mirror with your lives – crack it and face misfortune, for it is a terrible mirror – see how it has returned to you even after disaster?' He turned to Hui. 'Are you attentive?'

'Ah!' Hui's face was puckered with excitement. 'Do we fish with gunpowder, too, sir?'

Po Shan nodded. 'You may fish as our Hoklo neighbour, Fan Lu, fished with gunpowder. The fuse was faulty and took him early, and the primer went. The primer went and his hand exploded, and the bones of his fingers passed over his face, ripping out an eye. There are some begging on the streets less fortunate – men without eyes and hands, whose families picked from the sea the shattered fish and their own, living flesh. Aye, lad, you have my permission to fish with gunpowder.'

My poor little Hui hung his head in shame, and Po Shan said, ignoring him:

'No cats aboard, remember, for a cat can foresee the poverty that brings dilapidation and therefore rats and mice.'

'Then may I have a dog, sir?' cried Hui in his strange treble.

'A dog, but not a bitch, unless her pups are for eating, for a litter of pups with white tails can spell disaster, and personally, I do not like dog, the flesh is tasteless.' He paused. 'Smile if you will, but all this is deep-sea custom – Feng Shui, the influence of wind and water. Now the last custom I will tell you – the most important. Let no glass or cup be emptied aboard this junk for this will foreshadow empty nets, and by those nets we flourish or starve. Heed me!' He rose to his full height. 'Being a man I cannot strike a child for this is an assault upon the child, who cannot strike back. But Tai Tai will beat a child for this in my name – the empty glass. There is but one Old Man aboard this junk and I am he. Nobody shall call me Chu Po Shan, save Tai Tai, and Suelen who is of qualifying age, for it is not respectful. I am a proud man, for I am Tan-gar, of the true water-folk. My blood, like yours, is of the Indo-Chinese Empire – we are not simple Cantonese. Neither are we bred with the ferocious Hoklo. Be proud of this and do not take back-chat, least of all from sampan-dwellers and land-sliders, the stiff-legged people.' He looked around our intent faces, then lit the hurricane lamp and the shadows leaped into his face. Softly, he said, 'My woman sleeps. She has laboured hard, do not wake

32

her. Let this be known. Tai Tai, my lady, is first aboard this junk after me, Suelen is Second Lady, and you, Pei Sha, being youngest in the women, are least of all. Therefore all the menial work is yours – the swilling of buckets, the cleaning of bowls and pans, and the waiting on Tai Tai, who does cooking.'

I bowed to him, so firm and sure was he, and he said, 'Being strong, Ming Suelen will work like a man, but she is less than Hui who, until Tai Tai is better, will be my second-in-command. But I am always first – the Old Man. Call me this now and get the sound of it.'

'Old Man, Old Man,' we said in chorus.

'*Ah!* Now then. Waste from the body goes over the side – not into pails – not even with women, for pail-sitting is a filthy habit and worthy only of sea-urchins.' To Hui he said, 'When a woman is sitting aft you and me will turn away our faces, for she is a woman and entitled to respect. Nobody will sit aft in harbour or within sight of another craft, for this is scandalous. And all will sit away from the weather side lest another receives that which someone is discarding. Hear me again. . . .'

His deep voice droned on, rule after rule, law after law. Drooping, I listened, seeing through the window the kerosene lamps of Hebe Haven flaring skirts on the waters, and tangled in the spars and rigging of a hundred junks the headlights of the motor-cars beamed and flashed along the road to Clearwater Bay. The tide was coming in, the *Cormorant* savaging her anchor cable to its swill and strength. I heard Po Shan say, 'This girl sleeps . . .' and I knew the power of him as he lifted me.

And I awoke to a clear, bright morning, to the thumping of timbers and three mastheads swinging over the September sky, to the excited chattering of Hui, the bawling of Tuk Un, and the Old Man shouting for breakfast.

I leaped up from the straw of the aft cabin and ran, suddenly full of strength.

For the clouds were rose-tinted and flying before a southerly wind and the *Cormorant* bellied her bat-winged sails before it in the flying scud. The sea was deep green, the rollers running like snowy sheep before the barking of the big diesel. The wind thundered, the waves came foaming over the stern rail from the big tide building up along the coast of China.

Shivering with joy I gripped a mast, my feet braced to the plunges and rolls, and the sickness was gone for me, for this, being Tan-gar, was my birthright.

'*Heeah!* Ming Pei Sha. *Tan-gar!*'

It was the Old Man.

'*Ah!*' I cried.

4

EVERY HAND WAS busy that morning under Po Shan's bawled instructions and the bad language coming from the tiller was enough to singe blue devils. Suelen was mending sails, I was strangling a hen. Hui was already with the Old Man under severe sea instruction when Tai Tai came through the door of the aft cabin. Twenty-four hours after a three-day labour she came out with Tuk Un in her arms. Here was a woman born to the sea. With a wide grin on her broad face and her sun-hat on her neck she came, legs splayed to the rolls and lurches of the big junk. She held Tuk Un up before me, shaking him at the sky and he bubbled and cooed at her, the ghost of my mother.

'No fool baby, this one,' she cried above the sea. 'The big god Chang despised me when I prayed for a safe delivery, but he has beamed on this beauty, *ehaah*!' And I pitied her that her god despised her, the great Chang Hsien who roams the sky with a spear, hunting the Heavenly Dog who seeks to devour a mother's young. Chen Fu Wei also disdained her, saying before we left Sai Kung that she had a breast of stone. This was untrue, and I was glad, for now Tai Tai was feeding my brother in the aft cabin, in darkness, so that nobody should know of her save he, she being a woman of great modesty.

All that day we beat towards the coast of China, and on the morning of the third day the sea grew rougher and we wallowed in the deep, blue troughs with the fish-town of Swatow leering at us through mist and spray. Po Shan shouted:

'Right, then! Hui, down on deck with you! Tai Tai – back into the cabin with that baby. Suelen, Pei Sha – nets, nets. *Work*, the lazing is finished!'

Hui was first away, his bare feet scampering on the slanting

34

deck, dragging out the fine white nylon nets and cork bob-floats, bunching them at the rail for casting. I leaped beside him. Roars and groans from the tiller at this and threats to terrify, though the three of us worked like tigers. Tai Tai came from the cabin and said, 'This is part of the teaching. Do not heed him – forget the bullying, listen only to commands. Lower, lower – kneel, child. Aye, all is well, Suelen – two handfuls closer . . .'

'What the devil is happening down there, woman? Hui, *boot* them!'

Tai Tai said, 'Ignore him. Grip the bob-floats, Pei Sha.'

Grasping, straining, we lifted the nets to the rail and my bare foot splayed on the streaming deck. I fell. The line snaked.

'Idiot!'

The *Cormorant* heaved and spat at the sea, hissing and wallowing, and the sky went racing over the masts. Tai Tai said, 'Easy, girl.'

'Come about there! Horse's arse! God, where is a man?'

Tai Tai yawned. 'Wait for commands, this is only insults; soon it will be a dirty mouth, but he fishes well.'

'Down middle sail six feet – *move!*'

'*Move!*' shouted Tai Tai and dragged Hui away, pushing him to the mast. There she reeled off the fore-sheet with skilful sweeps, and Hui helped. The rope waved and streamed in the shrieking wind. The *Cormorant* swung slowly, kicking at the sea, and the back-sail flapped and thundered.

'She comes. Watch, *watch her . . .!*'

Tensed, fearful, we crouched in the lee of the gunwale, gripping nets. The boards bucked beneath us, the prow came round and the canvas roared in irons. Tai Tai tied the mainsheet and strained it to a bollard. Muscles aching, I straightened.

'*Down*, silly bitch!'

'Kneel,' whispered Tai Tai instantly beside me, and as I did so the big boom hissed over my head as the mainsail took the new wind. *Inches*, my head nearly off. Laughter from the stern.

"That's how they learn. Stand higher next time, one less Ming!'

The junk shuddered, the sail billowed. I saw Po Shan braced against the tiller, then ease her as she suddenly ran before the wind.

'Right, be ready!'

Tai Tai said, 'Ready, now – tell Suelen. Swing from the right, cast them high, up into the wind – do not fight the wind, make it work.'

'*Cast!*' yelled Po Shan.

'Throw!' shrieked Tai Tai, and the three of us flung the bob-floats high, grabbing handfuls of cork and nylon. Float after float went out and instantly I knew my hands were cut. Within a minute my arms were heavy, my spine threatening collapse, and bright red spots were staining the nylon. Po Shan was cursing us for faster above the roaring of the sea; down in troughs one moment, up to the heavens the next, with the wind whining and the big junk straining every plank and sea-bolt as the swell took her. I staggered and fell to one knee, dragged myself up again, fighting exhaustion, and I heard Po Shan call:

'*Wei*, Missus! She rides easy now – come upon the tiller!'

'He comes,' said Tai Tai, and left me, and within seconds Po Shan was elbowing me aside. 'Good girl!' he shouted. 'Lay flat and rest and back in five minutes. Hui – away up to Tai Tai and take a strain with her – God alive, it is either cholera or miscarriages. *Away!*'

I laid flat on the deck and listened to the song of it, the marvellous confusion of it all, and saw above me a fisher-sky filled with racing mackerel clouds. It was magical, a new plan of life, a primitive call that raced through my blood, and despite the pain I could have shouted with the joy of it. I had taken the nets wrong and my fingers were streaming blood, but I did not care. Raising myself I saw through a gunwale hole a long line of bob-floats snaking like pearls across a crested sea. Po Shan stretched himself, saying, 'Aye, well laid, though I expected better – you,' and he pointed at me. 'Do not double the lines in your hands or next time you lose fingers.' He gripped the lead and flung his weight upon it, shouting, 'Wei, *wei!* Stand ready. Ah, fine, Missus, fine – fetch her port. Hold hard all of you – anyone overboard swims, remember, and there are Swatow sharks.' He laughed at the sky. 'Hui, lad – aloft, hey, *hey!*' He swung a slap at Hui's backside as he ran past. 'Up aloft to the baskets and watch for the shoal, for I can smell them churning,' and little Hui, who had never seen a mast before, leaped at it like a monkey and went up hand over hand. 'Pei Sha, on your feet now, here they come!' Bending, he hauled me up against

36

him and I smelled the sweat of him and felt the teak hardness of his fine body. He pointed at the sea. 'Look, look – see the crests? Look, girl – look – a shoal!'

And above us came Hui's thin falsetto, a shrill cry in the bedlam. 'Fish, Old Man. Snake-fish, I do see them. Snake, *snake!*'

'Down and help Tai Tai on the tiller, then!' Po Shan wheeled. 'Take her port, Missus – heave here – port! Suelen – up and help Tai Tai!' and Suelen ran aft. Tai Tai joined me, grinning.

'He's a rough one, that – a hard master, but you watch now. Nets, child, nets!'

'Can you hold her, Suelen?' Po Shan again, hands to his mouth, bawling aft.

'Aye.' Suelen's reply was caught and strangled by the wind.

'There's a woman! Hui – back down there. Come, grip the nets, Pei Sha never mind your hands.'

I snatched the lead-rope and Tai Tai and Hui came running to help. Po Shan took the big strainer and spat on his hands.

'Heave!' Feet braced against the gunwale, we fought it, and through a rift in Hui's hair I saw Suelen on the tiller, feet braced, her body rigid, her face turned to the sky in the straining agony of it, for the sea was running full now, and it needed Po Shan.

'Missus – away out of it or you'll be dropping another one!' Po Shan again, and he levered Tai Tai away with his knee. 'Rest, woman, we can do it. *Heave!*' and he stuck his bare feet against the boards and flung back his weight. Sweat sprayed from his neck and shoulders as he fought it, for we were but punies and it was laughing at us. The lead-rope stuck, then flew, and as it came in yards Po Shan began a salty old sea-song a thousand years old. '*Ai-yah, ai-yah, ai-yah, ai-yah, ai-yah!*' we sang, getting the rhythm of it, and to my horror a giant garoupa appeared on the rail, blinking, its great jaws snapping at the lead-rope in the moment before it overbalanced, slithered down, and dove between my splayed legs, and I shrieked with fear: then another, and another – now in twos and threes they came, more surprised than me – slapping their huge bodies against the bulkhead, spinning in mad, gasping circles of froth. Ankle deep, now knee deep we worked then, yelling the dirty sea-song

Po Shan had taught us, and I saw Suelen's stare of horror from the tiller. But I did not care, for over the rail they were coming in a flood once we got them shifting, and I ignored the snapping jaws, the threshing spines. Now a baby shark, outraged at the indignity – up and over with him and he snapped at my leg then bit deep into the flank of a giant cod in the moment before I kicked him clear. But I was dying of labour now, the sweat running in hot flushes over my face and body. I shuddered to a sudden slant of deck, fighting the bile rising in my throat, and I went down on one knee. Instantly Po Shan was beside me, his face strangely tender, and he whispered, 'Ah, this is the sea-girl. Rest, child – finish. No more today,' then he went back to the nets, yelling, 'Empty, empty – Hui, run aft and lash that tiller – bowline, remember, and bring big sister down – aye, she will hold, but lash her hard. Fish, fish!' he stamped about like a madman. 'Women, get them down. Off hatches. Tai Tai, where the hell is Tai Tai?'

'You told me rest.'

'Now I tell you work. Down, down!'

'*Suelen!*' Tai Tai was the tyrant now, caught in the magic of the catch, the flapping, leaping mass of silver that poured into the flooded compartments, seeking escape in furious rushes at the bulkheads or vengeance on each other in swirls of foam.

'Keep her on tack, Hui!'

'Take that fool-woman off the tiller – Ming Suelen, Ming Suelen!'

'Po Shan!'

'Come down with Missus.'

I closed my eyes to the sudden sickness, then opened them. I put my hands before my face, slowly flexing the fingers: claws, red-blood claws, these, not fingers; the skin stripped from them like the skin of a conger, stark white, the ridges of the cuts welling blood even as I watched, and such was the pain of the brine in them that I could have screamed. Instead, I wept, softly. Presently, soaked with spray and sweat, I laid back and slept, and blood was on my mouth when they wakened me, they said. They fished again, said Suelen, and that before midday, for the sun was molten. And Po Shan fished again and yet again on the homing run, she said, and loaded them in, and Hui worked like a man. Never had he had such a catch, said Po Shan, except in the long winter hauls off the China coast, and that was trawler fishing.

And at dusk next day the shimmering reefs of Port Shelter came through the mist, so we hauled her over to starboard to avoid the stupid play-boats of the Hebe Haven foreign devils, and them nothing better to do but to cut across our bows with their show-off running-on-water, said Hui. Taking Sharp Island to windward, for we were still on sail, we took the Narrows past the Stranger's Grave and dropped anchor. Then, because it was late and our ice was low we ferried the catch across harbour to where the private dealers were waiting. There, we stood around our lovely, brimming baskets, and the dealers watched, unspeaking. We had risked our lives for this catch, but never have I seen men with so little interest.

Listen, for this spits of Hong Kong: in the alleys, in the finance houses, in the bars; in the fisheries, the place of the loan-sharks.

'A dollar a cattie,' said a dealer, looking over the jetty, for Chen Fu Wei had come in her save-life sampan to greet us and most beautiful she looked with her hair running free in the wind, and he was buying her, not fish.

'One-forty,' said Po Shan, bored.

'One-twenty-five,' said the dealer, and his face held the jovial scowl of a dog snarling in play. The wind whispered along the sorting-floor, ice in its sighs. Breath held, we waited.

'One-forty,' said Po Shan.

'Thirty!' This from another, one of blubber fat, with neck-laces of sweat and shadow – this one a loan-shark for sure; later I learned that children had died because of him, but he had not noticed. Smiling, he smoothed his stomach with slow, fat fists, and said, 'You are tied hand and foot, Po Shan – sell and have done with it.'

'I have been tied hand and foot before,' Po Shan answered, 'but not bested.' Turning to us, he said, 'Ship the catch back. I can sell in Tai Po tomorrow for more.'

'You can sell in Aberdeen for two dollars,' remarked Dog, 'but the wind is out so you'll burn a fortune in diesel doing it.'

Po Shan emptied his hands at us. 'You see – they control

everything, including the wind. Handle greed with greed, it is the only weapon. Take the baskets back – *move*.'

'Right, you,' said Dog, 'One-forty a cattie.'

'Too late – baskets back. Hui, Suelen!'

'One-fifty, then, and may you rot in hell,' muttered Dog.

'You also,' answered Po Shan, polite, 'and money in advance, please. I know you plug-nosed swines.'

'It is robbery!'

'Aye, and done in daylight. Next time I will wait for the wholesaler if the catch goes bad. You sit here like vultures making fortunes of death.'

They groaned, threatened, but they paid. The bargaining over, the catch delivered, I watched, sickened.

For the labourers were getting busy with razoring knives and hatchets in a flying of fish scales and entrails and sighs; a rising and plunging of choppers biting deep into the blocks, a blood-stained mutilation of the innocents who, writhing alive, were methodically gutted and cut to pieces. Now a great lobster, as brightly coloured as a summer butterfly, red, gold, satin-black, his pincers wide in the eternal challenge, weaving for an opening, his pop-stalk eyes following the darting, scarlet fingers. Up he went, and *splash!* And I saw him rise once in the boiling froth of the simmering tub, rigid with shock as the shell armour of his body, cold in sea-depth for a million years, grew warm, then hot, then scalding to the scream, and he shrieked once, though none but me heard him, and sank in torment, and died. Amid the faint hiss-sobs of bubbling crabs, the glazed eyes of giant cod and snapper, expressionless in their gory disembowelling – the rigid, throat-hooked, tail-anchored skinning alive of eel and conger, I stood in running blood in a savage public execution of innocence, and to my shame did nothing.

I wept.

To the god Hung Hsing, the fisherman's Divinity, I prayed for the spirits of these little ones who die that we might live.

Next afternoon, after the deck scrubbing, I left the junk deck where Suelen was basket-weaving, and took the save-life sampan just to be alone. With nothing better do to than to sit on the Sai Kung quay and watch the big American motor-cars slide by, I ferried myself across to Yim Tin Tsai, this being an island waving green and sunlit and with yellow sands along its shores. The sea, I remember, was burnished silver and flashing blue in the glass lagoons where the sand-pipers played and wagtails sipped the sea, for though summer was on its death-bed the birds still sang a spring chorus. Though of sea-gulls there are none in this part of China called Hong Kong, all refuse here being consumed by humans, and this is sad, for there is a fine white purity about a soaring gull. High above me as I plied the stern oar two vultures fanned wings in narrowing circles, with beaks to rip and tear the indolent fish or adventurous rat. Reaching the island I pulled the save-life sampan up the beach and laid there among the tufted dunes, thinking and watching the vultures.

Strange, I thought, the enmity of the gods, that they make vultures; some with wings for this soaring beauty before the plunge and scream; some like Dog and the other loan-sharks of the fisheries; two-legged, mostly foreign, says Po Shan. Though you don't have to be foreign to be a vulture, Suelen said – you can be a Chinese landlord who eats the dog and rents the kennel, or a millionaire middleman who floods the markets with imported chickens and makes a fortune while little chicken-farmers starve. Or you can be a rug importer in a Colony where even the poor snatch at the drug for dreams, and release from the terror of their hungry lives; or you can be an official most respected and dining plush while your servants are in prison, or a lackey, a perverter of contracts, says Po Shan, a pimp, a procurer, a briber.

All such exist here, says Suelen, in Hong Kong, and God knows what Hong Kong has done to have to put up with them.

Through the fierce light I saw a white junk heeling in the bay; all white she was, sails, stem, masts – as a white heron with wings outspread. And even as I watched it the junk veered, went about expertly and tacked across Pak Sha Wan, then came round full and ran goose-winged and free, straight for the island. As it came closer I saw a man sitting on an out-rig, naked save for a pair of scarlet shorts and sun-fire flashed on his brown body and light hair as he keeled over, his head skimming the sea. Nervous, I sat upright, then laid back in the sand as he flung over the tiller and beat back to Hebe Haven harbour. The heat took me. I slept. When I awoke Pak Sha Wan was deserted, so I took off my clothes and went down into the breakers, for washing was difficult with Po Shan and Hui about and too much sweat brings sores. Wading in, I swam, seeing below me in bright depths the lazy bindweed waving in current like the hair of a woman drowned, and this was my hair. In contorting, shimmering shadows I saw my body sweeping over brown pebble beaches and bucking slopes of sand, the mirage of noon. Now, diving, I swam underwater, glorying in the silent coldness, forgetting the threat of sharks, and rose in a joy of cleanness after the carnage of the sorting-house floor. With the tips of my fingers I touched the racing fry and baby snapper, enjoying the flashing terror of their mass escape, losing myself in an elemental joy, at one with the sea where I was born. Rising in the shallows I looked towards Sharp Island and instantly flung myself back into the waves, for not a quarter of a mile away the white junk was coming with foam at her nose, at speed — straight for my beach. In gasping haste, I ran up the sands and behind the first boulder of the dunes I knelt, peering.

The junk came veering into the shallows, and the boy, one little older than me, leaped overboard and waded beside it, and in that vicious light his hair was white, his body steeped in sun and as brown as a Tan-gar's. And it seemed to me that there was only the two of us in the world just then, and I knew a shameful trembling. Secure, I turned behind the boulder, and sat, waiting for him to go.

It was then that I remembered my clothes. My blue jacket and trousers, with sandals to hold them down, were folded neatly on top of a rock clear of the sea, not a dozen yards from his boat. I peered.

The boy was lying on his back on the sand, a corpse flung up by the sea, and I rose on tiptoe, for a better look. His head was towards me, his feet in the sea and I judged the distance between me and the clothes. Soon he would sleep, this was a habit of the foreign devils whose eyes were upside down; they would lie in the sun and sleep and when they awoke the skin would peel from them and they would rub ointment on the raw spots and next day come down to the beach and sleep in the sun again. The surf was pounding the beach, killing all sound, and I came from my hiding place on tiptoe, arms outspread for balance. I was

42

three yards from my clothes when he spoke, not moving, in perfect Cantonese.

'Oh no, you don't!'

And I was back, diving full length in the sand, face down for cover. The wind whispered, the breakers thumped, the shingle screamed, and I lay stiff, my heart racing. Anger followed shock and I sat upright behind the boulder, hugging myself. Shells were tinkling. I listened. His bare feet were slithering in sand, and he began to whistle in a high lilt of a tune, something I had heard before.

In Cantonese, from the other side of the boulder, he called, 'Sai Kung girl, you hear me?'

I did not answer. Strangely, there was no fear in me, for this was not a man but a boy, and I knew boys. He would tease, he would shame me, but he would not harm me.

'*Ahya,*' said he. 'No clothes. Answer a few questions and you can have them.'

Furious now, I did not reply.

'Three questions answered and you can have them – Sai Kung girl!' A pause. 'Or I come behind this boulder.'

'No!' I said, wishing him to hell with devils behind him.

'What is your name?'

I did not reply.

'Sandals for your name.'

'Ming Pei Sha,' I said, and had I got my hands on a stone he would have got more than my name. The sandals came over.

'Hoklo or Tan-gar?' His accent was good, it could have been Po Shan speaking: Cantonese in the mind and heart, this one, for all his European body.

'Tan-gar!' I yelled.

'How old?'

'Fifteen.' I screwed at my hands. Somebody might come and this boy would go – he would run to the boat and sail off, leaving me with the shame, and it would be all over Sai Kung and among the fishing fleet that Ming Pei Sha was seen naked with a foreign devil on Yim Tin Tsai, then no decent Chinese boy would know me.

'Please go!' I begged.

'If you promise to meet me here again.'

'I promise, but please go.'

43

He laughed and the samfoo jacket and trousers came sailing over and I snatched at them in mid-air and fought myself into them. The boy said, 'I will leave you while you dress and when you are finished come to me and I will take you back to Sai Kung.'

'Aye,' I said, without the slightest intention.

Pebbles rattled as he went away, and after a while I peeped over the boulder. He was standing in the shallows again; quite beautiful he looked standing there with the islands of Pak Sha Wan waving green behind him, and I knew again a sudden and shameful longing for him in which there was no great difference between East and West. This yearning grew to a pain, as if some secret inner being was reaching out black arms for him, and the spit was suddenly dry in my mouth. It was a new terror, for I knew that had he turned at that moment and called, I would have gone to him. Now he was full length in the sea, swimming with easy grace, white foam puffing at his ankles, and the passion of his youth flashed between us, and he did not know. I held him, I touched him, and he did not turn to me.

'*Ai-yah*,' I said, and snatched off my sandals and ran. From boulder to boulder I went in a swaying run and did not look back until I reached the save-life sampan behind the north rocks. Leaping into it, I pushed off, frantically thrashing the stern oar. When I looked for the boy he was running like a hare down the beach to me.

'Ming Pei Sha!'

'Go to hell,' I said, and turned my face to the sea, furious at what he had done to me, for I was sweating buckets.

In a moment he had brought me to a torment I had never known before, and I had not resisted him. In this, I think, is no honour: better, I believe, is the fornication of the body, so much cleaner than the fornication of the mind.

So I hated him and turned in the sampan. '*Wheeaah!*' I yelled. 'Horse's arse!' I spat towards him.

'Ming Pei Sha. Ming Pei Sha!'

Bats were planning for dusk when Suelen came from the jetty, she and Hui having been drinking in the jetty house of Exalted Virtue, which was very apt, I thought. Stars were sitting in the middle cabin window when she came back and leaned over my bed.

44

'What is wrong with you, old moper?'

'You leave me alone,' I said sharp.

And I closed my eyes to the pain of it, the entreaties and the sweetest love-making of the boy on Yim Tin Tsai.

Suelen, disturbed, came back, frowning, and said, 'This is a queer old face – never seen one like that on you before.'

She had not, and neither had I. After she had gone I rose from the bed and knelt before the Ming mirror, peering. Suelen had seen the face of Pei Sha the girl for the last time. What she would see in the future was Ming Pei Sha, the woman, she who had longed for a man.

5

COME SPRING WE had covered hundreds of miles at sea and the gipsy *Cormorant* was waterlogged with catches, for Po Shan knew the secrets of the shoals. But he was also a hothead and he quarrelled with the fishery man, saying that middlemen traders were taking his profit. This cut us out as surely as if they had shot us, and in desperation Po Shan turned to the private vendors – men like Dog and others.

But when, on the first night, we came in loaded with fish, the private dealers would not buy. They first offered us a fine price per cattie and in delight we ferried the big catch over to the jetty where they wandered around it sniffing and sniggering in their whiskers.

'Are you buying or not?' demanded Po Shan, but they were trifling with us, and did not buy. So Po Shan loaded the catch back and sailed it round to Castle Peak. There the merchants were waiting, including Dog who had come round by motorcar: they sat looking at the sea, arms folded, this to break Po Shan's spirit, so he flung Tai Tai aside, hit down two of them, toppled another into the harbour, came back raging, and took us out to sea.

And to none would he speak, not even to Tai Tai, his missus.

There, at sea, we drained out the old stock-water and pumped in fresh water to the holds but the great catch slowly died. Then we came back on diesel and lay off harbour while the private dealers took revenge and the stink of the rotting fish grew revolting: none would take the catch except the refuse-barges, who sold it to the Hakka farmers for dung. Twice we lost fine catches this way before Po Shan the Great learned that at sea he was master, but that ashore his masters were the middlemen – those who had never seen a big junk gibe in anger.

Also, the squeeze was on to pay his 10 per cent – the money he had borrowed from the loan-sharks to buy his fine junk, for the middlemen whom he was defying owned the finance companies, too. Next came letters of threat, to seize and sell his beloved *Cormorant*, and Po Shan, who would have sold his missus before he parted with a spar or deck plank, was in misery. Loan-sharks, finance companies, trader middlemen, fish subscriptions to the Communists, who would be a junk man? said Po Shan, *ai-yah!*

Suelen, whom nothing missed, said one day, 'Ming Pei Sha, this life of the sea is not for me. I am a Hakka, and of the land.' And she squatted on the sun-bright deck with her rattan basket craft between her knees, and the pattern she was weaving was of lovely shape. None could weave a rush pattern or rattan like Ming Suelen. She said, while Tuk Un sat blowing bubbles, 'The old man calls me a Tan-gar throwback, saying I was born for the sea, but he needs to carry my belly: my guts go bone-dry when we take it green.'

I picked up Tuk Un and kissed him. 'You have never complained before.'

She answered, 'Give me a hoe and a mow of land, I have had my fill of fishing. Only little pond fish I will raise on my five-mow-farm, Pei Sha, and hang them out to dry – you can keep your stupid great garoupa – just me and five mows, and farming.'

'Just you?' I asked, innocent.

'Ah,' replied Suelen, but I knew she was lying, for I had seen Mr Kwai To Man in Sai Kung, the Hakka who used to follow her home when we lived in Fo Tan. Also, there was lately a change in Suelen. Last three times into Sai Kung she was washed and dressed before Po Shan heaved the anchor, sitting on a deck coil in her new purple coat and trousers, her long hair virgin-plaited and pinned under her blue-rimmed, black Hakka hat.

'*Oi, Oi,*' Po Shan had said.

46

But how Mr Kwai had traced her to Sai Kung we never did find out.

There was, however, a letter. The coming of Suelen's letter I will remember until I die.

We had been out night-fishing, I remember, far beyond Rocky Harbour where the Hoklo children died. In a sudden squall the sea of night glass chopped up and fled, then became mountains in a roaring gale. And the sampans, caught in the fury, took it green and the children of one, all six, were swept off the deck to die. All that night the can-drums banged, red lights flashed, and the big junks pulled on their sheet anchors and began the search for bodies. We got two in our nets – a girl of ten with her baby brother still on her back. Under a dawning moon of fatal white we found their Hoklo parents and gave them back, and their mother, with four more dead at her feet, made no sign of grief, but took them in her arms, kissed them, and held them on the homeward journey, she being of the sea.

But back to Suelen's letter – the postmark was Kowloon, for quite by mistake I had noticed this when I took the envelope from Chen Fu Wei, our sea-postman. Chen said:

'This is great excitement – a letter for Ming Suelen. And the postmark is faint – also, one edge of the envelope has been turned up as if somebody has been trying to get inside it.'

'This is scandalous,' I replied. 'It is Suelen's letter,' and I held it up to the lamp. Tai Tai elbowed Po Shan aside and said, with authority:

'Sometimes, if you hold an envelope up to the sun with a mirror behind it you can see what is written within.'

'Shall I bring the Ming mirror?' asked Hui, keen.

'It does not work, for I have tried it,' said Po Shan. 'The envelope is too thick – not that I would have read anything, but such experiments are pleasing.'

'The easiest thing is to open it,' said Tai Tai.

'How dare you!' said Po Shan, shocked. 'Put the envelope on Suelen's bed for if we bandy it about much more we will be inside it, and she will have grounds to take us all to law. I am ashamed of you all – understand?'

'Most ashamed,' we answered, virtuous.

And in the evening when Suelen returned from the Tea-house

47

of Exalted Virtue where she had been selling her weave baskets to the fishermen, we all gathered around to greet her.

'Here is a surprise,' said she, eyeing us, and we squatted on the floor around her bed in the middle cabin while she took off her big hat and combed out her hair, watching us all with her great, dark eyes – especially Po Shan, who should not have been in there, a virgin room. I said:

'There is a letter come for you, Suelen.'

But she did not reply: just went on combing, unheeding, and her lovely hair hung in shining waves to her waist. Hui said, '*Whee!* It be a wonderful thing to get a letter. Old Grandfather Ching in the tea-house has never had one in his life, and he is ninety.'

'There are letters and letters, though,' said Tai Tai, nuzzling Tuk Un. 'It is what is inside that do count, I am told,' and Suelen said, with pins in her mouth:

'Pei Sha – tomorrow we are going to Kowloon – with the Old Man's permission, of course. So tonight you will wash and iron your samfoo, and see to your hair, as I.' And she looked at Po Shan, who hastily nodded permission.

'Especially welcome,' said he, 'since it may have to do with that letter on the bed?'

Crossing to the bed Suelen picked up the letter and held it against her. 'This letter is my business, Old Man,' she said. 'Out – everybody out. To all men, day and night I do bow and scrape, but this is my bed – and my secrets, Po Shan. How dare you pry – out, *out!*'

We went in scrambling haste, Po Shan head first, sheepish.

Next morning I rose early with the sea-mist setting fire to the village and the curlews shouting drearily over the harbour, and I put on my best jacket and trousers. With my hair washed and oiled I sat on the rail trembling with excitement at the thought of a visit to Kowloon. Waiting for the rice to boil, I listened to the sounds of the waking junks – the tinkling of bowls and pans, the creak of sleeping-boards. Groans and yawns stole about me in the still air; babies wept in petulant cries for milk, grandmothers cursed the morning aches and daughters-in-law, the Old Men barked and grunted. Distantly came the whoof-whoofing of the homecoming diesels and prows grew from the mist like invading ghosts. Drenched with last night's rain the fishing fleet

48

came in, its families sleeping off the dawn, its Old Men carved in stone at the tillers. And with their coming Sai Kung village flung off its shroud of sleep. Doors slammed, cocks crowed, dogs were booted as the dawn came flaring up on the rim of the world. As a curtain of life raised, the sun shot down daggers of fire and the grey sea was washed blue by an instant brush of an azure sky; great white clouds lumbered across the caverns of the sun like white-bearded, pot-bellied old men grieving for the death of another summer. I stood, staring at the astonishing beauty of the morning, and pulled my coat a button closer as the wind bit me. Turning, I saw Suelen by the middle cabin door, combing out her hair into the breeze.

She called, coming nearer, 'Remember the date, Pei Sha?'

This, I knew instantly, was not my adopted sister, but Ming Suelen, the Hakka. This was a woman of Anwhei and Honan, one who had fled from the butchery of Kiangsi and Kwangtung when the world was young. There was a sudden nobility about her, an almost barbaric splendour, and there was a chasm of time and race between us that no love could cross. Coming to me she said, her expression strange:

'Sometimes you are little Pei, the learned one, sometimes Ming Pei Sha, the rough Tan-gar fisher-girl. Have you thought of the difference?'

I nodded, fearful because of this strangeness, and she said, laughing at the sky:

'And sometimes I am mother to the Mings, or, like now, Hakka Suelen. This morning I am miles from dirty old Sai Kung and its stink of fish.'

'You are going to leave us?' I asked, reading her.

Sitting on a rail she drew from her breast the letter envelope, and read:

> ' "Woman of Anwhei!
>   Never did I dream that you would turn to me,
>   A fickle lily courted by the stream
>   Amid a thousand lovers.
>   As the white rose opens to her mating sun,
>   Or the black gull cries from Shansi Hill, for wife;
>   So I do turn to thee, Woman of Anwhei,
>   To share my life." '

I said, 'That is very beautiful, Hakka Suelen.'

'Ah,' said she, and folded the paper and put it against her. 'But it is something more, for a man do want me, Pei Sha, to take me to his village, and me to bear his child.'

I would have laughed because of the way she said this, but kept my head.

'For wife?' I asked.

'What else, for God's sake? He do say so!'

'And you will marry him?'

This shocked her greatly and her head went up. 'The poetry he sends is beautiful, but do I leap into the arms of the first man who wants to bed me?'

'I am sorry.'

She walked about, looking knives, then said into the sun, 'Nevertheless it is good that a man aches for me.'

'It is excellent.'

With her back turned, uncaring, she added lightly, 'I am not much to look at – this I realise.'

'Not if he has looked on you,' I said with care. 'Is . . . is it the little Hakka man Kwai To Man who seeks you?'

'My business.'

She was precious to me, and in this mood most delicate, like frosted lotus petals. The wind whispered around Pak Sha Wan and there was brine and blood in him. Suelen said:

'Never mind about men. This is a special day, do you remember?'

I said with confidence, 'Aye, it is the day of Ching Ming, the festival of the graves, when we sweep the stones and offer tributes to our ancestors.'

'It is not!' whispered Suelen. 'Think, child, think!'

But I was addled and could not think, and she said sharp, 'It is the birthday of Orla Gold Sister.'

'I am sorry,' I said, my head low.

'For shame! It is terrible! Do the Mings forget their own blood while I, who am not a Ming, remember?' She went to the rope ladder that led to the save-life sampan. 'Come,' she commanded. 'Kowloon!'

6

SUELEN SAID ON the way to the New Territories taxi,
'First we go to Ladder Street ship's chandler to buy eighteen
bob-floats for the Old Man's nets, also a new rattan for my
weaving; after this we will visit Orla Gold Sister.'

'In Tai Po?' I asked, incredulous, for this was miles.

'In Kowloon – in a bar. Which shows what can happen when
you sell a child.'

I was appalled all the way down Middle Street Sai Kung.
The sun was bright, the birds furious with chatter because the
day was ignoring them, bull frogs coaked from the rice-fields,
the cicadas fretted in whispers, worn out with last night's moonlight and loving. Through the rising haze I saw Yim Tin Tsai
green and golden, and thought of my boy in a flood of shame and
redness. To change my tune, I said:

'What is Orla doing in a bar?'

'It is indecent, we shall not discuss it. Nor would I bring you
but I cannot go alone. And when we reach this bar stand with
your eyes cast down, lest men demand you.'

'May I not even look?'

'Not at such men,' said she, and I remembered that she was of
Old China, and there it was once believed that a virtuous girl
could come to child through a glance from a Manchu warrior. I
smiled, wondering how many had used that excuse.

The breakfasts of the Hakka guests were dainty on the wind as
we went through Choi Hing and the squatters of Diamond Hill,
leaving the bus at the Ferry.

Great was the activity here, the people like flocks of famished
and well-fed birds, and we pushed a path through the claws of
beggars and the smart business people. Here were the cheongsam
ladies off to work on slim, stockinged legs, their fingers dipped in
blood, chattering, gesticulating before their toothpaste smiles:
there a gowned scholar deep in contemplation, the fighting
peasant mother, one baby on her back, a second by the hand, a
third in her stomach, and all their coffins in her gold-filled
mouth: here an insane heroin beggar, his hair over his face, his

51

smile wide to the brilliance of the morning. And I heard the background music of China, a symphony of bus-growl and pig-shriek and a chorus of hoick and spit and spatter. For as the birds sing before breakfast so we sing our throat-rending song of soprano rasps and basso booms with shrill children piping up like piccolos in the hot, summer air. Suelen bought the tickets and we went on to the ferry, jostled by the barging crowds. Taking a seat by the rail, I stared before me, rooted with astonishment.

For the boy of Yim Tin Tsai was sitting in the third row from the prow.

I saw him in profile against a turmoil of foam as the propellers got shifting into roars. Ropes were cast, commands shouted, but I was not there in the din of the ferry. I was running on the hot sand and him after me demented, and in a moment I feared and loved him and closed my eyes to the terror of it, and the joy.

Tin Au!

He did not turn, so I ate him with my eyes, closing them to a sudden delight as he kissed me, and when I looked again his gaze was upon me. He smiled. Swallowing hard, I smiled back, got a bit of Suelen's coat and hung on. It was unbearable. Hot fingers were touching my throat and breast . . . he who had seen me naked.

He winked, and I was astonished, sitting bolt upright.

'You all right?' murmured Suelen.

I did not know. It was his eyes. So clear and amazingly blue, those eyes, and they held for me a strange and awful command. I remembered with horror the legend about the gaze of Manchu warriors.

'Look,' said Suelen, 'the harbour!'

But I did not see the harbour: I saw only my boy on Yim Tin Tsai, for the making of love, says Orla, can be done with eyes, and why waste them on harbours?

Until the last few days I had feared even the thought of love, and had burned in the whispers of half-taught girls. These were the *kiss-me-dare-me* girls who began with students and ended with rickshaw boys, said Suelen, take no examples from them, for you are Ming Pei Sha. Also, I thought it all a little shocking – that the god who invented love should have such a sense of humour. Strange that he should give such nobility to the soul of a woman and then drape her body before the desires of men, and such vulgarity in this man's body. Fit for nothing but ducks, Orla once said, and I agreed with her. Were I the god of love I would devise a mating sweeter than honey, a conception of the mind, a delivery in smiles. This I put to Orla, and Orla laughed, saying, 'Do not interfere with it, Little Sister – you have it your way, I will have it mine.'

Very hot with me, very cold, for the boy was still smiling.

And Suelen, beside herself with delight, shouted, 'O, look, Pei Sha, the ships!'

The bucketing, crested sea was torn with prows and sails. On its breast went the bucking sampan, the rollicking walla-wallas in a deluge of foam. Past us flew the sleek motor-yachts of the taipans, the white naval launches slicing to nowhere, all tweeting and whoofing through the great cargo-bummers of the South China Sea. Barnacled, frowning they sit, screwed by dumb-bolts to the bed of the ocean, their crane-arms moving in disjointed slow-motion, and one by one they bellow for lighters. Here the Oriental liners doze at their berths after ten thousand miles of sea-waste – *Oriana, Iberia, Chusan* – the six-course diners of the richer than rich towering above the poorer than poor, and above them drones the white heron of Macau, wings outspread. All this I saw in a dream and prods from Suelen, for I was not really with her on the Hong Kong ferry. I was still on Yim Tin Tsai, running in hand with the boy who was nearly a man, and thunder muttered and slammed along the rim of the world as he took me in his arms and kissed me. And in that kiss the ferry rumbled obscenely, the big jets of Kai Tak airport exploded and whined like a typhoon wind, and all was sun and loving, far purer than I had dreamed. Later, the boy rose and left me lying in sand, and went down the beach to the sea where the white junk was waiting. Turning, he waved. I waved back.

'Goodbye,' I said.

'Goodbye,' said the boy on the third row from the prow, though he made no sound.

For the ferry was into the Hong Kong Praya. It bumped and bumped again, protesting to the bruising timbers. Heads rose in a towering mass about me and the boy was gone. A gangway crashed down and I went on tiptoe, frantic for another glimpse of him, but the shoving humanity, animated and chattering, went pell-mell for the butchering streets.

But he was waiting near the entrance, one eyebrow slightly raised, as if in question.

'Yes,' I said, and he looked relieved.

No need to go back as far as the Ching Dynasty. I think he knew that I had conceived.

The sun was a rod of fire, the streets flared. I looked again, but he had gone.

'What are you smiling at?' asked Suelen.

After an experience like that you can't help smiling.

We climbed the steps of Ladder Street into a kitchen of thieves, for Ma Chou Wong and the infamous Chui Apo, the pirate of Stanley, had traded here, dragging in their bloodstained loot from the caves of Bias Bay. Here on the stalls were the jade and jewels that had graced long-dead Portuguese ladies of Macau or forgotten Victorian maidens long since dust. Amid the junk of a modern society flashed and tinkled the chandeliers of the merchant princes who had plundered China and poisoned her with opium – men reviled by China since the ancient days of Commissioner Lin, who today stands responsible for the multi-million-dollar traffic in drugs – Jardine the Terrible, others – whose names, with the age-old pen of greed, are inscribed on the rolls of English honour. All this I was taught by my missionary man – also that the nooks and corners of Upper and Lower Lascar Rows are haunted by the ghosts of Old China, for Chui Apo himself had landed his armed junks under the noses of the British frigates in Tytam Bay and swaggered down these alleys, now a breeding ground of pestilence, a sink-pit of which Hong Kong ought to be ashamed.

At a little stall we bargained for and bought a tiny silver-plated bracelet for my sister Orla, and on the bracelet was printed, 'Love, Modesty, Wisdom, Humility, Virtue.'

'It is very beautiful,' I said, holding it up to the sun, and then looked at Suelen. She said, paying for it, 'Do not look like that at me, Pei Sha – all those qualities Orla still enjoys. She was sold by Papa, she did not sell herself for gain,' and thus I learned the difference between sacrifice and prostitution. Then Suelen said:

'Now to buy perfume for Lily Ting, Orla's friend.'

'Orla's friend?'

'The girl who is with her in the *Eastern Maid* bar. She is a loose woman, so we buy her perfume, to sweeten her. Pity this one, she needs such pity, so do not look at me so ghostly. You had chances, she had none, being sold into *muitsai*, the infamous girl-selling, at ten years old.'

'Child service can be honourable,' I said sharp, for she was talking of Orla and this Lily Ting in the same breath, and it displeased me. Suelen answered, smelling perfumes, 'But in the wrong house it can be living hell. Lily went into the service of an aged man – her mother was penniless since her man had taken another as wife, and deserted them. For three years Lily was happy as a serving-maid in a big house at East Point, but then the eldest son came home to visit. And on the night of his arrival he and his aged father drank themselves stupid on Japanese wine, and the father fell, and slept. While he slept, the son, believing himself to be in his own house in Macau, shouted for a woman. It was cock-call time and Lily Ting was up, she being the menial. Hearing the son's cries she went to him, and he took her despite her screams. Being a virgin, she bled much. Awakened, the mistress of the house came from her bed, and saw – this was the mother.'

'And then?'

'Then the family were greatly afraid, fearing a scandal. In the Old China Lily would have been whipped from the house for seducing a son, or given to the men servants for their pleasure. The parents feared. They sent Lily away. Today she is much older and she works in the *Eastern Maid* in Kowloon, with Orla.'

I did not reply at once, for this story was unlike the stories of Suelen. Never had I heard her speak of such things, or of such people.

'This shocks you, Pei Sha?'

I nodded.

'Better be shocked than be as Lily Ting,' said she. 'See, I buy her perfume, and this will sweeten her day, also her hatred of people. Let all your days be sweeter than hers, my precious,' and she put out her hands to me. 'Come.'

55

WE BOUGHT BOB-FLOATS for Po Shan and coils of
bright golden rattan, and Suelen bargained in high shrieks of
astonishment and disdain at the unearthly price, then we crossed
the ferry back to Kowloon side and searched the alleys for the
Eastern Maid bar until dusk was treading on the gown of night,
and at last found it within sight of the great Peninsula Hotel.
Already the neon lights were flashing in the harbour waters and
beneath the diamond-studded wealth of the big Peak houses the
harlot Wanchai signalled the lanterns of her erotic pleasures.
Strange Wanchai, I thought, watching it – the waterfront bawdy
town, an oasis of lust in a so-called civilised society, its existence
made fragrant by the films and the whispers of the tourists who
do things on other people's streets they would never do at home.
Womb of bar-girl suicide, tolerated by a God-fearing society
that beats its breast on Sundays – a relic of Victorian England,
the poor in suffering for the pleasures of the rich.

And Kowloon was happily up-to-date with the slaughterhouse
of Wanchai, said Suelen – bars everywhere. We were talking of
the Taoist beliefs, Suelen and me, as we walked, me staggering
under bob-floats; we talked, too, of the English congregation
and their white-frocked preachers.

'But what do these English preachers say?' I asked her.

'Let us find Orla Gold Sister,' said Suelen, 'the preachers are
indifferent.'

A pimp was sitting outside the door of the *Eastern Maid*, a
pie-faced Northerner by his looks, round and rosey-faced with a
long nose cocked up. I said, lowering the carrying-pole and
bob-floats:

'We have come to see Ming Orla, our sister.'

'Ho ho!' said he, scalding us with garlic. 'She has come to see
Ming Orla!' and he made faces at the bright lights, cleared his
throat, and spat past us with a wave of dismissal. Suelen said:

'Please, we will pay you two dollars, sir.' This she said with
great civility, which, with Suelen, was prelude to the savagery of
an alley cat.

'*Away!*'

Behind us, tipsy and boisterous, a group of beefy American sailors were gathering, and I knew by their hot glances at me that they were in longing, and I pitied them this pain, which I had suffered. I nudged Suelen, whispering:

'Inside or away out of it, girl, or the sailors will have us.'

The doorman rose. 'Two lousy Egg-Women with a load of stinking bob-floats – away before I bring up my boots. Sailors!' He waved and beckoned. 'Sailors! Very pretty girls inside, you come looksee?' this in English, most uneducated.

'Please let us in,' said Suelen. 'We must see our sister.'

'Get out!' the doorman shrieked, and up came the sailors just as Suelen hoped.

'What's wrong, lady?' This from an enormous sailor, pushing people aside.

'We only want to see our sister,' I explained in English.

'Say, she speaks English!' Up they came, sleeves going up, looking for trouble, and then there was a lot of barging and pushing in Chinese and English, a fetching of the landlord and other high officials, and big argument as to whether we were on our way in or out, and if we were in please would we be bringing the bob-floats?

'Bob-floats, also,' said the big American, lifting people aside, and into the *Eastern Maid* we went on a tide of sailors.

Never have I seen such a place or such people.

Lit by strips of brilliant light the room was all shining gold and gilt, and through the packed shoulders of men and half-bare hostesses its curved bar flashed and winked from a hundred bottles beneath a canopy of artificial stars. But the men! American sailors and marines eyeing each other, British soldiers thumping for English beer, French blue-jackets and a hundred and one nationalities ranging from Aden to Peru – the leering faces of men who would love to and dare not, the arrogance of those who dared – buying out girls with their fat wallets. Harsh music shrieked from a juke-box, couples danced languidly on a postage-stamp floor, clutched in a slow-motion heroin of sex: bawled conversations, screamed laughter, the low commands of the *Mamasan* who bought and sold, her dark eyes everywhere on lonely men. I watched, knowing the lust of the male from landlord to client; seeing for the first time a brothel legalised by the gigantic lie – that nothing was happening on the premises, for nothing did: this, the Hong Kong drug to decency that allowed such tourist attractions. This was the home of the *yum yum* girl which Hong Kong sacrificed in the name of prosperity; the unwanted pretty turned out of home; ex-concubine, desperate young wife, deserted lover, the hungry child who sold herself or the older woman graduating from a disgraceful *muitsai*, the infamous girl-selling once notorious in Hong Kong. This place, said Suelen later, was more than the home of Orla Gold Sister; it was but a step removed from the bawdy shamseens, the floating brothels of Wanchai and East Point where the perfumed mist and flower ladies once tiptoed on their crushed feet, attending to the desires of the late Victorians. Safe in the knowledge that brothels were illegal, the Government turned away its face and the houses of worship conveniently forgot.

Meanwhile, a commotion was growing about us, for there we stood in plain samfoos, one with a pole and bob-floats, the other with rattan. Heads slowly turned, mouths gaped, and high officials came running, arms flaying, their faces screwed up in stuttering horror.

'Come,' cried a voice, 'or you will be the death of us!'

Turning in joy, I saw Orla. Another girl seized my hand.

'Quick, child,' whispered Lily Ting.

This was not the Orla Gold Sister I remembered. She was only seventeen, but her work in the bar had aged her, her youth was flying in the lusting beds. Under the high mascara arch of her brows her eyes were strangely bright, and her smile, though wide and joyful, was not what she was, but what she would have been – before her death by men. Obediently we followed her up a narrow staircase, me still with eighteen bob-floats and getting jammed in the corners and cursing Po Shan. The room we entered was small, having but a narrow bed, a wash-basin, a chair. And in the grubby attic window glowed and pulsated a jewelled Kowloon and a mad criss-crossing of clubbing chimneys and garotting wash-lines, where dropped the coloured flouncies of a hundred tragedies.

And immediately Orla closed the door a man's voice yelled: 'Orla!'

'Coming, sir!' She turned to her friend. 'Lily, talk to them. I must go but I will soon be back.'

The door closed behind her, leaving us alone with Lily Ting. The strident music of the bar below trembled at our feet. Suelen said, sitting on the bed:

'You are Lily Ting? I am Ming Suelen – this is Orla's sister – Pei Sha.'

Lily Ting bowed. She was middle-aged, small, perfect in every detail, and there was dying beauty in her oval face, her skin transparent, her make-up bawdy, and the flesh was stretched tight across her high-boned cheeks. She said:

'You have come to fetch her home?'

'We have come to visit her,' replied Suelen, 'for this is her birthday. Until I received her letter I thought she was in Tai Po.'

'She ran from Tai Po,' said Lily Ting, and nodded sideway at me. Suelen said:

'Do not mind Pei Sha. We all have to learn of life.'

'And so did Orla,' Lily replied. 'The house in Tai Po had three grown sons. It was a man-eating woman they wanted there, not a child.'

Suelen bowed her head. 'God help her.'

'God help Orla if they find her here, for she is under contract with the go-between.' Lily opened her hands to us. 'She ran here, she begged me to help her. What could I do?'

'She should have begged of me, she would have been safer in Sai Kung with us. Where does she live?'

'We share a room in Prince Edward Road. I have a child, a little boy. Neighbours care for him by day, Orla and me love him by night.'

We waited half an hour until Orla returned, her high-heels clip-clopping along the landing, and she burst into the room with a cry of joy, slammed the door and leaned against it.

'Now then! Suelen, Pei Sha!' and she ran straight into Suelen's arms.

This was a very different Orla Gold Sister. I saw her close. Her eyes were bright with an inner fever and moving swiftly in her powdered face; her lips were vermilion, her hair sparkling silver dust, and her low-necked gown of satin black was stretched and curved about her fine figure. She was jabbering excitedly to Suelen, and I was forgotten, but I did not mind. The chasm between us was now too wide to cross. To my astonishment she took from her silver purse a cigarette and snapped a lighter at it with nervous fingers, sighing in and out a cloud of smoke.

'Oh, Suelen, it is beautiful, beautiful!' she cried then, holding the bracelet up to the lamp bulb. Turning suddenly, she kissed me. 'And you remembered, too – O, Pei Sha, Pei Sha!'

Her joy was pathetic: it was the excitement of one unwanted, who had been returned to love and warmth. I thought, I hate, I loathe, I *spit* on men. Closing her eyes in a sudden ecstasy, she said, seizing me, 'And you are so beautiful – did you know?'

'She knows all right,' said Suelen.

'Hui, Tuk Un – are they well?'

'They are hunters and fighters – the Sai Kung lads and Po Shan's missus.'

'You are happy with this Chu Po Shan?'

'We are of the sea-junks,' said Suelen, explaining all. She looked at Orla, mutely begging.

'No,' said Orla. 'I shall not come back with you.'

Suelen said: 'But one more mouth would make little difference.' She nodded at me. 'Ask Pei Sha, it is the life for her.'

Orla said, 'She is Pei Sha, and of the junks. I am Orla, and I am of the bars.'

'Is she a terror for the boys?' Lily Ting now, nudging me.

'All over the coast they come hunting her,' said Suelen. 'Even from Tolo, and the Tolo men are pirates!'

I laughed, they all laughed. Anything would do. Suelen said, 'Orla, Orla, come back with me! We will care for you.'

The door rattled to a man's knock. We froze. Orla ignored it, drawing hard on her stupid cigarette. Lily Ting stiffened, screwing at her hands. He knocked again, calling, 'Lily Ting, I can hear you in there – open the door.'

'What does he want?' I whispered, apprehensive, and Orla rolled her eyes very old-fashioned at Suelen. Lily called, 'All right, I am coming, sir.'

'Where is Ming Orla?'

'I am here,' shouted Orla.

'It is the big American.'

'Tell him I am busy.'

'You will come now. He is asking for you, and no other.'

Lily said, to lighten it, 'They all want Orla, she is very popular,' and my sister Orla drew herself up, saying to Suelen:

'See now, how I am needed here? Was I wanted at home in Fo Tan? And would I be wanted on the junk? Do not pity me, for I need no pity. Let me explain. The big American wants me. This is good, for he is a good man, and a man from the sea has a need for a woman. But there are men who call me to sit and talk, and these are lonely men, and to these we give another comfort. So do not despise the girls of Wanchai or the Kowloon bars, for we are friends to men.'

The man outside the door shouted angrily. 'He is buying you out, Orla, and he will not wait all night. Are you coming or do I call *Mamasan*?'

'Coming,' said Orla over her shoulder, and in that single reply, in the coarse manner of her I saw, for the first time, the prostitute. Suelen said, as she opened the door:

'Lily Ting, you should have brought her to me . . .'

'Goodbye,' said Orla.

'Goodbye,' we said.

The door closed. Suelen said, 'O, God, you should have brought her to me . . .'

Lily opened her hands. 'She has chosen the life. She is over sixteen, which is the legal age. You cannot guide Ming Orla – she has a will of her own. I sent you the first letter, remember? Nobody can say I did not tell the Mings.'

It was cooler in the street. With me under the bob-floats and Suelen clutching her beloved rattan, we waited for the New Territories taxi back to Sai Kung, and did not speak.

8

THE NEXT YEAR of my life passed in magnificent haste, as if eager to have me over and done with. The month of Clear and Bright by the old Chinese calendar came and went at a gallop. The summer solstice blazed into slight and great heat, the sun dripped naked in his sea of flame. Autumn nudged him out of it, and the heat ended. So swift this year on her winged feet that the Feast of Excited Insects became a faint March memory. Cold dews wreathed the shining land, frost winked at the frangipani leaves, and relented. It was January, the Chinese month of Great Cold.

Tai Tai, the wife of Po Shan, shivered in her bare feet, but not with cold – with debt. The New Year was snapping at her heels, a time when all debts are paid, and Po Shan was in debt, with no money to pay.

He was not the only one in trouble, so were the Mings.

Many times the dealer in women at Shatin sent his agents begging and threatening for the money he had lost on Orla Gold Sister, and every time Po Shan sent them back to Shatin empty. By God, the Mings will pay for this fraud, the dealer cried. The fraud has been paid for in full, said Po Shan – paid by the violated child, Orla. Away, away – running dogs, sons of bitches, *away*! And he ran down the slanting deck kicking them out of it. But there is more than one way to kill a monkey, and the Shatin dealer was an octopus, with tentacles.

'Six per cent interest as usual?' asked Po Shan at the sail-maker's.

'Payment in full, and now,' came the reply. 'A letter from head office.'

You are two days behind in the junk instalments, said the finance company who had never seen a junk. I will lend you the money to pay the instalment on the money you have borrowed from the finance company, said the loan-sharks – only 18 per cent interest. Pay now, said the kerosene merchant or no more kerosene: paint sold out, said the paint-seller during barnacle-scraping time.

Thus we learned that the money-lenders who owned Hong Kong owned us also.

Po Shan said, 'All this because of my weakness and stupid heart. I curse the day I ever heard of the Mings, their women and children.'

'Why the Ming women?' asked Tai Tai, his missus. 'Why not curse all women?'

And Po Shan barged about and muttered, and Tai Tai said of him, in his hearing:

'Listen to the big oaf. He is a great sweaty bear and he curses women – all save one woman, and her name is Chen Fu Wei.'

'I will not believe it!' exclaimed Suelen.

'Sleep with a man and know the man,' said Tai Tai. 'And I know the man within Po Shan – the hoary ape you do not know. By day he scorns her, for she disturbs him. By night he calls her name. She is the rice in his belly, the water on his throat.'

'He will take her as mistress?' I whispered, shocked.

'Not while I live, I am not enduring such wickedness.'

'Then as second wife?' asked Suelen.

And Tai Tai, Po Shan's missus, bowed her head. 'As a concubine by Ching Law. This I would allow.'

But the Great Cold seemed to freeze Po Shan's desire for Chen Fu Wei, the sampan girl, and not until the spring rains did he become sporty. I was at the rail, I remember, and Chen Fu Wei was in the sampan on the sea below me. Mistaking me for her he came behind me, his arms about my waist, and turned me swiftly about.

'*Wheeaho,* my little beauty!' and his lips crushed mine.

Terrified, I bit him, and he dropped me like something scalded and he stood above me, staring down while I preened and smoothed and patted myself, disgusted.

'Damned woman,' he whispered, 'You are the pod-image, your smell is the same, even your mouth betrays her.'

'Shame on you,' I said, on my dignity, 'not even on shore. On this very junk, indeed, within hearing of Tai Tai, and she your legal missus!'

This is spring, of course. Many do blame this kind of thing on the vernal equinox.

But although he pined for Chen Fu Wei, Po Shan took my brother Hui as his own son. Together they were as knotted twine, in the same salting-cask as herrings. At dawn's light Hui was out of bed rope-splicing, tarring, binding ends, and Po Shan gloried in the adopted son with the fine little muscular body, for Hui was nearly twelve years old now. In his spare time Po Shan taught him the charms of Chang Tao-ling, the Master of Heaven – such as on feast days when he would take him aft and there, in secrecy, put bangles on Hui's wrists and ankles so that devils, should they come, would believe him to be a girl and pass him by as unimportant. Having no silver chain and lock to fasten Hui to life, Po Shan would tie around his neck a dried chicken leg so that, if bad times came out of the debts, he would still be able to scratch a fair living. He even begged of me my Ming mirror. This he placed at the foot of Hui's deck mattress while he slept, facing east, so that tampering demons would see their own visage, and run, horrified. Suelen said of Po Shan:

'Tai Tai, treat this big man easy. Chen Fu Wei is not his dream of beds, she is his dream of sons.'

Hearing this, Tai Tai wept, for she was empty of sons, and she would not be consoled, except by her man, but Po Shan would not come.

The sun was rising blisters on this particular spring, I remember, but I remember it for greater things than that. All that April, day after day, the white junk would beat into Sai Kung harbour from the sea and the boy of Yim Tin Tsai would be standing at the tiller, shielding his eyes as he looked for me. But I had eyes of the sea, and saw him early, and was sharp below deck in the middle cabin. There I would watch, holding myself in hunger for him, dying for him, but terrified. For should he see me and call, my life in Sai Kung would be ended. There would be much talk and a wagging of fingers and tongues, and let us put an end to it, and down to the village with her quick and have her appear before the bald elders.

For what decent Cantonese boy would wait upon me after contact with a foreigner?

And on one such occasion Po Shan and Tai Tai were by the middle mast, speaking in whispers, and I listened, hating myself. Tai Tai had Tuk Un at her breast for feeding, Pa Shan was double lashing hawsers for the back bollards. They sat, and did not speak, until Tai Tai said:

'Look, my husband, this Ming Tuk Un could be your own boy. See how he grasps at me, believing me his mother,' and Po Shan answered gruffly:

'But he is not your son, nor mine. Do not deceive yourself, woman. A hungry child will suckle at a cow. Cursed is your womb that you cannot bear even a living daughter,' and he rose, flinging down the splicer steel. I heard Tai Tai say, in a voice of tears:

'Chu Po Shan my husband, I would die to bear your child. Seek your boy elsewhere, then, but do not curse my womb lest one day it bears a cripple. Take Chen Fu Wei as second wife if this pleases you, but do not curse me!'

'Blood of my blood,' muttered Po Shan. 'Flesh of my flesh. O, Tin Hau, Queen of Heaven, grant me a boy!'

Later I saw him prostrate before her altar in the aft cabin, with joss-sticks lighted, and he was weeping and beating his breast, for he was Tan-gar, and the men of the Tan-gar live and die by their sons.

Let nobody sneer who does not understand, for we are Chinese.

I wept also, for Po Shan and Tai Tai, his missus.

Other things were happening, just as disgraceful.

Ming Suelen, my adopted sister, was coming broody.

You can see the same kind of things with fluffy old hens who ought to know better.

Up they get in the morning barging everybody else off the perches, blowing up their wings to sharpen the neighbourhood, and strut and preen themselves before the cockerel standing in his spiked silence, his red eyes blinking his hellish thoughts, for cockerels spend time making up very obscene rhymes. Then they sit and moan and rock themselves on the eggs, calling their harsh love-calls, and then hide their faces, praying to the god of hens for answers, and getting nowhere but into pots.

So it was with my beautiful Suelen. The rumour went that a little Hakka called Kwai To Man had been seen in the vicinity again, minding his own business, as Hakkas do.

To make things even worse, Chen Fu Wei, the sampan widow, was also at it.

Hui was ashore in the Tea-house of Exalted Virtue, playing mahjong and fighting his new cricket, and Po Shan was on the prow of the *Cormorant*, doing his exercises of Grand Terminus Pugilism, the shadow boxing, which is a manner in which the heart and mind are strengthened. Fine he looked in his slow-motion contortions, his big body flashing sweat. The packed harbour craft creaked and groaned about us, the water-vendors swept their sampans up and down the water-alleys, their voices torn on the mud-caked air. Drowsy in the eyes I looked past Suelen's net-shuttle to distant Yim Tin Tsai but nothing stirred in its bright lagoons. Turning to Sai Kung jetty I saw Chen Fu Wei coming in her save-life sampan.

'She comes in a panic,' said Suelen.

Down from the prow came Po Shan, waving, and Chen waved back. I rose, watching. She was most beautiful to see, her baby Yin Yin bright-shawled on her back, her sampan swaying to the rhythmic sweep of her stern oar. Nearing us she laughed up and her eyes were slanted in her sun-black face, her teeth row-white in her Hoklo smile.

'Is there a welcome aboard?' she cried, and she scrambled up the rope ladder Po Shan tossed her, and slung a leg over the thwarts, looking glorious.

Tai Tai, from the stern rail, watched, and did not speak.

I have always been fond of Chen Fu Wei, for she was pure. There are some like her who ride the night sampans in other ports, plying the stern sweeps with muffled oars – the painted ones who carry no lights, but work in darkness and the hot blood of fishermen; thieving by night, husbands, lovers. Chen was virtuous. This was her strength and Tai Tai knew it. Now she said, gasping after the climb:

'Is anybody excited?'

'Why should there be excitement?' asked Po Shan.

'About the meeting?' she asked, innocent, and I knew she was with mischief.

'What meeting?' I demanded.

'The courting of the Hakkas. I have found the man, you see, but I have yet to discover the woman.'

'She is dozing in the head,' said Suelen, squatting on the deck, weaving rattan. 'She is a babbling bundle of nonsense.'

And Chen Fu Wei winked and threw back her head, laughing. She pointed. 'See – he waits. He has been there hours. Ming Suelen's man!'

'What is happening – who waits?' demanded Po Shan, on tiptoe.

And I saw, standing on the end of the jetty the little Hakka, Mr Kwai To Man, and by the look of him he was settling down for months. Suelen said, her face dark with anger, 'You should be ashamed, Chen! A grown woman and you carry scandal like a child. I will see to him,' and she rose, flinging down her rattan.

'He will need some seeing to,' shouted Po Shan, enjoying it. 'There is not much body on him but he has a saucy old air –

66

even from this distance,' and he slammed his fist down on the rail and went double with laughter.

I pitied Suelen. With a fine pride she went down the rope ladder and into the sampan and ferried like a mad thing over to the jetty where Kwai was waiting.

'To work,' said Po Shan. 'We have had our fun and now we do not stare. This is Ming Suelen's business.'

I said, bitterly, 'You have angered her. See, she raves at him, poor little man. Look, he is going.'

'But he has the scent of her. Do not worry, he will come again.'

Thus the hunting of my sister began.

Two weeks later this Mr Kwai of Ho Chung village again had a run at her.

For three days the *Cormorant* was up on the chocks and beached for a scraping of the barnacles and seam-caulking. Also, the engineers were coming to remove the big diesel engine because we had not kept up the payments. Henceforth we would fish by sail. The loan-sharks have their hooks in me, said Po Shan, and they suck my life-blood. They will not be content until they drive me to the land. And in his desperation he was turning more and more to Chen Fu Wei, which is a thing men do, losing their troubles in a new face, seeking in youth the lost strength of their purpose.

I well remember this day, for once a month the beauty expert came to the village from a parlour in the city, and with the children whooping about her she had set up a box on the waterfront for curling hair and plucking eyebrows. On my way to fetch kerosene at the stall I passed this woman, who was preparing a young bride for her wedding, and there sat the bride in a circle of onlookers with a high colour in her cheeks, which is the manner of brides. And the women, who were not of this village, were baying and shoving, whispering coarse jokes, pushing and tormenting the little bride until she was in tears, and the lady-women of Sai Kung were scandalised. Coming near them, I heard, and was disgusted.

'Marriage is not like that!' I shouted, and the beauty expert raised her face to mine. No paint or powder could have saved that face, which had died. She asked, hands on hips, facing me:

'And how old are you, little owl-talker?'

'Old enough!'

At this the coarse women threw up their hands, shrieking with laughter. It was a stupid answer and I was ashamed.

'And how many men have you known?' asked the expert.

I did not reply and this put the women in fits. I saw the wrinkled skin of their thrusting faces, the crone champing of aged jaws, and they hooted and stamped about me. The beauty expert said, 'Listen, and I will tell you of men. The Emperor Chow of the Shang Dynasty cut open the stomachs of women in labour for a wager on the sex of their children. He broke open the bones of men in winter to see if the marrow had frozen. Such is the unnatural cruelties of men in power, and a wife has no power to face a husband.'

Suelen said at my elbow, and I swung to the shock of her voice, 'That is not true of all men, I have known many who were gentle.'

'But not, I am bound, in a bed!' and the beauty expert and her friends flung up their arms and shrieked with laughter again. I felt Suelen stiffen, saw the muscles of her fine body cord and tighten against her jacket. She cried above them:

'Are you women or devils? Must you pollute the minds of children?'

'The mind of this bride is as moon-dust,' cried the expert. 'Better she knows the facts of life from me than learn them later from a man!'

'Then she learns them from me,' shouted Suelen, and thrust people aside. 'You and your kind have never known marriage. Get back to your rat-alleys and your painted whores and harpies!' and she kicked the beauty box flying.

'You swine Hakka!'

'Aye,' shouted Suelen. 'One pig kicking another – out, *out!* Away from a decent village lest the widows find you – they who mourn their seamen husbands.'

The friends of the expert clawed at her, but she clubbed them away. One clutched her and she flung the woman headlong. With her back to the sea she awaited them, and as the beauty expert rushed, shrieking, Suelen stooped, seized her, and threw her high. The woman screamed, and fell, splashing into the harbour.

'Next,' said Suelen, and the strangers shrank away from her. My sister smoothed back her hair. Reaching out she raised the girl-bride. 'Come, child,' she said, and led her through the crowd.

Later, with the village agog at this, I was buying binding-twine and kerosene as Po Shan had bid me, and a man was there at the stall. This was Kwai To Man, the Hakka; he was small, handsome, and I recognised him instantly. The vendor said:

'You heard of the fight today?'

'I saw the fight,' said Suelen's man, and slapped down money.

'The Mings were involved,' said the vendor, not seeing me. 'They live with poor old Po Shan – he keeps a tribe of women. It was the big Hakka, she fights like a man.' The vendor laughed. 'Ugly is as ugly does – did you see her?'

And Kwai To Man turned slowly, his dark eyes narrowed. 'I saw but an ugly beauty expert. The one who fought her was a beautiful woman. Mind your tongue when you speak to strangers – this one honours Ming Suelen.'

That evening, when we were all scraping barnacles off the *Cormorant* and Po Shan was sad because his engine had gone, Kwai To Man came down to the beach. I was starboard, working on the seams with Suelen. Hui and Tai Tai were port side, brushing on tar. If my sister saw him she made no sign, and Kwai stood there, waiting for Po Shan to return with pails and brushes. He said:

'Chu Po Shan, are you master here?'

Po Shan nodded, towering above the Hakka guest – he coming from Canton, his father also, though his mother hailed from Shansi where the men are tall and the women have glorious breasts and the dignity of queens. Mr Kwai pointed at Suelen, who had turned her back, and said, 'Then I would speak to you about that woman – in private.'

'Speak public,' replied Po Shan. 'We are one family, we keep no secrets.'

The Hakka's eyes snapped open in his dark face. 'One family? Are these three wives, then? How can this be. The big one is a Hakka, the other two are Tan-gar by their looks. The tribes are opposite – the sea, the land.'

'Speak straight,' said Po Shan sharply. 'You have seen a woman who takes your eye?'

'I fancy the big Hakka. She works well enough for you, she could labour for me.'

'As a labourer?' Po Shan's eyes were twinkling.

Kwai moved uneasily. 'As wife.'

'Have you invited her?' Po Shan now, hands on hips, booming bass, loving every minute, and Suelen worked on beside me, trembling with anger.

Kwai said, 'I write her letters by the village writer, and she does not reply. I visit her, and she raves at me. Has she ears, even?'

'She can hear a nit in ship's timbers, she can hear brown grass growing.'

'Then she has no tongue!'

'Easy, little man, take care . . .'

Suelen said, 'Go, Hakka, before you get the length of it. Find another woman you can make look easy.'

And Kwai's eyes grew round in his face. He exclaimed, turning to Po Shan, 'Did you hear that, sir? By God, she has a voice of gold when gentle, and her accent is as my mother's clan, she who dwelt by the Wei River!'

My sister's expression changed, I noticed. Po Shan said, 'You displease her. Go, little man. You do not tempt her so her back is turned to you. You are wasting my time,' but Kwai To Man did not heed him. With his hands together as if in prayer, he said to Suelen:

'Hakka, listen. For years I have followed you – improving myself for you until I became a man of substance. Now I have a hut which is registered under the Government – I have four mows of wheat and another two of standing rice, a buffalo, a plough. All this I would share with you, if you will be my wife.'

'This is a different tune,' murmured Tai Tai. My sister did not move to him.

Kwai said, his voice rising, 'I have pledged my life to you, Ming Suelen. I lost you, now I have found you. We are Hakka. The stink of things dying must sicken your nose – you are made for things growing, not slaughtered. *Ai-yah!* Must you stay and work with the sea-heathen?'

And still Suelen did not turn her face. Po Shan replied softly, '*Oi, Oi!*' and I admired him, for Kwai was insulting and with one blow Po Shan could have felled him, but did not.

Tai Tai said loftily, 'She dismisses you. Look, she does not turn her face. You do not show humility, and Suelen is humble.'

This infuriated Kwai. 'With all this land under the hoe – need I be humble? By the gods!' In desperation he swung to Po Shan. 'For years I have sought this woman. My guts are dry for her yet she rejects me – I who can have my pick of women north to Fanling and south to Stanley!'

'Such is life, my friend,' said Po Shan easily. 'There are things in my own life that do not come my way,' and I knew he meant Chen Fu Wei.

'But why, *why?*'

Tai Tai said, turning from my sister, 'Listen, Hakka, I speak to you a woman's language. You are not well-mannered. You have demanded, not requested. There are women in this life who cannot be bought with money or flattery. Let us know your standing. Where were you born?'

'By the Han River, in the clan of Kwai, which is much respected. But I know best the song of the East River in the province of Kwangtung, for this is where I grew.'

At this Suelen turned slightly, her face radiant, but still did not face him. Tai Tai said, 'This woman has laboured on a building site. She may not be your equal.'

'I, too, have laboured on building sites, before I started for a farmer.' He came closer to Tai Tai. 'Missus, speak for me when I am gone, for I want this woman to share my life.'

'I will speak for you. Come again, and when you do, bring humility. And remember that we are Tan-gar, not sea-beasts. Do not refer to us again as heathen or I will not check my man and he will kill you.'

'Yes,' said Kwai, most subdued.

'Go,' said Po Shan, 'we are busy.'

I looked at my sister after Kwai To Man had gone. She had not turned to him and I thought her displeased with him. Then she went at the seams like a mad woman, with the barnacles hopping out of it.

I mistook this energy for anger, but I was wrong. It was a strange woman-mixture of sadness and joy.

Suelen was smiling, her eyes with a hint of weeping.

'That is a queer old name,' I said carelessly, 'Kwai Ming Suelen.'

71

9

TYPHOONS CAME AND left us gasping, sweeping before them blood-stained dead. Tossed on the crests of tremendous seas, we laid on cable, and the *Cormorant* held. While big cargo ships steamed into the storm full speed and dragged their anchors, while junks and play-boats foundered on the rocks of Pak Sha Wan and Tolo, we held, lashed by Po Shan's tongue. Drenched, bewildered, we held her into the copper dawns, then dropped, sleeping on the streaming decks. The Tan-gar and Hoklo of Kwangtung, sick of it, began their dreary processions to the land and the slavery of the building sites. Landslides began in whispers and ended in shrieks. Hundreds of squatter huts collapsed, families were trapped in mud-slides; boulders, running amok among the shanty hillsides, crushed men, women, and children to death. People were homeless and destitute, wandering and begging. The rich cursed the big winds, swept out their flooded terraces and cancelled their parties with regrets – or came from the shelter of the plush hotels. The poor huddled together in their smashed huts or squatted on the sidewalks, waiting for the eternal Christianity of the World Lutheran Service, the Roman Catholics, the Street Sleepers' Association, and countless other Christian organisations. The Government, which forbade begging by law, begged for community relief.

And Chu Po Shan, with the debts to the usurers higher than ever, took us to sea on sail far up the China run, and went after the shoals, but there were none to be found, for the typhoons had cleared the waters and the fish were not there. And Po Shan went into the aft cabin and there prostrated himself before the little red altar of the Queen of Heaven, and begged.

But the fish did not come.

Suelen said to me, 'Pei Sha, the Old Man is in deep trouble. He is gentle enough, but in his heart he reviles us. I have made up my mind, I am going from here.'

'To labour on the building sites for the employers?'

'To marry Mr Kwai To Man of Ho Chung village.'

72

'But only weeks ago you sent him away.'

She smiled. 'He will come back. On the day of White Dews he will come back for me.'

'This is a different song,' I said, watching her.

And she rose, staring at the crested sea where the spume was flying on the homeward run, and said, 'I am singing a song for Kwai To Man. Ah, Pei Sha, it is something to be wanted!'

Next week we were south of Amoy and a Communist police boat came out and boarded us, all very polite. By this time we had big red snapper aboard, and they took twenty catties of this catch, which was fair enough, said Po Shan, since, after all, the fish were Communist.

'Some might call them Nationalist,' commented Suelen slyly, baiting him.

'These fish are large,' said Po Shan gruffly, 'they are bound to be Communist,' and he glared.

Tai Tai said later, 'He is glaring because he wants Chen Fu Wei, not because of the politics. Chu Po Shan has hair on his chest. He does not care who is ruling China so long as he rules the roosters in the aft cabin. I do know for I do sleep with him. At the moment he is on one hen, but he is needing two.'

Later, nearer home, we went in search of the bright lobsters and crabs off the coast of beloved Kwangtung, in moonlight. The wind was rising in swathes of sea-ripple, I remember, shepherding the mist into billows of fleece, and these we drove quietly before us for the market pens of Sai Kung, sheep most beautiful to see.

In this moonlight, with the Old Man stark black at the tiller, Suelen leaned on the rail and said to me:

'Kwai To Man will be waiting for me. And this date I would find suitable. In these days of autumn Mr Kwai will seek me for labour in his fields.'

I feared for Suelen, whispering, 'And you told him to learn humility?'

'I have a need for this man, Pei Sha. I am like him now in his need of me. I have no pride.'

'Suelen, do not beg. Not you, I could not bear it.'

And she smiled. 'No need to beg. Mr Kwai will be waiting for me on the jetty. It do take a Hakka to know a Hakka.'

But when we arrived in Sai Kung, Kwai To Man was not waiting on the jetty, nor had he come by the English September. And one day, coming back from Yim Tin Tsai, I swept the save-life sampan up to the *Cormorant* in dusk, and climbed the rope-ladder like a cat, for somebody was sobbing. Through the middle cabin window I saw Suelen lying full length on her straw, weeping in shame, she having lost face before everyone since there was no Mr Kwai.

So next morning I awoke with a raging toothache and borrowed from Suelen a dollar for the fare to Yaumati where the wonderful American missionary held his clinic for the poor. But by the strangest possible mistake I got off the New Territories' taxi at Ho Chung, the village of Kwai To Man and his papa. And next day Mr Kwai put on his best coat and trousers, which were of Shantung silk thread, and took the New Territories' taxi to Sai Kung, and Suelen.

These are the things we do for those beloved.

We were all down on the beach sorting a catch when Mr Kwai hove in sight. Suelen saw him first, of course, and went very self-satisfied and smug, saying to me, 'There now, what did I tell you? I snap a finger and he comes running,' and she adopted an air of cold indifference.

'Good morning, sir,' said Kwai to Po Shan, shaking hands with himself.

'Good morning,' replied Po Shan. 'Unless I am mistaken you have gone even smaller.'

'So would you if you had my labour,' said Kwai, eyeing Suelen who was flopping king garoupa from one basket to another and back again until they wondered if they were in Hong Kong or Tokyo. 'Sweat and labour is my lot, for I have no woman – only an aged father, and him too old for work. Also, in spare time I am building a barn.'

'Labouring?' Po Shan looked up. 'That is women's work.'

'Aye, but it is nearly finished.' Kwai brightened. 'Its beams are already hung with onions and garlic and there are thirteen jars of reed weave within, all filled with grain from the winnowing.'

'Thirteen jars, man?' Suelen the Hakka lifted slowly from the waist, staring askance. 'At this time of year? Don't tell me you are also making money?'

'I cannot handle more,' explaining Kwai, 'for in spare time I make flour.'

'A miller also?' Tai Tai now, with Tuk Un in her arms, most interested.

'Ah, for at festival time I make bread and cakes – even moon-cakes and rice-balls special for the Moon Festival.' Sitting on the sand he wiped his sweating face. 'These, of course, have to be delivered.'

'That is work for a child,' I said brightly.

Po Shan sighed. 'We are back to Kwai's troubles again. How can he have children if he hasn't got a wife?' Bending, he lifted a fish basket that would have ruptured a donkey, and grunted. 'Your trouble is height, man. Is there no little woman in Hong Kong island who might suit you? The Hakkas are too long round here.'

Kwai considered this. 'Size is nothing since women vary. There are garlic- and pork-eaters with drooling mouths, gossip-women who are an abomination, women as scraggy as Nanking beggars and soft-bellied ones with drowsy faces, hankering after sugary foods when they ought to be labouring in fields or child-birth – long or short makes no difference.'

Tai Tai said gently, 'You will not find perfection, Kwai. Ming Suelen, have the good manners to face him.'

The admonishment turned Suelen, and Kwai said to her face:

'I shall ask but once more, then go, for I am a proud man, and shall not lose face before any woman. Ming Suelen, will you share my life? Would you marry a Tan-gar fisherman, however admirable? (and here he bowed to Po Shan) and spawn a litter of half-breeds? Or have your birth-pains over a junk labour-tub when I could hold you in barn straw? Ming Suelen?'

He knelt, which astonished me, and people on the beach wandered up, some with their fists already in their mouths, and these included Po Shan himself, even Tai Tai, for the boat-people are unused to begging, and poets. Mr Kwai raised his face, saying, 'You demand humility? Here I show it, before your people, and this is unusual in my clan. Two years I have loved you, Hakka woman. Would your child taste brine in your milk? Must you steep your hands in the blood of things slaugh-tered when you can kneel beside me, planting, your fingers deep in rich, black soil? Ming Suelen?'

Since it was not his custom so to prostrate himself, I loved and admired this little brother-in-law-to-be, Kwai To Man.

But of a sudden Po Shan bellowed his explosive laughter, and the crowd took it up. I saw their faces in panic: cackling roosters, cawing crows of faces, cruel, eyes slitting to the coarse booms of laughter, black caverns of mouths and champing jaws; the yellow teeth of the wicked aged, I saw, for age is bitter and the cruellest of all. And I took a great breath to shriek.

'*Silence!*'

In the ring of people stood Suelen, glaring, her fists up, and they lowered their faces before her and shifted their feet like scolded children. And in the silence she raised Kwai beside her, and held him. 'Come, Hakka,' she said, 'away from these rough people.'

10

BEFORE THE YEAR was out my sister Suelen married Mr Kwai To Man of Ho Chung village, Chu Po Shan took unto himself the sampan widow Chen Fu Wei as second wife, and I took the save-life sampan and found a new world on my island, Yim Tin Tsai.

Important people first, my beloved Suelen.

Tragedy was already in the air for her, for she had no mother-in-law: Kwai's aged father was his only living relative, though Ho Chung village, it appeared, was full of dead ones. Personally, I would never marry without a mother-in-law, for how can one show love to a husband without giving obedience to his mother? However, Kwai's father was beloved by all, and most sensible he proved in the wedding negotiations for he immediately adopted Po Shan as Suelen's First Brother, and to him he sent forty small rolls of the highest quality wheat flour, eight pounds of best roast pork belly, and eighteen cream cakes – real cream, from Dairy Farm, not tinned, and all this was most impressive.

The customary gift of money, however, was strangely absent.

Po Shan said severely, 'Steamed rolls, cream cakes, pork belly, but no money.'

'Sai-law!' exclaimed Tai Tai. 'She is marrying into a school of skinflints.'

'Please, it do not matter,' said Suelen.

'Do it not? And on whose authority?' demanded Po Shan. 'Do they expect a solid gold bride free, the half-chit land-sliders?'

'Leave it, I beg you. It is humiliating.'

But next morning Po Shan rose well before cock-shout, shaved extra close, cursed old Fu Tang, the Sai Kung tailor, for not delivering his new silk jacket and trousers, and took the taxi-bus to Ho Chung. When he returned at sun-above, Suelen was richer by four hundred and eighteen dollars, money he had squeezed from the belly of her prospective father-in-law despite his groans and protestations.

'Three hundred dollars,' said Po Shan, and counted them on to the table.

'What about the rest of it?' asked Tai Tai, watching him.

'The odd hundred and eighteen I keep for myself,' he answered, pocketing it, 'to pay for my new wedding coat and trousers and the sundry expenses of First Brother,' and he went down into the save-life sampan to visit old Fu Tang, the tailor.

'His wedding coat and trousers are for his own wedding,' said Tai Tai to Suelen, 'not yours.'

'He takes Chen Fu Wei as concubine?' I asked, timid.

'Within the month I expect to name her,' said Tai Tai.

Suelen said later, 'Look on this one and see her well, Pei Sha. It is a big woman.'

Never in my life will I forget that cold October morning of Suelen's wedding day. For a week now all aboard the *Cormorant* had been scrubbing and polishing for the Ho Chung matrons coming to claim the bride. Also, the word of it was spraying like fire, for this was an unusual wedding – a Hakka being given away by the boat-people. Hui was aloft in the rigging fixing bright-coloured streamers and pennants, and a twig brush on the tip of the mainmast to scare away devils. But the devils were with us still, for although Tai Tai was accepting Chen Fu Wei after Suelen's wedding, she was skinning Po Shan alive at every chance. Even on the bridal morning when he came hopping mad from the aft cabin, cursing the tailor because his new trousers were too long, she said, 'What is your new fancy woman up to – can't she use a needle?'

'Come, I will shorten them,' I said with business.

'Indeed you will not!' Tai Tai was bristling, her face as red as a turkey wattle.

'Please, Missus,' whispered Suelen, her hand out to them.

'Leave him! And his trousers!' Tai Tai raved. 'He does them himself.'

Po Shan bawled. 'And I am surrounded with women!'

'And soon you will have another and she will give you more than trousers!'

'*Tin Hau!*' Po Shan hopped and blasphemed. Later, pitying him, I went secretly to the aft cabin and took a few inches off the legs – for Suelen, for this was her day of wedding.

The old sun came up golden, knowing it was for Suelen, and in its midday radiance the Sai Kung virgins trooped aboard the *Cormorant*. Led by the lovely Chen Fu Wei, they came, and their purple and white samfoos gleamed and cut new ironed creases. There was Kin, eldest daughter of Lai-Tam, the hero, and her two young sisters. There was Pao the Precious, only surviving daughter of the family Woo who lost six children off Tolo in the last sea-bitch. There was Little Lin, a midget child but of perfect proportions, sister of Ho who owned the junk *Up-You* and its save-life sampan *Up-You-Too*, both named by an American sailor, once a friend of the family; and Dal the beautiful – all came trembling for the forthcoming battle with the Sai Kung matrons who would attack to capture the bride, this being Hakka custom. And Po Shan took one look and scrambled down the rope-ladder to play mahjong in the Teahouse of Exalted Virtue, there to bewail the taking of his junk by women. Tai Tai I saw next, glowering at the stern rail, staring at Chen Fu Wei. I said softly:

'Be happy for Suelen, Missus, do not spoil things.' For the virgins, led by Chen who was matron-in-charge, were dancing about the deck and pulling gambling sticks for the honour of being in the front rank to protect the bride.

Tai Tai said with canker in her voice, 'See how that Chen preens her beauty, and dances. O, Pei Sha, I could take her eyes!'

Suddenly sick of her tantrums, I turned away, saying, 'Give some charity, woman. Pity all the sonless Po Shans but stop pitying yourself!'

For the jealousy was ripe within Tai Tai these days. It allowed no sense, no argument, and even now she did not hear me, so intent was she on Chen Fu Wei. But in her heart she knew that one woman is not enough for a man of strength like Po Shan – or two, or three even for those who are lithe to their mates with the sinews of a leopard. In sudden impatience I left her and went to the aft cabin which had been made most beautiful for Suelen with artificial flowers, streamers, and red paper. The beds had been cleared away and there was nothing left but the Tin Hau altar and a great carved chair in which Suelen sat. Already dressed in her many white petticoats she sat motionless, unsmiling even at me, while the maidens of Sai Kung combed and oiled her hair, plaiting it into the proof that she was a virgin, coiling it around her head. And while this was being done Pao the Precious read from a paper the advice on marriage. Over a rail nearby was the bright mandarin gown hired from Kowloon. Outside on the deck Hui and his friends were pasting lucky red paper on the thwarts, doors, even on the decks, and hanging red lanterns either side of the gangplank to greet the invading matrons when they came aboard. And at two o'clock sharp the aft cabin door was slammed shut and locked lest the bridegroom's matrons should steal the bride away before her time. As I took a last look round the tidy decks I heard from the Sai Kung road a thin cry, and shielded my eyes from the sun. The sentry look-out was standing with her arm upraised.

'They come!' I shouted, and ran, thumping the cabin door as a signal. Back at the gangplank I waited tensed, for a thin line of women were coming down to the jetty. So bright those coloured samfoos! All the glory of the great flags! Dust rose to their tramping feet, their excited cries drifted on the clear autumn air. Then a fine sedan chair came next into view, crimson, gold, with silver shafts, this to collect the bride. Carried by four bulky Ho Chung farmers, it came, followed by the Ho Chung matrons, their sleeves rolled up for the battle ahead, and after them came the urchins of Pak Sha Wan spoiling for the fight. Trembling, I raced back to the aft cabin door.

'They are coming – bolt up hard!'

'Aha, Pei Sha!' It was Po Shan, tipsy with the Japanese wine already, running aboard, taking up a defence position beside me.

'Away, or the women will have you!' I cried.

Now crowds of fisher-folk were jamming down to the jetty and our friends fought to keep a passage for the Ho Chung matrons and the chair, for they were coming to claim a bride and were not to be impeded except by virgins, for this was a mixture of custom, Hakka and Tan-gar. Even foreigners were there in twos and threes, fingering cameras and not daring to raise them. The procession came nearer, nearer, and when they reached the head of the gangplank the aft cabin door came open and the defending girls came out, showing their fists and threatening. One locked Suelen in the cabin and slipped me the key and I put it down the front of me.

'We demand the bride!'

The crowd went quiet. The sedan chair was set down on the jetty. The Ho Chung matrons came closer, threatening.

'We demand the bride!' This from a glorious Hakka woman, one of great height.

'Ha, ha!' yelled Po Shan, guarding the gangplank, and they murmured among themselves, these women, for a man was impeding them, and it was against the custom.

'Chu Po Shan!' I cried, grabbing at him, but he shook me away, grinning and flexing his muscles before the scowling matrons.

'All right,' I said, 'take the consequences.'

The women grouped, whispering, then rushed him. Some took the plank, some leaped over the gunwales, and in a moment Po Shan was enveloped in a shower of paper cudgels and mock staves. Tripped from behind, he went sprawling; he bellowed like a slaughtered bull as the Hakka women lifted him. For a moment he tottered on the port rail, begging, protesting, then took the plunge in waving arms and legs to an accompaniment of shrieks and laughter. Crouching behind a deck coil I watched the valiant fight of the San Kung maidens, who were allowing themselves slowly to be defeated, and one by one they were pulled down on to the hot deck while rough hands searched them for the key of the aft cabin door, behind which Suelen was patiently awaiting her fate. Never will I forget that scene and its sounds. The sweating, fighting matrons, the wailing protests of the defending attendants as they were dragged away from the door. Urchins were cartwheeling madly along the jetty, children yelling with delight: I heard the coarse guffaws of labourers, the cackling of the crones, the high shrieks of watching girls. All this I heard as if it was yesterday. Ming Suelen, my adopted sister, is not with me now, but I see her still – sitting in her gorgeous red mandarin gown behind the locked door, while the women of the bridegroom fought for her in Sai Kung.

'The sister!'

They remembered me. The cry was shrieked and caught up by a hundred throats, and Pao the Precious, keeping the custom, betrayed me, pointing at the deck coil.

'Ming Pei Sha, sister of the bride!'

The Hakka women rushed, snatching me down as I ran to escape. I wept, I fought, and their hands went over my body, searching for the key. A cry of triumph and they cast me aside while on my knees I begged them to give it back. They wheeled like birds scenting the wind, then ran for the cabin door, unlocked it, and threw it back. I rose to my knees. The crowd went silent. It was so quiet I heard fish gossiping. In simple dignity Ming Suelen sat there in the doorway, most beautifully prepared by the Sai Kung maidens, the red flannel of her humility covering her face. This was not my sister, but one from the walled cities of the Yellow River, of pure blood, while mine was mingled with that of the dark people. She was of the Sung invasions, one flung southward but never defeated. And I saw in her that day a nobility I had not seen before.

'Suelen!'

As I called she rose, and did not heed me. In barbaric splendour she stood there, inches taller than the Ho Chung women, and she was regal. A hand went out and slammed the door in her face. And I went to a quiet place below decks and wept, because she was going to leave me, but not only for this. I wept because Kwai To Man would put her to the tub and have her in the fields from light to darkness. She would bow to his father, she would wait upon them with the servitude of a menial: by day and night she would serve Kwai To Man, and there would be no sound of her in the junk, no sight of her at meals: the world would be empty for me, because she was Suelen.

An hour later the aft cabin door opened again, and Suelen stood there again, beautiful indeed. Motionless she stood with the eager, shoving women about her, the prisoner of Kwai. The sun flashed on her red and gilt gown and on her head was the plain paper crown of the Hakka bride. They led her forward and her face was covered, and she could not see.

'Suelen,' I whispered as they took her past me, and she paused for a moment, her foot searching a plank. Nor did she speak, but her face was wet beneath her flannel mask. She made no sound.

Silence. Not a whisper from that jetty crowd. The men were gripping themselves, even the children were hushed.

"Goodbye, my precious,' I said, but she did not heed me, for to do so was weakness.

Then the cry went up. 'Punish the chair!'

The people chanted. 'Punish, punish the chair!'

Three times Suelen kicked the sedan chair because it was taking her away from the people she loved, and thus she fulfilled the custom. Somebody opened the door of the sedan chair. Blindly, her hands searching, she found the mirror on the seat which had been keeping devils away, for no bridegroom wants a bride's devils to come along, too – he having enough of his own. They helped her inside. The red velvet curtains were drawn, the thick-shouldered bearers got into the shafts and lifted, then went along the Sai Kung road at a swaying trot. The snake of procession grew longer and I took my place behind the chair with Po Shan and Tai Tai immediately in front of me. Behind me was Chen Fu Wei and Hui, my brother, and Hui was weeping.

It was sun-shy when we breasted the rise of Ho Chung village.

With great joy I saw the boy of Yim Tin Tsai aboard his white junk anchored in the harbour. He was standing on the deck of the companionway, staring at the wedding procession. I hid my face lest he call to me and shame me before my people. But he saw me, I think, and waved.

This I ignored, the only thing to do with such bad manners.

Down to Ho Chung we went and there was Kwai To Man and his father waiting, and everybody in the village dressed in their finest attire, all most formal, and Kwai had got his new water-buffalo tethered across the path so nobody would miss seeing it, and a herd of young goats grazing on his field – nothing at all to do with Kwai.

'Welcome!'

They gathered about us, the children, the wives and husbands.

'Welcome, welcome!' The great hanging drapes of firecrackers began their ear-splitting blaze, the people took up the chant of welcome, the clearing thundered sound, and Po Shan, standing near me, shouted to Chen Fu Wei:

'Aye, aye, welcome indeed. Soon, *soon* my sweet – that is the first of the Mings sent in the right direction.'

11

SO I LOST my sister to Mr Kwai To Man, and when Po Shan brought me home from the sea I would kneel before the Tin Hau altar and give thanks for her happiness, for she had struck a decent house. Often, after the fish markets, I would take the sampan over to the island, but the man I sought seemed to have gone forever. Sometimes, too, I would walk down to Hebe Haven, but the white junk was never in harbour. Then the boat-boys would squat on the road outside Wan Kee and shout after me, asking if the fishing was better at Sai Kung now that I was there, and was it right that Po Shan was swinging double hammocks. For they knew me as their own blood, and it was their ambition to take me as Kwai had taken Suelen, and this frightened me because I was not made for their blood, but for the boy with the white hair.

Now there was a great loneliness in me. Hui was full of the sea and fish and boys: Tuk Un belonged to Tai Tai, who fed and cherished him with mother smell. Nor were things right between Po Shan and her, for Chen Fu Wei was the ghost lying between them, and you could take chunks out of the silence of the aft cabin and fry it and hang out the black looks for bleaching.

'Pei Sha,' said Tai Tai. 'My man is mad, so beware.'

'Mad?'

She said, 'And were I not such a bitch of a woman I would bind Chen Fu Wei hand and foot and throw her at his feet, to ease this madness. But I am not a woman, I am a wife. *Listen!*'

This Sai Kung is a heroic village, she said. For when the patriots wrecked and burned and spat in the faces of the Japanese they ran for their lives to the coast of Mother China, and they set off from Sai Kung by night. On the black nights of cloud they slipped out of the harbour in the big junks, their lives held on the tips of their fingers. And it was Po Shan who received them, fed them, shipped them, and the Japanese suspected. They came to Sai Kung and took him to the tea-house as a friend and men heard them laughing and bantering, Po Shan also. They asked him what he liked best in the world, and he answered bad women, and after bad women good wine. Po Shan was drunk for eight days, said Tai Tai, but even in his ravings he did not tell of the people manning the junks, nor those who harboured the fighters, nor how many patriots had gone. So they took screws to his thumbs, he said, and he did not enjoy that quite so much as the wine, for the wine was from Shamsui, and of good brew.

'Ming Pei Sha!'

It was Po Shan, ragged, bearded, undergoing the torture of the wine. Swaying before me he gurgled in his throat and said stupidly, 'You are her and yet you are not her. You stand in my Chen's likeness, every inch: her eyes, her face, her hair – even your voice.'

I sat down, ignoring him, stirring the chow-fan.

'Up when I speak to you!' He covered his face. 'Your every move reminds me of Chen Fu Wei. I am sick to death of the Mings down to the third generation. I will feed Hui because of his labour. But you and the brat Tuk Un – away!'

I was prepared for this for the lusts were in him, and said, 'Old Man, if I repay you the four thousand dollars my father owes you, will you keep my baby brother Tuk Un also, and teach him the sea trades?'

He stared down at me, mumbling, and, as the echo made sense he rumbled laughter, then threw back his head, clutching at things and shouting laughter. 'I would keep the devil himself for that money – ten thousand devils and Tai Tai also!' He peered. 'Explain to me, Pei Sha.'

I turned my back upon him.

'Later,' I said.

The sky was an ocean of red petticoats as I turned the save-life sampan towards Yim Tin Tsai next day in the hope of seeing my boy before I left Sai Kung village. And the danger of the sea was calling me, for a tropical storm was blowing off the coast of the Philippines and the sea was high in wave-swill, the rocks like white bears feasting. Finding a deep channel I took the sampan through them, reached the beach, and leaped out knee-deep in foam. Lying on the beach I lost myself in the thunder of the sea, listening to the piping of sea shells, the misty tinkles, the dull booms of the caverns. Despite the lateness of the year the sun was hot, and it was a consuming by heat and water. I thought, in sudden lunacy: just lie here and let the sea take you, or fly out to the rollers of the Wu Tan ledge. There, with a boulder cradled in your arms you can drop three hundred feet, they say, to the caverns where the big octopus and manta-ray go – to the piled bones of the old pearl-divers whose masters forgot the last pull up to sunlight, because they were old. I thought: let your bones mingle with theirs, one with the light-flood – you, Ming Pei Sha.

Enchanted with this escape, I sat up.

The boy of Yim Tin Tsai was standing beside me and I nearly died of shock.

'Pei Sha,' he said.

It was intolerable, an impossible impertinence. I leaped up, walking away.

And he walked beside me, undisturbed, as one walks with a friend, and I saw before me the little white junk in the shallows of the headland, and cursed him in whispered Cantonese that he should so pester me when I had a score of young men to pick from in Tak Long Middle Street. The sun burned down. I closed my eyes to the sweet intimacy of his nearness, gripping my anger, and he knew of this anger but was not perturbed. He said:

'I have been here eight times, in Sai Kung harbour every other day, but I have never found you. Are you listening?'

'No.'

'So I made enquiries and learned that you are employed on

the junk of Chu Po Shan, the fisherman, that the two boys I thought his sons are not his sons, but your brothers, Hui and Tuk Un: that your sister Suelen has married a farmer of Ho Chung village.'

'Indeed,' I said.

'Also that your parents died in a typhoon and that you possess the heirloom of your family – the Ming mirror.'

'That is very clever,' I said.

'But I learned more. I learned that you turn up your nose at the boat-boys and are never seen in a tea-house or playing mahjong.'

'And how did you learn all this?'

He said, touching my shoulder, 'If you stop this round-the-island race I will tell you.'

Sitting on a rock with studied carelessness, I listened, and watched. This was the body of a sun-fed Cantonese though his hair was English, as white as clouds. In build and lazy strength he was a miniature Po Shan, being wide in the shoulders, and the sight of him flooded me with shame. For although this was he who loved me, he moved before me without my supplication, he spoke without my desire, and did not speak of love. In the warm cabin, in the fierce nights off Tolo or Kwangtung, he was a dearer, sweeter thing of love and whispers, and very obedient to my wishes. Now he said, kicking at sand:

'I was in Hebe Haven when your sister Suelen married and saw the chair go past. I saw you also, and waved, but you did not wave back.'

He spoke again but I did not hear him. Eyes closed, I willed him near me.

'Are you listening?'

'Aye.'

He smiled. 'Many times I came here, and waited – once all night, but you did not come.'

'I did not promise to come.'

'The boat-boys told me you were Third Sister of the Mings. They also said that you were cold to them because you are educated. One day she will marry a millionaire, they said, she will not sniff at boat-boys.'

'That is one lie,' I retorted.

'Then one said . . .'

'Did you have to talk of me with boat-boys?'

'I had to know of you,' he said.

It was enough.

He squinted through the sun. 'Do you want to know about me?'

I did not answer, so he said, 'I am Jan Colingten. My mother is Dutch, my father English. I am nineteen, and I was born in Victoria.'

There was an enchanting simplicity about him. The wind stirred between us, the breakers thumped, the shingle screamed. I said uncaring:

'I was born in Shaukiwan.'

'Then you are a British subject.'

'I am not. I am Chinese.' I glared at him.

His eyes were incredibly blue. This is the difference, I thought, the eyes, the skin, the hair. Compared with a black-haired Tangar boy this was an albino, the egg of a sea-gull and blackbird mating. This was unusual, for most of these foreign ones are black and swarthy, the men with matted chests and tumbling hair. Mate with this one and you will be in trouble, I thought.

'I am off,' I said.

'Please stay.'

'I cannot stay. Soon the junk will be going. Po Shan never waits.'

'Will you come again, Pei Sha?'

'I do not know.'

He said, coming nearer, 'Come again, and we will take my junk round Stonecutters' Island and go through the Cupshui-mun in moonlight.'

I looked at him very old-fashioned, which is the same look in any language. But he was innocent, saying, 'Po Shan need not know. We will watch the Aberdeen fleet come in past Tytam Bay and the searchlight flashing from Lamma.'

I said, walking past him, 'Somebody is suffering from typhoon nut and it is not me.'

'You will not come?'

Perhaps it would have been best if I had agreed – more, if I had gone with him that very moment, and sailed to the rim of the world.

'No,' I said.

Turning, I went down the beach towards the save-life sampan. Hesitating, I stared.

The sampan was not there. Shielding my eyes, I watched it flowing towards the mainland. Taking the surf at the Point, it swung starboard for the Narrows.

'*Ai-yah!*' said the boy, watching it, and I swung to him.

'Pig! You loosed it!'

'You dragged it, you did not tether it.' He watched the sampan, rubbing his chin, very interested.

'What shall I do?'

He opened empty, expressive hands.

'But I cannot get home!' I pleaded. 'I cannot get back to Sai Kung.'

'There is always my junk,' he said.

It was the way he looked at me. Not such a fool, this one.

'Take me!' I cried.

'Hei-*up!*' he seized my hand and we went like maniacs down to the white junk and waded out to her. Scrambling aboard at the stern, I took from my pocket a lucky red paper, licked it, and stuck it beneath the roof of the little companionway, thus preserving myself, for the thought that the save-life sampan had run away was terrifying. The foreign boy would not know this danger to us; this preserved him also.

For there are those who watch, says Suelen, and arrange such things.

'Sail up!' cried the boy, and I ran to the mast, untied the cleat, and pulled the sail up, and it was new and red. Flinging the strainers across the companionway roof I took the tiller and shifted her into the wind a moment before the little diesel began to thump. The boy rose beside me, wiping his hands. Heeling into the wind, we carved Port Shelter like a China clipper, and before us, a speck on the tide, the save-life sampan rose against the sky before sinking into green troughs.

'After it!' he cried. Down past the Narrows we went on to the edge of the open sea and the little junk put up her nose at it, loving every minute. We were taking it green from the west when we reached the escaping sampan and I leaped aboard it, gathered its painter, and flung it into the wind. The boy caught it, knelt, and hitched it up and I jumped on to the prow of the junk again, expertly.

'This is a crew!' he shouted.

Reaching out, he caught my hand, and I did not move away. The junk was carving back to Yim Tin Tsai in a bellying sail, shuddering to the thump of the sea, and the spray came over the roof and lashed us, and we did not move.

There was a great need in me that he should kiss me, but he did not. He only ran his hands through his hair and shouted at the spray and we ducked as it came again.

'Pei Sha, look!' he cried, but the wind snatched his voice. He pointed seawards, but I did not look. I thought: I love you. It is stupid, but I love you, and have done so from the time I saw you. Soon I will go from here and you will seek, but not find me. You will wait on Sai Kung jetty for the *Cormorant* to come in, and ask Po Shan for me, but he will not know. Neither Po Shan, Tai Tai – even Hui; none shall know where I am gone. Then you will go to Hebe Haven and ask the boat-boys, and even to Ho Chung village and ask of Kwai and Suelen, and they will say: 'She is not here. Go to the big junk of Chu Po Shan in Sai Kung, for that is her home, and you will find her.'

Now he was kneeling at my feet, his fingers busy on the sampan painter for the rope had snarled in flight, and he looked up and flashed his smile at me, and bent to the knot again.

'I love you,' I said, but he did not know of this.

Getting up, he looked at the sky. A hint of storm was wind-staining the mating with the sea: he thought it was a typhoon, but I knew better; the season was late.

'Take me back,' I said.

Unspeaking, we went back to the island, and there he left me.

'You will come again, Pei Sha?'

I did not answer. The birds of Yim Tin Tsai were shaking out beds for the coming of bat-dusk when I left him, having no words for him.

Sitting on the prow of the junk he watched me ferry the sampan back to Sai Kung.

I did not turn to him, I did not even wave.

12

WHEN I RETURNED to the *Cormorant* Tai Tai was standing alone on the stern, weeping.

'Pei Sha, have you seen Chen Fu Wei?'

'She is still nursing her sick mother on Cheung Chau. Why is she important at this time of night?'

'Because Po Shan calls for her,' said Tai Tai. 'All my years I have been taught to obey a man, and I do so now. Until my twentieth year I kowtowed to my father, now I am humble before my husband.'

Hui came from the middle cabin then, rubbing his eyes, and he vaulted the rail and gripped the rope-ladder.

'Where are you going?' I asked.

'For Chen Fu Wei – the Old Man commands it.'

'But she is in Cheung Chau,' I said.

'She is not. She is in the tea-house.'

'You shall not go to her,' cried Tai Tai. 'I am wife, this is my privilege, for I have failed my man.'

'Missus!' I called, but she only wept more. I cried, 'Have sense – wait until morning. It is Po Shan's task to fetch his own concubine.'

'It is mine because I have lost face,' whimpered Tai Tai, hugging herself. 'This is my penance, to call the Second Wife.'

In this weakness I despised her, hating her blubbering face, her swollen eyes and quivering lips.

'Go with her, Hui,' I ordered, and he helped her down the ladder. Tuk Un was climbing the leg of my trousers and bawling to fetch out ancestors because his Tai Tai was going from him, so I lifted and soothed him and pushed at the door of the aft cabin. Po Shan was not in there so I laid Tuk Un in the bed and cooed and rocked him, and he slept. Then I went into the middle cabin which I shared with Hui, and lit the lamp, and read.

The stars came out and yellow lights began to wink down the road to Tai Mong and still Tai Tai and Hui did not return. Through the window I watched the pirating fleet come in from the sea, its red and green lanterns thrusting deep in the ebony waters. The junk gnawed at her anchor chain with the change of the tide and as the land lights died in mist the sea-going sampan of Fan Lu, our half-blind Hoklo neighbour, slid alongside and he called:

'*Aho!* Chu Po Shan, you aboard? Lobster and big shrimp coming in deep off Tap Mun, you heard?'

Po Shan did not reply.

'*Aho!* Chu Po Shan!' again the voice of Fan Lu, the mutilated gunpowder fisher. 'Away to sea, man, you are missing a fortune.'

I went to the window and called, 'Fan Lu, I will tell him!'

'Chen Fu Wei?' He waved his stumpy arm in greeting.

'It is Ming Pei Sha,' I called back, laughing. 'He is slipping cables at dawn – he will not sail earlier, man, for he is on the bottle.'

'*Sai-Law!*' He gestured his disgust.

The sampan crept away into the land mist, its lights dimming. Wondering if Po Shan had also slipped ashore, I went out on deck, shivering to the shadows of the empty junk. Moonlight lay in thick swathes of silver across the boards; jet shadows moved to the tide-heave: blocks creaked, ropes tensed and tired. Going back to the middle cabin I laid on my bed, then stiffened, listening with hawk ears, for a foot had slurred the deck outside. The door was ajar, searched by a beam of moonlight, and the beam widened to a man's hand. I watched, slowly dying. The door opened wider. I sighed with relief. It was Po Shan. He stood in the doorway, staring down in the lamp-light, and his face was red and black with strange shadows. Stripped to the waist as usual, caught in the ropes of the moon, he was wonderful in size and strength.

'Chen Fu Wei, you have come,' he said staggering, and I remembered the wine.

I laughed, saying, 'You have got the wrong woman, Old Man. Did you hear little Fan Lu go by shouting? There is big lobster and shrimp off Tap Mun – didn't you hear him call?'

Nearer he came and knelt beside the bed: reaching out, he took my hands in his, saying, 'I have an old frowse of a missus who is past it, and she is barren of sons. From you will come forth all my pleasures,' and he took me into his arms. 'Chen Fu Wei!'

'*Eeaah*, Old Man! Lay up!' I shoved him away, furious.

'Hush, my precious.'

'Chu Po Shan!' I twisted in his strength, fighting him, growing afraid, and as his hands searched me I hammered him with my fists, begging him, but he kissed away my protests. Terrified, I bit him, tasting the salt sweetness of blood, but this only brought him to a greater, crushing strength and he chuckled deep in his throat.

'Chen, my little wildcat, my sweet,' he said. 'I am a man now I have you for wife.'

I fought, I pleaded, I lay beneath him in growing sickness, eyes clenched to the sight of him, teeth gritted to the smothering pain of him. And amid my cries he took me in a knifing blade of pain in murmured words which he called love. In agony I called to him, for I was new to a man, but he did not hear me, for his was a panic of joy. Then, in husky whispers he told his gratitude in words I did not understand, for there was a coldness sweeping over me that moved slowly from my belly to my brain. Turning my face from him I took myself away to the green tumult of the seas, leaving my body for torture.

I wept. I called for my mother.

'Chen, Chen, hush, my sweet!'

His breath was heavy with the Samshui wine.

When he had finished with me he left me in the shadows. I did not move. Even later, when he knelt above me, one hand stroking my hair, weeping, I did not turn to him.

I could not bear his face.

Nor could I bear the gathering terror of his mood. I could have torn him with my tongue. I could have screamed the accusation and men would have come in fury, for Po Shan was not of lovely Sai Kung. They would have ridiculed him and served him with the reins and feed of a mule – the animal which mates beyond its natural kind. But I did nothing. Rising, sick, weak and in great pain, I pushed aside his prayerful hands.

'Pei Sha, Pei Sha!'

'Do not touch me,' I said.

Leaving him, I went to the prow and there wept for my boy of Yim Tin Tsai, because I was defiled.

In the morning Chu Po Shan acted very sheepishly at his rice-bowl, turning his pained face this way and that, full of sighs with him, as if he had suffered the outrage and I had had the enjoyment – dropping the stuff down the front of him and making a great show of wiping it up.

But although I watched his every movement he would not meet my eyes.

Tai Tai said, smelling Tuk Un and sighing, 'Pei Sha, best you know this. Soon perhaps even today, I am receiving my husband's new wife, and will name her.'

'Aye, Missus,' I answered, and Po Shan glowered at the table, knowing I was wondering in my pain how many women a man needed. Tai Tai said:

'This is Ching Law, and Customary Marriage.'

'Of course,' I said. 'Name her kindly, Missus.'

The custom demanded that the legal First Wife shall receive the proposed Second Wife into the family and name her in the presence of witnesses. There are other forms of marriage in Hong Kong which demand but the presence of two witnesses for the taking of other wives, but this is not true concubinage. A concubine properly married into a house under Custom Marriage has a respected and legal status – she is a wife – a second, third, fourth, or even a fifth wife, but her position in the family is recognised by law. This is the root of the trouble, as Suelen explained to me. With the example of legal concubinage constantly before them, women were readily agreeing to other systems of multiple marriage. Children with no claim to legal fatherhood were being born in thousands, unwanted by their fathers from whom their mothers could claim no support. Beware now, said Suelen.

Now Tai Tai said, 'I will name her Chieh, which stands for purity, for she might as well start that way even if she's not quite the same after Po Shan has done with her.'

I said quickly, 'I have red and white streamers from last New Year in my box, also lanterns from the Moon Festival. These I will hang in the aft cabin.'

'She is not sleeping there,' said Tai Tai.

'Then where?' asked Po Shan, naturally interested.

'You can have her in the sampan if you like, but not beside me.'

Po Shan rose in a sudden anger. 'All this bitterness because I want a son!'

Tai Tai rose with a sniff. 'Is it a son you want? Some might say a fresh woman.'

'Please do not quarrel,' I begged, for I was sick of it; of the pain, of the very sight of Po Shan, the prospect of having Chen Fu Wei on the *Cormorant*.

They rose together in a tumult of insults and I gathered up the rice-bowls and left them to their undignified squabbling. And as I washed the bowls on the prow my brother Hui came and squatted beside me. With precise and delicate fingers he held a great lobster on its back and bound its claws with rattan thread, whispering to it words of consolation, for these were his friends these days, Po Chen having forgotten him in the beam of Chen Fu Wei.

'Why are you weeping, Pei Sha?'

'I am not weeping.'

All night I had been in agony in the middle cabin while Hui slept, for Po Shan was great and I had never been used before; also, I was terrified at what he had done to me. Now the pain was bringing tears. Hui said, peering, his voice gentle:

'There is salt in your eyes, is it?'

'It is the misery of woman in me, do not heed it,' I answered.

He touched my hand. 'Ah, Pei Sha, Second Sister! First Sister now that Suelen has gone?'

'You need me, Hui?'

He did not reply to this, his eyes serious in his man's face, then he said:

'Yesterday, launching a new play-junk at Wan Kee's I did meet Suelen, and she asked of you.'

I nodded. 'Soon I must visit Suelen and Kwai.'

He made a face at the sun. 'And Suilen did say that there was room for me and you in the hut with Kwai, if you fancied.'

'Farming would be a change from the sea.'

He rose, holding the bound lobster before him, 'See how beautiful he is? No farming for me. When Po Shan has taught me the runs I will do the Kwangtung coast deep-sea and take a big three-master into Aberdeen Fish-City – out on high-tides only, she being long-keel.'

This was his language. He looked, he smelled, he was of the sea. I said:

'But things may change aboard when Chen comes, you think?'

'Yes, Old Man will be happy. Chen's a woman for any man's eye, and ten years is long enough with any old missus.'

One and all, these men were the same, I thought.

I said, 'Hui, listen. Soon I will be leaving the *Cormorant*.'

'Leaving? For Ho Chung farming with Suelen and Kwai?'

'My business,' I answered. 'When I go, will you take care of Tuk Un?'

'Tuk Un belongs to Tai Tai.'

'Perhaps, but he is not her blood, he is a Ming. Also, he is a baby still, remember.'

He said softly, 'I will watch him with the rail, for he is my brother.'

'For Mama, Hui. Watch him?'

He nodded, as boys do, and left me. But at the middle mast he paused, looking back. 'You are going, Pei Sha?'

'Yes.'

'Is it good for you to go? Who will care for you?'

'I will care for myself.'

He said at the sun, 'I shall miss you, for you are my sister. Tuk Un is my brother and he is important. You are not important, but I shall miss you.'

'Thank you,' I said.

An hour before Chen Fu Wei's arrival aboard the junk I was kneeling before the Ming mirror plaiting my hair when Po Shan came dancing out of the aft cabin, swiping at things and cursing women because his trousers were up to his knees, and behind him came Tai Tai holding her stomach, going purple in the face and shrieking laughter. He flung back the door of my cabin.

'Did you shorten these wedding trousers?' he demanded.

'Aye. Three inches, but they needed more,' I replied.

At this Tai Tai crowed to wake the harbour. 'And I had two inches off them, too, and so did Suelen!'

'No!'

Trembling, Po Shan stood before us with his beautiful new trousers up to his knees while Tai Tai shrieked her delight. 'And Chen lifted them, too, says Hui,' she cried.

'*Sai-Law!*' cried Po Shan, furious. 'Damned women!'

95

'Another six inches and he would be showing things!' Tai Tai rolled about. 'A new fashion for a wedding – Chen Fu Wei with her skirt up to her waist!'

'Your trouble is too many women, Old Man,' shouted Hui, and he turned, pointing. 'Too late to alter them. Chen Fu Wei is coming!'

Gaily the red streamers and bunting fluttered in the wind as Chen's sampan came alongside, stern-rowed by one of her relatives, and there they sat, all seven of them huddled in cold misery as if it was a funeral instead of a wedding, but they had done us well, Tai Tai said later. Chen's father had sent the customary gifts, including a fine leg of roast pork (and this Chen deserved for she was truly virtuous), rice-balls by the hundred, a sack of Tientsin cabbage, and nearly a thousand dollars – which showed his keenness to be rid of her, Tai Tai added.

And Chen sat sedately in the stern of the sampan, her hair oiled and shining black, her samfoo neatly ironed. To my surprise she still wore in her hair the emblem of mourning for her late husband, and her eyes were cast down with due humility, for she was coming as a concubine, a second wife, and so was junior to Tai Tai. This is the tragedy of concubinage under Ching Law. Although it is a lawful union its dignity is reduced by other forms of marriage, where lovers are taken with the assumption that they are legal concubines. While allowing the husband the privilege of multiple marriage, it reduces the principal wife in the eyes of her family; it allows the concubine little more than a living and forces from her constant subservience to the first wife who, liable to be thrown out on the mere accusation of mischief-making, laziness, or even failing to bear her husband a child, must accept the concubine's children as equal with her own.

To some, however – women like Chen Fu Wei, it offered security, for her own man was gone and she had a baby to feed.

To others, like me, it offered a chance to those we loved.

The sampan tied up alongside, a rope ladder was dropped, and Chen Fu Wei and all her relatives trooped aboard, while the boat-people of the harbour pulled on their cables and drew closer for a better view. Had it been a first bride there would have been firecrackers and cheering and bunting flying everywhere, but the women of the junks were silent, each wondering when her turn would come for her galley to be invaded by a younger woman, and they pitied Tai Tai. So it was all very formal, just a whispering and shoving along the deck to get into the right places, and the wind blustered, plucking at unwary streamers, blowing up gowns.

Tai Tai, dressed in her best samfoo, sat in a rattan chair before the middle mast. She called to me, and Hui and I took our places behind her, for she had no living relatives. Standing in a group by the port rail was the bride's party, still whispering and nudging each other, looking self-conscious, and in the middle of them was Chen, her hands screwed together, her face pale. Po Shan stood directly in front of Tai Tai's chair, his face blood-red, his jacket bone-tight across his massive shoulders, his fine silk wedding trousers flapping about his knees. And as the junks and sampans of the harbour rowed closer I saw the sober faces of their crews.

This was not a wedding, I thought: this is a funeral. This, I told Hui later, was the hell these marriages made for humans.

Po Shan looked over his shoulder and put out his hand and Chen Fu Wei came from her father's side and stood by Po Shan, her head bowed, and Po Shan said, his voice strong and clear:

'Missus, I bring you this woman Chen Fu Wei as Second Wife. Before these witnesses I ask you to name her.'

'Name her kindly, Tai Tai,' said Chen's father, a little bald shrimp of a man. 'Her mother is ill in Cheung Chau and cannot be here to beg you – name her kindly.'

Silence. Tai Tai did not move in her chair.

Po Shan approached her. On the table he placed a red envelope containing lucky money; another such envelope he held out to Chen Fu Wei, and her fingers touched it. He said softly, 'Tai Tai, this is my second wife. She will bear me a son, and this will be your son. I ask you again, name her, and she will kneel to you.'

Tai Tai rose, and I feared, clutching myself, for I knew her. Above the sigh of the wind and the wave-lap, she said:

'Chen Fu Wei, I welcome you aboard this junk as Second Wife to the Old Man. I accept you as *tsip*. But I am Tai Tai and you will remember that I am first lady here.' Then she took from the table the red paper envelope which called for longevity, wealth, and many sons, and Chen took it, her hands trembling, her eyes beseeching. I caught my breath as Tai Tai said:

'They ask me to name you, and this I do. I name you *Hsia To*, because the galley on this junk is too small for one woman, let alone two.'

'Tai Tai, for God's sake!' I whispered, but she continued:

'My husband calls for sons but he cannot beget sons. This you will find to your grief – that he cannot beget any child. Do you still want him?'

And Chen Fu Wei wept, her head bowed. Her relatives shifted their feet and murmured angrily among themselves.

'Do you still want this man?' Tai Tai's voice rang out, and I despised her. 'A man who is barren?'

'Yes, Tai Tai.'

'Then serve me.'

There was a look like knives in every direction, with Po Shan glaring down at Tai Tai and Chen's relatives threatening mutiny, but Chen did not heed them. With due humility she poured the tea from the old Wei-Hei-Wei tea-set and filled a bowl and took it in her two hands and brought it to the feet of Tai Tai and knelt before her, offering it. Tai Tai took the bowl, and drank, and Po Shan said, his voice vibrant:

'My principal wife has named Chen Fu Wei, and she is my second wife. She has taken the gift of tea, she has given Chen the lucky money. Stay, everybody, stay – eat and drink!'

But they were already going. In black looks and furious whispers, they went, staring over their shoulders, hating Tai Tai, and in the end only Chen was there, still kneeling before the empty chair, and she was weeping, having lost face before her relatives. I pushed Po Shan aside and raised her.

'Hush, hush,' I whispered as she sobbed against me.

Such was the insult.

The name *Hsia To* means One-too-Many.

13

SPRING GOT INTO us, and I was still on the *Cormorant*. We sailed under wind a hundred miles and more in search of the big shoals running down the coast of China and scoured the homes of the shark and snake-fish, the sea-scavengers who kept the shoals running.

Because of his debt to the finance company, Chu Po Shan was glum despite his new wife: because of this, and his shame, he never turned his face to me once, hating me, hating all the Mings – even Hui and Tuk Un, because we owed him money.

We sat becalmed on shimmering seas, we fought the winds of Kwangtung, tossing along the sea-lanes of the big liners bound for Taiwan and Sing-no-more, now lazing in the eddy and swirl to Nowhere, watching the forests of sea-flora weaving their fantastic shapes above beds of coral and mother-of-pearl. These were days of spring heat, of crimson sunsets and seas of blood-stained jade. And sometimes I would sweep the save-life sampan over to Yim Tin Tsai in search of my boy and go to a quiet place of bushes and weep, beating the earth with my hands for what Po Shan had done to me.

The boy with the white hair would not want me now.

Po Shan, however, was going very strong in one direction. From sea-sweeping he had turned to love-making. Nothing moved behind the prow-cabin door in the heat of the day. And at night, like nocturnal birds of love, he and Chen Fu Wei would come out hand in hand and stand embracing against the stars with moon-dust in their ears. This is not a sea-junk, said Tai Tai, it is a boudoir for a sing-song girl of Willow and Flower Lane.

This was most insulting, but the canker was in her heart.

I needed money to escape, money to leave Hui and Tuk Un in safety, and fed: big money, not a wage. So I wrote letter after letter to the go-betweens of concubinage, but received no replies. I offered myself for a pittance, but they did not reply. Desperate, unhappy, I stayed on, labouring for Po Shan, losing

99

myself in a new love – the baby Yin Yin, Chen Fu Wei's son, for Tai Tai had got Tuk Un.

This was a sweet baby, all wrinkled fat and bangles, and he loved me back, for Chen, his mamma, was so full of loin-love that she had no time for him. Neither, it appeared at first, had Tai Tai.

'Missus!' Hui once called. 'Yin Yin is crying. He is crying great tears of hunger and still his mama does not come.'

'Let him howl,' Tai Tai replied. 'Am I foster-mother to every stray?'

Later I saw her with Yin Yin on her knee, feeding him rice-congee and soothing him, while Tuk Un, steeped in sun and love, lay asleep at her feet.

I wrote more letters to go-betweens. Po Shan had his Chen, Tai Tai her children, Hui had his sea. There was no need for me here.

But after a while the lovers grew tired of their loving, which is understandable, said Tai Tai, for even Pekin Duck becomes tiresome if you have it too often. Out on to the deck came Po Shan full of his old command, and happy: doing his pugilism on the prow, bellowing the old sea-songs, and soon Chen Fu Wei followed. One morning she stood in the doorway of the prow cabin with her son Yin Yin in her arms, and said:

'Bring the Old Man,' and we whispered among ourselves and sent Hui aft for him. Po Shan came, his big body grimed with oil and he was scowling, for it was beyond the rules to command the Old Man to come for anything, even ship-wreck.

'Chen has something to say,' I explained.

'Then speak, woman – let them all hear it!' he bellowed, delighted.

Chen drew herself up.

'I am with child,' she said.

'You see?' shouted Po Shan. 'She is in child, and by me. Me, Chu Po Shan, I am going to have a son!'

'How long?' asked Tai Tai, her voice flat.

'It is the second month.'

Po Shan opened his arms to her. 'Today she speaks, though for a week we have known it. Wonderful woman, glorious woman!' and he put his big arms about her, scowled at Tai Tai, and took Chen within the prow cabin and slammed the door.

And we did not see him for another week.

Tai Tai wept and would not be comforted. The junk was now a shambles of love and jealousy. The birth of Chen's child would lay a spark to the gunpowder keg.

Before this happens, I thought, I will have a reply from a dealer in women, and then I will go from here.

Thinking of dealers I remembered Orla: remembering her I remembered Shatin, and Wing Sui, the merchant who bought her. Going into the middle cabin I wrote my last letter applying for concubinage. The Mings already owed this man money from Orla Gold Sister. Perhaps, I reasoned, this debt would fetch him.

Two weeks later, while in Sai Kung, I received his reply. The water postman handed me a letter. Like on Suelen's, the postmark was Kowloon.

And the letter had been delayed. I was demanded at Shatin that very day.

When I had burned Wing Sui's letter I went to the cabin and knelt before the altar of Tin Hau, the Queen of Heaven, giving thanks to her and my grandfather Ming, to whom I had prayed for help. Although he had hailed from Canton he had, in his time, rode the infamous Hankow Bore, which is a wall of water. The reply from the dealer in women had been swift: the grand-daughter of a man of lower estate might have waited months. After I had given thanks I washed my body. My hair I oiled and plaited with white ribbon. From my box I brought out the black cheongsam I had worn after Suelen's wedding, and this was made of Shantung silk. Kneeling before my Ming mirror I put lipstick red on my lips, enough to enhance my looks, not enough to suggest looseness. On my feet I put the black, high-heeled shoes I had bought for this occasion, and I stood on the stilts before the mirror and decided I was better than most. Then I packed up my bundle in sail-cloth and went out on to the deck. Po Shan was there awaiting me, for I think he knew something strange was afoot. His old confidence was back now he had a son under an apron. In debt to his eyes, pestered by the businessmen, haggled after by stall-holders, he was in penury with the junk slipping from under him, but he was whole and proud.

'I am leaving,' I said.

His eyes moved over me, first with scorn, then with veiled interest, pausing on my feet, and I knew what he was thinking. Chu Po Shan was of Old China, the China of the crushed feet, the peony-decorated five inch shoes that tiptoed around the gorgeous boudoirs of the ancient dynasties. Po Shan, the uneducated, was as unreal as the over-educated, the suffering poets. But I knew my feet were large, and I was ashamed. I was ashamed before the English shop-girl from whom I had bought them. 'Size two,' she said, after a lot of fiddling and measuring, and she was such a time finding a pair I knew they must have been enormous.

'You go when I say,' said Po Shan.

I glared up at him. 'And who will stop me? You shall not dictate to me, Old Man.' I added, 'With a word I could sell you up and send the *Cormorant* to the breaker's yard in Fish City. I am going. I know you. Soon you will tire of Chen Fu Wei, and then I will be third wife.'

He did not appear to hear me. Mention of the breaker's yard had stilled him. Slowly he sat on the thwarts, saying, 'Little matter if you sell me up. The loan sharks have beaten me at last. The Government forbids a fair profit on fish, and this has killed me. Go, then, and within a month or two we will follow you to the land, which, for the true Tan-gar, is but a place for burial.'

I did not reply, so he said, 'They force me from the sea and I know nothing but the sea. They have taken our birthright, squeezed us dry, uprooted us, and turned us into labourers, and we have been in the Pearl River delta for a thousand years, we are a proud people.'

I said, unpitying, 'If I go now you may not be forced on to the land. I will pay you the money my father owes.'

'You are selling yourself?'

'For a better price than I got from you, Old Man, so do not talk so pretty. And if you tell of me and my sister Suelen knows, I will never let you rest, Po Shan. Even beyond the grave I will lie with you and between wife and son. I will never leave you.'

'I will never tell,' he said.

'I will send you the money – what I can get. Teach Hui and Tuk Un the sea trades, and over the years I will pay the Ming debt. But never tell. Swear it!'

'I swear it, Pei Sha.'

He would have embraced me, I think, but I drew up, freezing him, and he lowered his big hands. I said, 'Now I am going. Tell Hui and Tai Tai that I am taking a post as a Hong Kong amah. Do not say more, man – leave it at that.'

I lowered my bundle and the Ming mirror into the save-life sampan, leaped from the ladder on to its stern, and swept it through the packed craft of the harbour, and the lovely people of the boats came to the rail and pointed wildly, for here was a lady in a cheongsam rowing in a sampan, but I did not heed them. Through the water alleys I went at great speed, and once clear of the craft I turned the prow towards my beloved Yim Tin Tsai for the last time. The sea, I remember, was calm and glittering, the tide low in timid wave-laps as I climbed bare-footed on to the sand of the island. Going through the dunes I sought the high places, looking over Inner Shelter towards Hebe Haven where the play-boats sailed, and standing there I remembered every detail of this beloved place: the early cries of my brother Tuk Un, Hui's shrieks of joy, Suelen's low singing at evening when the sun sank red-hot and hissing into the rim of the sea. Here were all the beloved sights and sounds, this, Sai Kung! – target of the homeward run when the sea was with tigers and spewing anger. Of all villages on the coast of China, this is the most heroic, and the best!

'Jan!' I called, but there was no answer: nothing but sea, land, and sky.

And standing there I seemed to see him swimming in the bay below me with his long, easy strokes, the foam puffing at his feet. Now he was standing above me, and I saw him clear – as clear as light I saw him, and he spoke, I think, but I did not hear him.

'Jan, *Jan!*'

It was ridiculous that I should stand there calling.

I wanted to weep, but this was loss of face. One day he might know that I had stood here weeping.

Anyway, there was too much between us now; nothing could break the barrier of custom, race, creed, and the thieving Po Shan.

'Goodbye,' I said.

14

NOW I STOOD in Shatin village, my own land, and watched the red bus blunder through the crowds towards Tai Po. With the Ming mirror under my arm and my bundle dangling, I walked through the bustling people, and loved this return. For the children were dressed in their brightest colours for a local festival; wayside stalls were selling windmills on sticks and rosettes and streamers, and the air was brittle with excitement. Wreathed in a white halo of cloud the stately amah of Amah Rock stood at her enormous height, dominating the estuary, waiting for her man to come home from the sea; the beloved amah carved from stone before whose solemn face the English boys had died by bayonets. And below her were spread the rice-fields, once the finest in Hong Kong, a tapestry of delight for generations of Emperors. The fishing fleet was in from Tai Po when I left the bus, its urchins cart-wheeling in the alleys; little girls squatted in the gutter playing the finger game and shrieking laughter, their unweaned babies clutching at their backs, mothers before their time: Hakka bent in the fields, maidens in black samfoos shouting their shrill soprano cries over the mud-caked valley. And the elders of the village sat outside the tea-houses in the half-drugged contemplation of the aged. Near the level-crossing now I paused, watching the train roar north to Canton and the other China beyond the Sham Chun River, and I remembered Suelen. For she had told me of the great names of the lost years – Commissioner Lin, the agent of the Emperor; the devils who had poisoned China and the devils in England who had let them – it would take some Chinese crackers to shift these people from the soul of the country, she said. Already sweating in the heat and dust, I smiled, remembering her, knowing a sudden joy and relief: Suelen, Hui, Tuk Un, all were safe.

A man was sitting outside a stall and his eyes flicked open as I bent to him.

'Sir,' I said, 'I seek a man named Wing Sui.'

He turned his face to me and I knew him for blind, and he

was poor. But the scholarship of his life leaped into his expression, and he smiled. 'You sound young, woman.'

'I am not so young.'

Aggressively, he replied, 'There are three Wing Suis in Shatin, and all are rich. There is the merchant himself, his brother the undertaker, his cousin the florist – and I expect I could pull out a bandit and monk if I went down the family line.'

'Wing Sui the merchant,' I said.

'Ah, the pimp! What are you doing with a pimp, child?'

'My business.'

'And mine. Are you girl or woman?'

'I am woman.'

He spat. 'Then pay for knowing – learn the first lessons first – nothing in life is free. Back to the level crossing. The first big house up the temple road – fifty cents.'

I paid him and he gripped my wrist, whispering, 'Now the second lesson, child. If you are dealing with the Wing Sui you are with soft-bellied men of hard fists and harder hearts. Take a dollar from them and they bleed to death, so take. Take, *take!* They have lost the power to give.'

'Aye,' I whispered back. 'Goodbye.'

'Goodbye. Go then – deal with the Wing Sui who deal in women; they will find you a florist for your wedding and I the Wing Sui monk for your funeral service – remember me.' Spitting on the silver he slipped it into his rags and rolled his opaque eyes at the sun. With frightened looks over my shoulder I left him, for what he had said brought visions to me. He was a wayside fortune-teller. What he had told me would come to pass, and I would be alive to suffer these prophecies, some unspoken, when he was safe and dead.

'O, God,' I said, and ran.

The memory of the typhoon, the drowning of my parents flooded into me as I pushed through the crowded alleys. New shacks now stood on the once-devastated hillsides; terraced fields were hazed with green shoots. Where children had died wheat and maize would rise in profusion. It was home and I wanted to cry with the joy of it. Through the head-loads and vendors' cries I went, breathing again the smells of beloved Shatin – fish-stalls, frying-stalls, even the gaudy colours of the distant floating restaurant, all brought memories of Fo Tan, the nearby village of my childhood. From a stall I bought sweet cake and fruits and took the lane that led to the graves of my grandparents, the place where we had rested before the great wave. I knelt. The leaves of autumn covered the graves so I swept them clean, and there prayed. Alone in the family unity, I prayed, and offered the tributes, and people passed me, mostly lovers hand in hand, but I did not turn to them, and one girl said, 'See that one kneeling there? She is praying before the grave of somebody beloved. But the bones are not drawn and the grave is ancient. How can this be?' I heard, and did not reply, knowing this to be stupidity. The waves had long since taken the burial urn, and the sacred relics; only the decayed graves remained, and to these I made my supplications. Later, I ate the fruit and cakes myself, for beloved ancestors give willingly to the living, then at sun-go-down I rose, taking the road that led to the temple and the house of the merchant of concubines.

The sun was shy below the rim of the mountain when I reached the mansion of Wing Sui, and I took a deep breath as its ornate iron gates clashed and clanked behind me. I feared, but I would have feared more had I known of the life ahead. The back door of the house opened by magic as I raised my hand to the bell: I knew this for a house of eyes.

'Your business?' This was a northerner by the size of his nose, as big as an American sailor and fair in complexion, but his eyes gone sour in his cavernous face. I said with an effort:

'Sir, I have business with Wing Sui.'

'She has business with Wing Sui?' He perked, his head on one side, bird-like in the cruel mimicry, and his voice was shoved high to a eunuch falsetto. I despised him, preferring men whole. 'Ah, pretty one, but has Wing Sui business with you?' He peered, delighted, his hands wringing beneath his black cotton gown. Lift that gown, I thought, and you smell the pain-killing lotions of the eunuch butchers: half a man: by bandits, they told me later. Disdainful, I looked past him, saying:

'Tell him that Ming Pei Sha the Tan-gar is here, and your master will come.'

He drew himself up. 'In his good time, Egg-Woman. Wait,' and he slammed the door.

Such tantrums from a servant.

With renewed confidence I took a firmer grip on the bundle and Ming mirror, and wandered the lovely courtyard.

Here was a stink of money. The air was embalmed in perfumed stillness, dead with grief for the end of the day; two stone lions with cubs under their paws, therefore females, guarded the main gates. Around the marble portico flowered bloodstained petals, convolvulus creeper, green and white, strangled the magnificent columnades, and beyond the rolling lawns, dainty, cushioned seats and bowers shouted lolling wealth. Here, in birdsong, was cleanness, a world removed from the rotting seaweed and the tossing, spewing junks: this was dignity after the night-soil bucketting of the harbours, the frothing excrement of Hong Kong's lavatory, Gin-Drinkers' Bay. Yet its beauty was impure; its wealth whispered of vulgarity, its perfume stank.

It is the way you make the money.

'Ming Pei Sha?'

I did not turn immediately.

'Miss Ming?'

It was a sallow ghost in a mandarin gown, and I recognised him through the years: Wing Sui, three years older, more prosperous than ever with a hundred women and more behind him. He bowed, beckoning, and Eunuch haggled about me, shaking hands with himself under his coat.

'Away, running bitch,' I whispered, and bowed to Wing Sui, going past him into a lovely room. Hanging tapestries I saw; great Kiangsi vases spraying artificial flowers. All around me was the gleam of brass, jade of many colours and flashing tiger's eye.

'You are Pei Sha, the daughter of Ming of Fo Tan?' He was astonished.

I nodded.

He said, 'I wrote, but I did not dream you would come. You are the sister of Ming Orla who broke her contract and ran from the house in Tai Po?'

I said, to settle him, 'I am the daughter of the man who owes you money.'

'Four thousand dollars?'

'Two thousand,' I said. 'The rest you never paid us.'

'Ah, yes.'

I followed him through bead curtains into a chamber of astonishing opulence, scented with the heady-sweet smell of opium. Here was the loot of the ancient traders; gorgeous carvings in yellowed ivory and amber, figureens, the peony fairies of the dynasties, tortoise-shell, and vases of rock crystal. I faced Wing Sui. Age had shrunken him. His was a skull on sagging shoulders, hairless and objectionable. The pupils of his eyes were dilated with the drug; a long, silvered pipe lay still smoking on a tray. I said, 'I have come to apply for concubinage.'

He nodded. 'Yes, but be warned. To apply for bed-concubinage before the age of sixteen is against the law. You know this?'

'I will be eighteen on the day of White Dews.'

The old talk pleased him. 'You look more like fifteen, but all the Tan-gar shed years. Tell me, what happened to your sister?'

I did not reply and his yellow teeth rolled tipsy in his smile. 'Will you prove the same – a concubine who shrieks fury at her first man?'

'The house at Tai Po was not concubinage.'

He shrugged. 'One son more or less should make little difference – this is the proof of quality. The house is better off without her.'

His feet were soundless on the Tientsin carpet. At a window overlooking the garden, he paused. 'Well, you are selling, not me. Name your price.'

'You will find a house for me?'

He turned. 'There is always a house for a beautiful girl, though the market is low these days. A surplus of women brings the price down.'

It was not so easy. I stood, ashamed, and in growing anger. Beyond an open door a timber staircase swept upwards in graceful lines to a ceiling mirrored, as a garden pond reflects in sheen the hanging day. Doves whimpered from the trees, cicadas were tuning on their lyres of love. I thought – all this loveliness for a bullet-headed northerner flung south by revolution, a hawk of humanity. His eyes drifted over me in mute assessment of dollars, and I wondered how many women had stood before these sullen eyes, the value of their merchandise scaled in lust.

For, to me, although it was my last resort, concubinage was only a cloak over the sensual need. As a great man had said, 'I have heard of people dying of hunger but never of the sexual urge.' The bed, not the cradle, Suelen had once said, and she was right. The demands came from the rich, the women came from the poor. The need for an heir being the usual claim, this was a system of rottenness that had flourished in China since the Yellow Emperor Huang Ti. In the Chow Dynasty, for instance, the sovereign commanded twenty-two wives, a feudal prince a wife and five concubines, even a poor scholar could take two mistresses: war-lords exploited the system for erotic pleasures. And wherever the demand, one found the go-betweens like this Wing Sui, the ten per cent traders of a modern city – brothers to the 100 per cent profiteers in the blood of slave girls of lost generations who were flung on the mercy of families who treated them like animals and beat their children for sport. These were the pimps and procurers from the educated Wing Suis who dealt with the rich to the scavenging, tom-cat traducers who dealt with the dregs, waist deep in human misery. All these once infested China until she was cleansed by the new régime. But Hong Kong, flying the flag of ancient history, protected the practice of multiple marriage by resolutions against it that never became law, and so the custom existed twenty miles from the border where the sin against human dignity had been condemned. Under Council after Council, the farce of a token resistence was condoned by a system which had taken a hundred years to clean up girl-selling. High officials winked at it, the pulpits ignored it. Under the umbrella of an English God Wing Sui waxed fat.

'Are you deaf, child?' he asked now. 'I asked your price.'

I answered, 'One pays for quality so the price is high. I speak English, I also know a little Shanghainese. I have simple qualifications in Chinese classic history and obtained high marks in literature.'

'That is astonishing for a Tan-gar.' He was impressed.

'I went to school – the teaching bought with my grandfather's money. Later, because of ability, an American missionary man gave me private lessons in geography and arithmetic.'

He was not really listening, but said, an eyebrow raised, 'I have for you a Chinese house, if the master accepts you, but knowledge of English could be an asset. So we shall test you, Ming Pei Sha,' and he said in perfect English, 'Where is Unicorn Ridge?'

'In Kowloon.' I replied in the same language.

'More, please.'

'To the east of Lion Rock which stands above the finger of Kai Tak airport.'

He nodded, amazed, saying, 'Now state your price, in English.'

'Six thousand dollars.'

With a gesture of disgust he turned away. 'Do not be ridiculous. English, German, French – all the European languages – I shall not pay that price. I am not buying an interpreter.'

'As you please.'

'Indeed, too much learning is a disadvantage. I would rather sleep with a braying donkey than an educated woman.'

I shrugged, picking up my bundle and bending for the Ming mirror, knowing that my revered grandfather had not yet done with him. Wing Sui said, aloof:

'You know your table manners?'

'In the Chinese, of course.'

'In the English?'

'They have no table manners.'

He accepted this. 'You do not like the foreigners?'

'A few.'

'This is good. As a *tsip* in a high-born house you may have to entertain them.' He wandered the room clutched in thought. 'Are you a virgin, Miss Ming?'

'Did you ask my sister Orla this question?'

'I did not. It was only a trifling possibility.'

I did not reply immediately. I could have told him that I was not a virgin, that virginity is lost in the mind, not the body. More, that although Po Shan had owned me in drink, even this cruelty had not robbed me of the virtue of the heart, but he would not have understood: of exquisite education, he would not have understood, for his learning was of the brain. This is the learning of greed, the education of the grab. This one knew but the sale of flesh, not the sale of the soul. His eyes went bright with interest when I answered, 'Yes, sir, I am a virgin.'

'You are sure?'

'I ought to know, it belongs to me.'

He was overjoyed. Even the terror of my price had not frightened him away. It was for the sullying of this virtue that he paid the highest price of all. He said, 'I ask you again – how much. And this time do not be ridiculous.'

'Six thousand dollars.'

He moved in agitated disgust and I knew the price was right. If wrong I would have been out by now with Eunuch standing over me. I added, 'Naturally, the amount includes the sum owing you for Orla Gold Sister, so you are really only paying four thousand.'

'Aye, but six thousand dollars is a terrible price for a woman.'

'There are women and women.'

He was worried and I was delighted. With the Ming mirror held against me, I watched him. Behind him, framed in evening clouds, I saw the baked outcrops of Shatin Heights and the star-lit hotel. The coming of night was brittle with heat. He sucked his teeth noisily, weighing the profit and loss. It was an immense decision. He turned.

'Take off your clothes.'

This was the real humiliation. Even before Po Shan I had managed to cover myself. I had never been naked before a man and I could not control the trembling of my hands. Seeing this he smiled and went around the room pulling each curtain with muttered protests.

'My sister Orla was not seen naked,' I said.

'Your sister Orla did not ask six thousand dollars. Come, take off your clothes. Much more will be expected of you.'

Bending, I drew the cheongsam over my head. Sitting deep in an armchair he watched with professional interest, then lit a cigarette, and I snatched at a strange consolation – that the smoke rising between us was a veil to my approaching nakedness as I removed my underclothes. As bare as birth I stood before him and he rose, walking around me, grunting appraisal like a buyer at a meat auction.

'You will not take less?'

'Not now, not a dollar.'

He patted my shoulder. 'You would be a fool if you did – you are a beautiful woman.'

'The money now,' I said, snatching at my clothes.

'Such indelicate behaviour! And you talk of education.'

'I am Tan-gar. I know you long-nosed thieves. Money now, or I go.'

Going to a drawer he drew out bank notes and counted four thousand dollars on to a table. 'Come, let us do good business, Pei Sha. You sell, I buy. It is an honourable transaction – we will leave the clawing to cats. Four thousand dollars. The debt of Orla is cancelled – here is my copy of her contract.'

Taking the contract I tore it into pieces. 'Now leave Chu Po Shan alone,' I said.

Later I joined him on the lawn. The Shatin estuary was now a sheen of quicksilver. In gaudy green and gold the distant floating restaurant shot the sea with light.

'You already have a house for me?'

He turned. 'In anticipation. One of the oldest and most respected, also one of the richest. The money was made in King-tung – some say a hundred million dollars.'

'When do I join this house?'

He lifted his eyes impatiently, and sighed. 'Listen to it! By your standards you are educated. By the standards of this house you are a rough Tan-gar. The wife would jeer at you, the servants despise you, the relatives make sport of you.'

'The master has no children?'

He spread his hands in outraged innocence. 'Of course not. Why, otherwise, would he be taking a concubine?'

It was an appalling hypocrisy and he knew I recognised it, but said, 'The opportunities are boundless, and must be carefully handled. You play your part, I will play mine. You will be perfect when I deliver you, for every trade in the world has to be learned and under the hands of the craftsman rough ivory takes shape in polished form and beauty. This is a noble profession. The Europeans take lovers, or prostitutes, which is worse. This is a part of their decadence. We Chinese take concubines, and the role of concubine is respected by law. The rich expect from me great service. From barren men I bring forth. I am a foster-father to a hundred sons, and upon perfection I have built my name.' He drew deep on his cigarette and exhaled noisily. 'The cheapest commodity in the East is rough women, the dearest is the finished product. Six weeks you will stay with me under tuition – everything found.'

'Six weeks!'

'It is a necessary period for instruction, and the suggestion is honourable, unfortunately I am beyond the charms of women.' He took my arm. 'Come, it is getting late. We will dine together and discover how you eat.'

The bow-lamps of the Hoklo sampans were crumpling the sea with skirts of silver, I remembered, the errant night winds starting blusters among the crags of Shatin. Po Shan would be hauling her out of Sai Kung by now, for the tides were right for deep-keel: he would take her two points east-nor'-east with up-sail on the middle mast and the others half furled, tack into the wind along the Narrows, and then run free and goose-winged to the fishing grounds. Little Fan Lu, our anchorage neighbour, would be there by Wednesday dawn, for he was slower: Leung Ho Cha with his two sampans and two wives would be there in the grey mists, his ten children shrieking from the little islands. And tonight there might even be the glow of a camp fire on Yim Tin Tsai; or tomorrow, in sunlight, Jan might run there, watching, waiting, and I would not come.

Eunuch, the half man employed from another age, moved across the room, bowing as he passed me, and softly closed the door.

15

FOR SIX WEEKS I lived in the house of Wing Sui, the merchant, learning better manners than I had read about – excellent manners, as Wing Sui said, being as universally admired as the language of love, in which I was a natural mistress, this coming naturally. In the paradise of a garden we sat together while he read from the ancient books: in his study I sat, eyes closed, listening, learning, sometimes smiling, for Wing Sui was of Old China, feckless in his beliefs, his roots fixed in the Dynasties; but he was learned. Spring was on her deathbed, warm breezes came in from beloved Tolo, a consolation to the street sleepers of Victoria after the bitter pavement cold.

'You speak of a husband, but never tell his name,' I protested.

'His name is Lo Hin Tan; he is rich, he is great, soon he will come for you.'

On the hook of this expectancy, Wing Sui dangled me, stuffing me with knowledge.

The garden flashed gold and green, whispering about summer in its quiet places. Outside a tiny love-pavilion we sat together, Wing Sui and me, and he read, but I heard nothing but wind-cry and smelled nothing but the brine of the estuary, dying inside for the sea.

'Even today Lo Hin Tan may come,' he said. '*Ahya*, my precious Pei Sha – you have the impatience of a child. Look, see my watch – even this midday he might arrive. Therefore, recite again for me from the Record of Rites.'

'I shall not. They are outdated, and foolish.'

'They are T'ung Shing, the authority of custom, therefore the law!'

'Mr Lo Hin Tan, if he chooses me for his concubine, will have no time for such a stupid Record.'

'Lo Hin Tan is highly educated in classic history. He is a scholar of Chinese culture, he despises Western creeds. He may test you. Be obedient. *Recite!*'

I sighed and said, ' "Therefore, concubines, if your years have not overflowed five tens, must wait on your lord every fifth day. . . ." '

'Proceed,' said Wing Sui.

I rose. 'But what if Lo Hin Tan shall seek me on the fourth day also?'

His face was impassive. 'I doubt that.'

'But what if he does, do I attend him?'

'You show him obedience, but he also has a principal wife, remember. Also, since he is a gentleman he will probably have paltry mistresses to amuse him.'

'But I will be a legal concubine?'

'You will be *tsip*, this I promise. It is a virtuous position under Customary Marriage. Come, you have a beautiful voice, Pei Sha. Recite.'

I said tonelessly, ' "When about to wait on lord the concubine shall purify self, rinsing mouth and bathing: shall straighten her garments, comb hair and draw on fillet. . . ."' I looked at Wing Sui. 'Fillet?'

'It is an ancient fashion, do not bother yourself – learn only the words. Recite.'

'". . . And lay broad hair-pin across back of head, draw hair into place, into shape of horn and brush dust from remainder."'

'Excellent! Pray continue.'

I said at the sea, '"If wife be not there then concubine-in-waiting shall not venture whole night with lord,"' and I thought, charmed with peace and sunlight: the money I seek buys land, women, houses, but not a single ounce of sea-spray. Sitting there I longed for the cries of the water-vendors, the bucking leaps of the junks, the crimson massacres of the little innocents after landfall.

Wing Sui said, 'You have a wonderful memory. To prove it again, tell me of the woman Yu, the wonder of the T'ang dynasty. First, her period with the history of England?'

'She lived when the North Men were burning Britain. She was named Sweet Orchid because of her beauty. She was a poet and played wonderfully on the p'i pa. She was Second Wife to Li Tzuan and loved him.'

'Quote from her poems.'

I said, '"Under an opal moon your loveliness I share in secret. . . ."'

He exclaimed in admiration. 'And her end?'

'She became unholy, enduring many men. Tiring of this, she entered a monastery, but she had made enemies. Falsely accused of murder, she was imprisoned.'

'But her end?' His eyes were wide with sustained joy. 'Tell me!'

I rose, disinterested. 'In the year eight hundred and eighty-two she was led to the execution ground of the City of Eternal Peace, and there destroyed.'

'Pei Sha, you are astonishing! You read, your mind photographs – you could know of all China.'

'When will Lo Hin Tan come?' I asked.

'In his good time. You are worthy of this man, for he is one of tremendous business. Marrying his first wife in Kingtung he raised a vast fortune in land, sea-junks, cotton, and oil. When the Communists came he ran east to Hong Kong with but a skeleton of his former fortune. Now he owns a dozen companies, has shares in many more.' He trembled with suppressed emotion and shook hands with himself under his gown. 'When you have fulfilled all your ambitions, Pei Sha, I beg you to remember me, the one who made everything possible.'

'I will be a second wife. Under Ching Law I can claim nothing from this man.'

'But he will be generous. Such knowledge, such beauty – no man could be otherwise.'

'Not even my children will be my own.'

'But they will have equality with the children of the first wife – to carry on an honourable name. Once having a son you could claim great privileges. With the game played right, Ming Pei Sha, fortune could be yours.'

I was thinking of Hui and Tuk Un when a sudden, terrifying thought came to me. Dragging myself from the bedlam and joy of the distant *Cormorant*, I turned.

'How old is this Lo Hin Tan?' I asked.

'There are varying opinions on his age. Some say sixty, but I met him some two years ago and I would have judged him at nearer seventy.'

I left him. Walking swiftly across the lawns to the house, I did not look back.

'Ming Pei Sha!'

Even at the door I did not turn.

Nothing was more revolting to me than the feeble clutches of the ambitious old: better the fist and strength of the brutal Po Shan.

Next afternoon, I was standing by the window overlooking the estuary. From here, though none will believe it, I could see Fo Tan village, where I was born, and I remembered Suelen and her patient, enduring smile; I remembered Hui and the shrieks of his boyhood, the whimpers of Tuk Un on my mother's breast, the appalling poverty of that childhood, the two-bowl-a-day existence on rice and water. I remembered once begging in the Shatin market place, and a tall, cool American girl giving me fifty cents. She would come to Shatin dressed in white and the people would follow her, saying that she was one of great purity and goodness. Alone she came to Shatin with her bag, visiting the beggars, and one she visited had the dreaded wasting disease, he being one from the leper colony of Hi Ling Chau, but now was cured. Lacking hands and feet and eyes he would sit near the village, begging, and the foreign girl would kneel beside him and feed him from the bag and he would drink from a flask she brought, although she was clean and he was not. Later she ceased to come and people looked and asked for her, and they said she had died, though not of leprosy. At the time I thought it cruel that she should die while the leper lived: now I thought it cruel that she had lived at all in a world where leprosy can be cured, but never greed.

Now Lo Hin Tan was expected and I stood before the mirror of my room with all my Tan-gar past dead behind me. This was an incredible Ming Pei Sha, one stripped of the labouring samfoo. Now I stood on stockinged legs, like a hobbled donkey on the stilt of heels; cramped by the gold cheongsam that chained me despite its high slit at the thighs, neck held rigid by the high collar; hair piled high by the visiting hairdresser, face powdered and rouged, eyes shadowed and eyebrows pencilled – I saw in the mirror the new Pei Sha, one far removed from the sweating labour of the junks, the girl Suelen loved.

Sitting on the bed, my hands folded in my lap, I waited the coming of Lo Hin Tan, prepared to go if he should choose me. Beside me was my suitcase and the Ming mirror, neatly wrapped and guarded against breakage, and I listened to the wind sighing over Shatin and the rice-terraces of Fo Tan, my village.

'Miss Ming!'

It was Eunuch from the lawn below, his falsetto voice strained high to a note of panic. I had to smile. Wing Sui was a century behind the times. The ancient game of China being played to the end – eunuch and concubine in these days of petrol-fuming Hong Kong and the giant air-liners pounding down the airport runway of Kai Tak.

'Miss Ming!' He called again and I rose and looked through the window. A big car was standing on the gravel drive before the entrance gates; a uniformed chauffeur sat in the front and a man at the back, though I could not see him. And even as I watched, Wing Sui approached the big car, bowing profusely to the back seat. I looked at my watch. It was exactly midday. All was timed to the moment with the hand of the expert – the location of the meeting, the way I would stand, the moment I would bow, the first words of introduction. Now footsteps hammered on the stairs and Eunuch burst into the room without knocking; life for him being dull indeed without such minor compensations, said Wing Sui. Once he had caught me getting out of the bath.

'Come, woman!'

'In my good time,' I said, sitting on the bed again.

'But your husband waits.'

'Waiting will cool him – Wing Sui also.'

'By God,' said he, 'in my day . . .'

'This is not your day, it is mine!'

'Miss Ming!' He made faces of agony, screwing at his hands in abject servility. 'The master . . .'

I rose. 'Away out of it,' I whispered. 'Running dog! *Bastard!* Away, or you will get some Tan-gar fisher-language – Wing Sui and Lo Hin Tan also. Tell them *wait!*'

He went, whimpering, and I sat on the bed again.

But Wing Sui, in his knowledge of women, did not hasten me.

Ten minutes later I descended the stairs. The two men were standing in the hall, and they stopped their whispering to look up. I came down slowly, my hand on the rail, and if Wing Sui noticed my air of disdain he did not show it. I could afford disdain. A month ago I had visited Po Shan and paid him four thousand dollars, which for him was the difference between life and death, and to do this I had pledged myself to a stranger. If it was not the man Lo Hin Tan it would be somebody else – Wing Sui would see to that; also, with luck, it might be somebody younger. Now the merchant stood in black severity, his mouth a thin line in the yellow wrinkles of his face, calm, possessed. But the man Lo Hin Tan was fidgeting like a nervous boy. Reaching the hall, I joined them, smiling. Wing Sui said softly:

'The girl Pei Sha, sir.'

Mr Lo Hin Tan returned my smile, and bowed.

Once, in childhood, I had seen a vulture caged, though some called it a Hong Kong eagle. This was the same barbaric head screwed on a starved neck, and it was hairless, for the curse of wealth, says Suelen, balds them quicker than shears. His nose was flattened, the nostrils with sensuous flares. Through slanted, pouched eyes he regarded me with the brooding intent of the hunting male, his eyes switching, taking in all at a glance.

Wing Sui was kind when he judged his age at seventy.

And I returned his stare, remembering dimly another man of fantastic riches of whom I had once read: owners of hundreds of labourers, of alley slums, and tenements which collapsed and took life: owner of land in the New Territories where the teeming Hakka toiled for cents while he made millions: with money in a Swiss bank without a doubt and a sea-going yacht oiled and fuelled for the last escape. For every one like this thousands in Hong Kong hungered and fretted, huddled in their hillside shanties the better to serve him. Lo's voice, when he spoke, was unexpectedly beautiful, being full, vibrant, and possessing a sort of dreamy exultation:

'I am honoured, Ming Pei Sha.'

'She pleases you?' Wing Sui now, better at the classics than formal introductions, and I saw the annoyance touch Lo's face. He gestured with a finger and Wing Sui faded from his presence.

'You are very beautiful.'

I did not reply. Through the age and extreme ugliness there seeped a charm of manner; his every word and movement evinced good breeding. Inches taller than me, there was a sinewy grace about him that spoke of youth. He said:

'Wing Sui has told you that I seek another wife?'

'He has told me that you want a concubine.'

Instantly, 'My wife is barren and I need an heir. Many years ago I married for the second time, my first wife having died. The marriage was contracted under Ching Law. This permits me to take another wife.'

'And your wife agrees?'

Wing Sui, having drifted back to us, interjected. 'Pei Sha, how dare you!'

'She has a right to know,' replied Lo. 'No, Pei Sha, my wife does not agree to me taking a *tsip*, but she will come to it – most wives do.'

'She will receive me?'

'My wife is a lady. Yes, she will receive you.'

'You have relatives?'

'For God's sake!' whispered Wing Sui, appalled, and Lo replied:

'Not on my side. But my wife has a considerable number, all of whom I appear to support, as you will see. Now you, Pei Sha. Some questions about you?'

'You know about me,' I said, and moved away.

He was not having me easy. He angered me and I wanted him to know this. The need for an heir was the excuse for desire, and I would have liked him to be more honest. Also, I was remembering his name from my childhood, remembering a wall on one of his construction sites whose hoarding blazed his name, and a Cantonese woman who was working there for ten dollars a day to feed her children. And the wall, which was in Mong Kok, fell, burying her, and men did not know. Two days later her eldest son, aged seven, came to the site in search of his mother, but she could not be found save for a hand clutching at air, and Lo Hin Tan had the wall removed and the body of the woman given back to her family. No compensation was paid, said Suelen.

'One important point,' Lo raised his voice. 'Your age?'

'She is above the legal age,' said Wing Sui.

'I ask the girl, not you. Your age, Ming Pei Sha?'

'I am seventeen. I will be eighteen in September.'

'You have proof of this?'

'No. My birth was not registered.'

Wing Sui said, bowing, 'Sir, examine her for intellect and you will find she is a woman – look at her bearing – she is beyond the age of carnal knowledge.'

'You have a relative I can interview to obtain written proof of age?' He asked this with great kindness.

'None whose name I will give you, but I swear to the truth. I am nearly eighteen.'

Lo nodded, glancing about him. 'You have luggage?'

Wing Sui waved and Eunuch, hovering near, went scampering. Lo opened the car door and I went within, sitting in the luxurious back seat.

'Goodbye, my child. May fortune attend you,' said Wing Sui, bowing.

I turned my face from him. He had done well through pimpery: a few lessons in deportment, table manners, ancient custom, the art of entertainment – and a profit of thousands of dollars. His labour had ended, mine had just begun.

Eunuch brought my suitcase and the big Ming mirror. The car started.

We took the road to Kowloon along the Golden Mile of Nathan Road where the property speculators, unchecked by Government, were making fortunes. Lo Hin Tan did not speak. With a world between us we sat contained by glass amid the lunatic rush of the city, me clutching the Ming mirror, he surveying the bedlam outside with tired eyes. In no way did he acknowledge my existence. It was as if he took home a new concubine every day of his life. On the ferry at Yaumati with the Kowloon shore receding, he spoke for the first time.

'It is hot in here, Miss Ming. Let us stand in the wind,' and we left the car.

His voice was indeed beautiful, as one buried in a grave years before its time. The harbour was about us now, rolling green and alive with craft. I stood beside him at the prow, remembering another trip by ferry, when, with Suelen, I saw Jan for the second time.

Now engines were cranked into roars. The big Buick whispered into the teeming Praya. Here is a bustling humanity, sweating peasants with the load-poles bouncing, crying for a passage through the packed crowds of coolies; businessmen in well-cut suits, waitresses and shop girls from places like Sincere's, Wing On, and Lane Crawford's. Pig-tailed Hoklo and Tan-gar were there from the heaving junks, chicken-sellers with their hens craning from their big rush baskets, their squawks accompanying the pig-shrieking lorries bound for the slaughterhouses of Kennedy Town: brown-clad policemen ballet-danced in slow motion, pointing with accusing fingers at the crawling dragon of chromium plate and glass. We edged and hooted into the traffic and took the way to the Peak up Garden Road. The chauffeur slowed into a drive and then stopped the car within immense iron gates.

This was the garden of the House of Lo. We left the car and walked.

Flowering azalea and calendula waved along the paths; amid great lawns stood oasis of wild iris, its great violet flower tinged with orange: nun orchids with their white petals and purple lips lorded it over the yellow creeper and wild jasmine, and persimmon, black as an English funeral train, edged the borders and bed of glorious rhododendron. Now a new vision of beauty – the great house of stone, its red roof of curved Chinese tiles giving it a hostile splendour. We walked slowly, passing marble fountains and falling sprays of light, and bowers where sat small and beautiful love-pavilions, their glaring whiteness decorated with scarlets and greens, the creeping convolvulus. Here, I thought, could be ancient China: here could have walked Pearl Concubine with her caged parakeets and chattering love-birds of the Imperial Court; the priceless jades and talismens, fawning courtiers and royal eunuchs with their intrigue and strangling cords. The wind moved and it was perfumed and I remembered the steaming alleys of Ho Man Tin and Hung Hom.

'You think it is beautiful?' asked Lo.

'I have never seen anything so lovely.'

He sighed. 'In the middle of Britain I have tried to build an island of China.'

The stupidity arrested me, but I said nothing. Hong Kong island, stolen from China was, to me, still China – every grass blade and leaf, every ounce of bright red soil, and it was impossible to believe that an intelligent Chinese could think otherwise. On the edge of the lawn before the house, Lo paused, saying apologetically, 'Here we wait to be received. The family have seen us arrive, soon my wife will call us. Are you nervous?'

'Of course.'

'There is no need to be. Wing Sui tells me you are a scholar – we will talk of the classics, this will pass the time.'

'Wing Sui is exaggerating.'

'But you read greatly.'

'Every book I can find.'

He smiled, delighted. 'The last book you read, and when?'

'*The Dream of the Red Chamber* – part of it again last night, this book I love.'

'Its author?'

'Ts'ao, but there is doubt about that.'

'Excellent! I seem to remember a verse he wrote on the subject of the story. . . .'

I began, '"These pages tell . . . a string of sad tears they conceal. . . ."'

He stared at me. 'Pei Sha, that is quite remarkable.'

'It is not. It is simply that I love the poets, and have studied them.'

The wind moved between us, scented with flowers. Nothing else stirred in the radiance of the day. I thought: this missus is taking her time; strange indeed that a man as powerful as Lo Hin Tan should wait with such humility to be called like a child.

Now he said, glancing apprehensively at the house, 'You will have read of Bright Concubine?'

'The lovely Ming Fei!'

'You mean Hsiang Fei – she was born on the banks of the Yangtse-kiang, and was both beautiful and virtuous. Come, we will honour the classics. Tell me what you know of the Bright Concubine.'

It was most difficult, I did not want to hurt him.

'Ah, I have caught her – she does not know!'

I said, 'There is nothing lower than a boastful woman, sir.'

He grimaced. 'But you are wrong! To show knowledge of wonderful things is not to boast, Pei Sha – it is to honour. Tell me of Bright Concubine!'

I said, 'Being beautiful, she was desired by all men and sold to the terrible Shan-yu of the Huns by the Emperor Yuan, and carried away to the land of the Tartars.'

'Clever! But do you recall her lament? It begins, "Mistress to a savage king, a nomad's life I share . . ." Come, try, your voice delights me.'

I repeated, ' "Mistress to a savage king, a nomad's life I share, a bargain for my people's freedom; longing for the sweet-sour earth smells of my fields, the wallowing buffalo under a China moon, my heart is winged. On earthbound hope I fly to my sweet land beneath a China sky." '

His eyes moved slowly over my face. 'God,' he whispered, 'that was beautiful.'

I was disturbed. To stay silent was deceitful, so I said, 'Sir, I quoted you that lament because it was the one you wanted, but it is not Bright Concubine's.'

'Who, then, if it is not the Lady Chao's?'

'It is the song of an earlier traveller – none know her name.'

He waved me down. 'Would you teach me the classics, child? The poets are my life-blood. Listen. The Bright Concubine

123

was Hsiang Fei – you called her Ming Fei earlier and I let it pass, but do not provoke me.' He was plainly angry.

'I am sorry.' I bowed to him.

'Do not bow to me, it is servile. Only allow that I am right.'

'You are wrong,' I said sharply. 'The name of Bright Concubine was Ming Fei – some called her the Brilliant Lady. Many poets confuse her with Hsiang Fei, so you are not alone in the error. Wang was her family name and she was born in Chingmen. To mistake her for others is a popular trend – one followed to this day by the poorer scholars; she is not the Fragrant Concubine of the Emperor Ch'ien Lung, but the one who set out for the Jade Gate in the Han dynasty.'

'God,' he whispered. 'Where did you learn such things?'

'From the books, from the bald men of the tea-houses and the monks of the little temples.'

He was about to reply when a voice called from the house, and we turned. A tall woman was standing between the great columns of the entrance, her hand upraised. Even from a distance she was beautiful, her scarlet gown enhancing her fine figure.

'We are called?' I asked.

Lo took my arm. 'My wife's people are waiting, Pei Sha.'

Mrs Lo Hin Tan was still beautiful despite the drag of the years, and all sounds faded for me as I stood before her. Her brow was high; her hair, streaked with grey at the temples, was plaited in shining strands over her head; her eyes were rimmed with shadow, her face classic in line, and impassive. It was as if the knowledge of me had quenched the once fierce anger in her: she looked sick and empty of tears. Lo said:

'So you received my letter.'

'Letter!' she turned away her face. 'Have we drifted so far apart that we now have to write?'

He waved her into silence. 'Words achieve their end with reasonable people. Your tantrums are such these days that you won't listen to anything. This is Ming Pei Sha, and she is joining this house as *tsip*. I ask you to welcome her.'

'With a little effort you might rake up some dignity, Lo.'

'I am finished with dignity. Are you accepting her or not?'

'If I do not you will only command it.'

'Of course.'

Lo Tai's faded eyes moved over me. 'In your letter you said you were bringing a woman. Instead you bring a child. How old are you, girl?'

Lo answered sharply, 'She is over sixteen and she comes of her own free will.'

'Let her answer for herself.' She turned to me. 'Your name is Pei Sha?'

'Yes, Lo Tai.'

'Have you received money?' Her voice was strangely kind.

'I have received money from an agent.'

'And you come of your own free will? You are not owned and being sold?'

'I am not, Lo Tai.'

She bent to me. 'Listen most carefully now. How old are you?'

'I am seventeen, Lo Tai. I will be eighteen in the month of September.'

'You have a birth certificate?'

'My birth was not registered.'

'Why not?'

Lo said testily, 'She is Tan-gar. She was born at sea.'

'That is no reason why she cannot show a birth certificate. In what year were you born?'

I told her.

She raised a finger. 'Now, do not lie to me, Pei Sha, for you will have to certify your age before my relatives. My husband intends to have physical knowledge of you. If you are under the age of sixteen you will both land in serious trouble outside a bed. Do you quite understand?'

I lowered my head. 'I understand, Lo Tai.'

There was a pause and she said quietly, 'You are very beautiful.'

I was sick and ashamed. Her very kindness and concern for me was heaping on me degradation. Sighing, she turned to Lo, saying, 'Well, since you are so determined I suppose she will have to stay.'

'Thank you, Lo Tai,' I said.

Lo replied sharply, 'She is not begging, you know, and neither am I. She comes quite properly – under the laws of Customary Marriage.'

'Under your law, Lo, not mine. I do not now accept Ching Law.'

He was exasperated. 'God, woman, you married me under this law!'

'Laws, like men, change with time – standards alter them. I do not accept it.'

'Whether you do or not it is a fact. What is more, Pei Sha has equality with you in dignity – remember it.'

'In dignity, perhaps, since she is a woman – but she is equal in no other respect. I am mistress of this house.'

'Nobody is denying it. Come, do not waste time.'

His wife turned. Lo took my hand and we followed her into the hall.

'Do not let them frighten you,' he whispered. 'I am master here – do not be afraid.'

This was a hall of treasure, of statues of amber and jade; of panelled walls beautifully carved, ornate, arched ceilings; floor tapestries from the weavers of Pekin and Tientsin. And beyond the great vaulted walls, side rooms shone with gorgeous brocades. It was a pirate-lair of brass and rosewood, with great ivory pagodas depicting every dynasty. Beside Lo, stiff with fear, I went, with Lo Tai leading us as to an execution through a millionaire's dream of art. Turning through a door we entered a small, red-carpeted chamber. To this day I remember the great bench table of polished teak where stood the tea, wine, and foods for the greeting meal, for behind the table sat the relatives of Lo Tai in order of age. Thus the custom of centuries was about to be revealed; a marriage fulfilled and sanctified by the mere formal presentation of the husband's choice of a second wife.

And I was suffering the terror of the concubine.

The relatives stiffened as we approached, their feet shifting nervously, their hands clasped across their stomachs, their eyes switching up at me.

These were the relatives of Lo Tai, the principal wife of Lo Hin Tan.

Take the most important first, the smallest, Lo Tai's father. Here was a little five feet wisp of a man with sinewy, fumbling hands where the veins stood proud to his life of farming. His jowls were hanging on pin-bone cheeks and straggled with white beard. Leaning heavily on his stick, as if to call from me the utmost reverence, he champed his jaws in my direction. And as I neared the table he waved the stick at me and cackled from a crimson mouth, till smothered by whispered consolations.

This was the head of the tribal executioners.

Next in right was First Brother, and I despised this one on sight; a man stuffed up with wealth and property, all earned by Lo, I suspected. His face was lined with excess, having the creased chins of the grossly overfed. He squeezed and pampered his outraged father in a voice of piping protest, between times shooting agonised glances at Lo over the table, disassociating himself from the tribunal: plainly he owed Lo money.

'First Brother,' said Lo, and I bowed.

'Second Brother,' said Lo, and I bowed again.

This second brother, blessed with the bountiful fat of all the brothers, bowed back, wheezed, flushing red with dislike for everybody, concubines in particular.

'Third Brother,' said Lo, and down I went again.

The youngest was a miniature in sloe-eyed innocence, not much older than my precious Hui; but fat, *fat* – bangled wrists, knees knocking beneath his satin trousers, buttons in agony across his tight waistcoat, he was flinging nervous glances at First Brother in case he put a foot wrong. But he was a child. I smiled and his face became mirthful. Delighted, he smiled back, and First Brother elbowed him.

'My mother,' said Lo Tai, then, and I took a great breath.

This was the root cause of the obesity, the fat-lined womb. And by the narrowed eyes that shifted in her paunchy face, this was the schemer of my promised execution. She did not bow; in fact, she did not move or make a sign of recognition, but stared through me at the pattern of brocade on the wall behind me.

There was a pause in the introductions, and I wondered why. Then a door opened and a woman came into the chamber, one gaunt and grey, with the face and body of a ghost – the ghost of a woman who had died of hunger. And in the eyes of this woman there was neither expression nor light; the bones of her pitiful body pinned the rich silk of her gown with her every movement: a family skeleton who had found the key to her cupboard, and uninvited, walked in.

Heroin.

To my astonishment she smiled with sudden brilliance, bowing. I bowed back.

'Yee Moi is my name,' she said.

'I am Ming Pei Sha,' I replied.

'My sister is ill,' said Lo Tai softly.

Her sister was dying.

They looked, they moved awkwardly in the seat of justice. Silence, a shivering silence, one you could have split with an axe into a gale of words – insults, hatreds, threats – all save Yeo Moi, who regarded me with her lovely, idiot smile.

Lo Hin Tan said with care, 'I have been married for twenty years and have no son. I have an empire of business, and no heir, and without a son a man is like a comet flashing across the sky. Therefore, under the law, I bring this woman Pei Sha before you. She shall be my second wife. Through her will my name endure.'

Its very sincerity lent it more beauty, and Lo Tai's father, suddenly reformed, stamped his stick on the floor and muttered approval, till silenced by withering glances.

'She is Tan-gar, I hear,' remarked Lo Tai's mother, 'and I do not like the Tan-gar. I do not like the boat-people at all, for they are not Chinese.'

'She is Chinese, of pure blood, do not mistake it,' said Lo.

'Your Hong Kong age, girl?'

I hesitated, turning to Lo. She said, commandingly, 'I asked your Hong Kong age – now tell me.'

It was a trap and I recognised it. By Hong Kong law I was two years younger than by the Chinese calendar. I told her my age and she turned away with a sniff. 'She looks more like fifteen to me. You have proof of her words?' she asked her daughter.

In this house so far I had met nobody I could hate save this one. Her florid face and girth told of her good living at Lo Hin Tan's expense: her body is fat with inner riches, Lo told me later, for in it the body of her husband is stored. On him, before the coming of Lo, she had battened and fed like a blood-suck spider, draining him of his youth with her driving ambitions, dulling his intellect with her incessant, peasant chatter, killing his pride by her insults before the servants.

Lo Tai, her daughter, said wearily, though it was a lie, 'Leave it, I have the proof.'

Then First Brother drew himself up with a fine pomposity, saying, 'Come, Lo, this is an outdated custom. Besides, I deny your need of an heir. There are enough males in this family to inherit the wealth of us all.'

'My wealth,' said Lo, 'you have none.'

First Brother ignored the jibe. 'Ching Law is not accepted beyond the border, Lo – concubinage there is outlawed.'

'But it is the law obtaining in Hong Kong, and I invoke it. I do not invoke the law of the Communists in one breath and revile them with the next.'

Despite the situation, this delighted me.

'Nevertheless,' said his mother-in-law, 'were you fifty miles north of Lo Wu you would be arrested, tried, and convicted on moral grounds.'

'A law is moral wherever it stands,' said Lo. 'In Red China, in Hong Kong. What would be a mistress fifty miles north of Lo Wu is a wife here.'

'I shall never agree to this union,' said Mother-in-law. 'It is an outrage to my daughter's pride.'

'It is an outrage to my pride that I possess no son.'

'I accept her,' said Yee Moi, the sister, quietly, 'I accept her because she is beautiful, and she will bear Lo a son.'

'Silence!' they shrieked at her.

And her father said, 'Take her, Lo. This is Customary Marriage.'

'It is immoral,' whispered Mother-in-law, and Lo said blandly:

'The customs are changing with opinion, it seems. Father-in-law accepts this girl as my second wife because there is more than one in this very room who did not spring from you, Mother. This is good, for now you have three sons instead of only two daughters!'

'This was my sorrow,' she replied. 'I do not wish my daughter to suffer what I have suffered.'

We stood in another silence, and Lo reached out and deliberately took my hand.

First Brother shrugged, turning away, 'He is intent on the folly, Sister. Name her and have done with it.'

Lo whispered urgently, 'I beg you to remember her beautiful name.'

His wife lowered her head and said softly, 'I name her Pei Sha, which is her name. I give her this name because she is too young to know the hurt she has given me.' Smiling sadly, she looked about her. 'I accept her as *tsip* because I have no choice under the law – she is forced upon me. But if she bears Lo a child I shall never recognise that child. The law may claim this, but I do not accept it. Give her the gift of money.'

Still beside me, Lo opened a packet and brought out two red envelopes containing the lucky money. One envelope he gave to me, the other he placed on the table before his wife. To me he whispered, 'Now serve her.'

Under the cold gimlets of their watchful eyes I poured jasmine tea into a bowl. Taking the bowl in my two hands I knelt before Lo Tai at the table, and she took the bowl and raised it to her lips, but she did not drink, so gave me no compliment. Then she placed the bowl on the table and took up the second envelope of red lucky money and this she gave to me. I took it and raised myself, standing before her.

And Lo Hin Tan clasped my hand and led me to the other side of the table, saying:

'Eat, drink! Let everybody place the seal of family acceptance on this marriage.'

But they did not turn to him, not even Lo Tai's sister, the heroin Yee Moi. One by one they left and did not drink, and we were alone in the red chamber.

'Come,' he said, 'I will take you to your room.'

16

ON THE DAY of Grain Rain which is in the month of April by the English calendar, Lo Hin Tan took me as his second wife to his bed, and consummated his marriage.

The night of his love-making stands clearly in my mind.

The sky was brilliant with stars, I remember. From the

garden of the house on the Peak I saw the harbour pinned with light. Far below me the roof-dwellers steamed in mumbling sleep, for it was strangely hot, and the sea-front pulsated and sparkled the crimson of its midnight pleasures. The great sleepless traffic-dragon of the Praya writhed and gleamed; rickshaw coolies, stupefied by exhaustion and weak congee, walked between the shafts along the road by Tamar. Unable to sleep, I watched, expecting this call from Lo, for I had been ten days in the house and had not even seen him. Ah Ying, the little maid he had appointed to me, said he had gone to Manila, and according to her had returned that evening. In a house of whispers and hostility the family passed me on the stairs and did not speak. Even Father-in-law, who, said Ah Ying, had known enough concubines to land him on his death-bed, did not spare me a glance.

Now Lo was home again, they told me. In the desperation born of loneliness, I longed for him to call me.

I turned in the garden as a tracer of light shot the lawn. Standing in shadows I followed the track of the hunter, seeing Lo from instant to instant, room to room, from light-switch to curse and out on to the landing again. I could almost hear him swear when I was not in my bedroom. It was reasonable, this impatience. When one pays several thousand dollars for a woman one expects to find her accessible. Now the light bloomed on the first floor, now in the hall with gathering speed. He must have been galloping by the time he reached the front door; it was extremely flattering.

'Pei Sha!'

After the brutal courtship of Chu Po Shan I did not fear the aged Lo Hin Tan.

Still in the shadows of the garden I watched, and did not answer.

'Pei Sha!' It savoured of command and I did not like it.

Resplendent in a white dressing-gown, Lo stood in the doorway, then crossed the lawn to the bower, looking astonishingly young in that blue light. Seeing me, he approached slowly, and I was aware of a sensation of lost time and period. Dressed as we both were in white silk, it could have been an assignation between Emperor and mistress, a whispered love-making in a dynasty of terror. He said, taking my hand:

'I rang for you, and you did not come.'

'It was late, I did not expect you.'

'I went to your room and you were not there.'

I said, moving away. 'Only the maid said you might be back – your relatives do not speak to me. You have been away many days and not one word have they said to me. How do I know where you are?'

'I am sorry.'

I wandered, and he followed, adding, 'I came in later than expected from the airport, I was tired, and slept. Then I awoke, remembering you. I had a dream and the experience was terrible. The plane crashed and I burned. Have you ever had such a dream?' I did not know that he was foretelling the manner of his death. I shook my head.

'It was quite horrible.'

His hands were trembling. He was like a child who was afraid, and I pitied him. And as I took his hands I saw in the cruelty of the moonlight a face savaged by years, a corruption of weariness: in a moment he was old again. I said:

'You have a tired head. You have been working too hard, Lo.'

He nodded. 'Another company in Manila. It goes on and on, one company after another. It is gross stupidity and I often wonder what will be the end of it.'

'It is ambition and greed. It can only have one end.'

He was plainly surprised. 'It is not greed – neither is it ambition, for I have fulfilled all ambitions. You are too young for great wisdoms, Pei Sha – it is habit, pure and simple.'

'Can't you give it up?'

He hunched his thin shoulders. 'Business is a dog-fight. If one breaks off the other dogs tear you to pieces.'

'You must enjoy doing business with dogs,' I said.

It amused him, and he replied, 'You are fascinating. I came down here to carry you to a bed. Instead, I am inveigled into superficial conversation for which I am far too tired.'

'You'll find conversation a lot less tiring.'

I walked, and he followed, taking my hand, and it was better for me. Here, beside him, I did not see his face. Dreams could be conjured in this make-believe, for his hand was young and strong, his voice filled with the resonance of youth. Close your eyes, Pei Sha, I thought, and this could be Jan and Yim Tin Tsai. I opened my eyes to find Lo looking into my face.

'Are you back with me?' he asked.

I smiled for answer, and he added, 'I have known you for but a few hours and yet you are mine only for minutes. Do I bore you?'

'That is not possible.'

He moved uneasily. 'Do you despise me?'

'Why should I despise you?'

'Because I seek your youth, and I am old.'

'If this were so I would not have married you. There is more to marriage than age, sir, there is intellect.'

'Is one concerned with intellect when one is not yet twenty? Perhaps I should know, but I forget.'

I replied, 'I have come of my own free will. I am your wife. Shall we go to your room?'

'Not yet, Pei Sha.' He looked at the sky, whistling softly at its beauty, as a young man might do. I detected in him an occasional impish humour that was most attractive; humour, I find, is a balm to many blemishes. He said softly, 'You must know about me. My past is interesting. I was born and raised in Kingtung, in a mansion on the Hong Kong road, by the strangest coincidence. A week after I arrived my father swaddled me against the snow and took me down to the nearby village, to the cottage of the poorest and most insignificant woman he could find. He did this for three reasons – first because I was the first son of his loins, by his fourth wife, a serving-girl of low intelligence, and my father reasoned that since I had to leave the house the milk that would suit me best would come from the breast of a commoner. Secondly, to keep me in the house on Hong Kong road would court disaster. From three other women he had sought sons, and produced unimportant daughters, and the devils who were determined to cheat him of this son-ship would surely seek to kill me. Thirdly, he was terrified of kidnappers, for he was one of the richest men in the city. After I had been spirited away he took into his house a tiny girl-child whom he named Loi, and this child he raised as his own daughter. So that there would be no possible mistake about the sex of his new offspring, he would himself accompany the amah around the streets, showing this child to friends and neighbours, speaking loudly of his lovely baby daughter so that the evil ones would be left in no possible doubt as to their success, and his failure to produce a son. When I was six years old the village woman brought me home, and for the first time I met little Loi, my adopted sister. She was a dark and beautiful child, and I adored her. On bright nights, when we grew older, we would play games of make-believe. On nights such as this, for instance, we would pretend that it was the Moon Festival. These games allowed us many privileges, which we granted each other. You remind me so much of my Loi. Money was never short in my family, but we endured a lonely childhood. Bring her back for me, Pei Sha! Tell me, have you eaten your mooncakes yet?'

'Are we playing a game now?' I was a little frightened.

'Oh, come, you must be quicker than that about make-believe. Have you eaten your cakes today?'

I said, 'When I was a child in Fo Tan village we had mooncakes on the mid-autumn festival, also melons and pomegranates, though this custom seems to have died.'

'My sister Loi ate pomegranate seeds by the mouthful to guarantee sons, but she had six daughters. Also grapes for fertility and peaches for longevity. Neither did the peaches serve her, she died at thirty.'

'Which legend do you believe?'

He sat on a garden seat, drawing me down beside him. 'My darling Loi believed the legend of the Queen of the Moon, of the wife Sheung who swallowed the pill that brought her immortality and the name Moon Goddess.'

'That legend has no substance of truth,' I said. 'Mine is better.'

He replied with feigned smugness, 'Now you are going to tell me the myth of the Yuan dynasty rebellion.'

'It is no myth – hundreds of thousand – millions of people believe it. Look at the moon, Lo Hin Tan, and swear that you do not believe it.' I stared into his face. 'Swear,' I said.

'And the penalty if I do not?'

I said gravely. 'Under the Huns of the Yuan dynasty the country was in ferment. . . .'

'Which version is this one?' he interjected, but I ignored him.

'. . . So oppressed were the people that the hated Mongols allowed them one table knife among ten families, and installed in every cottage a Hun spy, and this man had sport with the women. Family life was threatened – the root of existence, so the Chinese plotted. The women cooked cakes and baked secret messages within them, telling the date of the rising – instructing all that in the absence of knives, bamboo canes would be sharpened. And on the fifteenth day of the eighth moon, at the same hour, ten thousand Huns fell by stabbing, and the rule of the Mongols was ended.'

'I have never heard anything like it. My sister Loi would have been appalled.' He rose, smiling down at me.

I said, 'I enjoyed the make-believe, although it was grotesque. I like you that much better. I am ready now, and will come.'

'Commendable obedience, but who invited you?'

'Now you do not want me?'

'Come when you are called – this is the custom. And don't let us be too ancient or intense, Pei Sha. First some hard facts after the fun. Why did you become a concubine?'

'For money.'

He saw the sense of it, and nodded. 'But a woman of your ability need never want for money, surely?'

'Quick money,' I replied. 'And in a lump sum, not a wage.'

'There must have been a reason.'

'The reason is my business.'

'Mine, too, now you are my wife.'

'You bought me – must you have more?'

Behind him the black waters of the harbour were festooned with light, a galaxy of masts and spars, and the Hong Kong Yacht Club glittered and shimmered in the blackness, for the moon was spent.

Lo reached out and drew me against him, his arm hard around my waist.

'It is enough that I have you,' he said. 'Come.'

I had expected the fussing ardour of the aged, even the smothering strength of Po Shan, but it was not so. He was strangely gentle with me, and knowing of women, he was cool, cleaving to me as a young man, whispering words of love. And but for those whispers I could have imagined a sweeter place

135

than a bed, and a dearest in the loving. The room was heavy with tapestries, I remember, the bed a sea of gold and scarlet. It was brief, for the knowledge of me soon spent him, leaving him silent beside me, as one approaching death. There is neither rank nor ruler in love save the strongest. He slept. Later he rose in the bed, whispering to me. I did not heed him, for he was as nothing to a woman. With early dawn, as the sun came up red and raging over the world, he awoke, holding me in his arms, and he wept. I pitied Lo Hin Tan. He who owned finance houses and rents, shares and properties, even a thousand people who worked for him to the point of slavery, could not command one as insignificant as me. The wind came up with the dawn, blustering in from the sea, and it hammered at the windows and slammed the doors of the house. I shuddered. Lying there in the wind sounds it was as if death itself with all its perfumed mould, aged face, and disobedient limbs had crept into the bed and was lying in my arms. I stirred.

'Do not go, Pei Sha.'

He was clear-minded, wide awake. I said softly:

'Lo, it is dawn. I have already stayed too long.'

'My wife is in Macau.'

'That is what I mean – I should not be here.'

'Sleep, for God's sake, sleep.'

Despite the crying wind, he slept, and after an hour I rose and left him, because he was old. Standing by the window I watched the heavens grow bright in a ripped crimson bed-sheet of a sky, for the wind had got children by the throat now, the harbour was green and storm-tossed and the children screamed and screamed.

On the landing I fumbled with the light-switch. A door came open in the light of the window. Lo Tai, the wife, stood there. Unmoving, she stared at me.

Running swiftly down the stairs I reached the great hall and turned at the balustrade, staring back.

17

'LO,' I SAID, 'tomorrow I am going to Ho Shung village in the New Territories to visit my sister Suelen.'

In a passion of coolness after the incinerating heat of the June day, Lo Hin Tan lazed in the garden in his long rattan chair. This chair interested me. From Foochow it had come, according to First Brother, and it had cost Lo twenty dollars from a way-side stall in Kowloon City, which, until the Japanese came, was actually walled.

I said, 'Are you listening, Lo?'

'For you I am wide awake, ears shivering,' he replied.

'Then think of the journey. Think of the material – I know the price of rattan because my sister Suelen was an expert with it. Think of the artistry required, the back-breaking labour, and you will understand the state of the peasants in China.'

'It worries me considerably.'

I continued, 'Take the beautiful lace-making – another ex-ample. The peasants give their eyesight to produce such art, and we buy these table-clothes for a pittance – have you thought of their pitiful wages?'

'It is quite scandalous.'

'Hong Kong is no better, but the wages are low for another reason. The trade unions have no real negotiating power. They try to represent the workers but it is a losing battle. Take the tram crews, the bus crews – this is their trouble. They are grossly underpaid, many are actually underfed. Yet there are about ninety banks in this place and most are flourishing. With a Colony coining money as fast as this one I think it is dis-gusting.'

'Disgusting.'

'And even if a bank goes bust it is the poor who lose their money,' I said.

'But think how little they are losing.'

'Nobody cares. Take this chair and the price you paid for it – this also represents official attitude.'

'If in doubt blame the Government.'

I said sincerely, 'There is a direct link between this chair and the economics of Hong Kong. Wages low, profits up, very rich, very poor – it is a simple system. All the time you have an autocratic authority – a benevolent dictatorship instead of a democratic rule – you will have such injustices.'

'Yet it is an excellent chair,' said Lo.

'It has got to be or you wouldn't have bought it. Why didn't you pay more for it, Lo?'

'Because the man only asked for twenty dollars.'

'Is that really true?' I put down my needlework. 'He must have been weak in the head – I know the price of rattan.'

'Well, he did ask for thirty-five, but I beat him down.'

'That was greedy of you.'

'That is how I make my money.'

'Aren't you ashamed?'

'Of course not. I admit I am greedy. I adore the state.'

'What about the man who sold the chair – don't you ever think of him?'

'I do – he'll have to sell a few more chairs.'

I got up. 'It is terrible. Enjoy your money while you can, Lo. One day they will come and take it from you.'

'God, listen to it!'

I said, 'I think it is astonishing that an intelligent man like you cannot see what is coming – and, what is more, do nothing about it.'

'*Oho!* Communist!'

'I am nothing of the sort. I am talking common decency. You don't have to be a Communist to demand a decent standard of human behaviour.'

He rose awkwardly. 'I am quite reformed. Tonight I shall go to that stall-holder in Kowloon City and give him the other fifteen dollars.'

'Lo, you are kind in so many ways. Please be serious.'

Angrily, he said, 'God, what a house! It is full of spongers, gamblers, and reactionaries – and I refuse to be serious about this damned chair. Half my life I spend watching the share index or sitting in board rooms explaining to dome-headed speculators how I make their money. Now Father-in-law is in the Philippines, Mother-in-law in Canton again, and my wife in Macau – all at my expense, thank God. By day I laze – all this week, anyway; at night I make love to you, sometimes with success. With such peace and satisfaction how do you expect me to be anything but a capitalist?'

He was infuriating. I said, 'Tomorrow the company will be much more sincere. I will visit my sister Suelen in Ho Chung village.'

That night, after the evening meal, Lo said, as we walked in the garden:

'Tell me more of this fine big sister Suelen.'

It was possible to love him, too. I told him of Suelen, of Kwai and how he courted her, and he laughed. Sometimes, in his pouched eyes, I saw affection for me. In the garden the moonlight was kinder than in the bedroom, its blue radiance lending him a grace that deserted him in his failing, frantic love-making. Dressed as now, in his green gown, he seemed of another, more refined age. Now he said:

'And does Suelen know you are married to me?'

'She addresses her letters to Ming Pei Sha. She thinks I am here as a servant.'

We stopped at a rustic table. Lo poured himself more jasmine tea. Sipping it, he said, 'Is this wise? A double life rarely remains a secret, and most concubines have enemies – it is a natural state in the jungle of life.'

'It is a risk I prefer to take.'

'This is good tea,' he said.

It was his habit to drink lotus tea in the garden at dusk, the light being gentle to his eyes, he said. By his request I would drop the seeds in the lotus flowers at dusk, and, with darkness, the petals would enclose them. In the morning I would gather the seeds and put them into a container, now deeply scented with the perfume of the lotus. The scent of the tea revived half-forgotten memories of youth, said Lo. Now he lowered the cup, saying:

'Presumably this Ming Suelen disapproves of concubinage?'

'I am sure she would.'

'Is she a Christian convert?'

'Not a convert, but she is interested in Christianity,' I answered.

'Most Christians condemn concubinage, yet they have tolerated prostitution for centuries. They will not face facts, but we pagans are very much wiser – frankly one woman at a time has never satisfied me. Once you accept this as a biological necessity you accept multiple marriage.' He moved testily.

'Why the outburst?' I smiled at him.

'Christians sicken me.'

'Suelen is a woman, her opinion is unimportant.'

'And what do you think?' He glanced up.

'I am a concubine, I am not paid to think.'

'Assume you are not a concubine?'

'I would outlaw it tomorrow.'

'What would you put in its place, then – divorce?'

'No, marital loyalty.'

'You are too intelligent to be such a shocking prude, Pei Sha.'

I said, 'Men are immoral. Anything moral they condemn as prim, this is their defence.'

Lo gestured angrily. 'Man is polygamous, this is a natural law – and you are confusing ethics with a sensual need. The need in men is so strong that women can neither understand it nor hope for loyalty. Conscience doesn't enter into it. The only reason why a man doesn't sleep with every other woman he meets is either because she won't let him or there is a chance of somebody finding out, and men are sensitive to criticism. Adultery is the alternative to multiple marriage – once women accept this simple fact they accept the essence of the problem. Divorce on the European style is rejected in China because the children suffer, and children are the heritage. No, Pei Sha. Customary Marriage endures because it is best. The husband is reborn in the youth of his young wife, the old wife retains two vital assets – her man's respect and the love of her family. Thus the unity of the family – the very basis of Chinese life – is protected.' He meant every word of it. It was supremely honest.

'And the concubine?'

He spread his hands. 'No law forces her to be a concubine.'

'Except the law of poverty – in many cases. What about the wife?'

'The principal wife is still the accepted head, if not the leader of the house.'

'In her opinion.'

'It is so in this house, Pei, you cannot deny it.'

'You really think Lo Tai is happy, don't you?'

'She has every reason to be, she costs me enough.' Lighting a cigarette he exhaled the smoke noisily. 'She cannot expect too much, you know – she has had twenty years of love and attention and has given me little in return.'

I smiled. 'No son.'

He did not reply. It was the age-old excuse – the indictment of the first wife for failing to bear a son. This was the fantasy in which Lo Hin Tan hid his marital conscience. For the simple sin of barrenness a first wife could be cast aside; for illness, disease, alleged laziness, mischief-making, even for the sin of jealousy. Only public opinion was left to her as a protection should her husband decide to dispose of her under Ching Law.

I said, 'Ten minutes ago I was perfectly happy, now I am stricken with conscience. Who began this stupid conversation?'

'Ming Suelen,' replied Lo. 'She disapproves of concubines.'

'Which reminds me. Tomorrow I must visit her.'

'Tomorrow you are coming out with me, so you may not visit her. It is the fifth day of the fifth moon.'

'The Dragon Boat Races!'

'Come,' he said, and drew me against him. 'You are lovely, you are talented. In your youth I regain my old desires, I am most thankful to the ancient law.'

Hand in hand we entered the love-pavilion.

So I did not visit Suelen and Kwai To Man next day but went in the big car to Tai Po in the New Territories, it being blazing summer June, and the anniversary of the sacrifice of Wat Yuen, the poet.

The holiday crowds were thronging the streets of Shatin as we passed through. Queues of people in their best clothes were waiting at the bus stops outside Fo Tan, my village, and as we passed I saw its beloved roofs and the haze of its gardens. I saw the lane which led to the graves of my grandparents, the place on the road-side where my mother stumbled and fell in the tidal wave; the same blind scholar outside the tea-house, even the road that had led me to the house of Wing Sui. Lo, sitting deep in the back seat, had sunk into one of his inscrutables silences, which was the time when he was really making money, said Lo Tai, and sitting there I knew a sudden and acute longing for my own people. The train to Lo Wu was coming, I remember, and the Buick stopped at the level-crossing near the estuary. Here a crowd of villagers were waiting to cross, and with the curiosity born of villagers, they peered into the car, chiefly at me. I saw the wide eyes of the children, alive with incredulity at the luxury before them: the eyes of the women traced me from the top of my back-combed hair down to the tips of my shoes and back again, holding in their gaze the calm mockery born of their virtue. The men stared in blatant admiration, one or two faintly nudging each other, enamoured by the prospect, if unattainable.

But it was the eyes of the children that troubled me. All this, they were thinking, in the midst of our tremendous poverty: these, many of them from my own village, Fo Tan, held hands and stared, and I was embarrassed before them.

The train came hurtling down the rails towards us. The children left me for the new sensation, and I leaned towards the window for a better look at the train, and stared straight into the face of Kwai To Man, Suelen's husband. Clad in his black Hakka costume, with his bamboo shoulder-pole lying loose in his hands and his load at his feet, Kwai's face held an incredulity that surpassed that of the children. And he lifted his head with sustained interest in the second before the train crashed down the lines between us. The barriers swung clear, the car surged forward. By now, my heart thumping, I had opened my compact, holding it before my face, the powder-puff acting as a mask. But in the reflection of the mirror I saw Kwai To Man standing motionless by the roadside, looking back.

'Oh, God,' I said softly.

Lo turned instantly. 'Are you all right, Pei Sha?'

'Perfectly.' I snapped the compact shut and put it away.

He said next, 'You have gone very pale.'

'I am perfectly all right, I tell you.'

'Is it your period, darling? Perhaps you should not have come out.'

'Lo, for heaven's sake!'

He said, as to a child, 'It is only because I am so concerned about you.'

I was frightened and furious. Kwai had seen me without doubt, and Kwai was so damnably prim. Women, to him, were either virgins or harlots; his tiny mind, baked as it was in the ruts of his soil, could discern no significant difference between immorality and sacrifice. And he would go running to Suelen braying that he had seen me done up dainty in a rich man's car, that he had never seen an amah like that before. Suelen, outraged by the suggestion, would deny it, and then he would pry to prove his point. He would pry and lever and open the box, lifting me before her without a shred of respectability, and Suelen would be shamed before him and his people.

For smaller crimes good wives had been cast out.

While this prospect was terrifying, Lo was infuriating.

These days he was examining me under a microscope. With the desperation of a man who has but three more copulations left in him before the abyss of impotency he was measuring my state of health and morning complexion with vague enquiries, constant insinuations, and sidelong glances of hopeful anticipation, for he was son-mad. Now I wanted to shout that my periods were my business, that I had not conceived nor could he hope that I would conceive unless he could shed twenty years over-night. I was being unforgivingly cruel; Lo was gentle, as usual.

'My dear girl,' he whispered now, taking my hand.

I snatched my hand away.

Tai Po came up through the mountains, baked brown mountains straight from the sky oven; their forests flashing green floated in mist above the sugar-sheen of giant Tolo, the lovely Tolo I had fished for a thousand years on Chu Po Shan's *Cormorant*. I sat upright in the seat now, hands gripping, shivering with excitement, and Lo Hin Tan watched me with sustained curiosity, but I did not care. For we used to take the stormy Tolo wastes by night, I remembered, and await the shoals crowding down from the north; tail-flipping darts of phosphorescence, the shrimpy-big-boys, cried Hui, at nearly half a dollar a time. And the mass of them would heave and surge and mound the sea about us, the moment of the prawn – alive, *alive*, begging for the capturing nets and slaughter by scalding in the simmering vats of Pak Sha Wan. There, under the winter moons we would take them in their hundreds, tackle blocks and ropes creaking under the swinging nets – countless tragedies for the clattering chop-sticks and chow-fan bowls from Kennedy Town to Little Sai Wan.

'Look!' said Lo beside me, and the lovely vision passed.

For the foreshore was a sea of bright umbrellas and the Dragon Boat crowds were flooding in from Black Point to Tai Long and Star Ferry. Even from the bridge over the estuary I could see them, the brilliant dresses of the Europeans, the Indian saris of gorgeous colours and the coloured bunting and pennants streaming in the wind above a sapphire sea. The car stopped and we got out into a press of laughing, chattering people, for the Cantonese are at their best on festival days. Pushed along by the crowd we battled towards the stand amid the blaring jive of pocket transistors – the students out for enjoyment; a new generation of China, its youth radical and ambitious; removed from stories of the old tyrannies, kowtowing, and subservience.

These, I thought, are the new Cantonese emerging from the smoke of the Opium War: through these will Hong Kong find herself and free herself from the old colonial ideas, which are as outdated and unwanted by the mass as the Old Victorians. Five years from now these will rule Hong Kong, the final edict in a process of Asianisation since the British made the generous mistake of educating some of us.

'Third row from the back,' said Lo.

We took our seats in the stand.

I looked about me but there were few students here, and these, I feared, were very different people.

Below me on the sea the Dragon Boat crews were marshalling on the yellow beach; bronzed, half-naked giants marching down to the sea with the sixty-feet-long boats carried between them, this a part of the tribute they were paying to the poet Wat Yuen. Earlier, in a drumming of firecrackers, they had run these boats three times towards the grandstand where stood the red altar of Tin Hau, the patron of the boat-people. Now the races were about to begin. Beside me Lo sat in easy grace, bowing greetings to many about us, and I envied his unruffled calm. With clutched hands I watched the massed summer hats down the trestled tiers of seats: here were the elegant coiffures and fashion plates of the right people, many of them Colonials; but many, too, were the snob upstarts fighting to inject new life into a system long since dead. Some were possessed of the hawk-like visage of the chandelier rich or the cockatoo arrogance of those who sacrificed good manners for the smart reply; who didn't dislike the Chinese, but preferred northerners while in the south and southerners while in the north. These were the gabbling plum-in-mouth half-humans, and I hated them and all they stood for – the coarse banter of their forced male laughter, their garrulous female shriek. I closed my eyes and turned from them, my inferiority flying, knowing a sudden gladness that I had sprung from Tan-gar and true nobility, the coolies of the sea.

Lo Hin Tan, I noticed, was receiving his usual share of approbation: wealth, I had discovered, was a quicker passport to attention by the people who mattered than welfare. Below me a young European nurse sat alone, unnoticed.

There were quiet families – they could have been Greek, Dutch, German, or English, with their children gathered about them, self-contained and whole, kind and well-mannered. But there were also the others.

This, I thought, must be part of the social education, but I wondered if it was necessary to know of such humans in the search for knowledge – the pink-faced, chubby men, the swarthy war-horse men of square blue jowls and bass booms; their women fussy with artificial gaiety, enwrapped in their searchlight smiles and total isolation: they who were raiding a colony gutted with poverty, who lived like princes while Chinese children roamed the gutters of Shamshuipo and Ho Man Tin.

'I will soon be back,' whispered Lo. 'They are not as bad as they look – nurture such respectability,' and he rose.

It came as a shock that he should leave me for friends. They were waving from the edge of the stands, a group of beautifully dressed Chinese and elegant women. I rose as the Governor entered and took his seat, his manner serene, one beloved by the Chinese. Forgetting Lo, I stared, having never seen him before.

So intent was this stare that I did not see Jan Colingten standing beside me.

'Good morning,' he said, in English.

Unaccountably, it was no great shock to see him beside me: indeed, it appeared to be a logical sequence of events. Often I had considered such a chance meeting. This was his life and I had invaded it, therefore I was in some degree prepared. A race was in progress now and this helped me; the sea was in a turmoil as a hundred paddles plunged and whipped up showers of light-spray; the crowd roared and swayed. Sitting down, looking straight before me, I said in Cantonese:

'I am afraid I do not know you.'

He smiled. 'Don't say you've forgotten me!'

I was dying inside for him, my heart hitting against my body, for the old emotion was leaping at me now that he was near again. But I was wishing him to the devil also, for any moment Lo would come back. Jan said:

'Next you'll be saying you do not even remember Yim Tin Tsai.'

'You have made a mistake,' I said. 'I have never seen you before. Please go. Soon my friend will be back, and . . .'

'Ah yes, I have seen your friend. I will not embarrass you. You must forgive me for the mistake. It is amazing – your face, your voice – you are the image of a girl I met at Sai Kung.' All this he said in Cantonese, adding, 'You don't speak English?'

I shook my head.

'Then that's the proof of it. This girl was missionary educated – although she was Tan-gar she spoke English fluently – astonishing for a fisher-girl.'

I sat in silence, screwing at my fingers, and to my horror he sat down beside me, saying, 'Look, I'm quite sure your friend won't really mind. Now I am here will you explain to me the legend of Wat Yuen?'

'You know it as well as I do.'

'Only in outline.'

I thought: Oh God, soon Lo will come, and I will sit here like a dunce between them fishing for words. It was dangerous. Lo was no fool. Desperately, I said, turning, 'Jan, please go, I beg you.'

'When it suits me. Your friend has you now but I will have you in the end – he might as well get used to it. Come, talk naturally – don't look goofy – people are watching. Pei, you are beautiful, and I've missed you. Now then – the legend.'

I said with an effort, 'The . . . the boats symbolise fighting dragons. Their fighting is thunder and this brings rain . . .' I faltered.

'Is that all?'

'The . . . the races are held to honour the memory of Wat Yuen, a poet and minister of the old China court of the King of Chu who reigned three hundred years before . . .' the words fell from me as from the teacher's lips at school, and Jan took them up, saying, 'Three hundred years before the coming of the Christ. At first Wat Yuen flourished, but later fell from grace, and the king no longer heeded his protests about the wickedness of the court. So the king banished him to the Yangtse valley. As an exile in Hunan he wrote the famous poem Li Sao, then drowned himself in the River Milo, giving his life as a protest.'

The crowd bawled about us, the jackanape people leaped and cheered. I said:

'You are cruel. I did not know you could be so cruel.'

'And the dragons sought his body, so the people, relenting, threw offerings of food into the river to appease their hunger.' Jan rose. 'Think of it, Pei Sha – two thousand years ago – a time of torture for conviction, the great scholars, the famous mistresses and concubines. Yet the Chinese still pay tribute to a man who died for decent things.'

'Jan, for God's sake!'

'You would do even better in Taiwan,' he said. 'There men actually hire wives, and when they tire of them, hire others. Come to the stalls, Pei, and we will buy rice-dumplings and throw them into the sea – concubinage – the old legends, these are things worth keeping.'

I knew by his face that there was no hope for us now. The crowd was cheering again, a massive poetry of noise and power, for another race had started and boats were running prow to prow, their drum-men beating frantic tattoos to keep the rhythm of the flashing paddles.

'Please go,' I said.

'You bet.'

Through tears I saw him find his way through the people. He entered a front row of seats. A man of tall and resolute bearing rose to let him pass. A woman beside him smiled into his face, talking with animated joy, then turned and looked towards me.

'Goodbye,' I said.

And as if to end the act a moment before the fall of the curtain, Lo came back immediately and sat down beside me with a grunt. 'Sorry about that – business friends. I couldn't call you over – wives were there.'

A concubine is rarely introduced to wives. He added, 'I hope you weren't too lonely.'

'You must have noticed that I had company.'

'I don't miss much. Young Colington, eh? Friend of yours?'

Lo was always too full of surprises ever to surprise me. I nodded.

With a grin he said, 'I thought he was never going. He knows you're married, I hope.'

'Of course.'

He took a cigarette and snapped a lighter. 'Naturally you want young company. I don't expect to command every moment of your life, but be careful who you pick – his father's a big noise. Handle it with care or we'll both be in trouble – especially you – make sure your husband never finds out.'

18

I WROTE TO Suelen four times that summer and she did not reply. Aching to see her but too ashamed to go, I wrote yet again. Lo said, 'I do not understand you. For weeks you have been threatening to visit your sister Suelen, yet you do not go.'

'My sister Suelen knows of me,' I replied.

The Great Heat faded, the big winds came tearing in from the South China Sea with violins and thunder, and took lives, as usual. First the little stream-beds, the stones calcined by the blazing summer, began their trickles; then came cascades spewing from fissures of the sun-baked mountains. The cascades spumed into torrents and the torrents into huge gushes of water that foamed and misted into waterfalls, deluging the valleys. The water-courses were brimming, the nullahs alive and foaming, and still the rainbanks swirled in from the sea. Then the giant out-crops, once cemented into rigidity, began to move. Tiny earth-falls grew into spills of rock and little boulders, and these spills charged the great crags and broke them off, and the bright red soil, baked into cohesion by sun and wind began to landslide, and the mountains trembled. Leaping, spraying debris, thundering, the avalanches came down the slopes, seeking the homes of the shanty poor. Down in the slums of Poor Man's Peak the old women prayed to their ancient gods, and naked urchin boys, sweating in the ramshackle bedrooms of the scabrous streets, came running with wild cries. The slum houses steamed with the onslaught of water; walls bulged, timbers groaned, and buildings collapsed in roars and screams. And from the rubble where the people died strange smells arose; dead cats and rats, confined till now to a gentle but rank decay, burst their putrescence upon the humid air. The accident sirens screeched; the fire-horns of the heroes bellowed from disaster to disaster. Calcined by summer, fevered by the rains, Hong Kong steamed and fretted in a shroud of water that wallowed over the streets to the mothering sea. Slowly, the mortuaries filled.

Lo said from behind his morning newspaper:

'I see that in the State of California the practice of wife-exchanging has begun. Further proof, if more was needed, of the degeneracy of the Western world."

I did not reply. Lo's overcrowding sin was artlessness. His newspaper came down. 'Surely you have views on this?'

'Aye, but not for airing.'

'Come, Pei Sha. Nobody in the house has an inch of tongue.'

'All right, then! Wife-exchanging is no more primitive than concubinage.'

He got up. 'My God, don't start all that again.'

I wished desperately that he would go to the office. There seemed no escape from him: it was torture by solitary confinement, and from his prison I longed for Jan and the abandoned freedom of Yim Tin Tsai. Lo said petulantly:

'What is wrong with you these days? Aren't you well?'

'I am perfectly well, Lo, but I must get away from this house.'

He spread his hands. 'Name the place, the time, we will go.'

'You always say that, but when I suggest somewhere it doesn't come to anything.'

'Have my people been annoying you?'

I could have told him that his people never even spoke to me: that the moment his back was turned I was the complete stranger. With Lo Tai perpetually in Macau at the gaming tables, the place was a funeral parlour. They would pass me on the stairs, ignore me at table – all except Yee Moi, the sister, and she was demented with heroin. But in Lo's presence they were all wheedlers, particularly the brothers, their excessive politeness bordering on cynicism, but Lo never noticed this. Ah Ying, my young maid, was my only companion. Sometimes, in desperation, I would take the car to the city and walk the length of Des Voeux Road, just to be with people; or stand on the waterfront and watch the junks. Here was peace and companionship. I would call to them and they would answer me in their harsh, Tan-gar voices, and the children would wave. There I smelled again the acrid, savoury stink of fish entrails in the pan, the bubbling noodles, chopped meat and garlic, and heard the sobbing of babies in the stifling air of the hooped canopies. Now I said to Lo, 'Next time you fly to Singapore, will you take me?'

'I usually take Lo Tai.'

'I know, but will you take me?'

'My dear, there are some things I can do and some I cannot.'

'Because you are ashamed of me!'

He replied impatiently, 'It isn't a question of being ashamed, darling. It is a question of custom. The First Wife enjoys privileges that you cannot share. You are leading a wealthy life, Pei Sha, you can't have everything.'

'But I entertain your friends here.'

'That is different.'

'It is not at all different. If I can do it here I can do it abroad – you bring Lo Tai back from Macau. It's time she did some entertaining.'

As usual, my anger drew him. Instantly, he was beside me. 'You entertain me, my sweet – leave the guests to Lo Tai.'

'Leave me alone,' I said, pushing him away.

He stood before me, hands clenched, pale with anger. 'How dare you!'

I shouted into his face, 'For heaven's sake leave me alone!' and ran to the garden gates. There, I screwed at my hands, enduring a trembling emotion that I could not control. I heard Lo's footsteps on the gravel behind me, but did not turn.

'Pei Sha, you are ill,' he whispered.

I covered my face with my hands. 'Lo, for God's sake!'

I was sickening of his love for me, even hating my youth since it induced in him this longing for affection. And his very gentleness, his great respect for me heaped upon me degradation, for I was betraying him in every thought and action. As the days dragged on I longed for Jan with an intensity that was almost overpowering. In Lo's arms I saw his face; amid Lo's sweetness and tremendous understanding of me I heard his voice. Now I gripped Lo and held him hard against me. 'Forgive me, forgive me,' I said.

In such nightmares he held me, and did not reply.

Then, too, there was a fearful night; the night Yee Moi came, the sister of the drugs.

I was in the pin-drop numbness before the stumble into sleep when the handle of my bedroom turned. I opened my eyes in moonlight, watching it.

'Ming Pei Sha!' A whisper from the landing outside. I got up, pulled my robe about me, and unlocked the door.

Yee Moi was standing there, an apparition in white, her nightdress pinned and tented by her skeleton body. With her black hair straggling over her shoulders she stood, unspeaking, her fist against her mouth, the parchment of her face skinned tight across her humped cheeks.

'Pei Sha,' she said, coming in, and the moment she spoke I knew she was under the drug: for this is a slurred speech, and throaty. Her eyes were fixed, her thin lips drawn back, exposing her large and beautiful teeth.

'What is it, Yee Moi?'

'First Brother sends a message.' She stared vacantly about her.

'What message?' I took her thin hands. She said at nothing:

'First Brother keeps the key of the drawer. Tomorrow he will not open it, he says, unless I bring the message.'

I held her and she was shivering. She said, 'I cannot sleep because of tomorrow. I will go mad if I do not have the medicine.'

'I will get the key, Yee Moi. Tell me the message.'

She turned her pitiful face to mine. 'First Brother makes you an offer. Go back to the boats and he will pay you big money – Lo Tai also, for they spoke together. Send Yee Moi, they said, and Second Brother agreed. They will pay you twenty thousand dollars if you will go back to the boats. Let Yee Moi take the message, they said, for Lo Hin Tan will never believe the Tan-gar if she reports it, for Yee Moi is mad.'

'You are not mad,' I replied.

'But you will leave here?'

'Not until Lo himself tells me to go.'

She opened her hands. 'But you are useless to him! You have not conceived.'

'And who knows that I may not one day bear him a son?'

'Lo Tai knows. Only tonight she said that the Tan-gar is empty.'

'The Tan-gar may be making a pretty fat son for all she knows. One day my boy will rule this house – go to her now and tell her that also.' I opened the door.

'And the medicine?' She suddenly clung to me, in an agony of apprehension.

'Go to First Brother and demand the medicine – do not beg it, Yee Moi – demand. Tell First Brother that if you do not have the key by morning, I will deal with him.'

She wept, she ran. I stood in the doorway of the bedroom and watched her running on tiptoe down the long, crimson corridor.

Watching her, I knew that I had to see Suelen. Although she would despise me, although Kwai, her husband, might even turn me away, I just had to see Suelen.

Hope, who makes a restless bedfellow but a happy breakfast, was with me in the morning, and I awoke to a sun-streaming day and the birds shouting their nuts off in the thickets of the hill. We dined alone, Lo and me, although Lo Tai was in the house. We ate breakfast on a table of mother-of-pearl inlay amid the bright colours of the garden, and Lo said:

'The house is in a ferment. People have been up and doing all night; the in-laws are restive, my wife is impossible. Last night she soaked me with tears and protests. I am quite sick of women.' He began to fold his newspaper with slow, deliberate fingers – always a sign of nervousness with him. He glanced over his bowl. 'What will you do – stay here?'

'Why, are you going somewhere?'

'I told you – I am flying to Singapore today. For three days I will be out of it all.'

'You did not tell me this.'

'Then I must have told my wife. I forgot. I've got so many damned women about me that I forget everything these days.'

I rose from the table. 'Then I will visit my sister Suelen. Is . . . is Lo Tai going with you?'

'No, thank God.'

'Would you like me to see you off at the airport? It is on the way to Ho Chung.'

'I would like that.' He snapped his fingers and began an urgent discussion with the Number One houseboy about what time the car was needed and what he wanted packed, and I looked past them to the terrazzo floor of the verandah where Ah Ying was squatting, for she was only makee-learn maid and full-time amah. Despite her ungainly posture I saw the dignity of her labour, for this was my beautiful Suelen's squat borrowed by another: the straight back, the angled knees, the thin cotton of her blue samfoo straining to a scream across her strong, smooth buttocks. I loved this little Ah Ying, aged sixteen – only three years younger than me. She earned a hundred and twenty Hong Kong dollars a month as a virgin amah, less than I would spend in a day as an old man's pretty, but I envied her freedom. After work in the house she would escape from the snaps and frowns of the other servants, for everybody was her superior, and leave by the back entrance and take the big red bus to Ho Man Tin and the squatter hut where she was born. Then, in the evening, she would oil her hair and plait it with white ribbon, put on her best samfoo and clog sandals and stroll the evening markets with her boy, eating chow-fan from the wayside ovens and rice-congee steaming hot from the cans of the kerb-criers, sucking the food through her strong white teeth, belching, gesticulating meantime, bantering, threatening the hawking, chattering crowds. Then, after dark, if her fancy whispered, she might go to some cool place of starlight and there make love in kisses and slaps where the naked urchins of the junks fished along the sea-wall. After this – home for Ah Ying, with no harm done and nothing on her conscience – hand in hand with her too-shy lover whose sole ambition was one long kiss without a single slap – home through the paddy fields of his mother's house in Tai Wu and the sweet, sour earth-smells where the buffaloes wallowed under a big China moon. And in the morning she would wake in virgin straw, untroubled, bow to his mother, and begin again this little pain of sweat and labour by day, earning the pleasures of her exotic nights.

'Ah Ying!' I bent to her, whispering.

'Aye, Missy?' She scrambled up, her eyes bright with the inner fever of her youth. I straightened. Behind me I heard Lo's cracked commands, the house-boy's urgent cries. 'It doesn't matter,' I said.

But I did not move, for her great, brown eyes were holding me. She was demanding my youth in a house of age, bridging the gap between us with all her understanding. I thought desperately: I will go *Tan-gar*. I will visit Suelen and Kwai and take them gifts of food. I will take the bus to beloved old Sai Kung and dangle my feet in the sea again and watch the fishing junks come in. I will bawl insults at Missus and Po Shan and hear Hui's shrieks of joy at the sight of me. And as a rough Tan-gar I will dress again and take a save-life sampan to Yim Tin Tsai, and if the gods pity me I might even see my boy. And the delight of this promised freedom brought me to a stuttering gladness. Bending, I seized Ah Ying's soapy hands and danced her in circles on the lawn, and her apprehension changed to pleasure, then to brilliant joy. She shrieked, I shrieked back. And we went round and round shouting at the sky and kicking up our legs in a sudden abandoned orgy of youth. The bucket went over and this brought us to fresh, uncontrolled laughter; giddy, we staggered, hanging on to each other, and then collapsed on to the lawn with the bucket rolling and clanging between us.

'Ming Pei Sha!'

Still sitting, still hand in hand, we stared.

They were grouped together outside the French doors, rather like three generations awaiting the family photograph: Father-in-law, Mother-in-law, the three brothers, their jaws dropped in shocked surprise; Lo Tai, her head up, well on her dignity, even Yee Moi, head low, most distressed, and Lo himself. Disengaging himself from the family tree he slowly crossed the lawn, standing above us.

'Pei Sha, how *dare* you!' he whispered.

I got up, dragging Ah Ying after me, and faced him.

154

'With a servant. In my own house – before my own people!'
He was shaking with anger.

'Go to the devil,' I said.

'*Pei Sha!*'

I shouted, 'Go to the devil. All of you, do you hear me? *Go to the devil!*'

Turning, I seized Ah Ying's hand and ran her across the lawn towards the door.

Pak Sha Wan, Sai Kung, Yim Tin Tsai, *Suelen!*

19

LO FLEW FROM Kai Tak airport under threat of typhoon, a girl who was screaming her fury along the coast of Luzon and winking her eye at the trade routes to Hong Kong; winds were already moving in the harbour. Over morning tea in the airport lounge, I said to Lo, 'If you were wise you would delay this trip, you know.'

He stirred his tea abstractedly, not completely pleased with me: apparently my behaviour with my maid having caused consternation among his relatives and nearly a riot among the servants, where Ah Ying's stock had risen considerably.

He said, 'I must go. The others are already waiting in Penang.'

Lo did not die on this flight to Singapore, but his insistence on going under threat of typhoon gave me a further insight into the mind of the speculator. It appears that the risk of death, like all risks, is examined, and in the ice-cold brain its possibility is set against the possible profit. If the profit is big enough then the risk is taken and the manner of dying discounted: the distended, bubbling suffocation of death by water being one with the incinerating shrieks of death by fire. The fact that once you're dead money is no good to you appears to be forgotten. I said:

'Lo, you own God knows how many companies now. Another can await a two-hundred-mile-an-hour wind.'

'You are becoming prosy. Anyway, Otaka Wan is too important to miss – this is a merger, not a company – big stuff.'

'Otaka Wan?'

'Japanese.' It was the way he said it. People said that Lo suffered badly during the Occupation, but they forget all sins in the grab for money.

'He sounds important.'

'Most important. He's coming to Hong Kong soon and I'd like you to entertain him.' Rising from the table he glanced at his watch. 'Time I was getting to the gate. And don't look like that – I'm sure you'd do it so much better than my wife.'

A thread of suspicion touched my mind. Some concubines are expected to entertain guests to things more enticing than tea. Lo added, 'Enjoy yourself with your sister. I'm quite sure you'll find her a lot less barbary than you expect.'

'Goodbye,' I said.

He looked at me so strangely that I was seized with a sudden panic that he might kiss me in public, an unforgivable act, but he did not.

I went through the turnstile on to the waving platform. A crowd of Service people were seeing a plane away; cameras were clicking, children wailing, a forgotten amah standing in solitary desolation, grieving for another woman's child. Above them the flags of the airlines streamed in the wind.

Lo's plane, a great Mandarin jet, was standing on the runway area and I waved him into it, then leaned on the rail, watching with pride.

This great, glorious, courageous Kai Tak!

Many times in childhood I had walked Kowloon with Suelen while this edifice to labour was being built. Like all great and successful projects of its kind the engineers claimed it as theirs, the craftsmen boasted of it, an architect said it was a gift to posterity – like one or two other gifts architects have perpetrated in Hong Kong – but it belonged, in essence, to none of these. Under molten skies thousands of coolie men, women, and children had snatched this million-ton tarmacadam finger from the sea : with a thousand bamboo shoulder-poles and many thousand rush baskets swaying, they had carried the bright red soil, an army of crawling, diligent ants patiently working, patiently dying in the hoicking, sweating dust of the diggers and drag-lines. Standing there I heard again the dull explosions that blasted my childhood, the clamour of the machines, the hoarse commands of foremen and overseers, and saw again the long, ragged lines of women wending homeward to their shanty beds. Yet when the most important people arrived at Kai Tak they spared no thought for this sacrifice – the cheap labour, so much regretted by the politicians – that had tramped over the border at Lo Wu: they who had built Kai Tak with their bare hands had little better in reward than the slaves who built the Pyramids.

To me, to Suelen, this great Kai Tak, the Gateway to the East, is their dirt monument. And Hong Kong being their China, it is a gift to their own posterity.

Lo's plane moved. Waddling in rumbles and wing-sag, the big jet reached the end of the runway, then accelerated in blasts of turbulent air, clubbing aside the beauty of the morning. Pounding down the tarmac, dragging a wreath of smoke by its tail, it turned its nose up at the gap of Lyemun. I watched it until it was a tinkle of light in the sky, driving for Sing-no-more.

Leaving the airport I called on a cheap tailor, bought a simple, white samfoo stained with purple flowers, also clog sandals from a stall. In the tailor's parlour I changed into the samfoo and brought down my hair to my waist, plaiting it either side of my head in the way Suelen admired; the ends I tied with white ribbon. Next I bought fresh eggs and garlic, rice, dry noodles and pork slices, also two packets of Three Fives cigarettes, the kind Mr Kwai smoked. Leaving my best clothes at the tailor's I walked the alleys of Kowloon City, ate rice-congee at a kerb-stall. Squatting among the legs of the market crowds, I watched a beloved life go past. Later, I boarded the New Territories taxi-bus for Pak Sha Wan. It was late afternoon when I left the bus and stood on the deserted road. Before me the Inner Shelter was a sheen of silver with her clustered junks and yachts, and the wind breathed faintly the perfume of distant Sai Kung, for the typhoon had died in hours. I turned, seeing Ho Chung village all green and gold, with white, linen clouds straight from the river wash flying in the wind above the steeples of Ma On Shan. I took a deep breath, gripped my hands, and walked. Lo would have had a stroke had he seen this performance.

There was a path down which naked children played and brown ducks walked with the clamorous quack-quack of authority. Grunting piglets stubbed at the teats of a slovenly sow, hens scratched, cockerels strutted; Hakka women splashed knee-deep in green water, working the hoe, their noble faces burned to ebony beneath their curtained hats, and to each one I bowed, my duty as a stranger.

Kwai To Man, Suelen's husband, I saw next, kneeling, his fingers in earth.

'Good day.' I bowed, fighting for calmness.

He frowned up, then wiped his forearm across his sweating face. Staring, he rose slowly to his feet, then smiled broad, his eyes screwing up with delight.

'Ming Pei Sha!'

I felt weak with relief. At the Shatin level-crossing, then, he had not recognised me after all. Flinging down his dipper he cupped his hands to his mouth, shouting, '*Wei, wei!* Kwai Ming Suelen!'

The village stirred in its drowse of heat. Dogs barked. A little boy came running down the path and Kwai seized him, turning him back. 'Back to Kwai Suelen, boy. Run! Tell her Pei Sha is here. *Run!*'

Now there was a confusion of people and activity, scampering children, wives nudging and gossiping down the path, girls of my own age examining me and turning up their noses, for the Chinese are terrors when it comes to competition; dogs threatened and subsided into scratches and slavering grins; the old ones came in ones and twos, regally, without committal. And amid the shouting my sister Suelen ran, elbowing people aside, her hands covered with flour. She stopped, staring, her eyes going big in her brown face. Her hands rose, and fell. She straightened, beaming, for dignity, whatever the cost, must be preserved within sight of the neighbours. She bowed. I bowed back, following her and Kwai up the track to the door of her cottage. This cottage being built of real brick and timber, I did not dream that Kwai was so successful. We entered, and the neighbours followed us within.

'Head Man Kwong,' whispered somebody, and we stood in respectful silence.

He came through the crush of the people. His head was shaved in the manner of the Taoist mystic, his presence was made severe by his long black gown. Suelen announced with pride:

'Head Man, this is Pei Sha, the family Second Sister.'

He bowed. 'Welcome to Ho Chung, Pei Sha.' His voice was deep and held a fine authority. 'Your sister Suelen and her man Kwai are much respected in the village.' He looked about him and there was much nodding and wagging of heads from the elders. Turning to the door, he cried, 'Bring food and drink to greet Kwai's relative.' To me he said, 'Have you come for work, child?'

'No, sir, I am already working on Hong Kong island.'

'That is a pity, for the festival of the Cowboy and Weaving Girl is upon us, a time of romance, and there are fine bachelors here for such a beauty!'

This brought banter and laughter, and I joined it, fearing him. For this was Head Man and his power was absolute.

'Where are you employed?' His fine eyes regarded me intently.

'In a house on Hong Kong Peak, sir. I am Second Amah.' Desperation formed the lie, and it brought excited discussion and beams from the people. Head Man said:

'This is excellent. With industry and application you may soon be First Amah.'

'She is most industrious, sir,' whispered Suelen, clutching herself.

'You will do your best, Pei Sha?'

'I will try, sir.'

'Fine, fine, but why have you not visited us before?'

Kwai said instantly, 'My sister-in-law has been ill, Head Man.'

'I am most sorry.' He leaned to me, his face kind. 'You are better now, Pei Sha?'

'I . . . I am better now, sir.' I glanced at Kwai.

'And you know the great news – that Suelen is with child?'

I forgot them all, and swung to her; she stood before me, her eyes cast down like a scolded girl. Head Man said, 'You will come help deliver Suelen at her time?'

'I will come.'

At the door, he said, 'Now go, everybody. Until the women bring the food, let this girl be alone with her relatives.'

With relief I watched them go, realising the chasm between us; the danger of forgetting the authority of Head Man, and wondering about Kwai's blatant lie which had saved me. And the moment they had gone Suelen leaped at me, her arms encircling me.

'Oh, Pei, it has been a life-time!' She held me away, her bright eyes sweeping over me. 'And you have grown so beautiful! It is ages since I have seen you. Why didn't you come before?'

I thought: you do not know of me. Kwai has not told you of me, he has also lied for me because he loves you. I said, 'It . . . it is a very strict Chinese house, Suelen. Only when I attain the post of First Amah will I get free time.'

'But I have written three times and you have not replied!'

I hung my head.

'Oh, my poor sweet,' she whispered. 'I had forgotten – you have been ill – why did you not send for me?'

'Forget illness and letters. I am with you now!'

She warmed to me again. 'The money – do they pay you well?'

'A hundred and fifty a month – and twenty dollars extra for the English language – everything found.'

'*Wheeah!*' She turned. 'Kwai, do you hear that?'

'He has gone,' I said.

'But it is a fortune, and I am so proud.' She caught my hands. 'And what about your studies?'

'I study every night – when I am twenty-one the bank will consider me – it has all been discussed with the Bank of China.'

'The Bank of China!' She stared her disbelief, then slowly straightened, adopting a playful arrogance, her nose high. 'I Suelen, known here as Ming Hakka, am married to Mr Kwai To Man, a farmer of some standing, and I have a relative working in the Bank of China. Kwai, oh, Kwai, where are you? Come!'

'And I have a relative in child?'

Her expression changed; she whispered, 'Pray for me, Pei Sha, that I give my man a son.'

'With a tail front and back to make sure of it,' I said. 'When?'

'I am five months away.'

'Then next December I will come to you. Have you seen the boys?'

'Not since spring when Tuk Un was running and Hui with a hair on his chest, a man!'

'And Missus?'

'Time and Chen Fu Wei have settled Tai Tai. Chen has a second son coming, she hopes . . .'

She spoke more. Indeed, now she had started I could not stop her, and did not try. All the lies had been worth it, none of the pain without reward. She said next:

'And Chu Po Shan has come into a fortune, they tell me. A relative died in Canton – four thousand dollars – think of it, *whee!* And so he was able to keep Hui and Tuk Un, God bless him.'

She looked at me and there was a strangeness in her eyes.

'Aye, a good man, that Po Shan,' I answered.

I heard, with relief, the people coming back. Led by Head Man they came in with their joss-sticks and food and their gabble, and I snatched at them, for Suelen had a nose for the truth. Now they were about us with bowls of steaming congee and noodles. An old and lovely crone cried at my elbow:

'Ming Pei Sha, you are the prettiest in Ho Chung since I was a maiden. Women, make her stay for the Double Seventh and join with the girls in prayers to the Weaving Girl!'

'Some pretty good cowherds in Ho Chung,' the men shouted. 'Stay!'

The children swept about me. 'Stay. Beg her to stay, Mama!' They tugged at my jacket, a child knelt in prayer at my feet.

'Head Man – order her.'

'Fetch old Kwai – where the devil is Kwai?' A new game now, everybody as sharp as needles.

'Other side of the duck pond with little Kam the widow.'

Uproar then; Kwai slandered, Suelen protesting. I thought: this is the simplicity and purity I have lost, this is all innocence.

They called for him, they even searched, and Kwai could not be found, and only I knew why.

Later, when we had feasted and the shadows had deepened, the boys lit the lamps and cleared the table for cricket-fighting, which I had always hated. But I lost myself in the orgy of cruelty, a sort of refining through pain. Cat's Claw, whiskered out of his tiny cage and into a fighting fury, took Red Jade by the leg and bit through it with his nip-pincers, and the cricket went in a circle of agony, dragging the stump. Cat's Claw bit and snapped, each click of his minute jaws dividing yet another piece of Red Jade's half-dismembered body, but he suddenly wheeled to his two-inch height, spurred by the terror of death through torture, and fought back, taking his opponent high before collapsing under his rending teeth. Money chinked. The eyes of the elders were drooping with insensate pleasure, and Cat's Claw bit and chewed at leisure. Disgusted, and unseen, I swept the dying cricket to the floor and stamped out his life. Money was changing hands: Suelen, in a corner, was telling a woman about the sea-life, her hands moving in joyful articulation. I opened the door and brilliant moonlight flooded over me.

Kwai was standing beyond the door, his face smudged with shadow; a corpse face in that funeral light: an undertaker.

'Come,' he said, and I followed him. On the far side of the pond, he turned.

'Kwai,' I began. 'I beg you, listen . . .'

'I do not need to listen, I have seen. Do not think, because we are poor farmers, that we are fools – that we cannot tell a maiden from a sing-song girl.'

'Please hear me!'

'Draw the curtains of your fine car when next you drive with the man who hires you.'

I turned away. 'Does Suelen know?'

'She does not know.'

'But she stared at me. Just now, again . . .'

'That is your conscience – do not blame Suelen.' He looked at the sky and his eyes were as jewels in that light, a trick of the moon with Hakka. He continued, 'You claim her as your sister, but she is not your sister by blood. You took her to the sea with all its stinks and slaughters, but she is not of the sea, and I found her and returned her to her own people. Perhaps there are no riches in Ho Chung, but she is happy, and she would rather see you starve than take to a rich man's bed.'

I turned. 'I am married to this man under a law recognised by the Government!' Angered now, I stared at him.

'Aye? Well, in the new China we are simpler. One woman,

one man. Had you been the wife of a rickshaw boy I would have admired you. As a concubine, I despise you. Years ago you would have been trussed in a pig-basket and carried down to the river.'

'Years ago you would have respected me!'

He waved me down. 'Stay for the night lest the old ones become suspicious. Leave the village at sun-come-up. Never come back.' Reaching into his pocket he brought out a packet. 'Here are Suelen's letters that I never posted, here are your letters that my wife never received. I lied for you, but I will not lie again.' Turning, he said, 'Remember – at sun-up. Never come back.'

20

NEXT DAY I took my leave of Suelen and her people with the excuse that I had to be back in the house on the hill before morning tea. But when I reached the Sai Kung road I turned left to Hebe Haven, to look for the white junk of Jan Colingten.

It was a gossamer-thread morning, I remember, with the big willow spiders slaving at it all night and the spit-gobs of drooling ferns hanging heavy in the webs, swinging and sparkling in the early sunlight. I walked alone, the world belonging to me, with my jacket flying open and the wind beating about my naked breasts in a fine frenzy – recompense for the sultry, sweating night on the boards in Suelen's cottage, the very brazen joy of that half-naked walk cleansing me and drawing into me the sweetness of the morning. The purse-seiners were out in Port Shelter, for I heard the rat-a-tat beating of their sampan drums and smelled the tang of their village fires, dear little people. Later, I saw their minnow catch staining the rocks sea-silver, a myriad, tiny tragedies glazing in heat who once flooded white on the rollers, sacrifice to the gorging mackerel. High above me the frangipani flowers spread their petals, their indolent beauty spiked by daggering bamboo: pink, fading chrysanthemums suffused the green of wayside lawns when I reached the houses, the rising sun shot ultra-violet splinters of light into green jungle of perfume and heat. I paused, savouring the beauty, knowing nothing so lovely in Lo's world of wealth.

I buttoned up my jacket as a young amah approached aimlessly, leading on a leash a small, flat-faced dog. Never have I seen such a stupid dog, panting up at me with its eyes crossed, its nose snitching, and its tongue between its teeth.

'Good morning,' I said.

''Morning. What you doing up so early?'

'Just walking,' I said.

She was small, fat, and dressed in the white jacket and black trousers of the house amah, and her virgin plaits swung either side of her pale, sallow face.

'Where you from?' she asked.

'Hong Kong Peak,' I lied.

'Aye, indeed? And I am amah to the Governor himself, and this is his dog, though if we stop telling lies you are a Tan-gar fisher-girl and I am from Wanchai.'

She delighted me, for some frumps come walking first thing in the morning. And although she was short and fat I pitied her loss of face, walking with a dog, for she had a fine dignity about her and the carriage of a princess. I asked, 'You work here?'

'All week, but Sunday off I go Wanchai.'

'Relatives there?'

'My mother. She's in one of the cages you rent from landlords – like the cages they have in Lai Chi Kok zoo – you been there?'

I said I had not.

'No need, girl – you go to Wanchai, or North Point, or Kowloon. It's the new idea – people in cages – forty dollars a month. By putting them in cages they can get more to the room, even on stairs and landings.'

'It is damned scandalous,' I said.

'It's worse being in one. There's girls coughing blood, girls in labour, school-girls, bar-girls, beggars, rickshaw boys – and right in the middle of them my little mother – eighty last week.' She put the tip of a finger into her mouth and looked at the sky. 'Last night I lay thinking, working it out. If you've twenty cages to the room and the monkeys are paying forty, that works out at eight hundred dollars a month. And if you buy two big houses and divide them into forty rooms you can call yourself a financier.'

After a pause, I said, 'A millionaire in three years.' I jerked my thumb at the houses behind me. 'You work here?'

'Third one down.'

'It's big enough – haven't they room for your mother?'

'Tin Au! If I suggested that they'd call me a Communist.'

'It stinks,' I said.

'It stinks and it must stop,' she replied, her eyes on fire. 'How the hell can I sleep with my mother in a cage? What's wrong with the damned landlords and the damned Government that allows them to be such landlords?'

The thing at our feet snuffled between us, eyes bulging, nose dripping, mouth gaping, panting; its cranium compressed for classical pedigree, the torture of inter-breeding for the delight of beasts called humans.

'What is it?' I asked her, stirring it with my foot.

'Don't ask me. But if I got the love he gets I wouldn't be an amah.'

'There's some sense in that,' I replied.

'That's where you're wrong, girl, there's no sense in anything.'

She got going. I called goodbye but she didn't answer. The thing nosed a bush and tried to put his leg up but she yanked him on, skidding him on his ear, which is a natural thing to do, I suppose, with him in the money and her mother in a kennel.

It is funny where you meet them, when you least expect them.

With views like that she was bound to be a Communist.

I wandered on under a glowing sun, shedding into the radiance of the morning the memory of the sleeping cages and the palatial beds of the stuffed over-rich; the neat, bright-faced children in droves on their way to school, and the under-privileged tens of thousands for whom there is no school: seeking to obliterate my growing shame that I was contributing, in my way, to Hong Kong's magnificent sin – her acceptance of the vulgarly rich and brutally poor. But the sense of shame became so great that I had to smother it, and this I found easy: one does it by canalising one's energy into a completely different realm, and for me this was the sight of Hebe Haven, jewelled in sunlight, her lovely harbour matron to a hundred clustered boats. I immediately felt better. This is the tragedy of Hong

Kong; this is why Hong Kong exists as she does and accepts such an existence, untroubled by her few dissentient voices, her morale supported by the few, labouring saints. Compassion has no undying limit. Misery after misery dilutes compassion; sadness after sadness brutalises, and eventually destroys the human sense of good.

I walked on, fighting the knowledge of my own, personal guilt; envying men like Lo Hin Tan their cataract of blindness.

The good, the best are here among us also, and in the unknown places, many of them. We can number them, multiply them fictitiously, and this is the easiest and best escape of all: in the last resort one can always admire the saints.

I paused on the road, lifting my face to the wind. I smelled Sai Kung on a flurry of air. I ran, and did not stop until I reached Tak Long Middle Street. Through the lines of shopping people I went down to the sea and its contorted imagery of rocks, and there I found the packed sampans and junks of the harbour I loved. Mothers were sitting in a line along the old stone wall, feeding or smelling their babies, old men were shuttling at nets in sun-fire. It was the old, delightful, unchanged Sai Kung, and I shouted reply to the astonished greetings and surprised calls as I ran along the edge of the quay, seeking the *Cormorant*.

'Ming Pei Sha!'

I stared down and a woman in a sampan below me waved her arms, her hairless, waxen face alive with recognition.

'*Ah*, Wu Fai!' I cupped my hands. 'You seen Chu Po Shan?'

She cackled with delight, wringing her hands and splayed her feet on the sampan. 'Never mind about Chu Po Shan — I got a message.'

'Who for?'

'For you, girl.'

'What message? Who from?'

She adopted an indifferent air, plying the stern oar with indolence, not caring if she saw me or not. I cried, 'Wu Fai Sung! I pay one dollar for that message.'

She shrugged, hoiked, spat, wiped her mouth, looking at the sea.

'How much?' I called.

'Ten dollar.'

'What for I pay ten dollar?'

'You hire this sampan – take you over Yim Tin Tsai, you pay ten dollar?'

'Why for I go Yim Tin Tsai?' I shouted, stupidly eager.

But she did not appear to hear this. Singing softly to herself she swept the sampan round in eddies.

'You hear me, Wu Fai Sung?'

'Ah, I hear you. Twenty dollar.'

'*Devil!*' I stooped to her, furious.

'I got message.'

In haste I rolled a stone into two ten-dollar bills and dropped them down to her. 'Wu Fai Sung,' I called. 'You tell me message now or I come down and damn skin you!'

Snatching the money from the air, she said, 'This very special sampan. Big white foreign devil he come and say to me, "Missus, you ever see fisher-girl Ming come these parts you tell boat-boy and he run telephone to me, eh?"' She preened herself in the sun. 'Me very special missus, very special sampan.'

My heart was hammering. 'When?'

'Day 'fore yesterday – maybe day 'fore that, can't remember, O *ah!*'

Excitement was suffusing me. Stupidly, I began to tremble. And Wu began to sing a plaintive Mandarin love-song I had heard before, its key minor and sad.

'You tell boat-boy, *now!*'

She jerked her thumb at the road. 'I told boat-boy.'

I straightened, looking towards the village. A lithe, half-naked figure was racing along the road.

'He go telephone,' said Wu. 'You go Yim Tin Tsai, and wait?'

'Aye,' I said, 'Yim Tin Tsai!'

She ferried the sampan towards the quay steps. 'This big devil say he come, maybe one, two, three hours, remember.'

I leaped into the sampan. 'One, two, three hundred years, Wu Fai Sung, I will wait. Away, Missus!'

'Ah!'

'Full speed!' I flung my arms about her and kissed her and her big Hoklo sun-hat fell over her eyes and she fought it, me also, shoving me away in Cantonese curses.

'*Ai-yah!*'

Bending, I scooped up the sea and flung it high in sparkling light-spray. '*Wheeah!*' I shrieked. '*Yim Tin Tsai!*'

Jan came when the sun was high, bringing the little white junk round in the lee of the wind and running it into the lagoon where I sat waiting. Anchoring her, he dived and swam, then waded towards me.

'You came!'

He looked bigger, more mature, his chest and shoulders burned deep brown by sun and wind. Sprawling beside me, he said:

'So you got my message!'

'What message?'

'The message from old Wu Fai Sung?'

'I don't know what you are talking about.'

This sat him up. 'Then how did you get here?'

'I have a perfect right to be here,' I said. 'I have been coming here before you even knew of it, it is my home.'

He nodded, grinning. 'So it wasn't a rendezvous after all?'

'You must be mad.' I stared at him.

He rose, laughing. 'Well, I suppose it serves me right – I behaved pretty badly when last we met. I apologise.'

'What for?'

He opened his hands to me, 'For my bad manners at the Tai Po races, but you must be reasonable, it was a bit of a shock.'

I said, getting up and brushing away sand, 'You are thinking of somebody else. I have never been to the Tai Po races.'

It stilled him. His smile faded and his eyes moved over me, taking in all; the simple samfoo, the sandals, the plaited hair. He said:

'I understand.'

'Oh no, you don't.'

He did not reply but touched my hand and there was a new sweetness in it. He said, 'The great thing is not to think too much – deep thought is the enemy of happiness. I believe in taking things at face value. You, for instance, must surely have a double. I saw your double with Lo Hin Tan at the Tai Po races. Believing it to be you, I spoke to this woman.'

'You must have felt very foolish.'

'Naturally. It was Lo's mistress. It would be pretty difficult to be a fisher-girl one minute and a rich man's concubine the next.'

'It would be impossible,' I said.

We walked on, our bodies touching, splashing our feet in the shallows, and the sun beat over us and it was glorious. I said, 'You know, I find you very confused. You called this girl a mistress then you said she was Lo's concubine.'

'The terms themselves are confusing,' he replied smoothly. 'What is a wife here is a mistress in my country.'

'But you are not in your country, you are in Hong Kong.'

'And I cannot interpret the way I choose?'

'Of course not – you have no right. While in Hong Kong you must live by Hong Kong law or you will never know where you stand. You speak fluent Cantonese but this does not make you Cantonese. No, you must not interpret, it is very dangerous; you must simply accept the facts. One fact is that you do not know this girl's background or her difficulties. Life has been too good to you – you snap your fingers and everything happens. You are even a different colour – how can you understand this woman?'

He said, without emotion, 'I do not understand her.'

'Then do not judge her. And do not call her a mistress, for she is not immoral.'

There was a place of shade and coolness within an arbour of rocks facing seaward, and we went there, lying together in peace, hand in hand. Beyond Jan I saw on the sea six great bat-winged junks making north with foam in their mouths; and I remembered Po Shan. I had become old, and Jan was impossibly young; men had owned me; compared with him my youth carried no conviction. And I knew what was going to happen. Soon he would make love to me, and because I loved him I would give myself to him, and this would be wrong. This would be immoral, because he was a boy and I was a woman. Amid the groping hand of Lo, it would not be a gift, it would be seduction.

Invading my thoughts, he said quietly:

'You know, Pei Sha, I read somewhere that the soul possesses two bodies, so it chooses as it pleases – one body for sadness, one for joy.'

I said, 'Or one body for service and the other for devotion?'

'It could be imagined.'

'Such isolation – such a division – do you think it possible?'

'Quite possible. This is why it was not you that day in Tai Po.'

I sat up. 'But I have already told you – I was not there.'

'Of course not.'

He spoke more. His words, perfect Cantonese, flooded over me. He told me of the triangular, cut-throat sails of the pirating junks, the men of the Pearl River delta who had pillaged and burned along this coast a century ago. Inflamed with rice-wine, crazed with the Jardine opium flowers, they had razed the mud villages and sailed through Mirs and Bias Bay with living bodies crucified across the prows.

He sat up, pointing towards Sai Kung. 'From there the patriots waited for the junks that would take them to the mainland of China. On dark nights they went through the Narrows with muffled oars under the noses of the Japanese pill-boxes, and fought in Burma and down the coast of Kwangtung.'

'You were here in the Occupation?' I asked.

'I was born soon after the Occupation. My parents were imprisoned in Stanley. They saw each other twice in over three years, but they were lucky. My uncle and his friend held vital information and they were tortured, but did not tell. They were both beheaded.'

'Tell me happier things, Jan.'

'Right. Do you know the legend of Yim Tin Tsai?'

I shook my head, knowing it well but wanting to hear his voice.

'You have never heard of Chui Apo and the girl from Aberdeen, his lover?'

'I have never heard of them.'

He said, 'They lived in Stanley over a hundred years ago. Their ghosts still walk this island, the old ones say.'

'Tell me.' I got up. He was too close for easy listening.

He laid back in the sand. 'Chui Apo was a pirate. He sold his loot in Thieves' Market. He had a little gunpowder factory near Stanley, and he and his girl met here often in secret. One day when the girl was visiting her parents who lived near Stanley two English officers molested her. She called for help and Chui Apo killed the officers, but the police caught him and sentenced him to death. So his lover walked from Aberdeen to Victoria and brought evidence of the officers' behaviour. His sentence was reduced to one of transportation for life, which in those days was something worse than death.'

He was handsome, I decided: never had I seen a man so handsome. 'And then?'

'So she smuggled a rope to him in the prison and with this he hanged himself, for he was a wild thing and she could not bear him caged. Most of the Chinese legends are sad, have you noticed?'

'That is because China is herself a tragedy. A scholar once said that the tears she had wept in the last thousand years would make another Yangtse River, and those over China's history another Yellow Sea.'

'China, my China?' he said.

I smiled, and he continued, 'It is the title of a book written by a missionary. I used to think it was a stupid, emotional title, now I think it is beautiful.'

I replied, 'Personally, I find it smug – and so few will understand it. Fewer still will read it. There are only two kinds of people – people who love China and those who do not understand her, fear her because of this, and therefore hate her.'

'A lot of this is your own fault, you know,' Jan answered. 'Not only are you geographically isolated but your damned silly pride over the last few centuries has kept strangers out while the rest of the world was getting to know itself.'

'Oh, no! Our pride, as you call it – though you really mean arrogance – has kept us free. If we had invited you in, you would have divided and enslaved us.' I added softly, 'I am in dread of the judgment of God for our national iniquity towards China!'

'Mr Gladstone has been dead a long time, remember,' Jan replied. 'Pei, surely, when all the sins are forgiven we have something in common – sense of humour?'

'I doubt even that, but does it matter? What we want to work for is mutual respect, and at the moment things are one-sided. Isn't it typically British, for instance, that they demand to be understood because they're British, but they don't take the slightest trouble to understand us? Last week, in Shaukiwan, a man was knocked off his bicycle. He was carrying on the cycle cans of kerosene – you know how they pile them up – and the cans burst and the road was flooded with oil. He just sat in the middle of it all and laughed. Europeans came up and thought he was mad. Then they got angry and tried to pull him out of it, but he just went on laughing, so they called the police . . .'

'He must have been mad!'

'He was quite sane,' I replied. 'Two days later he threw himself from the roof of his settlement block because the oil was his life's savings. His family was destitute. And as he fell he cried, "Take care of my children." Do you understand that?'

'No.'

'I do. The important thing was that he didn't lose face. What about that for a sense of humour?'

He made a slight gesture of helplessness, and although they had taught him my language, although he had been born where I was born, there was still ten thousand miles between us.

I looked towards the sea and he did not move in the sand at my feet.

'Do not go, Pei Sha,' he said.

The tide was coming in now and I saw the little white junk rise keel-free, swinging on her chain.

'Jan, soon Wu Fai Sung will be back with her sampan.'

'To the devil with Wu Fai Sung.'

'We cannot stay here together, it is wrong!'

'Why is it wrong?' He drew me down beside him.

'Because we do not know where it will end.'

'Are you afraid of Lo?'

'No, but I am terrified for you.'

'Yet you came – nobody forced you, Pei Sha.'

'Yes,' I said. 'You forced me.'

'If you leave me now you will never come back.'

'That would be for the best. Jan, we must be sensible. Your parents . . .'

'My parents do not run my life. Besides, I love you.'

The words had a miraculous quality, they took my breath. I laid with him in the sand and he did not touch me, and I was glad: had he touched me now it would have sullied all I had dreamed of – the sounds of those words, given with such simplicity.

Rising on an elbow he looked into my face.

'Come with me to the junk,' he said.

I did not reply and he kissed me.

The touch of him against me was like a scald, and his strength was not the feeble clutch of Lo Hin Tan, but the arms of a man. The wind moved about us, the breakers heaved and thumped, and I saw through a rift in his hair the half-moon sands of the island surging with foam.

'Come, Pei Sha.'

We walked unspeaking down the sands, but the white junk was dragging her anchor, so we quickened into a run, and as we ran I knew that this was the opium of love, the heady madness that is half desire and half loneliness. Jan dove into the sea and towed the junk back, and because I was dressed he lifted me in his arms and waded out to the gunwale.

'Up!' He scrambled over the stern, went for'ard and ran the red sail up to the masthead. The little junk nosed the wind, scenting a tack. I swung the tiller, pinned it, stooped, and dropped the centre-board. She heeled immediately, loving it: bubbling and foaming at the stern she ran for the open sea. Hands on his hips, Jan faced me.

'This one,' he said, 'is a professional.'

I did not reply.

We sailed, we did not speak much, for when you run an eighteen-footer out into the big junk winds you do not think much either, not even about love. With the tide now racing full we took along the shores of Bay Islet with a fine song in the sail and the tiller kicking alive under my hand. It was dusk by the time we had rounded Basalt Island and darkness had fallen when we anchored in Clearwater Bay, so Jan lit the red and green navigation lamps. It was lonely, and beautiful, the moon skinny with herself, hardly the moon for lovers. We did not plan this darkness or talk of it. The fall of night was as inevitable as the fact that soon we would make love, and the thought brought me dry in the mouth, and trembling. With the yellow lights of the traffic winking at us along the coast road, we stood together, in whispers, loath to break the magic of the solitude, and expectation.

'Are you hungry?'

We fried bacon on a tiny oil stove, we cut the white English bread and drank tea from cups and the darkness deepened over the Ninepins where the big Aberdeen junks slid past in faint moonlight with cotton wool on their snitches and their lights ghostly against the stars; there was no sound but the faint thump of diesels and the slap of water against hulls. Later Jan dove from the prow and swam around the junk with his long, lazy strokes, and I knew that he was naked, but it meant nothing. Squatting on the stern I called him in whispers, for the windows of the rich houses were blazing along the road, the yellow beams of car lights seeking us out in the ebony waters for obscene whispers and suggestions of the mob. Criticism was unimportant now. To me it was important only that I should possess him whatever the cost to myself: that I should be taken just once in love and give without the promise of reward. It was wrong, but I could not help myself: it was unfair to Jan, but I could not help this either. It was neither sin nor outrage, for the fight was over. This part of me was mine, it belonged neither to Wing Sui nor Lo Hin Tan. Now Jan was in the sea below me, gripping the gunwale, and the water was on his face and his hair comically tufted, the lights of phosphorescence playing across his arms and shoulders, like some blazing monster spewed up from the sea. Bending, I kissed his lips, tasting the brine, and I smiled in secret, thinking that he was elemental; that this kiss of the sea was a consummation of our love.

'Aren't you coming in?' He whispered it, and the junk rolled and heaved.

'I do not swim like you and it is eight fathoms, I know it.'

'You can drown in six inches.'

Kneeling on the deck I folded my hands and put them between my thighs. 'Also, there are sharks about – one was reported off Shek O only last month.'

'This shark will not eat you. Coming?' He pushed away with his feet and opened his arms to me from the sea.

Rising, I unbuttoned the front of my jacket, closing my eyes. It was absurd, but the thought of standing there naked before him was terrifying. And to stand there and brazenly take off my clothes seemed immodest, for he was no longer the shadow of my loving, but Jan, my man. When I opened my eyes he was treading water, regarding me with something like astonishment.

'What is wrong?' he actually asked, 'nobody is watching.'

Aye, I thought, nobody is watching except the sea and sky, and Jan who does not matter, and some of the purity entered me. I took off my samfoo jacket and trousers, and stood naked before him. Bracing my legs to the roll of the junk I untied my hair and let it fall free over my shoulders. And in the final nakedness the last protest of Lo Hin Tan died: I was no longer owned.

'Coming!' I called, and dove.

Reaching Jan I encircled him with arms, and my long hair was as a wreath about us, binding us even closer, and I knew a savagery of possession that was no part of the tiptoe, cheongsam world of delicate manners and dainty living: it was a new world of the Tan-gar, of conquest and strength. He held me, one amazingly strong, and I did not drown. Instead, we kissed in the sea with the long rollers of the now ebbing tide flooding over us. This was the beginning of love, a tuning of the mind for the unity of the body so soon to follow, and in the sea, under his hands, I died for him in gasping joy at his nearness. I swam away from him, doing my ungainly dog-paddle, for the Tan-gar are rarely swimmers, and he pursued and caught me with his long, graceful strokes. We hung on the anchor chain, we played hide-and-seek along the hull. Once I evaded him and levered myself half up the stern brace, but he caught my hips and pulled me back, and we wallowed in the sea hand in hand, looking at the stars and the plight of the moral, highly civilised world behind the distant, dull mountains where puppets walked, sipping their evening drinks, talking inanely, breathing but dead, making love but never loving. In this fine purity of the chase the night faltered and stood motionless. Gripping the thwarts I saw Jan's face in the faint light, and he was no longer smiling. This, I find, is the way of men: a fierce, explosive longing.

'Pei Sha!' he said, his voice strong and clear, and I knew him.

I had been the temptress. This was my responsibility.

Jan watched me as I pressed the rail beneath me and scrambled dripping on to the deck. There, I knelt, smoothing water from my hair, smiling down at him.

Behind me was the door of the companionway. After the coldness of the sea it was warm in the cabin. And within a minute the door opened and Jan stood there, and there was no shame in this nakedness, and nothing of fear.

'My sweet,' I said, and opened my arms to him.

The kiss is quiet in the beginning, and for all his passion there was no pain in his arms though his strength was greater than Po Shan's. Also, there was a cleansing sweetness in it, because it was Jan. And in all the tumult and stuttering breath there was yet a dignity, for this was not the smothering face of Po Shan or the reek of wine, but a strange and awful gentleness. Owning him, knowing the agony of his youth in the arms of one so old, I saw in the faint light a stain of blackness on his white shoulder, and this was my arm and hand: this was the hand of an ancient race, burned near black through a thousand years of sun, before his race was known. And as his wish for me grew I knew an exult-ant and tremendous joy, for I heard him and was glad for him, though my joy was not of his: mine was the greater, the re-moved. It was the beauty he was teaching me after the ravaging, tiger's lair of a man like Po Shan: it was giving, not taking. I held him, that I might bear his child I held him, kissing his face, whispering to him words of adoration, and even when the light-ning of his youth flashed between us I held him still, and would not let him go.

'Pei Sha, *Pei Sha*!'

I did not speak, for this is the time when the breed is played, and comes nobility, and I am Tan-gar.

I did not reply to him. No man in the world is having me as easy as that.

He called again but I did not answer, and he called again.

'Hush,' I said.

Soon, I thought, you will rise from this bed, and leave me. Being wise in the ways of men I know that this will happen. You will leave me, Jan, and stand alone, your face turned away from me, seeking a renewal of your manhood, your identity, in a rejection of our unity. You will stand still, and from here I will watch you, and in that stillness you will regain your in-dividuality. In your silence you will discover if this woman alone will suffice you, Jan: whether she is the one you have used and enjoyed or she is the one you love.

'Leave me now, Jan, do not speak.'

Sighing, he left me.

I thought: now go to the window port-hole, Jan, and look out on to the sea. With manhood cooled, regard your situation, and the result. If you decide to love me then turn your face to me and say you love me, or turn your face away, and hate me.

Lying there, I watched, breath held.

His face was smudged with shadow, and fine in profile. He did not move. Indeed, I could not even hear his breathing, which, moments before, had filled the cabin. Then he slowly turned and came to me, and knelt, smiling.

To me he said, 'I love you, Ming Pei Sha, I will never let you go.'

His hand was on the blanket and I snatched it to my lips, kissing it.

I could have borne his rejection without a single tear, but this I could not bear. So much for sea-breeding. I wept.

'Pei Sha!' he said, and held me.

So passed the night and we awoke to a brilliant dawn with the old sun coming up above the Ninepins, raging red in loops of glory.

'*Away!*' shouted Jan, and hauled up the anchor, pointing east.

For the triple sails of the big Sai Kung junks were rising scandals on the horizon.

Crank up the diesel, up with the sail and away full pelt with us across Port Shelter, although there wasn't enough wind to stir a magpie's breast. And had one been up early on the peak of Ma On Shan he would have seen a little white junk creeping across the forgiving sea, her tail between her legs, in awe, at the doings of the night.

But we sang. Hand in hand, we sang at the sky. There was no awe in Jan and me.

21

AND AFTER THAT first love-making Jan and I met often on Yim Tin Tsai, in secret. In the fevering heat of first love we met during the glorious summer ending, and Lo was content, believing that I was visiting Suelen. And Suelen, the virtuous, bloomed with the coming of her baby, walking with pride, her load bulging before her, a fine sight. Despite black looks and threats from Kwai To Man, I still continued to visit them, being wonderfully alive those days in my longing for Jan's child: for this I laid with him, to pleasure him and own a part of him. Should Fate divide us none could take this seed from me.

Now, in the foyer of a hotel I sat, awaiting Lo and his business friends who had just come in from Kai Tak – led by the important Otaka Wan. From a seat near the entrance I watched the arrival of the big cars and the guests spilling out of them – Americans mostly, raucous, lovable, with their cameras and women – giving of themselves to a scurrying, heedless Chinese humanity with an interest in nothing but the Hong Kong scratch to live.

'Excuse me,' said a voice, and I rose, smiling, half expecting this. For some time this man, and his wife, had been watching me.

'Can I help you?'

He said, 'Joe Burrows. This is my wife, Ellie.'

I bowed, and Ellie, diminutive, corsetted, regarded me with wide eyes.

'My name is Ming Pei Sha,' I said, and Joe replied, awkwardly:

'Reckon you'll think us rude – barging up and talking to a complete stranger.'

'Not at all.'

'Fact is, we're lonely, and Ellie wants to talk.'

'Of course. Will you sit down?'

'We haven't got time for sitting – we're only passing through – second day. We got to be back aboard the *President* at noon.' Joe looked about him. 'What a city!'

'I am glad you like it.'

'You born here, miss?'

I nodded.

'That makes you naturalised British, or something?'

'No, I am Chinese.'

His wife Ellie now, staring up at me with her round, mothering face. 'You like living here?'

I shrugged. 'It's my home.'

'Glad it isn't mine,' said Joe. 'They'd never stand for it in the States. Here they're renting out hotels for business suites while the poor live like little pigs in shanty towns.'

'Take it easy, Joe,' said Ellie.

'They even sleep in the streets.'

I nodded. 'But you must remember something, Mr Burrows. This is an exploding population. Twenty years ago it was half a million, now it is over six times that amount.'

'So what?'

'So they haven't done badly when you come to think of it – have you seen the big resettlements,' I looked at Ellie. 'It's a tremendous problem, you know.'

Joe said sullenly, 'Expect you'll think I'm rude – shooting my mouth off but this place is ridiculous. They've built just enough to keep folks quiet and not enough to boast about – I'm a builder – started from nothing and proud of it – and I know the speculators. There's something wrong with a community that builds office blocks while decent people are screaming for homes.'

'Relax,' said Ellie, and turned to me. 'He gets so burned up – not that he's a Socialist or anything.'

'For Pete's sake, Ellie, why should I be a Socialist just because I get burned up?'

I said, to humour him, 'A dollar or two on the income tax might make a bit of difference.'

'Now you're talking!' His fist went up. 'Twelve and a half per cent – if I was paying that I could retire tomorrow. Listen, with the cheap labour they've got here they've got it made. They're shouting that they're short of ground, but they've got enough ground to house another three million if they wanted to. Take Happy Valley. They could house five hundred people in that racetrack Totaliser.' He brought out a cigar and chewed at the end.

Ellie said, 'Joe, she just isn't interested in politics.'

'Who the hell's talking politics? I give this place five years. By that time China will have a seat in the United Nations and she'll just take over – very smooth, very polished – no bangs, nothing. And this they know and this they act on – big investment, big return, and get rich quick.'

'Joe, the lady's bored.'

'I'm enchanted,' I said.

He swung to Ellie, pointing with his cigar. 'Didn't Johnny say the same thing?'

'Johnny?' I asked, and Joe said:

'They're just doing enough to keep things quiet. Makes me wonder how the politicians sleep nights with those people on the sidewalks.'

I said, tentatively, 'There are the benevolent institutions, you know . . .'

This straightened him. 'Who's interested in benevolence? Decent people are interested in rights. Back home public opinion . . .'

'That's your public opinion, Mr Burrows, not ours – and you can express it. We have more difficulty. When the servants become masters, the ordinary man in the street can do little about it.'

Joe burst into a flood of vituperation that damned all governments and dignified all people, but I was not really listening for Joe Burrows was far too intense to be rational. I was looking at Ellie. Her eyes held dreams as she watched the tapestry of Hong Kong life flood down Queen's Road East – smooth-faced young executives, girls in flowered cheongsams, the sweating coolies. Yet, for all his brashness, Joe Burrows was one in a hundred in Hong Kong, I thought. He was opening his mouth and blasting. He was looking behind the gilt exterior and smug, self-satisfied attitudes and seeing the individual human tragedies of the shadows that have no place in statistics. And even if he was doing this with a biased eye, his outrageous slant could never equal the human insult of the thousands in Hong Kong who look, see, and turn a blind one.

I said, 'Mrs Burrows, your husband mentioned Johnny. Who is he?'

And she said, not turning, 'Well, I suppose Johnny's the cause of the trouble. He was our boy. He was in the Navy and he came to Hong Kong several times. He felt the same way as Joe – even in those days. Every letter he sent home was a protest. And he reckoned that, when the war was over and he was clear of the Navy, he was coming back to live here.'

'To open a clinic – he was studying to be a doctor,' said Joe.

'And didn't he do it?'

'He was killed at Okinawa.'

The foyer roared about us, yet all was silence. Ellie said, 'So we come back instead, year after year. We get a pass from HMS *Tamar* and we stand in the places where Johnny must

180

have stood; we eat at the places he ate, we go to the bars he went to – those that are left. Soon after the war we tried to find Kathie.'

'Kathie?'

'She was a bar-girl – she was Johnny's friend.'

'Time to be going,' said Joe, and put out his hand to her. Turning back to me, he said, 'Hong Kong's all right, I guess – it's just the way you look at it. This is your home, so our point of view is bound to be different. Being Chinese you'll find that pretty hard to understand.'

'You'd be surprised,' I said.

Life had timed it to a second. Out of the corners of my eyes I saw Lo and his friends approaching rapidly, and inwardly cursed them.

'Goodbye,' I said. 'Goodbye, Ellie.'

She smiled. They knew it all, I thought; self-made, uncomplicated, they knew life and the rending, tigerish order of things: they who had given a son for the Feast of Okinawa.

And Lo was at his brightest and best. Bowing, he said, 'Pei Sha, this is Mr Otaka Wan and his business partner, Nita Zorai.'

Down they both went into the ridiculous posture of the bow. Face down, bottoms up.

Japanese. Some had seen this base servility before mass murder.

I watched Joe's face as he took Ellie's hand. He sighed, shaking his head wearily.

Okinawa! I saw the flash of guns.

'Goodbye,' he said.

There was a girl beside Otaka Wan, a Chinese, one possessed of a bright loveliness that instantly took my eye: she had the flared, sensitive nostrils of a northern tribe, her almond eyes slanting in her high-boned face. Inches taller than the man beside her, the black and gold cheongsam she wore accentuated her sinewy grace. And as the men bowed she looked at me, one eyebrow raised in mute protest. She was most beautiful, and incredibly alive.

'Anna Toi,' said Lo, and gestured towards me. 'My little star,' he added, and I glanced at him sharply, for this was an endearment he had never used before. It put my status accurately – I was a concubine. It also indicated that Anna Toi was probably a mistress. Otaka Wan, I saw, was examining me with intriguing curiosity, a man with frightful ambitions. Lo said:

'I thought we might dine at Repulse Bay – the hotel there possesses the colonialism I find attractive. You would like that?'

'Anywhere,' replied Otaka thickly, flashing me a toothy smile.

'My wife is joining us later. Pei Sha – you will take care of Otaka?' asked Lo.

I bowed. 'Of course.'

'Anna?' Lo took her hand and led her away, and Nita Zorai, obviously her escort, trailed along behind us. I didn't like it. Otaka was undoubtedly the one Lo was trying to please and I began to wonder where such a service might end. Otaka took my arm, his square, fat face creased up. In lisping English, he said, 'Repulse Bay is most beautiful – come, we will share it together,' and he waddled beside me in his thick, stumpy middle age. I found him quite revolting.

'Have you been to Repulse Bay before?' I asked.

He gave me a joyful, gold-filled smile, but did not reply.

To escape him I began a process of mental isolation, pretending that he was Jan and very deep in thought, and that I must not disturb him. This reduced the embarrassment of our silence. After a bit I began to think about Lo Tai.

I had never dined in her company, and now I was dreading it. Also, I was surprised. Although a few wives shared the public view with their husbands' concubines, it was the exception rather than the rule, and to date Lo Hin Tan had done his utmost to keep us apart. Now, walking with Otaka to the car park I began to wonder what Lo was planning. His wife had been spending much more time at home lately; during the last few months, with the possibility of my maternity apparently receding, Lo and I were drifting apart, and I began to wonder if the gap between us had widened sufficiently for Lo Tai to creep through it back to his good graces. I was only tolerated now, and no doubt the fault was mine. The deeper in love I became with Jan the less I had accepted Lo's attempts to ingratiate himself with me, and I wanted desperately to release myself from the bondage of his clumsy endearments. Legally, if I left him, he could bring me back. I remembered Otaka Wan's presence with a little shock when he said now:

'Lo Hin Tan was right, Pei Sha. You are beautiful.'

I asked, 'This is not your first visit to Hong Kong?'

'This time I am here on business.'

It was a strange reply, but his face was impassive. We walked on towards the car park on Garden Road. Lo called from behind, 'Are you two all right?'

'Perfectly,' replied Otaka. To me he said, 'This place has more than its share of beautiful women. Zorai and I have an interest in bars – we are extending the business to Hong Kong.' He flashed me a smile.

'A few more will make little difference.'

'But ours will be of the most select kind.'

I nearly shuddered, for I knew Otaka Wan as unmistakably as if I had known him all my life; I had met his type a hundred times. Past his flat profile there rose a terrifying picture of roped prisoners and plunging bayonets, and I heard the screams of men. Now he was back with a quieter, less spectacular form of plunder in the age-old game of blood. Bars, not swords for Mr Otaka Wan; a return on capital outlay particularly high these days with the influx of tourists. There was very little difference between his coming twenty years ago and now, I reflected. The sigh of prostituted love sounds so much like a scream. It was cruel and unjust, and I knew it, but couldn't help myself.

We got into the Ford Fury. Lo was driving it himself. Talking in barks and door slams he, Nita Zorai, a slim bespectacled man, and Otaka Wan got into the front seat. Narrowing one eye in secret congratulation at being alone with me, Anna Toi slid into the back beside me. Her beauty took my breath. I do not remember seeing a more lovely human being. Only money could bridge the gap between such beauty and a man as colourless as Nita Zorai, whose only asset was a quiet charm.

Night was falling over the mountains as we took the Garden Road route to the Peak; weaving a tapestry of jewelled blackness against gaudy Kowloon and the neon-lit, pulsating brilliance of Wanchai. The Passage of Cupsingmoon was a stream of diamonds. Festooned with light, the big cargo-bummers of the trade routes pinned themselves on the night. I said to Anna:

'Will you be staying long?'

'Only a couple of days – Nita is investing.'

'So Otaka told me.'

She sighed. 'They go as the mood takes them, and don't be

misled – they're both rather nice unless you make up your mind too soon."

'But at the moment the craze is bars, eh?'

'And don't believe all they tell you – when you're deep in the market you need good cover.'

'I find it all far too complicated,' I replied, and Anna said:

'Don't try to understand them, just accept them. Being clever they are often misunderstood.'

It was an admonishment and we sat in an awkward silence until Anna said, 'You are Lo's second wife?'

'Third. One is dead.'

'You are lucky. I am only an escort to Zorai.'

'There is little difference.'

This turned her. 'There is a world of difference, Pei Sha.' She used my name beautifully. 'You have a legal standing – at least you are supported by public opinion – I have no such security. When first wives are around they actually put their noses up.'

'Why do you stick it?'

She took from her hand-bag a tiny, jewelled compact and held the mirror up to the back seat moon, turning her face this way and that, her lips pouting. 'Because I need the money. Why did you marry Lo, for instance?'

'I had my reasons.'

'We all have our reasons. My mother is a mahjong fanatic. She would gamble on the weight of a fly. We were in debt and stranded in Canton.'

'You come from Canton?'

She snapped the compact shut. 'No, Shanghai – at least, I was born there. My father was a Government official. When the Communists came we had to get out. My mother, Pi-Pi, and I came down to Canton – Papa stayed north.'

'Pi-Pi?'

'My baby brother. He was only three, then.' She settled deeper into the seat, smiling secretly. 'I loved my father and he loved me. The first house he bought was lost over the gambling tables – mother again.' She opened her hands in empty anger. 'It wasn't as if she ever won. She made his life a misery.'

I asked, 'Where are they all now?'

'Mother is in Canton – still dry-swimming – the mahjong.

Papa was wounded in the fighting up north. He wasn't a Communist, but if ever a man was opposed to a rotten, out-dated system, it was my father. He was wounded in the shoulder and somehow got down to Canton where he had rented a house for us – this wasn't a shack, you know – he still kept us in style. I remember that he came in the back way to avoid being seen. I was ill – something I'd eaten, and I awoke to find him standing at the bottom of the bed. He was clutching his shoulder and his face was ravaged – like something you see on the films. He asked me where Pi-Pi, his son, was, and I said he was next door in bed with Mama, but he wasn't. And when we went into the room next door she wasn't there, either – she was out dry-swimming. We searched the house for Pi-Pi, but we couldn't find him. Then we went into the garden, calling him. My father found him face down in the gold-fish pond. He had been dead for hours. My father wept. He sat there with Pi-Pi in his arms weeping and kissing him until my mother came back.'

'And then?'

'Then he gave the boy to her, kissed me, and left. A week later he was killed in the fighting around Nanking.'

'And your mother?'

'I told you – in Canton, playing mahjong, but now her stakes are higher. I give her the money, somebody has to. Confucius was pretty old himself, you know, when he made the law on filial piety.'

'It is a good law, Anna.'

She shrugged, turning away. I said, 'You could always leave Nita Zorai, you know.'

'Not with a mother as expensive as mine.'

The men were talking in the furious manner of the modern big business, inarticulate with rush, gesticulating, drawing graphs in the air, shouting with laughter.

I said, 'Does Nita Zorai know about all this?'

She rolled her eyes. 'Nita? Just look at him. Do you really think he would understand?'

22

AUTUMN HAD DIED so sadly. The crimson Flame of the Forest petals that had graced the entrance to the Repulse Bay Hotel were withered. Lo, with the Chinese delight in all things beautiful, took the car slowly up the flowered drive with care. There, amid the death-bed sighs of the cicadas we stood unspeaking, bewitched by Repulse Bay under the moon. About us the Grecian urns and white arches of a lost generation cast black shadows on the lawn.

'It is enchanting,' whispered Anna beside me.

'It is more,' said Lo. 'It is a tribute to the gentlemen who own it. They could pull it down and build another concrete block monstrosity by a modern architect, but they will not.'

'It hasn't changed,' said Zorai, and I looked at him sharply. Otaka said:

'Well, Jimmy's of Cairo is gone; Raffles of Singapore is in a built-up area. East of Suez this is the only famous old place left unspoiled.' He glanced towards the entrance. 'Is your wife here, Lo?'

'She will be here later. Come.'

On the dining balcony, Anna and I watched the blue-glass sea, the black, volcanic mountains spearing at the moon like hunters: the wake-lights of the fishing sampans burned great shafts of gold in the ebony sea; red and white navigation lights moved against sea-billow clouds of astonishing whiteness.

Lo was ordering drinks, Otaka and Zorai lighting cigars when Lo Tai arrived, driven by the chauffeur, and she made a planned entrance on to the balcony, straight from the beauty salon. Her hair was groomed in a chignon style, her diamond earrings of perfect length. She approached slowly, curved and youthful in a long, black gown. About her shoulders was a scarlet stole, and the manner of her walk lent her an unusual radiance; she came savouring the impression upon Lo, who rose slowly from the table, staring at her.

'*Tsao!*' he exclaimed.

Lo Tai bowed. Such was her charm and manner during the

introductions that I wondered if she had been drinking; she was particularly effusive to Otaka Wan, I noticed: it seemed that they had met before. I sensed she was up to something and did not blame her. It is a perpetual wonder to me how such women manage to tolerate their husbands' concubines. Now she said, nudging me:

'There beside you sits the most charming and incorrigible rogue in Japan.' She fluttered an eye at Otaka Wan. 'He is quite ruthless, incredibly eligible, and has never been cornered into matrimony.'

'Not with any high degree of permanence,' said Otaka.

'He is quite wicked and everything he touches turns to gold.'

'One favour for another,' whispered Zorai. 'Diamonds for beautiful women.'

Lo Tai spread her hands. 'You see what I mean? For the really good manners one has to go to Japan, Pei Sha.'

'Unfortunately we lack your good looks, Lo Tai,' said Otaka.

Lo Tai rose, pointing at the sea. 'But there are things one cannot buy with charm or money, Otaka, and one is Repulse Bay by moonlight.'

'We have our own bays and moonlights,' lisped Zorai.

'Look!' She pointed again. 'If you stand you can even see the islands of China – isn't that quite remarkable?'

'Astonishing,' replied Otaka, and winked at Zorai. I saw this, and was furious.

'They have been here before, Lo Tai,' I said.

She swung to Lo, crying, 'Oh, surely not – not to Repulse Bay! And we had so planned it.' She gestured her anger. 'Lo, that was most awkward of you, it was supposed to be a surprise!'

'They have both been here,' I said. 'To Repulse Bay – to this hotel.' I smiled graciously towards them.

It was becoming sharper. Conversation was difficult. I knew I was being bad-mannered but could not help myself. Their manner was one of revolting self-assurance; they were still possessed of the arrogance of conquerors, and I thought it deplorable that they should even be allowed to sit there, all wounds healed by their ability to pay – to buy the place, if necessary. Otaka was rubbing his chin and looking about him. He said, 'It has a fine soul, eh, Zorai? I wonder if it pays?'

'Do you think it has changed much?' I asked.

Lo was immediately on to it. He whispered, 'Pei Sha, please.'

But I was infuriated, by history. 'Twenty years is a long time, Otaka.'

Lo Tai interjected, with panic in her voice, 'Exactly, and things are bound to change – we change; our outlooks, points of view.'

'Not that much,' I replied. 'Were you here for the massacre at Stanley, Otaka?'

Lo rose in his seat. 'Pei Sha, for God's sake!'

'I was only wondering what Otaka remembers of the war.'

Drawn, Otaka replied quietly, 'Quite a lot, young woman.' He exhaled cigar smoke towards me. 'I make no apology for beginning in Manchuria, coming down the middle of China and ending up in Chunking.' He smoothed his stomach with a slow, ponderous hand, grinning. 'We were crack troops, eh, Zorai? But the war is over now, eh, Lo? And China is timeless, change-less – all her scars are healed; incidentally, I wasn't here in the war.'

'The scars you can see,' I said. 'For instance, I have a friend whose uncle was with the British soldiers at Eucliff. They tried to swim over to South Bay at night, for they were surrounded, but the phosphorus betrayed them. Next day the beach was strewn with bodies. Is it true that you sent home the ashes of your dead in the priceless Eucliff carpets?'

'This,' said Lo Tai drily, 'is going to be the most delightful evening.'

Something was happening and I did not know what it was. I sensed that Lo Tai was scheming against me; that it was she who had organised this meeting, and for her it was going to plan. Perhaps she could not have guessed I would make a fool of my-self, but she was now plainly delighted. Cunning is a woman's substitute for claws. Turning to me, she whispered for all to hear:

'My dear, this is not fair to my husband. Do control yourself.'

The attitude of Lo was now derisory; something just short of the open insult in which the Chinese are expert when the mood takes them. And Anna Toi, taking advantage of the temporary silence, said desperately:

'Oh, look, Pei Sha – the people coming in!'

I clenched my hands under the table, getting a hold on myself.

The presence of Otaka Wan and Zorai was having a devastating effect on me, almost as if I had eaten opium: it was enveloping; a head-spinning, frustrated anger, something I had never experienced before. I was remembering Po Shan's torture, the beheading of Jan's uncle and his friend.

'Look, Pei Sha!' repeated Anna.

The guests trooped on to the balcony from a cluster of little sports cars roaring up from nowhere, the girls in bright dresses, the men in the blue uniform of the Officers' Mess. And it had been a good night in the Mess by the look of things: they laughed; they chattered, they took the place over with their noisy banter, and I loved them, envying them the gaiety of their youth. Now they were crowding at the table, scanning French menus, shifting nervous bottoms, wondering what to order. Otaka Wan said:

'Delightful, aren't they, Pei Sha? Being anti-Japanese you are doubtless pro-British.'

It was very clumsy. I countered, 'It follows naturally, I suppose. Yes, I am quite fond of the British.'

He chuckled and I knew he was looking for trouble now, and I didn't blame him. 'I can't say I'm fond of them but I do admire them. If a war came tomorrow they'd still know how to die – but not what they were dying for, eh, Zorai? Come, let us continue this stupid, international hatred.'

Zorai replied thinly, 'I agree entirely. The British still live by their blind acceptance of their supposed omnipotence. That is why they are difficult to beat in war, hard to handle in politics, and impossible to do business with.'

I said, 'I thought they were doing passably well in Hong Kong, but perhaps I'm mistaken.'

Otaka regarded the young people over the end of his cigar. 'They are unchanged. They are exactly the same as they were twenty years ago, Zorai – look at them. Every damned thing belongs to them – Tokyo, Manila, Singapore, and Repulse Bay Hong Kong.'

I thought the vendetta was over, for the waiter was with us, and Lo ordered brazed shark's fins, sliced abalone, with pea-sprout.

'I cannot bear abalone,' cried Zorai. 'It is rubber – one just chews and chews.'

'Double-boiled wild duck with almond soup?' asked Lo, but nobody answered.

'Stewed turtle in oyster sauce. Otaka, aren't you listening?' demanded Lo Tai.

But Otaka was not listening. He was back twenty years amid the screams and slaughters of the Aberdeen hills, and the rape of Stanley. Glowering at the young British, he said:

'Yes, they would still know how to die.' He turned to me. 'Something we had to learn, too, Pei Sha. Or didn't we suffer so much?'

'You are making too much of them,' murmured Zorai. 'Come, Otaka – Lo Tai is trying to order.'

Aye, I thought, you are making too much of them, Otaka Wan. Only a generation ago such as these had bowled hand grenades down the west wing of this very hotel and fought the Otakas and Zorais in bloody hand-to-hand, tooth, claw, and bayonet for every yard of ground – nor grovelled, said Chu Po Shan, when their hands were tied with wire and they were booted into trucks for Stanley Prison or the blood-soaked execution sands of Big Wave Bay. And now they and the Otakas sat within knife-throw, dining together on a balcony along which, twenty years ago, they had rolled and clawed . . . under the same old China opal moon dragging her shot-up silver across the same old China sky.

The waiters were bringing the food. The smell of it alone made me feel physically sick. I do not know how I managed to sit there in full knowledge of the iniquity. Otaka recovered with the arrival of the food, grinning at me over his sharpened chopsticks, snapping at them like a dog at a fly. Cheeks bulging, he pointed.

'Another lot,' he said.

This was going to be a party. Another dozen young Britishers ran up the hotel steps, and among them was one of familiar gait, inches taller than his friends. I gripped the arms of my chair.

Jan.

It did not seem possible that we should be apart when, but only a few days ago, I had been in his arms: nor possible that he should be taking with such unbridled pleasure to the beautiful blonde girl beside him. Taking her arm he ran her up the steps, then left her to greet the party already at the table. I lowered my head, filled with loneliness, then rose from the table, briefly excused myself, and walked swiftly down to the garden. There, from the shadows of the lawns, I watched Jan in the red glow of the balcony lights. Mercifully, the blonde girl had left him and he was in the company of men, but without him I felt drained of life.

'Pei Sha!'

Lo Tai was approaching, her feet soundless on the grass.

'You are aware that your behaviour tonight is quite dreadful?'

She still commanded obedience. Wing Sui had done his work well. It was according to Rite and I hated the law, but she commanded it. I said:

'I am sorry, Lo Tai.'

She drew herself up with a fine arrogance. 'More is required of you. Otaka and Zorai are important to my husband. You will return and apologise.'

'I shall do no such thing.'

'You realise the outcome?'

'The outcome is clear. I am supposed to entertain Otaka Wan, and I shall not do it.'

'Actually, you are expected to sleep with him, if he wants you.'

'It is immoral and I will not do it.'

'The fact of your presence is immoral to me, but I have to accept it.'

I desperately wanted to cry. Jan moved in the light of the lamp and I saw him in profile, talking, laughing. Lo Tai said with business, 'Come, be a good girl. It is a wonderful opportunity and you never know where it might lead you. You intrigue Otaka – he is used to servile women. You anger him now. No doubt you will delight him later.'

I thought: I am due to meet Jan in four days' time on Yim Tin Tsai. There, in his love, I will wash myself clean, and I will not even think of Otaka Wan. Lo Tai said, coming nearer:

'Facts are difficult to accept when one is young, but you ought to recognise them.' She nodded towards the balcony. 'You know why Anna Toi is here?'

'To replace me.'

It surprised her. 'You knew this? That was very observant.' She laughed softly. 'You know, Pei Sha, it is an astonishing life when you stop to think about it. Yesterday we were worlds apart and without the slightest thing in common. Today we are in the same boat – discarded wives.'

'You will always be Lo Tai. I am the one discarded.'

She sighed. 'My husband is an astonishing man. His energy is incredible when you examine it – and really, there isn't much of him.'

'It is chiefly ambition now,' I said without emotion.

This made her smile, and she spoke, but I didn't hear her, for I was watching Jan again. It was a frightening omen that we should be apart, and I was trembling for the touch of him. Lo Tai said with command:

'Come, Pei Sha,' and held out her hand.

I stirred myself. 'I will not come with you. Bring Lo.'

Incredulity spread slowly over her face. 'But I am telling you – come.'

'Bring Lo.'

She clutched her dress. 'How dare you,' she whispered, and I swung to her, my voice raised:

'Bring him!'

Outraged by the menial, she swept away. 'I will do more. I will report this insolence to him and you will go to the bars where you belong.'

But she did not go. Stiff with repressed anger, she turned back slowly, and by some vicious trick of moonlight, her face, once beautiful, was aged. She looked hard at me, and sighed, and I think she knew by intuition that she was beaten.

'Tell him that I am with child. Tell Lo this, and he will come,' I said.

Her eyes widened with disbelief. 'You are lying!'

'I can give proof of it. I have told no one until now.'

'How long?' Taking my arms she swung me to face her: mistress and servant, one in search of the truth.

'Two months.'

She whispered, 'Oh, my God!'

'It is true. Bring Lo.'

I stood watching Jan as she went up to the balcony.

Lo came in a hurry. Finding me in the dim light he swiftly crossed the lawn, his hands out, his face radiant.

'Pei Sha!' He drew me against him. Over his shoulder I saw Jan standing now, drink in hand, and heard his laughter. Strange,

I thought, the power of one small human. From womb-darkness it lifted a finger, beckoned, and the rich and powerful came running. Lo held me, but I was still watching Jan.

'Two months and you did not say, oh, my darling!'

'I had to be sure.'

'But tonight of all nights! Why choose such a time?'

'Because you were giving me to Otaka.'

'Pei, it is not true, I swear . . .' I said, 'Listen, Lo – never that again, you understand? Not Otaka, Zorai – anyone at all.'

He did not reply. Taking my hands he caressed them, his eyes adoring me; it was a love renewed in seconds, and I knew the wretchedness of the sonless man. I also knew my guilt.

'Come,' he whispered. 'I will break the news to them. I will tell Otaka and Zorai, and they will understand you better – also, Otaka will be delighted.'

Not if I knew Otaka, I thought; tonight his would be a loveless bed.

At the top of the balcony steps, with Lo's arms about me, I turned to find Jan's eyes full upon me. I did not return his faint smile of greeting, I could not.

The moment was Lo Hin Tan's in the face of such betrayal.

23

LIVING IN LO Hin Tan's house was now a very different matter.

With the key of their fate in my stomach, so to speak, the young males bowed and wheezed their respects at every possible occasion. Second and Third Brothers went ram-rod to attention as I passed, now assuming the indifference of one in authority. First Brother, who but a century before would have abducted me to the imperial torture chambers and the strangling cords of the royal eunuchs, now paid to me the obeisance due to a high personage. Life for First Brother had taken a fatal twist. Poverty faced him should I bear a son. His career of the limpet was endangered. Even the birth of a daughter would reduce him to his last hundred thousand. So First Brother grovelled and whined, snivelled and fought to ingratiate himself with a concubine whom he detested and, with half a chance, would have publicly degraded.

Apart from a growing sense of shame I was enjoying every minute.

Even the arch-schemer – Mother-in-law – permitted herself a smile and whispered congratulations while nobody was about. Father-in-law, to whom the prospect of yet another full concubine was merely a part of the daily round, continued to pass me, but Lo's gratitude was pathetic. With his wife's consent he had moved me into his own room, the better to serve my every whim, and every day brought its new bouquets of flowers, or gifts.

And as the days went by my conscience grew.

With the coming of December, the month of Suelen's labour, I had been three months over the making of Jan's child, yet there was still little show on me, which is usual with Chinese, especially Tan-gar. I awoke one morning with mist billowing over the hill, rose from my bed, and went to the window. A bean-curd sky was flowing over the harbour, and I felt suspended in space, as one removed from visible earth, a spy from a falcon's lair in the clouds. Behind me Lo breathed deep in sleep, and I saw his face, drawn with age. And as I stood there I knew a flutter within me which was not the child but the grafting of a new sinew on the child, and the full knowledge of the deception came over me. Until now it had been the gasps and endearments of Jan's love, the sacrifice of position, name, life itself for him, if the need came. But now I knew, in the sight of Lo's sleeping face, that Jan's pleasure in me was a great and terrible betrayal of Lo Hin Tan.

There was but one enduring consolation.

'Pei Sha.' Lo whispered from the bed, and I turned.

The silence of the room was dust dry between us. I did not move.

His hand went out, beckoning.

This was now an old man. Yet, as if the knowledge of his success had revived him, he was a man transfigured, rejuvenated by his great love for me. And although I had told him repeatedly that I was carrying his child, he sought me at every turn, begging fresh assurance. This, too, was how I paid . . .

'Pei Sha, come to me!'

In extreme age, enfeebled, even when ill, there was always the dignity. When all else in life forsook Lo, this gift would be his to the grave.

In penance, and pity, I went to him by the bed, then knelt at his feet, kissing his hand.

'Pei, my little one, tell me about my child.'

'Hush, Lo.'

'Tell me!'

I kissed him again.

I held him, for this was a man who had lately died: this was Lo in childhood, and I liked him better, and he whispered to me, begging me to revive him that he might enjoy my youth. But I could not revive him, for he was dead. There is, in some old men, a big and stupid pride that their youth stands firm and proud within the flesh. Great are the lies they tell themselves, though they have less to offer in the way of love than kisses to a lady grasshopper, and gentleness alone is the balm of such madness.

Yet to give of gentleness in the face of another love is punishment in itself, and this was how I paid for the sin of loving Jan. Every day I paid, and did not count the sacrifice, and none knew of this. While the grip of Jan's thick arms ennobled and refined, the kisses of my husband died upon my mouth. But I did not reject him, and I was glad. I was his wife, this was my duty. But in his arms I would call to Jan, and hear him answer. In the shadows of Lo's room I ran on the sands of Yim Tin Tsai. In tears, sometimes, I paid the debt.

Lo said, broken:

'My manhood is over, but tell me again, Pei Sha, that I have a son.'

'I carry your child.'

He stiffened against me, his tear-stained face turned up, his welted eyes dragging in his face. 'But a son, Pei Sha – say I have a son!'

It angered me. I rose. 'A child,' I said. 'Can I guarantee a son, man – can I work miracles?'

And in a blind spell of rage he went full length on the bed, thumping the pillow, saying, 'Until you came my life was cursed. How wonderful and terrible that at this late age I sire a boy, yet in my youth I have loved two wives, both of high rank and pure breeding – they could not bear for me, yet you, a Tan-gar girl, hold my son.'

This is the greatest error of wealth, and insult – it claims nobility. I said:

'Ten million dollars will not buy a baby's eyebrow.'

It sat him up, scornful. 'But where does breeding lie?'

'I have the breeding,' I said. 'You have only wealth.'

He rose from the bed, impatient, pushing me aside. 'This is the old argument – the nobility of sea-breeding, but I do not believe it. My son comes from you, and you are beautiful, but nothing more. You are clever and of high intellect, but nothing more. My son does not come from a line of blood.'

'Be thankful that he comes.'

With disgust, he said, 'Women of great quality are often barren. Sensitive, those of the famous names – these often have breasts of stone. Yet the meanest and plainest beggar girl can spawn ten brats at the wink of a fiddler's eye.'

'That is the grief of beggars,' I said. 'That, in a world owned by a devil while the gods rest, is the punishment for poverty. You have a child coming, Lo – if you think so little of it – give thanks to that devil.'

All this, was how I paid.

Later, the morning was brilliant, which is the way of Hong Kong in December; the sun was golden on the trees of the hill fanning live in the wind and just enough English Christmas in the air to freeze a baby's dew-drop. Blowsy, stifled by sleep, Lo sat up in bed. Outside on the landing footsteps slithered.

'Ah Ying,' I said, and opened the door.

In she came with the morning tea and I thought she looked adorable. Dressed in her white samfoo, she glided behind her silver tray with her nose high and her arms stiff out before her. But although her hair was beautifully groomed and oiled there were the yawns of unaired bedrooms in her eyes, for Ah Ying was courting very strong.

'You have been sick again, Missy?' she asked, putting down the tray.

'I have not been sick, thank you,' I replied.

'That is excellent.'

This girl knew her way, her virtuous life was planned. One kiss a night before marriage and the back of her hand at the first improper suggestion. Six children before she was thirty, this was her plan: a brick squatter hut on Diamond Hill in which would live every relative in sight – hers and her husband's: bowing respect to her future sons, servitude to her mother-in-law, this was Ah Ying's ambition. Sometimes she swore horribly, she also prayed fervently to her many gods. She knew about Jan and did not really approve, but enveloped him in her love of me. She hated Lo Hin Tan, his house, his relatives, and everything to do with him.

Lo, I noticed, was watching her carefully as she put down the tray. Lo, so close to death, at last was failing.

This was his eternal lotus tea, and he swallowed it like a drunkard in thirst. Now the girl busied herself around the room. Sitting before the big Ming mirror I combed my hair, watching Lo as he sipped his tea, and his eyes never left Ah Ying, the virtuous, and I pitied him. This, the dictator of the company board-room, the paper tiger of an unrequited love.

I was in the bath when a knock came on the door. Covering myself with a towel, I opened it. Ah Ying was standing there shaking, gripping herself.

'Missy!' she whispered, incoherent. 'He tried to *kiss* me!'

It was outrageous virtue. I had to smile.

'Oh, Missy, *ah! Ai-yah!* Next time Master want morning tea he bloody fetch morning tea himself!'

Once there had been an English soldier-boy, and he had improved her vocabulary.

I was not surprised. I held her. 'Hush,' I said. 'I will see to it. It is not very terrible. Go now.'

Later, at breakfast, with Lo looking sheepish, I received a letter by hand, and it was from Kwai, having on the page the single word:

'Come.'

'My sister Suelen has begun her labour,' I said to Lo. 'Today I am going to Ho Chung village.'

After that I wrote a note and put it into an envelope, folded it, and gave it to Ah Ying, with the threat of death by skinning should she lose it.

'Take it,' I said, 'to Jan Colingten, the British boy.'

'The boy Jan, Missy? Ah!' She hugged herself in a torment of pleasure.

'And do not tell Master.'

Her face changed. 'I take this note for you – never mind Master, it serve him bloody right.'

I said nothing. We are all entitled to our opinions.

'Wheeah!' she cried.

The mist was still on the rice-fields when I left the bus at Ho Chung corner. In a quiet place of bushes I changed from my wealthy clothes into the simple blue samfoo I had brought with me, and hid my bundle in the grasses. Outside Suelen's cottage door a little knot of village women were standing, some kow-towing to the God of Women, and to him they offered food and pretties, the barter for a woman's easy labour.

But then I realised that they were giving thanks to him, and that Suelen's baby was born.

'Where is Kwai To Man?' I asked them.

One bowed. 'Kwai is laying his child before Head Man Kwong up in the brick house,' and they gathered up their altar and joss sticks, wanting no knowledge of me, being a stranger to them. Alone, the village nodded and whispered about me.

When they had gone I opened Suelen's door.

She was lying where they had left her, on the labour planks; and she was part of the debris of the birth.

'Suelen,' I said, coming near her, but she did not stir in sleep. I watched.

Her face was white and wet with sweat, her hair tangled about her. And even as I stood there the pain bloomed deep in her and she twisted on the planks, sighing. Anger seized me – that she should lie neglected and alone, with the rags heaped on her body and Kwai's child ripped from her for public presentation. In her sighs the vision of Mother China entered the room and stood between us. With a face lined deep with the labour, starvation, and childbirth of the centuries, Mother China watched, with me, and did not complain. Male expression, male comfort, male dominance was alone important to this old ghost – she who knew quite well that the pain of a birth would kill a man of strength. On China Hill she sat, nodding her approval to the whims of

198

husbands, while her women, only a few decades away from the agony of foot-binding, carried the loads of China; labouring in swamp or under the coolie-pole, giving themselves to rich masters by day and poor ones by night. But I was of the New China and I banished the old bitch in fury.

'Suelen,' I said, louder, and she opened her eyes.

'Pei Sha!'

I ran. I fetched water from the pond and stripped and washed her despite her weak protestations and her hands over her face, for Suelen was very modest. I found a white sheet and in this I dressed her, the property of Kwai's mother, long since dead, and Kwai will be furious with us, she said.

'Then she has no need of it,' I replied. Very pure and virtuous she looked in this winding sheet, and she laughed, seeing the humour of it. The birth, she told me, was easy, and she was as strong as a man. A day from now she would be in the fields with Kwai who was good to her and respectful of her womanhood. It was Kwai, all Kwai, her beloved. Had I seen him?

Waiting for, whispering to the lover who had deserted her in her time of need, she slept, her hand in mine.

But Kwai To Man did not come within the hour and still Suelen slept. I rose from the floor, for I had been thinking. Doubtless Kwai had sent for me on the orders of Head Man Kwong. Perhaps, when he returned and found me here he would rave at me before Suelen and order me away. I gathered up my things and opened the door of the cottage. Nobody was about, so I went down the track to the Sai Kung road.

Nearing the bushes where I had left my clothes Kwai came from the trees, and in his arms was his son.

'Pei Sha,' he said, astonished. 'You came, then?'

'I came but I was too late.'

'Her birth was easy – you have seen Suelen?'

'I have seen and attended to her needs. Thank you for the letter.'

He said, 'She has a good womb. It has made me a son without blemish. See now,' and he squatted on the ground and bared the boy on his lap, rolling him over on to his belly. Glancing up, he added, 'It is good, Pei Sha? See, he is perfect.'

'It is excellent.'

He rose, swaddling the baby against him. 'Also, she is full of milk, the women say, and that is a good sign. She will give me more and more sons until my house is crowded. Would you like to hold this first son, Pei Sha?'

'Yes.'

He pulled the red cloth closer about the baby. 'Hold him, because, though not by blood, you are his aunt, but please do not touch his flesh with your fingers.'

Most carefully, I took Suelen's son, and held him, and Kwai said:

'By the law it is wrong that I should be here alone with one like you. Yet why should I not love you? You are Suelen's sister by adoption.'

'I would like you to love me.'

He considered this. The baby stirred in my arms, whimpering. Kwai said, 'Do you know what my woman said?'

'Tell me.'

'Suelen said that to some the body is not important; also, that a woman can be a virgin in the body and a harlot in the heart. Would you agree?'

I nodded, and he continued, 'Suelen also said that although you act like a *yum-yum* girl, you are a woman of great virtue.' He took my arm, 'You will laugh when you hear what next she said. "So when next you meet my sister Pei Sha, kindly show her deep respect, for you are not worthy to clean her shoes." Did you hear that?' He peered.

I had no words for him.

'Do not cry,' he said. 'Your tears are on my baby's face.'

I said, 'Who told her all this of me?'

He shrugged. 'She is Ming Suelen – nobody told her. She knows all such things.' He put out his hands. 'Now I will take back my son.'

I gave him the boy with the greatest care, for I was impure to him.

'Goodbye, Sister-in-law,' he said, and bowed deep to me.

I watched him walking along the track to his cottage.

Later, at Pak Sha Wan, I looked through the window of the little fish restaurant. The tables were full, for it was a Saturday, a time when the rich flee from the bedlam of Kowloon and seek the calm of glorious Hebe Haven. Jan was awaiting me, sitting by a window overlooking the bay. The seat opposite him was vacant. Wandering in, I looked idly about me, arrived at his table, and took the chair.

'May I?'

He half rose, 'Please do,' he said, looking past me.

It was subterfuge, and I was sickening of it. A few eyebrows went up, I noticed, especially among the Chinese. Quite a few of the women would have had my eyes out: the more fervently nationalistic might claim a pollution of the race through contact. My only emotion was one of rancour. I wanted to stand on the table and shout down into their faces that he was mine, and I was his; that no matter how they glanced and sniggered, nobody would keep us apart. Sitting there I suddenly wanted to cry. The humiliation I had suffered with Kwai, the knowledge that Suelen knew the truth of me – all this, and a growing sense of loss within me, was reducing me to a tearful emotion, and emotion is so untidy. It was weak, and quite shameful.

Jan said, as to a stranger, 'Have . . . have you ever dined here before?'

In Cantonese, I replied, 'I have never been able to afford it.'

'It's a kind of land-locked sea-food restaurant. The fish are kept in water-tanks.'

'Oh, God, *no!*' I said, turning away.

'You are supposed to pick out the one you want when you come in. Surely you knew that?'

I had known and forgotten it. I said hotly, 'I think it is barbaric. To actually point one out is a betrayal of his innocence. To eat him after that would be public execution.'

'This is a religious objection?' He spoke like a stranger with another under medical analysis.

'It is an objection against indecency! It is brutal and without conscience. I have lived by fish and they are pure. Also, but this is not important to you, it is against the teachings of the gentle Hung Hsing.'

'Who?'

'The fisherman's Divinity, and do not look like that!'

'I did not realise you felt so strongly on the subject, I am sorry.'

I turned in my seat. 'I shall not eat here.'

'Of course not. It is an objectionable place.'

'It is a lovely place, but I shall not eat here.'

The mobbing bawls of the room flooded over us, the clicking chop-sticks, shouted arguments. The waiter came. Jan said, 'Just tea, please.'

'Tea, also,' I said to the waiter.

Jan said, 'The idea was to meet a girl here. The two of us were going out to sea in my junk – look, she's anchored in the bay.' He pointed. 'Now I am wondering if she is going to come.'

'Of course she will come.'

'If she does I shall make love to her.'

'That is why she has come – for somebody to make love to her.'

'Is that the only reason?'

'Chiefly. I know I should be ashamed, but I am not. I love you, therefore I need you. Physically and mentally, I am lost without you. It has been nearly a fortnight since I saw you. Do you know this pain? I thought I would go mad.'

He said, smiling, 'Do not be so intense. People are watching – one man particularly. He is middle-aged and fat – Cantonese by the look of him, and he is doing his best to lip-read every word you say.'

'I do not care,' I said. 'I love you, I love you, I want you – there now, did he get that?'

'More than likely.'

I said, 'Perhaps it was stupid meeting here in public.'

He smiled. 'The sooner they find us out the sooner they'll get used to it.'

'Jan, do you really mean that?'

He rose. 'Come,' he said. 'I will teach you how much I mean it.'

'I shall not get up.'

'Don't be so obstinate.'

'People are watching us. I shall not get up. It is very gallant of you but it is not fair to your people. You go. Take the junk over to The Sisters. I will meet you there by sampan.'

Jan put a five-dollar bill on the table, finished his tea, and left me.

Sitting there I watched him sail the white junk through the Inner Shelter.

An hour later, sitting cross-legged on the companionway roof, I said, 'And what do you do for a living?'

We were aboard the junk and leaving The Sisters, with the wind humming in from the Ninepins and the sea in deep green troughs. Jan said, swinging her to port:

'I smuggle jade to Foochow and diamonds into Amsterdam.'

The prow reared and bumped, spraying light, magnificent in colour, and all my fears were cleansed by the cadent beauty of the day, and the beloved sea: sun, wind, water, were combining to produce a single, brilliant chord of joy.

'Be serious,' I said.

'How can one be serious? Life itself is the eternal joke, death a laugh from the belly. Also, I am with you, and you bring me happiness.'

'Sometimes you are very young, Jan.'

He was wearing a white shirt, I remember, and shorts, and the shirt was open to the waist. In the sun his skin was golden, the faint haze of hair bleached white, and the muscles of his chest bulged with the authority of a man. Yet he was still a boy, and it seemed impossible that he was mine. The voice of loneliness and loss nagged me again, and I stilled it. Enough, I thought, that he is mine today; tomorrow we will scheme and plan for another day. We did not speak, but listened to the sea and the out-raged pride of the junk as she fought it, slapping it down her shanks. Now she leaned, whining protest, and we flung ourselves over in the counterbalance. Behind us the land grew misted in spray.

'All right?'

'All right,' I said.

Standing there with his arm about me I began to wonder what he would say if I told him I was going to have a child. It might be a good test of love to tell him; again, it might induce in him a mistaken sense of loyalty. Our love and the enjoyment of that love was as much mine as Jan's, and because I was so much older in life than he, it was my responsibility. I could have sullied the purity with precaution, but this would degrade it. Yet it did seem strange, standing there in Jan's nearness, that he could enjoy the best of me today without apparently a thought for the worst of me tomorrow; waddling, misshapen. And the child would be the child of Jan, without mistake – a Eurasian, brown-skinned child, the pigment of the Sino-Indian; the classical features of the European. Handsome men, glorious women!

And for the very first time the facts came home to me. If this proved so, then within a day of the birth I would be homeless. Lo Hin Tan would have me out – immediately. The moment was five months away by natural law. Jan now, I thought – every precious moment – *Jan*. And if I was alone in five months' time, then it would be Jan's son or Jan's daughter.

The task now was to still this growing sense of loss.

'You know, you still haven't told me what you do for a living,' I said.

'I tell you repeatedly, but you never bother to listen.'

'You're a broker, or something.'

'I am not a broker. I assist a broker.'

'What is a broker?'

'You probably won't understand, but if you had money to invest you would give it to my broker and he would invest it in somebody else's labour – and the harder they keep the labourer at it the more profit you'd make.'

'That is frightful,' I said.

'It may be frightful but it's the way they make their money.'

'And your broker?'

'He draws a percentage.'

'You subscribe to that way of earning?'

'I hate every minute.'

'Then why do you do it?'

'To please my father. Meanwhile, I study engineering – I told you this but again, you weren't listening.'

'You have passed an exam in it – that I remember.'

'I have passed two exams in it.'

We were alone on the sea. In sunshine, great, magnificent, reared the islands of China. Jan took her west on a tack towards Aberdeen Fish City.

Bending, he kissed me. 'Hold your breath,' he said. 'I sit my Finals in London – in July.'

It did not surprise me. All day I had been haunted by a groping fear, that soon I would lose him. Empty, I said:

'When . . . when will you go to London, Jan?'

'I leave in about a month.'

'A month!' I turned to him, appalled. It was the very immi-
nence of the loss that was terrifying. He said, as to a child:

'It is more than just taking the exam, Pei. Father has arranged that I work in a consultant's office for a few months
before I sit it – I'm lucky. Few get such an opportunity.'

'You want to do this?'

'Of course.'

'And after the examinations?'

'Then I will come back to Hong Kong to fetch you. My father
has a partnership lined up in the City, but I think I'm too young
for it. You've got to get some mud on your boots before you
can be a slide-rule engineer.'

I did not understand this, so I said, 'You will not take the
partnership?'

'That's the trouble with fathers. He wants to stick to his own
business.'

'He arranged this for you. He must love you very much.'

I had often wondered if his parents knew about me. True, they
had seen Jan with me at the Tai Po races, but it was only a
passing welcome, and they had probably forgotten it. It seemed
impossible that they would approve of such an association as this.
The European community in Hong Kong was too closely allied
to the old ideas for ready and perfect acceptance of inter-racial
marriage. The Chinese community, with its pride based on the
old Pekin arrogance, was little better, though things were improving. But one thing was certain: while Jan's parents might
accept a Chinese girl of good breeding, they would never accept
a Tan-gar who had been a concubine.

Jan said softly, 'We have come to it at last, Pei. When are you
leaving Lo Hin Tan?'

'I am bound to him by marriage. I cannot leave him.'

'It is Customary Marriage. You can leave him tomorrow.'

Turning from his arm I sat on the thwarts, staring seawards. 'Anyway, you have your career to study – how can we
marry?'

'We can leave Hong Kong,' he replied.

'What about your ambition?'

205

'I could get a job with a construction company in Manila tomorrow – with the right qualifications.'

'And your father – what about your father?'

'He is living his own life, Pei, he isn't living mine.'

'But he will find you a partnership, and you must take it whether you want to or not. He is your father and you must obey him.'

'Oh, no I don't!'

I got up. 'Talking like that – you should be ashamed!'

'I am not in the least ashamed. Give my old man half a chance and he'd be swarming over me.' His hand went out: he suddenly realised the awful affront.

'Do not touch me!' I drew away. 'It is terrible to hear you talking like that. God, I am ashamed of you!' I wrung my hands in the agony, horrified for him.

'I'm sorry.' He groaned at the sky.

'So you should be. About your own father. Your manner, your disobedience – it is quite disgusting.' I glared at him.

We did not speak for many minutes, and it was terror – this, our first quarrel. The junk did its best to bring us together, leaping and rolling, but I was quite firm. This was not an attempt to dominate him, nor was it unreasonable filial piety. No man could hope to succeed in life with such disobedience to his father in his heart.

Eventually, I said, 'When you come back to Hong Kong – what will you do, then?'

'Try to make my father change his mind about the partnership, the dear old boy.'

'Oh, Jan!' He kissed me and I held him and the sun danced about us; the day was sweet again.

'And if he agrees?' I asked eagerly.

'Then I will travel to Manila. I will go to Kai Tak airport with a girl called Ming Pei Sha, and take her First Class to Manila. There I will install her in a First Class hotel – all most respectable – separate rooms until she takes my faith, and then I will marry her.'

He looked hard at me, his eyes moving over mine. 'Until she takes my faith,' he said softly. 'We have never considered these things, Pei.'

'It is not important – I will take your god. I have so many

now, another will make no difference. But your parents – you will obey your parents? Oh, Jan, it is so very important!'

'I promise.'

We anchored the white junk in an inlet of Mirs Bay. We rowed the little dinghy ashore to silver sands, and there, among the dunes, we pitched our tent. Jan bathed, but I did not, lest he see the small curve and promise of his son. Hand in hand we wandered this new island, standing at the mouths of great wave-caverns, listening to the rush and swirl of terrifying water. Many times Jan kissed me and I clung to him, fighting away the threat of emptiness, the time when I might stand in these places and speak and hear no answers. In the lazy, warm December afternoon we watched the bat-winged fishing fleet sail out from Fish City, its course set for the crested tides of Kwangtung. We cooked sausages on a little stove and ate them between hunks of English bread, most unpalatable: the nauseating, sweet, black coffee I drank, also to please Jan, saying it was delicious. With the coming of night we climbed the highest hill, and there we looked over the sea-wastes to the land of China, and in that moment Jan was no longer beside me, for I was as one with my country, and she was immortal. She, with her countless generations and long dead prides and cultures, could command me into a sweet and silent communion of love that even Jan could not invade. Suspecting this, he did not speak. Later he turned me into his arms, but his love was mortal. It was the love he had sought and found in me, and he had called it forth, therefore it was mortal. And even in the moments when he kissed me I saw those black hills, and knew that my love of China was undying.

The knowledge of Jan's going, the chasm of emptiness that faced me – the inner desolation that I hid from him in these moments of love – all were sweetened.

Beneath the startling brilliance of the stars, the clutching exhilaration, the incandescent seconds of Jan's loving . . . there was a land beyond the mist of darkness. *China!*

As one with him, in the perfect and complete harmony of our union, he spoke from darkness and I answered him.

'You will wait for me, Pei Sha.'

207

'I will wait.'

He sighed deep in his throat, and whispered, 'Last night I dreamed of you and that I had left you. A child was born to you, and it was mine.'

'That was a silly dream.'

Beyond the sharp outline of his cheek, his hair, the lanterned blackness of the sky was a triangle of brilliance on the grey smudge of the tent walls; the crowded galleons of the Milky Way, of which Jan spoke, drifted white smoke over the night, most beautiful. Chu Po Shan and Tai Tai, Chen Fu Wei and the boys – all would be dreaming down the Kwangtung coast under this same lover's sky, I remembered.

'Why should such a dream be silly?' Jan's voice was deep in the tent-silence of breathing and sighs.

'Because I shall not have a child until it is convenient.'

'How can this be? Can you control such things?'

'Please do not speak of it, Jan.'

'But we must speak of it. I am going away. What will become of you if you have conceived?'

'I have not conceived. I would rather not discuss this, it is my private business.'

'I have never heard it called that before.'

I said, 'Be content that you are one with me. Don't I please you a little?'

He did not reply at once, then he said, 'You please me all my life, because I love you.'

'It would be scandalous if you did not. If you did not love me, this very act of love would make me into a common *yum yum* girl, your every kiss would be a betrayal.'

He said, kissing my face, 'When I return from England I will marry you.'

'Do not say that.'

'Why not? I love you and you will be my wife. At this moment more than any other I have a right to say it.'

'It is a promise, and I do not want you to promise anything, lest you break it.'

'You are strange,' he said.

This was a great and lovely peace, lying there with Jan.

That my world was savage and inscrutable did not seem to

occur to him: that we were divided even at this moment of
bodily union was unspeakable in cruelty, but true. For his land
was West and mine was East, and the eight thousand miles that
stood between us was as an inch compared with the division
created by creed and custom. I might carry his son, but I would
build that son in the fashion of my own blood, overwhelmed by
China and her centuries. And all the beauties, the sweetest
intimacies of our love were but gossamer threads binding us
compared with the chains that bound me to Mother China. Even
while he was mine in the greatest torment of his strength, even
while he clutched at me and honoured me with his body, I was
removed from him. One part of me was mine and no foreign
words of love could unlock the door and release me in the fullness
of love. At times, as if distraught with the knowledge that he
did not totally possess me, Jan would whisper Cantonese, as now,
but this did not release me from the bondage of the clan. The
time was too fierce, the years of enslavement to the tribe too long,
and the intonation of his words was wrong, the cadence stilted
by the foreign breath. Amid his sweetness, his gentleness, and
his great respect for me, he did not own me fully and completely,
and this he knew, as he knew it now in the fire of his youth.

I held him. Later he slept, but I did not sleep.

With Jan sleeping in my arms I watched the dawn come up
and saw the distant crags of Ma On Shan ringed with red light.
Through the flap of the tent I saw the sea, its sheen rose-tinted,
the butchery of another Kwangtung morning, and I heard
through sea-mist the big diesels thumping as the junks came
home. I knew their course by heart. Bound for the treacherous
Ninepins, they were on chart for Cape D'Aguilar. The wind
moved and I smelled their wet decks, the brine of their holds,
and through the blindness of the sea between us I saw their
thwarts stained with fish scales, their gutting blocks streaming
blood. I stood with them on the prows: in Jan's arms, with him
breathing beside me I stood there, peering with them for the
betraying foam of the East Ninepin and the long white surf of
Tai Long, for the pair of them were bastards to a junk a point
off course. Behind me the children croaked from sleep, the Old
Men grunted and cursed and commanded, the Tai Tais

grumbled replies: hens crowed from the aft pens, dogs barked to greet the dawn. And in this music Jan stirred beside me, his lips seeking mine.

I kissed him, my eyes wide open and fixed upon the sea, for the big boys were making shape with towering sails and prows snuffling at the waves.

'Pei Sha!'

'*Ah*,' I said. The junks came nearer, *nearer* . . .

Because I loved him I would have pillaged the world for him. I would have been broken in his hands to bring him the gift of a new, fragmented joy. And even as I listened to the junk music Jan knew me in gusty breathing, in a primitive strength he had never shown before, but I did not mind.

In the dawn of a tent prison I laid, and his love was sanctified by his very need of me. It was the spirit of love being tested by fire in the mansion of the flesh, for Jan. But I was calm. I called to him, I think, begging him to enjoy me before he left me, lest it proved to be for the last time.

Afterwards, I thought, could come the ravishing.

24

ON THE EVE of Chinese New Year, which falls in February, Jan sailed for London, and the day before that we met in public, to say goodbye.

We often met near Dai Dy Day, at a place called Possession Point, which before the war, was occupied by fortune-tellers. Here, over a hundred and twenty years ago, the British Navy landed, and took possession of Hong Kong, so Jan had told me; now the American Navy had landed and taken possession of the China Fleet Club, he said. This did not make sense to me, but I did not trouble to enquire further: little made sense on the morning of the day before he was going to leave me. These meetings were not the passionate trysts of Pak Sha Wan, but ones conducted with a fine decorum, for this was Hong Kong island, a place of broad walks where taxis slowed and curtains shifted at tiny windows; the alleys and passing cars were riddled with intelligence. It was always the same. Jan would arrive first. I would get out of the taxi and walk idly, like a woman whose thoughts are a void. Just as idly, I would reach the seat where Jan was sitting, and sit at the other end of it, looking out to sea. And in the mile between us Lo Hin Tan and his relatives sat, Jan's parents, eyeing me with distaste – and all the social behaviours and accepted standards of our twin civilisations – they sat there, too, grubby, skinny with their wasting slanders: they who tolerated bars and ball-rooms, who made excuses for the degeneration of the very best people in the name of art or temperament. And they, who for nearly a hundred years had protected the vice rackets by inaction and the infamous child-procuring, by their lack of compassion – all these sat in trembling anticipation, waiting for the touch of a finger or a glance of the love they could not hope to understand.

Jan said, not turning, 'My darling.'

The Fleet was in, mainly American, and the boys were flooding ashore, already boisterous, fending off the shoe-shine boys, winking at the girls – on their way to the bars, and some on their way to Church, the American sailor being a cross-section of life, said Jan.

'When . . . when do you sail?' I asked.

'Midday tomorrow.'

'New Year's Eve! It is a very thoughtless time.'

'You will come to see me off?'

'How can I? Your parents will be there – your friends.'

'Come just the same, Pei?'

'I cannot. But I will be on Queen's Pier and watch you leave from this side of the harbour.'

'I will look for you.'

Hong Kong roared between us. He said then, half turning, 'I watched you get out of the taxi just now. I thought you had the most beautiful legs.'

'Thank you.'

'Next time don't show so much when you get out of taxis, you are my private property.'

'It is a delicate operation, but I will try.'

'I also thought you looked very pale, and drawn.'

'That is an appalling thing to say to a woman.'

'You are not a woman, you are Ming Pei Sha. Are you all right.'

'Perfectly. Are you?'

He said, 'I will write to you – *Post Restante*. Here is my address in London.' He tore a page from his diary and put it on the seat between us. Taking it, I said:

'And what is this *Poste Restante*?'

'It is a method of sending letters. I write to the old post office in Pedder Street *Poste Restante*, addressing them to you, and you collect them.'

'That is fatal. People will open and read them.'

'Of course not – this is a post office.'

I said, 'Kwai stopped my letters to Suelen. Po Shan and Tai Tai talked of steaming open Suelen's letters, Hui held it up to the light with a mirror. It was perfectly disgraceful.'

'I doubt if they will do these things in Pedder Street.'

The tide was coming in, the sea slamming the stone wall, spraying high. Out in the harbour the battleships brooded and sulked in shades of grey, the walla-wallas foamed and bumped, an airliner circled the green finger of distant Kai Tak.

'I love you, Pei Sha,' he said. 'I will come back to you.'

We spoke more, of idle things, seeking oblivion in the normal, but the sea was already pouring in between us. Soon Jan would go, for he was becoming restive. He must have had a great deal to do at home, and I did not want to keep him.

'Go now,' I said.

'Another few minutes. God, how empty everything is!'

'It is not empty. It is full of love, but go, Jan. Quickly, catch it unawares. I will sit here until you have gone. Do not look back.'

The roar of the waterfront came between us like a physical blow: distantly, I heard the shrieking of a fire-siren. It came nearer, strident, imperative. Then it rushed towards us, bellowing for a path, plunging for two great smoke plumes standing motionless in the sky. Three engines, flashing red, a cannonade of brass and crimson, tyres whining, jolting, swaying. Now came the ambulances scorching behind them, sirens howling, and behind them the Hong Kong dragon of the Praya, the chrome and rubber monster who neither rests nor sleeps but roams and plunders through its twenty-five-hour day of Victoria's neurotic existence. The horns and sirens tinkled into the slums. Sounds grew about us, attaining their datum of normality. Only the sun was silent, burning down.

'Jan,' I said, and turned.

But Jan had gone.

Next day, the Eve of the New Year, I could have watched Jan's going from the bottom of the garden of the house. But to say a goodbye from this great height on the hill lacked warmth, so I took a taxi down to Queen's Pier just before midday. The very activity of the house allowed this brief escape, for preparations were growing in pace. Earlier, with Lo Tai, who was warmer to me, I had gone down to the kitchens, there to supervise the making of Nin Ko, the New Year pudding. And there poor Ah Ying, my maid, nearly died by execution, for in full view of everyone she had left a bared kitchen knife, thus cutting the threads of the family fortune. Lo Tai, quite naturally, flew into a rage and I cursed Ah Ying for her stupidity, then begged for her, so Lo was not informed. Then the servants were lectured upon the avoidance of bad language, the sacrificial cock was examined for plumpness, chickens and ducks made ready, little sucking pigs prodded and patted. Big fried balls of sweetmeats, plain and stuffed with sugar, were baked to tell the future – ill fortune attending if they are misshapen, and God help the cook, said Lo. The servants and their children were assembled in the yard and presented with lucky red money calling for luck, advantage, and wealth, pictures of the carp for success through endeavour, peach blossom and pine for longevity. And Lo Hin Tan, whose fortune originated from his grandfather farmer, then dedicated the first day of the new year to ducks, the second day to chickens, the third to dogs and pigs, and the fourth to cattle. Sesame was brought in for burning in the courtyard, thus banishing the lurking spirits of the Old Year. Oh, I so love the New Year customs and its devils and gods! Crackers then, to scorch the Skin Tiger, who thieves the cakes of the poor and carries them to the rich and the lamp is lit at the shrine of the Kitchen God, honey being smeared upon his lips so that he might give a kind report in the celestial regions on the behaviour of the household over the past year. In the morning the gate of the yard would be opened to fortune, and bows made before the altar bearing the family tablets and ancestral gods. Aye, I loved it, for when a sea-spirit I used to watch the big junks come in with their kerosene lamps blazing in the night, a gunpowder flash of fire-works and flaring paper to attract the love of the Queen of Heaven and Hung, the fishermen's Divinity, and the whole world was alight with goodwill and beauty. For there are no sweeter customs in the world than on Chinese New Year, a kindness which, for Hong Kong, only the New Year could liberate and sustain. It was a time of double pay for most, all debts paid and the eternal greeting of 'Kung Hei Fat Choy,' of incense burning and perfumed joss-sticks, forgiveness, the gayest and brightest clothes. And Hong Kong, like her gigantic mother of the mainland, was caught up in her yearly shout of joy. Loving it, I watched, but I was empty, for Jan.

I left the taxi near Queen's Pier and watched his ship clear her berth on the Kowloon side and swing her prow towards Lyemun. I waved as she steamed past me, but I doubt if Jan saw me; one small human waving against the gigantic backcloth of Hong Kong is insignificant. And I did not realise, as I watched him go, that I was losing him, perhaps forever. It was only when the ship had disappeared that I knew the full impact of the loneliness, and the sudden isolation was enveloping, a vacuum in which one might scream with pain, and hear no sound. For the holiday crowds were coming in from Star Ferry now, a commotion of rollicking, shouting people waving peach blossom, laden with gifts. And the taxis and rickshaw-boys attacked them, the latter with hoarse cries. The very presence of the holiday crowds increased the sense of utter loneliness. I turned away, and the great Peak faced me, spearing at the clouds.

Jan had gone, and at that moment it seemed right that we should be apart – divided by the great edifice of social distinction before me now – the Peak that Mattered.

For this was the Peak that belonged to Jan.

This was the very crown of Pearl Island, dominant, beautiful, studded with its great white houses, sweeping lawns, art treasures, and enormous wealth – wealth, it is said, that makes the standards of Eastern finance. Here live the merchants and princes of Hong Kong, dining and wining with grace and elegance – those at the top of the Colony tree. And since the dollar is the god around which Hong Kong revolves, the way to the Peak is one of wealth and status.

The Peak that belonged to me, Ming Pei Sha, sea-collie, is in another part of Hong Kong island. It is in Causeway Bay, and many call it Poor Man's Peak.

This is a mountain of crammed shanties where live the poorer than poor. Oil lamps are their chandeliers, corrugated iron shacks their mansions, which, in typhoon, collapse and whirr in the air, dismembering knives. Boulders, dislodged by storm, crash down the mountain in trails of death: fires rage here, fed by lamp explosions; the old die of exposure here, the young from wasting diseases brought on by undernourishment. This is a place of head boils and skin rashes, of rickets and the fat bellies of actual hunger. In scores of such communities spring the underpaid labourers of Hong Kong, the garbage-cleaners of Gin Drinker's Bay, or the sweating, coughing cement coolies who carry the bags through molten summers from the barges of Shamshuipo – modern slaves of Greed, Hong Kong's Pharaoh, with the lash of hunger to drive him. And his sister is the earth coolie on the building sites: his brothers the tram and bus crews, the street-sweepers, the hawker control – the mighty army of the expendable in a Colony of princely riches. These were my people. Upon their misery stood the great banks and finance houses: the little flower-makers of the winter pavements, the weavers of the factories . . .

I looked towards Lyemun. Nothing remained of Jan's passing but a thin wisp of smoke in the sky.

'Goodbye, my darling,' I said.

Mingling with the crowds, I walked slowly towards the ferry, loath to leave Jan's nearness and enter the house on the Peak.

'Good afternoon.'

I turned to the voice, recognising Jan's mother instantly, though I had only glimpsed her on the day of the Tai Po races. She was small, grey-haired, insignificant beside the tall man accompanying her, Jan's father. The crowd jostled, then swept between us.

'Good afternoon,' I replied.

The sight of Mr Colingten made me fearful; his austere bearing was enhanced by his great height, and there was about him an air of disassociation as he took his wife's arm and led her to a waiting taxi. Plainly he was a man not to be tampered with. Over her shoulder Jan's mother smiled her goodbye, and small apology? I wondered at this, walking slowly, watching their taxi in the congested street.

I was meeting everybody that day.

On the corner of the subway I met Orla Gold Sister.

'Good gracious,' she said, for we came face to face.

Here was a sight for a shore-leave sailor: upswept in the bosom, with a high slit in her cheongsam into which she had been poured, Orla looked the complete seductress, the beautiful. Her hair hung free to her shoulders, her bust sharpened above a waist for wearing a dog collar: she could hardly breathe.

'Orla!' I cried.

Standing away, she surveyed me, hand on her hip. '*Ai-yah!*' she exclaimed. 'This do not look like a Number Two Amah! Suelen wrote and told me. Or is it the Bank of China?'

'Do not believe all you hear from Suelen.'

Orla preened. 'She gets the truth from me.'

'You are fortunate, Orla, you can afford the truth.'

There was a sudden scuffle of people, their laughter dead: fish-eyed, intent on their blazing path of unconcern, they pushed shoved, elbowed: the very blossoms they carried in their hands were withered. Orla said, 'Then what are you doing now?'

'I am a concubine.'

She whistled softly between her teeth, adopting the mock primness of the *well-I-never* clan. It became her because I expected nothing more. To lie successfully one must nurture the falsehood and have more lies ready, and I was sick of lies. The one who lives a lie for the comfort of others must cover all eventualities, like having a spare set of false teeth in the coffin for use in the after-world. To all others I had lied – even to Jan I had pretended. Orla being my sister, it did not seem necessary to lie to her.

'Dear me,' she said, 'is he rich?'

I nodded. 'He doesn't have to wait to die, he's having his paradise now, or so he thinks.'

Orla was still beautiful. The years were treating me with a deeper savagery, and I envied her the lines of her figure; mine was filling under the corset where it should have been going in. She asked:

'Does he treat you well?'

'Much better than I deserve. He is old, not handsome, but he is a gentleman.'

Orla said, 'Old or young, gentle or otherwise, they are my business. Tell me his name when you are finished with him?'

'When he is finished with me,' I said. 'Where is Lily Ting?'

'Back in the bar. I am off duty.'

'At this time of the day?'

'It is under new management. Japanese – they're organisers. These days we serve afternoon tea – you wouldn't know the place.'

'Still the *Eastern Maid*?'

Orla nodded. 'You promised to come again, but you never did.'

'I am sorry.'

She shrugged. 'That's all right. We all have our lives to lead. But come again when you can – Lily and me would be pleased to see you.'

'Thank you. I promise.'

She appeared eager to get away, ill at ease. I did not want her to go. It was suddenly important that I should be with her. She was my blood, and it was the New Year. I said, desperately:

'Orla . . . what are you doing over the holiday?'

'You'd be surprised.'

'Come home with me.'

She made a face, whispering secretly, 'This I'd love, but what about the boys – it's their holiday, too.'

'I understand.'

'I wonder,' she said, and she was no longer smiling. She moved away, looking me up and down. 'I wonder.'

'Goodbye,' I said.

The air was suddenly cold. I stood watching Orla's slim, black figure clip-clopping towards the ferry. She waved, but not to me. He was a sailor, tall, fair, and impossibly young. There was comfort in the very sight of him. At least she would not be alone over the holiday, and looking at them now, at the joy of their meeting, hearing Orla's shrill laughter above the stampede of the crowd, there didn't seem a lot wrong with it. Orla, giving comfort, was one of the anointed.

Carrying Jan's child, in the house of Lo Hin Tan, there was a lot more wrong with me.

25

LO WAS WORRIED, but not about me. They were still doing their best, he said, to start a war in Southeast Asia, and any success in that direction would certainly affect his shares.

'To what extent?' I inquired.

'Nearly two million dollars is involved.' His glare told me that he was outraged by my calmness. I said:

'I shouldn't worry too much, my dear, you always have the odd twenty million or so to fall back on as loose change.'

Neither did this amuse him. Later he said that the Americans ought to take a much firmer stand, that he wondered if their heart was really in it and that unless somebody acted now we would all catch the insidious, creeping disease of equal shares for everyone.

'For some who haven't got much this would be excellent,' I said.

I got up, with an effort. Getting up was an increasing effort these days. The New Year was far behind us and I was very near my time. I have always believed it an appalling affront that in the business of procreation men were allowed to get away with it. I was an awful shape. No coolie woman with the promise of twins could have been uglier, and I hated myself. Thank God Jan wasn't here to see it.

'If we gave them half they'd want more,' said Lo, folding his newspaper.

'Who can blame them? You've had the cake and eaten it for years.'

He ignored this, saying, 'It's high time the Americans did something about it.'

Strange, I thought, that it always had to be the Americans . . .

'It is extremely worrying,' he said.

Vaguely, I wondered if he would be worried about the Americans acting in his interests or mourn a single life. Cut Lo with a knife these days and he would bleed Hong Kong dollars, and the onslaught of senility was not only dulling his intellect but inspiring in him a greater, more vicious greed.

I said, 'Show me a boy in California and I would not risk his life. I would not risk his fingernail to save a cent of your fortune, Lo. A hundred million dollars could not buy a single drop of blood.'

'I didn't realise you knew people in California.'

I looked at him, sighed, and turned away. Conversation was impossible. He was failing in all things except his perpetual, inner demand for more; he was now losing account with the rhythms and meanings of sentences.

He rustled his newspaper. 'Do you see this? It says . . .'

I tossed him the *Tiger Standard*. 'Try this one,' I said. 'Its views are independent, and therefore quite disturbing.'

Although it was hot it was cooler in the garden.

The summer was upon us in waves of strickening heat. The humidity steamed, the baked mountains flung back the radiance of a molten sky. Every week I wrote to Jan and took a taxi to Pedder Street post office to collect his unfailing letter. He was doing well in London, spending more time on building sites than in the office, and this pleased him. He was missing Hong Kong and me in particular. This month he was sitting the examinations. His father had agreed that he could return by air immediately they were over. This would bring him home by the end of July. They were dangerous letters. Every one said that he was deeply in love with me. I used to collect them, take them to the seat near Possession Point, there consume them, sometimes in tears, tear them into tiny fragments, and throw them into the sea.

Sometimes, weary of the weight, I would go to the end of the garden and watch the Kowloon wharf from where he had sailed, trying to recapture him as I last saw him. The house of another millionaire was being built down the slope below me, and I would lose myself in the miracle of its industry and the craft of the builders, envying the women coolies their fantastic energy as they shovelled and carried with their pretty, bouncing gait to the metallic music of concrete mixers and hoists. But there was more than this single house in labour – the whole of Hong Kong seemed to be building, and the sounds came to me on the heat-laden air; the bombing thumps of the pile-drivers along the reclamations, the midday and evening blastings when the whole

Colony pulsated and trembled to rock explosions. Stained with sweat and dust the ant-like labourers of the office blocks hammered and toiled amid the concrete jungle of the levels; then, spent with weariness, they wandered the mountain paths to shanty huts or Government hen-coops while the Europeans sought the shade of the club umbrellas, or swam at the smart resorts, cursing the lassitude of Chinese waiters.

It became even hotter with the beginning of June.

Then came the typhoons.

The big winds came swirling in from the South China Sea in whips and shrieks, missing us by a shave in their frenzied rush to get among the poor of Kwangtung. People died under falling signs and scaffolding, were crushed to death by boulders and suffocated under the rubble of their ancient houses. The homeless and destitute were packed like sardines into the school buildings and improvised First Aid posts; the Tan-gar and Hoklo poor returned to their storm-tossed boats in the typhoon shelters; the roof-dwellers climbed the ladders leading to their destitution, high enough to be forgotten, there to huddle among their soaked possessions.

Hong Kong, during typhoon, is at her most courageous best: a single nation who, amid the common danger and misery, flings aside the social injustices and biting sense of wrong. There are acts of courage and unselfishness from high strata Europeans and kerb-side beggars: king and serf are one. But Hong Kong after typhoon, in the apathy of her steaming slums, spewing with dirt and smells, in her tears, her grieving, is at her most brilliant; a shining jewel in the crown of an Empire. Eager with hospitality, public contributions, renewed benevolence, she becomes what she could and ought to be for the rest of the year – an example to the rest of the world of what compassion can achieve in the face of every obstacle.

To me, a Chinese who was born in Hong Kong, and loves it, its creeds, its many races . . . it is the tragedy of the East that this opportunity is being missed; that one more flag is being lowered by greed in the name of true democracy.

Lo said, after the typhoon, 'Pei Sha, you look weary.'

'I am shapeless, weary, I am altogether sick of life,' I said.

'Two more children have been burned to death in lamp fires, did you read it?'

'It is the typhoon,' he said. Like the French who blame everything on the war, Lo blamed everything on the typhoon. He took my hands. 'Come, I shall take you out. You have been in far too long.'

He drew me to my feet. Most afternoons I rested in his long rattan chair in the hall for here it was cool. And now, as I rose, I saw myself in the plate glass mirror near the front door, and smiled.

Ah Ying was standing nearby with the half-past-three bowl of soup held before her. There was another bowl of soup which came in the morning, at half-past ten, and one could tell the time by these entries.

'Soup, Missy,' she said, so I sat down in the chair again.

It was owl soup, and quite hateful, for owls terrified me even in trees. But I was given this for a reason. Excellent for expectant mothers, said Ah Ying, it practically guaranteed a child with the longest, darkest eyes in the Orient: the recipe given her by a revered ancestor on her mother's side, had never yet failed anyone. She would stand over me while I got it down. With the need to give Lo an apparently legitimate son and heir, I was naturally prepared to try anything. Jan's eyes were incredibly blue.

Earlier, in the privacy of my bedroom, Ah Ying had helped me to dress, and this she did with an autocratic command. A meat-fed tiger would have shown more pity had this palaver of getting dressed been disturbed by anyone less than Lo himself. With brisk action and her nose up, she would approach me with the next garment, aware of her competency, that I loved her and was her private property. Now, but a week away from labour, I was most heavy – even the doctor spent an indecent time listening to things with the stethoscope. First, with legs splayed wide to the weight of me, Ah Ying would haul me from the bed, and there I would sit, feet dangling, awaiting her next pleasure. This would be a savage, bed-kneeling, nightdress tug-o'-war – Ah Ying most violent, tongue between her teeth in sweating concentration. I could just as easily have dressed myself but dared not suggest it, for on these occasions she was mistress and I was maid. But on this particular morning, Ah Ying, having stripped me, did not appear immediately, leaving me sitting on the bed as naked as a baby, fighting to cover myself. I glanced over my shoulder. She was there all right and with my stomach-belt in her hands, but standing like something stricken. And as I looked she dropped the bodice, clapping her hands to her mouth.

'It is nothing to laugh about,' I said.

But when she sank to her knees, blue in the face, I smiled. Next, holding her stomach, she staggered to the big Ming mirror and held it before me; pointing at my reflection she rocked and stamped in shrieks, and I saw before me the mountain of ridiculous curves and bulges which men call motherhood. For this state in me Lo Hin Tan had prayed, grieved, and joyed; a son for his exploding greed, a daughter at the worst. I smiled. He, at least, was served. I wondered what Jan would have said had he seen me then. But no thought diluted the comical, for Ah Ying, paralysed with laughter, was now reeling around the room, so I got up, took a broad-rimmed Tan-gar sun-hat off the wall and put it on my head, parading round the room hand on hip in the manner of a mannequin, posing before Ah Ying's drooling protestations.

But we had not locked the door and in the middle of the performance Lo came in.

'*Pei Sha!*'

His hallowed posture was so completely false that I became the sea-coolie I was, and turned to him, tipping the hat to a rakish angle. Ah Ying was now on the floor, and crawling.

'Have you no dignity?' Lo commanded. 'Get yourself dressed!'

The fun was over. Ah Ying had wiped her tears. Dressed in my maternity samfoo, I was waiting for the car with Lo's arm on mine. The typhoon was over. Lo Tai was in Macau, as usual; all her relatives were on holiday in Japan or the Philippines. Like the dutiful husband whose bride is a barrel on legs, Lo was taking me out.

Maternity, after death, is surely Nature's greatest joke. I stood there with bulges, while she, the Womb-Spirit who had brought me to this state, with her long red nose and horns and her cradle under her arm, was winking at me round the corner.

'Pei Sha, you look delightful,' whispered Lo. He really meant it.

I bowed to him. 'Thank you,' I said.

We went, on my request, to Pak Sha Wan. This meant taking the car over Vehicular Ferry, and I reflected, sitting there in the big Fury beside Lo, that we had not crossed the ferry together since he had brought me to the Island as his concubine. Nathan Road was going at life with marrow-bones and cleavers, as usual, a sustained roar of traffic and building as we passed Chinese Products, the famous store; Kai Tak airport was bright with its coloured flags, now a place of international repute; once a place of execution, said Jan – the old pirates in long, squatting snakes, their pigtails over their faces, shuffling along on their haunches to the bright red flash of the execution sword: theirs was a placid amusement in the decapitations that had gone before, the prancing antics of the ceremonial executioner whose contortions, while prolonging their agony of life, lent some grace to the dreadful manner of their death. What men and women were these? I wondered.

'They were supremely unintelligent,' said Lo curtly.

'They were supremely brave, for they knew how to die.'

Sometimes I wonder about my people. Enjoying the twin virtues of tolerance and industry, we leave our enemies to discuss our faults. Reserved in public, we are amorous in private. We hold no time for unusual theories, seeking contentment in the normal, and whatever may be said of us, we have no ambitions to rule. We have been made war upon a thousand times. Because of this we have always been the conquered and rarely conquerors; this a war-like world despises. We dream greatly, but our dreams are sane, for we know, in the main, that colourful dreams, like dyed silk, will bleach in morning sunlight. If we have lagged behind the rest of the world in our five thousand years of civilisation, it is because we have preferred the flight of a king-fisher to the drone of machines, the laughter of children to the tramp of boots. Inventing gunpowder, we put it in festival firecrackers, not in bombs. While the world was in a cave we were considering the possibility of flight into the Universe, and wondering about radio while Europe was living under the club. We prefer the family table to the table of the board-room, age before youth, wisdom before beauty, grace before exhibitionism. Ours is a shallow world, chiefly reserved to the pleasures of eating and sleeping. If we love education it is because one can sit in peace to learn – it is the tutor who does the talking and standing. People will never believe it, but we have suffered too many famines, floods, massacres, *Squeeze-* and warlords to get together to plan a war; also, war is too energetic, and is only worth it in defence. If we have a national pride bordering on arrogance, we must be forgiven this, for we own little more. The cultures of the ancients have taught us to live at an even flow, blessing China when she is bountiful, bowing to her will when she starves us. With the same fatalism of the old Bias Bay pirates who met their deaths on the sands of Kai Tak, we accept death when it comes, as we accept the wonder of life.

'All of which is most informative,' replied Lo, 'but I doubt if you really believe it.'

'I believe it implicitly.'

'I do not. You have been reading far too many contemporary Chinese authors.'

'Of course. And one is deeply affected by what one reads. If you are going to confine your education to the Stock Market index you will only learn about shares and prices.'

It interested him, and he turned in his seat. 'I may be out of date with the new ideologies, but the contemporary authors, to my mind, say absolutely nothing newer than those of a thousand years ago.'

'That is exactly what I am saying. Don't you see the importance of that fact? Politically we might have changed, and who can blame us? But ideologically we are changeless. The ancient China speaks today, with the same tongue, the same fatalism, the unchanging basic *wish for peace* – and with the same unerring knowledge that she will never be understood.'

'I, for one, have no particular wish to try,' said Lo.

'But you surely understand. You are Chinese.'

'I am Hong Kongese.'

I gripped my hands. 'You are Chinese – you are of China's blood. She bore you, she raised you, and nothing can change it. *God*, what people!'

'Please, calm yourself. It does you no good to become heated.'

'You expect me to sit here cool and collected while you deny your country?'

But the heat, the effort of conversation, had exhausted him.

224

The car purred on down the road to Clearwater Bay, and we did not speak until the turning.

He said, 'Lately I find your youth exhausting. My mind is too set for change, Pei Sha, you should try your theories on a younger man. I have read, learned, and suffered before you opened your eyes to light. In my lifetime, which spans many wars, millions have died. In the Triple Slaughter of Kar Ding, in the ten days of killing at the siege of Yangchow a million people perished, it is said. This does not encourage a claim to race or creed, nor does it warrant the nobility of your ideals.'

'But that is defeat – Lo, can't you see?'

He sighed deep. 'Leave me, Pei Sha, leave me.'

I watched him, secretly proud, if angry. When raked from senility he was, as usual, my intellectual superior. I watched the hedge-rows flying past, comforting myself that he did not possess my perfect love of China.

By the time we reached Hirons Highway I was feeling sick, for the child had taken off its sandals and put its clogs on.

Lo was dozing as we drove past Ho Chung, and I sat upright in the back seat, clutching myself, staring over the fields. Suelen was standing in the haze of green; tall, erect, she stood with her baby slung on her back. And even as I watched in joy she cupped her hands to her mouth and shouted to Kwai, and he rose from a ditch and waved reply to her. Trees framed, then obliterated this sight of beauty. I could have wept, both for this sadness, and the growing pain. I was in labour, and had expected it since early morning, but if I had Jan's child on the beach of Pak Sha Wan, I had to see my glorious Hebe Haven. We reached the little fish restaurant where, a century back, it seemed, Jan and I had met. Lo awoke with a start and looked blearily about him.

'Where to now, sir?' called the chauffeur.

'Into the car park.' I answered.

The car stopped overlooking the sea. Lo said, 'Pei Sha, you have gone very pale.'

'If you examine me closer you will find that I change colour every other minute.'

'Do not trifle with me. I am worried about you.'

'It is a perfectly normal condition, and I am quite all right.'

'We have come too far, you are very near your time.'

'Lo, please.'

'God, what obstinacy!'

'Some women cry for lemons, others for sweet foods. I want to come here.'

The chauffeur looked through the glass at me, his expression agonised. I said:

'*Sai Law!* Tell him not to worry, I shan't have it in the car.'

Lo took my hands. 'Pei, why have we come here?'

'I must see Shelter Isle.' I grasped the handle of the door but he restrained me.

'Look, you can see it very well from here.' He pointed, but I could not see it.

'I want to get out.'

'You will stay in the car!'

'Lo, be generous, allow me this little privilege.'

He groaned. 'All right, but only for a minute.'

'Do not worry, I tell you.'

I told him this, but now I was becoming agitated. It had been a dreadful mistake, coming here. Lo's presence was sullying my communion with Jan, and I wanted to cry. Also, I was desperately afraid, but not of the birth.

It was the typhoon. I had forgotten the typhoon.

All over inner Shelter the bows and sterns of lovely yachts and junks were projecting from the sea. The shores were heaped with smashed hulls and debris. Lo said, 'Pei, you are trembling.' He held me.

'I cannot see from here, Lo, I want to go down to the beach.'

'Can't see what?'

'Does it matter? I want to go down to the beach – Wan Kee's.'

'The shipyard? Darling, the *steps!*'

'Please take me.'

'I certainly shall not!'

'Then I will go alone.' Pulling free of him, I began to run. The chauffeur overtook me and caught me, holding me.

'Missy, do not run,' he whispered, 'please do not run.'

I was behaving abominably, but I could not help it. Lo came up, furious with anger, and cried, 'You will come back to the car, do you hear me? Good God, woman, what has come over you?'

'Please let me go to the beach!'

People were gathering, Hoklo mostly, standing with their fingers linked, their eyes like the eyes of children, and I knew I was making a fool of myself. But near Wan Kee's yard stood the little fish restaurant with its pink-washed walls, and it seemed like adultery to be standing there with Lo, in this place where Jan had last loved me. I tried to pull away, but the young chauffeur held me fast.

'Take her,' said Lo.

'You want sampan?' She came up to us, a broad Hoklo woman, grinning a golden smile, and there wasn't ten dollars between us and our stomachs. Patting hers, she said, 'You man trouble, Missy?'

'Man trouble,' I said, 'and men do not understand.'

'You want go beach?'

'Down Wan Kee's,' I said.

'You leave her,' said she, pushing the chauffeur aside. 'We got same fat trouble. I take her Wan Kee.'

She took me down the steps. The pain was growing with every minute and I could not understand it. Standing on the slipway, I whispered to her:

'Woman, where is little white junk belong Englishman?'

'Little white junk?'

'Young master – Jan Colingten – big fair English ghost, he go away.'

'Ah?'

'Little white junk with red sail and English flag – you boat-take-care-woman?'

She lifted her face to the sun, fighting for intelligence, then grinned wide, and said, 'Twenty-four junks, all finish. Big typhoon, Missy.' Turning, she pointed to the distant shore, then swung her arm inland. 'Look! Little junk no good in big typhoon, see – he go first.' She made a queer whistling sound with her lips and rolled her eyes in grief. '*Ahya!*'

Lo called from the top of the steps, 'Pei, what are you doing down there?'

Within a few feet of where I was standing I saw, among the rocks of the Hebe Haven foreshore, the splintered framework of a white cabin, and this was Jan's. Piled high in the debris of other smashed boats was the unmistakable wreckage of a keeled hull; and jutting from the rubbish and seaweed, the filth, the mud, was a long, slim mast, unbroken, its pennant fluttering, its sheets tangled in a crimson sail.

I wept, my hands to my mouth.

The Hoklo prodded me but I did not heed her.

'Pei Sha!' called Lo.

It was as if life, in all its debasement, had taken our love and defiled it with the dirt of the world, mixing it with the common and unwanted.

'Missy, you come now? Master calling.' The Hoklo again, determined to do well by me. She whispered in my ear. 'You have easy birth, girl, do not be afraid.'

Strangely the pain had gone by the time I reached the car, but a coldness was creeping over me that had nothing to do with the coming labour. Ice was in my womb. Lo said, slamming the door, 'I hope you're satisfied – crying in public. You've made a show of yourself before all these people, and a damned fool of me.'

He spoke more, but I did not heed him. Head lowered, eyes clenched to obliterate all sights and sounds, I ached for Jan.

26

IT IS THE third hour of labour.

Earlier I was wandering about the house. Lo was at the office and everybody wanted to telephone him and bring him home, but I would not have this. I said it was stupid to bring a man from his office because his woman had begun the perfectly normal function of having a baby. This was midday. By two o'clock the pain was worse, so I called an amah and told her to bring me writing paper and a pen, for I wanted to write a letter to Jan. Yesterday I had received his letter and, quite naturally, wanted to reply to it. But Lo Tai came instead and said I could not write the letter – that she had never heard anything like it – wanting to write a letter at a time like this. 'Who is the letter to, anyway?'

'My sister Suelen.'

'Your sister Suelen?' asked First Brother, coming up.

It was the way he said it.

'It does not matter.' I went around the garden again, holding on to things and laughing softly at the pain, for pain looks a fool when you laugh at it: later it takes revenge for this, and makes a fool of you.

First Brother came waddling after me, wheezing his fats and creases. Here is a fine figure of a man for you: ungainly, flat-footed, his existence a gasping fight against a suffocating obesity; bald as a gnome, he followed me around the garden, my every sigh, every movement of intense and vital interest. In a few hours from now my loins will open and consume him, this he knows. No good can come of this for First Brother, whose life is one long drool of food and women. A daughter will be a shock to his bank account, for Lo, in family honour, must substantially reduce him: a son, Lo's delight, could mean penury, suicide the alternative to a pittance. Now, near the gates of the drive, he said:

'Is it bad, Little Sister?'

Never been called that before. I turn. He stoops, a near cringe before me, all fat thumbs and a gibbering expectancy, mouth gaping, head wagging in utter sympathy for the girl in pain. And under the bald dome, in the tiny sheep-brain, is moving a whistling, exploding pain that he would give to me: total obliteration by a shattering miscarriage – of Lo's son, his womb, and Ming Pei Sha, in agony.

I shut my eyes to the sight of him, moved away, gripping the gates, my face against the comforting coldness of iron, and smiled to myself. What a situation! Jan would have had a word for it. I clenched my eyes as the pain bloomed again, raking me.

'Poor Little Sister,' whispered First Brother.

Unmoving by the gate, I opened my eyes wide at him.

'My business. Go to hell,' I said.

Three love pavilions were in the garden to Lo Hin Tan's house. In two of these, during the long, sultry afternoons, Lo had made love to me, so these, quite naturally, I avoided. The third was in a wild and lovely sea of rhododendrons, willow trees, and glorious convolvulus, and from its tiny, leaded window one could see the harbour, and the junk fleet savaging the sky along the coast of Cupsingmoon. Here, in whispers, I made love to Jan.

'It was bound to happen,' he said.

'It is most unfair of me,' I replied. 'Please, do not worry.'

229

'It is not unfair. It is the reason why I loved you, that this should be.'

'Then it is unfair of you,' I replied. 'My dressmaker is Lai Wah of Kowloon City. Before I met you she said my waist was nineteen inches round, now it is more like fifty-six. If I were to give your name to my dressmaker she would certainly make an issue of it.'

He said, 'It is strange, you know, that such a perfect love should produce such gross imperfection – just look at you!'

'The love is not yet perfect, Jan, for it is incomplete. No, do not reach for me. Do not kiss me, do not even hold my hand. First Brother is looking through the window.'

He was there with me in the love pavilion, tangible, intangible. I was very near him sitting in a little cane chair, looking at the dragon of the Kowloon hills. Calculating that England was eight hours behind Hong Kong in time, I reflected that Jan would now be sleeping, and wondered if I was part of his dream. The second day of the examinations? Stupid thought. If he slept at all his would be slide-rule dreams of bending moments, moments of resistance, the enigma of the calculus. Strange, I thought, that such a brain could possess a mind of such endearing passion. Somebody tapped the window of the love pavilion. First Brother again, the bastard.

'Away!' I shouted, and added a pair of Cantonese fish-wife oaths to sharpen him.

He tapped again, and I rose, furious at the intrusion.

But it was Lo Tai, making faces on the glass. Sighing, I opened the door.

'Are you all right?' She was being the cold, efficient mistress, doing her duty by her husband's concubine. Her attitude was regal. This was enhanced by the brilliant scarlet of her dressing-gown. Her heavy eyes said she had been raked from sleep.

'I am quite all right.'

'How are the pains?'

'They are increasing.'

'Hold them, you understand. Do not bear down – not yet, for you are hours from your delivery. And Pei Sha . . .'

'Yes, Lo Tai?'

'Do not lock yourself in here. You frightened First Brother to death. He came and wakened me.'

'Yes, Lo Tai. May I write the letter now?'

'You are an astounding young woman. I have never met anyone like you. You are coming into heavy labour, and all you can think of is letter-writing. What letter can be so important?'

'It is to my sister Suelen.'

'If necessary we can send a car for your sister – anyway, the letter would not reach her in time – don't you see?'

'Yes, Lo Tai.'

'Won't you come into the house now? Lo will be home soon.'

'I would rather stay here.'

She wore an air of dissociation. 'As you wish. You know where I am if you need me. Anyway, the doctor will soon come.'

After she had gone I went around the garden again. It was hot. June is a stink of a month in Hong Kong, with only its beauty and sun-splinters to cherish it for the long brown lines of wor-shippers lying along the sands of Repulse Bay, Shek O, and Big Wave where the little Chinese patriots died. I waddled, I gripped myself, I moaned, I laughed a little, and above all, I sweated. It was a scandalous exhibition of sweating, a dripping, bucketing performance. No woman should be allowed to give birth in Hong Kong in the month of June.

At the sixth hour, Lo was still at the office, and I was still in the garden. For a while, during the afternoon, Ah Ying, my little maid, walked up and down the lawn with me. I noticed she was pale and asked her what was wrong. Childbirth, I find, is an astonishing phenomenon. She had pains in her stomach of such severity that I once actually had to support her; she claimed that it was something she had eaten, but I knew it was love.

After Ah Ying had gone back to the house I went down the gravel drive to the main gate again, and there I met Jan. He said distantly:

'You realise that you're in trouble, don't you?'

'Trouble?'

'The place is on tiptoe. Questions will be asked if this child is anything but pure Cantonese in form and colour. Why could you not have waited another month or two? It would have been much more convenient. We could have left for Manila together and you could have had the baby there.'

'This is family planning. What has this to do with love, Jan?'

231

'It has everything to do with convenience. What will you do with the child when it comes?'

'Leave it with Lo Hin Tan.'

'But it is not his child.'

I said, 'I have no option. I am alone in this. It would be easier if you were here to help me, but you are in London and I am in Hong Kong. Besides, it is better this way. Your parents would be scandalised if they knew the child was yours. It would be the end of your career.'

'It will be the end of you if Lo does not accept your word. Have you thought that the child itself might betray you?'

'The decision is the child's,' I said, 'we must leave it to the child. Have you any views on this?'

But he did not appear to be listening. He said, 'Not particularly.'

It was a reasonable reply, come to think of it. His poor head must have been full of the coming examinations.

On my way back to the house, after Jan had left, I met First Brother. This was no wheedler now. He walked along beside me with a new assurance and stature, saying:

'Are you looking forward to having this baby, Little Sister?'

I said, 'The pains are coming every twenty minutes. I will take just one of these pains and put it in your stomach, then you can tell me if I am looking forward to it.'

'I am sorry. It was a stupid question. Tell me, who were you talking to at the gate just now?'

'You saw somebody with me?' I asked.

'Nobody was with you, but I heard you talking, and you said strange things.'

'Women often say strange things when in labour.'

He said, 'You are a queer girl. I have never known anyone like you for talking to herself. For instance, a few months back I was in a little fish restaurant at Pak Sha Wan, and you came in and sat at a nearby table. Sharing the table with you was a handsome young European. Obviously he was a stranger to you. His face was turned from me and as far as I know he did not utter a single word. But you, on this occasion too, said many things. I could not hear your voice because of the noise in the restaurant, but I could have sworn you were speaking to him.'

I said, holding myself, 'You were mistaken. I was quite alone.'

'You did not know this man?'

'I had never seen him before.'

'And have you seen him since?'

I straightened. 'How dare you!' I said. 'I shall report this to Lo.'

'I have already reported it to Lo, but, as usual, he will not believe anything against you.'

I smiled. 'That, First Brother, is your biggest misfortune. God help you if my child is a boy.'

'And God help you, Ming Pei Sha,' said he, 'if your child is not Chinese.'

Lo flew home for lunch and flew back again, called by a board-meeting. The doctor came and said he would call back, since by the way I was going I would still be at it a week next Sunday. At five o'clock I suppose I ought to have been in bed, but preferred being in the garden because I could see Kowloon wharf from the garden and the glorious sea. From the bed I could see nothing but mountain and sky, and that is for the people of the land. Lo Tai found me on my knees and begged me to come to bed, but I disobeyed her for the first time. So she brought Father-in-law, who had just come in, and he waved his stick and threatened, so I gave him some rough old Tan-gar language. He was so shocked, and delighted, that he brought Mother-in-law. Stuffed up, pompous, she came in fearful authority.

'Pei Sha. Your time is close. Go to your room!'

'*Ai-yah!*' I said, on my knees on the lawn, hugging my stomach.

'Do you hear me?' She was appalled at being ignored.

First and Second and Third Brother came, and one asked, 'Ming Pei Sha, why will you not go to your room?'

'Because I am having a child.'

First Brother, cajoling now, 'That is why you should take care, for it is Lo's child. In law it is his child, not yours – do you understand? This child is not even your property. It is from your body, but in law it belongs to Lo.'

'I want to go to Tolo,' I said.

They stared at each other. 'Tolo? The sea? At a time like this?'

233

Strangely, of them all, First Brother knew, and understood.

'She is Tan-gar,' he said.

'And what has that to do with it?'

He replied, 'The vixen goes to earth with young, the bird to her nest. The spawning grounds of the little fishes are above the high waterfalls. Because she is Tan-gar she yearns for the sea.'

It is strange, I thought, how a bed can teach a man so much about women.

They knelt and tugged at me, but I would not go. They implored, they telephoned Lo. And then somebody had a wonderful idea.

They fetched Ah Ying.

She sauntered towards them, aware of a power that was real.

'Hey, you!' she said, and I looked up. She jerked her thumb towards the house. 'No more Tan-gar tantrums. *Bed!*'

I opened my arms to her.

In the bed, awaiting the coming of the midwife, I called for Jan, and Ah Ying rushed in, her hand clapping across my mouth.

'For God's sake!' she whispered, staring around.

I quietened, watching her in the strange, misted light of evening. She asked, straightening, 'Is the pain that bad?'

'It is not unbearable.'

'Then treat it so. You are behaving badly. Twice in the last hour you have called Jan's name, and he is in England. It is ridiculous, do you hear me?'

'Yes, Ah Ying.'

She busied herself around the room, whispering, 'Then hear this, too. Soon the midwife will come, and the doctor, and they have pixie ears. The whole bloody house has pixie, pointed ears. Grown men are stooping at keyholes, women holding their breath. Terrible things are being said, do you realise it?'

'What they suspect is true,' I said. 'This is Jan's child, not Lo's.'

At the wash-basin now, without turning, she replied, 'So it might be. You know it, I know it, and you ought to be ashamed. But they do not know for sure, so leave them to guess. Bite your hands if the pain is great, but do not call his name again. For the sake of Lo?' She came to me and knelt by the bed. 'My sweet.'

Once, when a child, I had seen a woman in a bad labour. Now I remembered all the panic of that birth, the midwife's shrill commands, the frightened cries of children. The boys said she had swallowed a toy balloon and they were trying to fetch it out of her, and I went to a corner and wept for so great a pain: the blue, distorted face, the heels drumming on the earth. Two days later I saw her working in the fields outside Fo Tan, with her baby in the shade of a banyan tree, and she was laughing with the men, throwing back her head in joy, showing her strong white teeth. But I did not hear her laughter now; I would have heard her shrieks above the tramp of marching armies.

Lo came home, stayed a while with me, then left.

It was evening, the twelfth hour of labour. The sun was smouldering in his arson of the sky; the moon appeared, fatal white, a lord of terror among his scattered stars. The cicadas began their night loving; outside the window a bird was going mad with joy.

'Jan!' I cried, but nobody heard me.

In the echo of my cry came the midwife, and I watched her drift around the room with her calloused hands and growled commands at Ah Ying, intent on her business of bowls and buckets, the artillery of birth being assembled before the attack on the bed. Yee Moi, the heroin-eater, came, smiling down at me with her great, wide eyes, then Lo Tai herself, then Lo, and he whispered:

'Be patient, my precious. Soon you will have your son.'

At midnight I said to Jan, I will fetch old Wu Fai Sung, the boat-woman, and she will ferry us out to Yim Tin Tsai where the white junk is waiting – just you and me, Jan. And we will sail through the Narrows and past the Stranger's Grave to the channel of the Great Ledge and the caves of the sea-cobras. Over to Basalt with us then, and you will make love to me in moonlight with the big diesels thumping through the night, bound for Amoy and the Kwantung snapper grounds. For us the world will die, Jan. Time will stop dead on the clock of joy. I call for you and you do not come, and every time I call Ah

Ying stops my mouth and threatens me with death. How stupid that I should lie here calling for you, and you eight thousand miles away and eight hours of life behind me. Yet in my heart I am glad you are not here to see this tossing, shuddering cage of pain, but the same thing happens, they tell me, to the very best people. This indignity is not reserved for the sea-coolies, Hoklo and Tan-gar.

It could happen, you know, with a tall, fair English girl, or a French or Italian girl, or even a pitch-black Negro girl as slim and small as me.

And class, most of all, has nothing to do with it.

We sweat and groan in mansion or shanty.

Near dawn, with the moon caught in a toil of my clouds, my son was born.

The room was quiet, I remember; the silence screamed of its immense, enveloping relief. With all pain gone, I listened; heard startled whispering, an exclamation from Ah Ying, and raised myself in the bed. Lo came in, then Lo Tai, and they grouped themselves in a corner, their heads together, like anarchists crouching over a bomb.

'Lo!' I called, and he did not turn to me. But I saw his face in profile as he slowly raised himself, and it was the face of an ancient, scalded white with shock; a face that had died in a moment of terror.

'Lo!' I cried.

He crossed the room, opened the door, let Lo Tai through it, and slammed it behind them. Ah Ying opened the door then and First Brother came in. I called to her and she came to me, gripping her hands. I said:

'Give me the child. I want my child, I want my son.'

'Hush, sleep,' she said softly.

'*Please!* please, Ah Ying?'

And First Brother came, pushed her aside, and stood by the bed.

With slow deliberation he folded his hands before him, smiling down at me benignly.

'Pei Sha,' he said. 'Your son is dead.'

27

THE COMING OF the Stillborn had an astonishing effect on the house. As if he had raised a spear of abortion and scattered them, Lo, his wife, and all his relatives vanished on a gale of horrified whispers. This, it appeared, was the new topic of scandal – I did not want the child. Lo, said Ah Ying, prostrated with disappointment, had flown to Japan. Exuberance took Lo Tai to Macau, flushed with victory for a new assault on the gaming tables. First, Second, and Third Brother, resting content in the knowledge of a wealthy future undisturbed by the brat of a concubine, were in Canton. All was joy in the hearts of the brothers. Father and Mother-in-law and Yee Moi, stupefied by the drug, were somewhere in the house but about to evacuate to a more respectable place.

I did not grieve for Jan's son, for I had never known him. I have known a woman stricken with grief over the death of a lap-dog, and this I can understand since she grieved for the death of love – if one can possibly bring oneself to love a lap-dog.

It might have been respectable to grieve for Jan's boy. Certainly I should have taken my sadness to Tin Hau, who loves us all, but I did not do this either.

I grieved instead for Jan.

August came, bringing her typhoons and storms, and Jan did not come. The house was empty of life. Only Jan's letter, arriving at Pedder Street with its message of love and promise, kept my heart beating. I was ill. The complaint was most private in nature, being a scalding in the water and peculiar to women, especially after birth. The constant pain ravaged me. There seemed no release from its savage attacks. I used to wander about the empty rooms at any hour, a ghost of silence in a long white gown, followed by the ghost of Nature with red pincers in either hand, determined to do well by motherhood and make it attractive. Ah Ying, in Lo's rattan seat in the garden, said:

'I have been considering it. I shall never marry. So much carrying, such humiliation and pain. Even when you have the child you aren't bloody finished with it. Drink this.'

She gave me my morning medicine, which I hated, but which guaranteed astonishing recovery from weakness. It was Chinese wine diluted with water to which was added the bright red and bitter fluid of a snake's gall bladder. A dozen glasses of this and the world was reasonable. I drank it with a shudder, not because of the bitterness, but because the snake, in order to serve me, had to be skinned alive. True, they were first drugged with the fumes of sulphur, but I could not remove myself from such terrifying cruelty. Ah Ying said now:

'I am a Buddhist, and if I marry it will not be for love. There is a boy in Tai Wu and he cannot polish ten cents, and he is cutting his throat for me, but I will not marry him. Once I thought differently, but I have changed my mind. Instead, I will pay a marriage vendor five hundred dollars, and he will introduce me to a clean and reasonable man. I will marry this man and take his name, then leave him. With my five hundred dollars he can buy himself a concubine. How is the pain?'

'It is better,' I said, for had I complained she would have brought another gallon of barley water and stood over me while I drank it. She said next:

'But it is important to be a mother, whatever I may say. When I feel I need a child I shall go to this man, demand him, lie with him, and have his child. Thus I will have respectability, and a baby. A woman in this life needs little more.'

'And money?' I asked.

'I will earn the money. I will be independent of a man, with nobody snapping at my heels for mahjong debts. Also I shall not wander the earth as a hungry ghost in the afterlife.'

'I am sorry for the man,' I said, 'having lost you.'

She tossed her head, getting up. 'He will have his concubine. And since he will probably be husband to other girls like me, he can buy many more wives – under the existing law he can have much enjoyment and money. *Wheeah!*'

'A delightful life,' I said. 'The men do not miss much.'

'Exactly,' said Ah Ying. 'But after looking round at a few of the sods they are certainly missing me, as I told my English soldier boy.'

She straightened, shielding her eyes from the sun. 'A car is coming up the road to the house.'

Instantly I was upon my feet beside her. 'A car? It will be Lo.'

'It is trouble,' said Ah Ying. 'It is Lo Tai.'

'Pei Sha!'

I was half way across the lawn to the house when Lo Tai called me. It was only a fortnight since I had seen her yet she looked suddenly aged. The years of rejection, the passionate loneliness of the gaming tables had struck her in the face; the hopelessness of her love for Lo had stripped her of beauty. She approached slowly, lowering her little travelling suitcase.

'Have you heard from Lo?' she asked.

I shook my head, and she said, 'I have heard, and most surprisingly – he actually wrote to my hotel in Macau, asking me to represent him.'

'To represent him?' I moved away. 'I do not understand.'

But I understood perfectly well. Lo Tai said:

'I am sorry to be so blunt with you, but I am also affected. He is bringing home another woman.'

'From Japan?' I smiled. 'What a man! He will have been right round the East before he is finished.'

'You expected this?'

'I am not surprised.'

'But so soon after the . . . the birth.'

'Time is short for Lo.' I laughed. 'And one must give him credit for trying.'

She turned away. 'I find it quite appalling – it is one wife after another.'

'I can't afford such a view,' I replied. 'I am one of the wives.'

She wandered past me in contemplation and I realised, in full and sudden pity for her, that I was treating it too lightly. She was still desperately in love with her husband.

I said, 'I am very sorry, Lo Tai.'

'You will be more sorry when you hear what I have to say.'

'I can guess what you have to say – Lo wants me to leave.'

'How did you know that?'

'Simple. A barren womb has no place in a house like this. A crippled one doesn't bear thinking about.'

'How honest you are!'

'I will be more honest. I do not know whether I shall go.'

She said, 'He is bringing the new wife by air soon. If you were still here it would be embarrassing.'

'Why?' I turned to her. 'There are men in this Colony with several concubines.'

'But none of Lo's social standing. Think of me, Pei Sha – how could I possibly face his friends? Please.'

I said lightly, 'I expect I know the new girl. Is it Anna Toi?'

'It is.'

'Well, well!'

Lo Tai answered, coming closer, 'It is strange, Pei Sha. When first you came I hated you, as tomorrow I will hate Anna Toi. Now, through rejection, we have something in common, and I understand you for the first time.' Quietly, she wept, her hands to her mouth, smothering the indignity.

'It is only through rejection,' I said, and did not comfort her.

She was Lo Tai and I had always respected her, despite her part in the vulgar intrigues against me, the studied insults I had endured. But now she was weak I despised her. Her type could be repeated many times in Hong Kong. Outdated customs were reducing their status as wives in the eyes of their friends and their pride in the eyes of all. But, instead of fighting with tooth and claw, they accepted their lot with faint protest, leaning on time and progressive public opinion to effect abrogation of an insulting law, bowing to its insult to their womanhood with resentment against the concubine, instead of public demonstration and domestic action against their husbands. Some clutched at the steady middle path, retaining the pampered existence of their lives, accepting the conscience generosity of their men, who heaped on them the treasure that kept them sweet: theirs was the attitude of the virtuous wronged, and an attendant hypocrisy that transcended that of their husbands. Many were rich and powerful women, and good ones. They supported the charitable institutions, they worked among the poor, but they did not lift a violent finger to sweep away the final insult against their sex – multiple marriage, which ruined the domestic tenor of their households and destroyed the lives of thousands of women in Hong Kong – the deserted earth coolie with children to support, living in poverty; the girl of fading beauty who had taken to the streets to feed a child; the ageing woman whose man had brought in a glamorous mistress – the thousands of a Colony where the helpless cried for help. Against these sisters the rich, the powerful, closed their ornate garden gates; waiting for the great healer Time, and the generosity of man-made laws, knowing all the while that even moral men, in their abysmal ignorance of women's problems, virtues, and tremendous capacity for love, would never begin to understand.

Lo Tai said now, drying her eyes, 'Pei Sha, I beg you to leave tonight. Anna Toi and Lo are arriving at Kai Tak soon. Otaka Wan is flying with them.'

I did not reply, so she added, 'Lo will not be ungenerous, this I can promise you.'

'I am a wife, not a prostitute.'

'Do not look at me like that,' she said. 'Please go.'

'Tell me, Lo Tai – where can I go?'

'To your sister Suelen?'

'Her husband would never have me.'

'Then back to the junk you came from?'

'Chu Po Shan already has two wives, also sons – he does not need me.'

I watched her frowning efforts as she searched her mind. 'Lo once told me, but I forget. Isn't there another sister somewhere?'

'There is Orla Gold Sister. She is in a bar. Surely Lo also told you that?'

'There are worse ways of earning a living.'

'Of course.'

She said, 'Many of the girls of the bars are truly virtuous.'

'Of course.'

'Then why not consider it? Why not see Orla?'

'Because I do not fancy working in the bars.'

'But it can be an excellent occupation, also remunerative.'

'If it is that good I suggest you try it.'

She drew herself up; the mistress. 'Now you are being impertinent!'

'It is long overdue, and something I have denied myself. You, with your suggestions, are being outrageous.' I moved away from her, and she sighed, her hand out to me, saying:

'All right, all right, I will give you money in advance. How much do you want?'

'I have not asked for money.'

She smiled. 'You have not, but you have done your best by

241

suggestion. Come, how much? Later Lo will open a pleasant little bank account for you – this can be in the nature of an advance.'

I said, 'Lo Tai, you and this house disgust me.'

She shrugged, shoulders hunched, emptying her hands at me.

'If we disgust you so much I suggest you do without a dollar compensation.'

'That was my intention,' I said, and left her.

And it was worth every cent. On the stairs I looked back at her. She was standing motionless, her expression bemused.

Without a doubt, it was something she had not expected.

That evening I packed my bundle. I could have taken one of a dozen suitcases, but now I was determined to leave Lo Hin Tan as I had come, with nothing. I took down the Ming mirror from the wall and wrapped it in brown paper, and went down into the hall. Ah Ying, forbidden to help me, was waiting there. We did not speak much as we crossed the lawn to the main gates, both knowing at the moment when the child was stillborn that it would come to this. Reaching the waiting taxi, I turned.

'Goodbye, Missy,' said Ah Ying, but I did not really hear her.

Looking past her over the great sweeping lawns, the love pavilions, the light-spraying fountains of the House of Lo, I was thinking that it was a century ago since I had arrived here, a trembling Tan-gar girl from the sea. I was now twenty years old, and aged; one versed in life with all its male demands, intrigues, bitterness. I thought: were the inner shade of me, Ming Pei Sha, to step from the bright green of this youthful cheongsam, watching people would say, 'How strange! See that young woman and the old crone beside her. They are dressed the same, in height and form they are identical twins: but one is a girl and the other is an ancient – see her white hair, her poor lined face.' And hearing this, I would know exactly what they meant, for I had left my youth in this house. Then I remembered, with a surge of relief, that pain and bitterness first stains the spirit, so Jan would not see this shade. Only the brightness of Ming Pei Sha he would see, and love. Then I thought of Anna Toi, who would continue the game where I had left it; Pi-Pi, the baby brother, who drowned; her mother, the mahjong fanatic – she and Lo Tai would have something in common. Lo would have to get moving. It would need a rising market to keep that pair going. Yes, I thought: soon these iron gates will swing aside and Anna Toi, Lo's fourth wife under Ching Law, would make her entrance, and the whole sad business would begin again, a whole new set of human emotions stirred in Lo's frantic and eternal quest for a son from his unwilling loins.

'Goodbye, Missy.' Ah Ying hung about me, her tears wet on my face, then pushed herself away, and turning, fled.

'Goodbye,' I said.

I can see her now, running against the background of the house and sky, her white samfoo a symbol of her purity. A back door slammed and I imagined her leaning against it, panting, head up, her eyes clenched to the scald of her tears. But I did not weep.

'Goodbye, Lo,' I said. The cab-driver came out and lifted my bundle. He looked at me strangely, then stooped for the Ming mirror.

'I will take that,' I said.

The moment the cab surged away down the gravelled drive I knew a marvellous sense of relief, and security. And with every yard the wheels covered this emotion grew until it attained the status of a wild joy. I sat up, gripping the seat. I could have shouted with laughter and relief. I was free.

The driver half turned. 'Where to?'

'Jan Colingten,' I said.

He frowned over his shoulder.

'Star Ferry,' I replied.

By now I was counting my money. I possessed a hundred and fifteen dollars and some odd ten-cent pieces – the remains of two hundred dollars I usually carried in my handbag. When with Lo one paid bills with a smile or nod, or at the most, the drop of a card. A hundred and fifteen dollars. Considering that I was homeless, it was a trifling amount.

The important thing now, of course, was to stop Hong Kong finding out; she had vicious plans for the destitute.

28

I CROSSED THE ferry. Lodging houses were cheaper on the Kowloon side. With my bundle in my hand and the Ming mirror under my arm, I walked slowly.

Down Pekin Road the street-sleepers – that great army of Hong Kong poor – were claiming their pavement pitches for the coming night. In the dusk mangey dogs delivered uppercuts at the garbage cans, skeleton cats cringed their tortuous paths down the alleys, bemoaning the fate of cats in China. Here was the wetting ground of countless little boys, each contributing, in his time, his arrogant fountains – contrast to the girls, his mother-sisters, who would rather die than so debase themselves in public. Along this road surge the night-going crowds, the great *Terraplane* and *Chrysler* cars with outspread wings. Past the rat-boxes and the little diners of the pavements go the spenders, each intent on the business of eating, dancing, drinking, loving, as the mood takes them, but never in this world the business of brotherhood, for this is a luxury which Hong Kong disallows. The very vastness of the poverty and pain, the very enormity of the complex human problem denies for any but saints the individual conscience. Individually important, microscopically unimportant, the crowds flood by, transitional on the giant sorting-house floor of the Hong Kong go-down: impermanent, self-seeking, ill at ease, fussing, fretting for the extra yard on and the extra shove, they go – oblivious of the rag bundles that are street-sleepers. Numbed by community decree that outlaws beggarhood, or the latest press report of a beggar worth his weight in gold, they ignore the beggars. Firm in the knowledge that everything can be left to the Hong Kong saints, past the stomach-bulging hunger of pavement children they go, vociferous, gesticulating in a score and one languages, every one knowing a dozen reasons for not belonging and why this transient life of couldn't-care is the greatest life on earth. Jostled, elbowed, I went with the night crowds. All this, I thought, is the bones of bitterness: all this wealth, hunger, tuberculosis, drugs – my God, no wonder they leap at drugs, one in fourteen in Hong Kong being an addict –

all this labour by day and sleeplessness by night, winter cold and tossing, sweating summers . . . does a city so have to suffer to bring out the sweetness of its people? Or is it merely to prove the fortitude and tolerance of its birthright? For all the frantic efforts of the World Lutheran Service, the Roman Catholics, a glorious Salvation Army and other Church organisations of relief, the thousands of heroes like the Resettlement officers, the Red Cross and the Saints of Sunshine Island – all is a mere pond ripple in a raging sea of human hopelessness and degradation, for it is a relief based on individual goodness and not public intention. I sighed, closing my eyes to the squalor, shutting off my mind and heart to the misery, and walked on in company with the night crowds. And against this backcloth, which was my home, I thought of Jan, remembering his stories of tea on English lawns, bee-hum, leafy lanes under an English sky, all the fragrance of his dreams. But my dreams were of this, in Pekin Road: of molten summer days, Hakka knee-deep in the rice-fields, the wallowing buffalo, the massacre of the sky over the China hills. Jan's was an ordered past since the cradle rocked by a nurse, his memories of blue blazers on sports days, the sedate quiet of a quadrangle in a serene English town – all this he had told me. My past was the bedraggled poverty of Fo Tan village, the eternal war between the pocket and the mouth; the barbaric seas off Lamma and Tolo, the outrage of Po Shan and the great and small insults that were a part of the daily round in the house of Lo Hin Tan. Perhaps, somewhere in the universe between Jan's planet and mine, the fates which devised our meeting might build for us a bridge upon whose crest East and West might love in peace, secure from the racial haggling, the dogs of West and East yelping at our heels.

Now it was dark and I was tired. Up Nathan Road, once condemned as a Folly, now applauded as a Foresight, the lights blazed with strickening brilliance, a giant conflagration of neon flashes and headlamps. I was remembering a cheap lodging-house I had once noticed, and found it almost instantly in Granville Road, not yet decimated by the giant reconstruction. How strange, I reflected, that everything in my world seemed to be dying at once. This great road, even, was on its death-bed; its ancient and loved stalls and vendors being slowly ground under the iron heel of the finance houses who were building shops and offices where Government should have been building homes.

At the top of rickety stairs I found the lodging-house; a single, enormous room, its walls flanked with sleeping cages. I had not expected this, and remembered that morning walk from Ho Chung to Hebe Haven, and the amah with the lap-dog – her protests about her mother living in one. I had to smile. For me, the wheel of life had, in the space of hours, turned full circle. I paid the room-keeper forty dollars in advance, and she gave me the keys of the cage behind the door. None of the other occupants were in, so I washed at a basin, and, refreshed, went down Mody Road to one of the eating houses. Kowloon was getting into its stride for the night revelries. Strident music came from the bars; Europeans in evening dress bustled out of taxis, Indian women in bright-coloured saris walked with elegant, dark-skinned men. I went slowly back to the lodging-house. In the morning I would cross the Ferry to Pedder Street post office and collect Jan's weekly letter. The thought of his home-coming brought me to a pitch of bright joy – all would come right when Jan came home. Now, back in the lodging-room I sought the security of the sleeping cage. Even the bars of a man-made prison have advantages. They may keep you in but they keep the world out. A group of teenagers were in the far corner playing a guitar and laughing with the shrill urgency of the young. Down the walls of the room, as night grew older, lay the labourers of the building sites; a blind musician with his child were close to me, the child on her haunches, examining me with sustained interest, but when I put my hand through the bars to her, she sought the safety of her father. He spoke, I think, but I did not hear him. In the new-found security of the sleeping cage, I slept, and in the noise, the smell of unwashed humanity, the throat-rasping hawking, the snores, I slept in peace.

For the first time in years no man was in reach of me.

In the morning, after the other occupants of the room had left for work, I rose, washed, and dressed and went on a bus to Prince Edward Road, to try to find my sister Orla. Not knowing the house I walked up and down in the hope of meeting Orla or Lily Ting, but I did not meet them, neither did anyone know of them from my enquiries. At midday I ate rice congee in an eating shop off Waterloo Road. After this I returned to Nathan Road, and went to the bar *Eastern Maid*, where Orla worked, but it was closed, so I took the Ferry to the Praya and called at Pedder Street post office in the hope of getting the weekly letter. It was there. The small, precise handwriting brightened the day. Consecrating the rite of reading Jan's letter on the bench near Possession Point, I walked down the waterfront with it clutched against me, loath to open it lest it tell of a further delay in his home-coming.

On the bench, oblivious of the passing crowds, I opened it. It was a scrawled letter, one written in haste, and its message was brief. He was arriving at Kai Tak on the last day of the month, and he begged me to come to meet him. I got up, I remember, staring at the sea, my mind fumbling for the date. Two days' time – he would be arriving by air the day after tomorrow! It seemed impossibly good. The post-mark on the envelope was scarcely legible, but I deciphered it; the air mail had been delayed. Flight 307 arriving at ten o'clock at night, at Kai Tak. It was an unbelievable joy. I could hardly contain it. A tiny shoe-shine boy arrived at the bench, his smudged face staring up at me, his head on one side in urgent enquiry. I said:

'You will never guess what has happened!'

His eyes narrowed with the studious intent of his childhood. 'Ah!'

Past his snub profile I saw the junks heeling in the sky, the wallowing sampans and crazy sails, rip-torn and flapping in wind madness.

'You want shoe-shine?' It was his world, composed of two parts: shoe-shine or no shoe-shine – food or hunger, with a thrashing from his bully-man if he came home empty.

I gave him a dollar and he hunched his shoulders, head lowered for the charge to escape. When you shoe-shine along the waterfront in Hong Kong you are never sure of humans.

'Wait!' His world, too, was ordered by command. Skidding round, he faced me.

'I go now!' he whispered, fearful.

'You wait, for I want you. Day after tomorrow someone I love come to Kai Tak. Do you understand? This is good, eh?'

'Your mama?'

The thought was inevitable. 'Not my mama,' I answered.

'Will you blacken my finger for luck, Shoe-Shine?' I held out my forefinger.

He grinned wide, showing his broken milk teeth, then stooped, unwrapped his bundle, prised open a tin, blackened a brush, and brought it across my finger. With great importance, I held my blackened finger up to the sun and turned it in a circle, peering at it, while he watched hypnotised by his sudden and tremendous power. I said, 'Shoe-shine boy say you come Kai Tak day after tomorrow – remember!' I looked down at the child. He was still kneeling, clutching himself, staring wide-eyed at my uplifted finger.

'He come Kai Tak,' I said softly.

'Ah.'

'Day after tomorrow.'

'*Ai-yah!*' he breathed.

I rose from the seat, and momentarily held his thin body against me. 'Go now,' I said, and he went, staring over his shoulder, his pace quickening in fear and pleasure. He finally ran, yelling.

I moved, too, and quickly. A minute from now I would be plagued by an army of tiny shoe-shine boys.

At seven o'clock that same evening I pushed open the door of the *Eastern Maid* bar.

Brothels were once legal in Hong Kong, but the outraged virtue of political visitors had them banned, so the brothels went underground. Sanctimony was now appeased, the Colony was cleansed, everybody was happy. Bars and ball-rooms sprang up; many were respectable clubs of entertainment staffed by hostesses, and nothing improper happened on the premises. The *Eastern Maid*, at a glance, was not one of these. If there was still an outcry against the danger of such bars, and some like this exist, it was discreetly kept off the front page. Indeed, talk of the girls who plied the trade was no longer hinted at by the popular press, it was accepted. The night whispers of Wanchai and other places, the bargaining for women, the showing of blue films was openly reported; which is probably a cleaner way of handling things than putting them underground. This fact you accept, when, like Government, you accept a trade in sex.

Five girls were sitting at the little gilt tables, others lounged

along the plush, cushioned walls. Some were playing cards, the popular pastime of the *yum yum* girl between ships and customers, some were reading. My sister Orla and Lily Ting were talking in whispers as I entered and did not see me until I stood before them, but the captain of this ship was the *Mamasan*. A hand turned me, and I faced her. There was a blowsy, tired look about this woman; she was now shapeless, yet in shadow, under the obesity of middle age, was a figure of beautiful proportions, and her Asian face held a sort of Mongol prettiness that all the years of travail could not conceal.

'Ming Pei Sha,' she said.

I was astonished. Orla and Lily Ting were now either side of me, but I was staring at the *Mamasan*. She smiled, and her words now were heavy with Shanghai dialect:

'You came here once before – with your big sister Suelen – remember?'

'That was over three years ago!'

'In this trade we remember,' she said, but I did not believe her. There was more to her memory than that. I said:

'I have come to visit Orla and Lily Ting.'

'Of course.'

I turned to them, and the *Mamasan* added, 'And perhaps, before you leave, you will have a word with me? There is always a vacancy here for one so handsome.'

'I will find my own employment. I have come to see my sister.'

She bowed slightly, still smiling. 'Orla, why not take Pei Sha to the rest room, it is more private there.'

The other girls watched with faint interest as we went through the bar: some were pretty, a few were quite beautiful. White-coated soda boys were getting busy along the ornate bar for the night invasion, for the Fleet was in, but they did not spare me a glance, the charm and mystery of womanhood having long vanished from their dreary, pimpish lives. In the room upstairs, the one in which Suelen and I had stood a generation ago, Orla said:

'You have been a long time coming.'

'I came when I could. I had a child a few weeks ago, and lost it.'

'I am sorry,' said Lily Ting, speaking for the first time.

'You did not look as if you were having a baby when I saw you.'

'But it is true.'

'And now he has turned you out?'

'Orla,' said Lily Ting, 'do not be a pig.'

Orla said, 'I thought she had come to see me. Now I know she has only come for help.'

'I came because I promised. I do not want help, nor would I ask you for it.'

Something was wrong and I could not identify it. Orla was naturally distant, a girl without warmth, but this was open hostility. Lily Ting, overspeaking me, said hotly:

'She is a little old pig. She is bad-tempered because her man has not shown up four nights running. He is a sailor.'

'With sailors you never know where you are from one day to another,' I said. 'The captain up-anchors and leaves fifty girls behind. It is sometimes extremely hard on the sailors.'

'My!' whispered Lily, 'you talk good. And you are beautiful. I would never have thought when I saw you last, with bob-floats on your shoulders, that you would grow so beautiful.'

'That is her trouble,' said Orla, turning to the window. 'All her life she has been clever, now she is beautiful. She has had everything. I have had nothing.'

Lily, in panic, said, 'And Suelen, how is Suelen?'

'She is happy farming in Ho Chung – you heard about her baby?'

'We heard,' said Orla, her back to us, 'Suelen, with her man, her baby, has done better than any of us.'

'A boy first time, too!' exclaimed Lily.

It was quite pathetic. Something was between us, something strange and unfathomable. Words were drying. In the perfumed stillness of the room I sensed the growing hostility. There is so much disappointment in the age-old call of blood. The love of a good friend is so often to be cherished above the love of a poor relative, who is demanding that the rewards of kinship are a social right. Owing nothing to Orla Gold Sister, I said, 'Well, I had better be going.'

'Where to?' asked Lily.

I fought down an urge to tell them about Jan. 'I don't know.

My English is good. I shouldn't have much difficulty getting a job.'

Orla said at the window, 'There is one here, if you want it.'

'So *Mamasan* told me, but I do not think so . . .'

'I suppose it isn't good enough for you.'

Lily said, her hands clasped, 'Do not come here, Pei Sha!'

'One day. Who knows?'

With her nose up, Orla said, 'My God, it's something to be able to pick and choose, isn't it? But whether we're educated or not, we all seem to finish at the same level. One can aim at the Bank of China, of course, but that pays peanuts compared with a job like this.'

There was no point in staying longer. 'Goodbye,' I said.

Lily opened the door and went down the stairs with me. On the landing she stopped me, her hand on mine, and whispered, 'Please, please do not blame her, Pei Sha – she is not herself today. Everything is going wrong. Her sailor stood her up, I told you. Yesterday *Mamasan* told her to prepare for an interview with the owner – he's the big-shot – owns dozens of bars and ball-rooms. She got very excited, she put on her prettiest dress. She danced about. I couldn't get any sense out of her. She kept saying it was her big chance. When she had the interview in *Mamasan's* office, the owner asked her if she knew where he could find her sister, Ming Pei Sha.'

'Me?' I stared at her.

'He said his friend knew you, and the people at your house.'

'Do you know his friend's name?' I asked, but I already knew his name.

'I know his name,' said *Mamasan*, standing at the foot of the stairs. 'Otaka Wan. He is trying to find you.'

'Goodbye, Lily,' I whispered, and hurried down.

But the woman barred the way. Smiling, she said, 'There are times in life when we make mistakes, Miss Ming. If you leave now you will be making a big one. From the day you left Lo's house Otaka has been trying to find you. He can have the pick of a hundred women, yet you have taken his eye.'

'He hasn't taken mine,' I said, and pushed her aside.

At the door, she said, 'Then what is wrong with a job here? An attractive girl like you could be rich within a year. The hours are good – six in the evening until two in the morning. You would be expected to dance, certainly to entertain. You would receive four hundred dollars a week wage and anything you get in tips.' She looked at me, her eyebrows raising. 'If you wish to be bought out it costs the man a trifling amount, and anything he gives you is your own.'

I was measuring the distance between her and the door. She was a powerful woman. For some unaccountable reason I kept thinking of Johnny Burrows, the son of Ellie and Joe, the Americans I met in the Hilton: Johnny who died at Okinawa to make a better world, and most of all, a better East. The *Mamasan* said:

'Our owner is a good boss, and very generous. A girl with a decent flat – and he will find you one – can command a thousand dollars a week.'

'That is excellent money,' I said drily, but the cynicism died on her face. 'Now, if you will excuse me.'

'But I have telephoned Otaka Wan's office.'

'All the more reason why I should be going,' I said, and seized her in sudden strength and pulled her away from the door. Off balance by the unexpected attack, she staggered, and I was through the door and slammed it in her face. As I reached the pavement the door came open again.

'Miss Ming!'

I ran. And even as I ran a big Ford car passed me and slid up to the entrance of the bar. I heard a squeal of brakes. Seeking an alley, I turned down it swiftly. She called again:

'Ming Pei Sha!'

I ran faster.

29

IN THE EVENING of Jan's return I knelt before the Ming mirror, finishing my hair. Earlier I had been to a beauty parlour and had it done in the chignon style which Jan admired. With a borrowed iron I pressed my green cheongsam, with my few remaining dollars I bought new shoes and stockings. Unaware of time or period, I spent freely, forgetting the need even to eat. Soon Jan would come. In two hours' time he would arrive by plane at Kai Tak and my life would change. After this could come the material rush and tear of the job-seeking crowds, the starched, exquisite, painted loneliness of the counter-girl in the big store – the China Emporium, Wing On, or Sincere's – at any of these I would stand a reasonable chance of employment – until Jan was ready for me. And then – Manila! The thought of escape to happiness brought me to a pitch of suffocating joy. Two hours – only two hours. After I left the hairdresser I had wandered the streets between Jordan Road and Star Ferry, then up and down the counters of the vast Chinese Products in Nathan Road, for I never tired of the loveliness of the Chinese trades, the gorgeous brocades and emperor's sleeves, the tiger's eye, and jades from Pekin.

But back in the lodging-house I was consumed with a sudden self-criticism, and the immediate effect on me was explosive. Given to instant opinions on others, I had never paused to examine myself. My assessment of Otaka Wan, for instance, had been cruel and unjust. As honourable as the next man, I had converted him to a lower order by an outrageous bias. Next I remembered Lo, and the memory of his kindnesses covered me with confusion and regret. I had rejected his many virtues, caricatured his faults, and used my youth to pillory his age. Obsessed with my love for Jan, I had forged Lo's betrayal. It was unforgivable. Yet no surge of conscience diluted my need of Jan or shamed my love for him. Beside such a love all other emotions paled, conscience was stilled. This is the price of love. Integrity, even honour, will die before its onslaught.

Watching my face in the mirror, the changing expressions of joy, I began to think about Jan. The very thought brought me to an emotional pitch of longing that I had never experienced before; it was a physical pain that could only know relief in his arms. In quieter moments I had examined this emotion. It was incredibly strong; deeper than the mere desire to be subservient and please the loved one, it was now demanding, a passion, rich, insatiable in dreams. Without him I was a discontinued existence. With him life attained a deathless creation, as if I had been fashioned for his pleasure and my own completeness.

Dusk was settling on the crown of the China hills as I left the lodging-room. I took with me my two possessions, the blue labouring samfoo and the Ming mirror wrapped into a brown paper parcel. My few other belongings I laid at the feet of the beggar child, whose father was fast asleep as I closed the door. I had paid my rent. Tonight my sleeping cage would be occupied by another, for that is Hong Kong; one moves out, another moves in. I crossed Nathan Road, caught a bus to Kai Tak airport, and watched the gaudy neon lights flying past me. Through the rear window I saw Kowloon against its incandescent sky. How beautiful it was that evening! A Colossus of light, the bawdy, ill-defined galaxy of wealth that commanded Hong Kong. Somewhere in the strangling ropes of road lamps was the House of Lo, I thought: Lo would be there with his usual command, bowing to the beauty of Anna Toi on one hand, enduring the insults of Lo Tai on the other, and dragging by the tail the obese flirtations of the brothers, but this was not to be, for Lo Hin Tan never reached Hong Kong; neither did Otaka Wan or Anna Toi the beautiful, for they also died. The private plane they chartered was lost in typhoon a hundred miles south of Yaku Shima, a ball of fire, it was reported, falling into the sea. But I did not know this as I sat in the big red bus that raced through Kowloon. So Lo begot no son and Anna did not serve him. In death, Lo Hin Tan was free.

The air was sultry with the threat of the typhoon in which Lo died, the coloured flags hung motionless: but the great airport was vibrant and alive despite its apparent torpor. The restaurant was almost empty; the sweet, savoury smell of food induced a sudden hunger, and I remembered with a little shock that I had not eaten all day. I knew I could not afford a meal in the restaurant, so I took one of the high seats on the coffee counter. It was a quarter to ten. Flight 307 was already signalled. Ordering tea and sandwiches, I ate slowly, though now consumed by a sudden ravening demand for food. People began to come in with the excitement and jubilation of the homecomers, for a plane had just landed. Now a great jet roared over the tarmac in a flash of silver and red lights winking. I watched it slow on the runway, turn, and waddle back to the control tower in a high shriek of jets and wing-sag. The restaurant began to fill. As if signalled by the incoming draft of big passenger jets, they poured through the entrances in chattering, gesturing groups, diverted momentarily from the pressing needs of conversation by the crackle and imperious commands of the public address. I thought, watching them: this is an age of people, it is no longer an age of kings; this is a new era breaking on an ancient world. Within a hundred years the frightful decapitations of Kai Tak had changed to a scene of touch-button modernity. The centuries when life was cheap will die. While, within living memory, nearly a hundred million humans have perished through slaughter, flood, pestilence, and disaster, this new world ushers in a great revival of human hope. And, with the aid of machines, this great new world, even in Jan's time and mine, could build a pure resurge of the human soul. I watched the people flooding in, knew the great bond of their humanity. And I knew that they, with the aid of the machine, would reach out hands of friendship to massive peoples once beyond their reach: cultivate enormous deserts for their food, and build a tower of sweetness and unselfishness to crush the gluttony of the modern age. A new gladness seized me and I knew that I loved them. All these chattering faces, happy with expectancy – the arrival of a loved one – held in their hearts the same capacity for love as me. I was so enwrapped in this new and wonderful discovery that I noticed a few staring at me, their smiles dying with interest. I turned back to the counter on the high stool.

'Good evening, Miss Ming.'

I turned to the voice. It was Jan's mother.

I did not recognise her instantly, but instinctively knew her before the moment of recognition. She was much older than I had realised, her face harassed by the years: only her eyes were young, the eyes of youth, bright and alive in her sallow cheeks. Now she said, quite simply, 'You have come to meet Jan?'

'Yes.'

'In his letter he told us you would be here.'

She was nervous. Her hands were trembling and, on the high stool beside me now she folded them in her lap with deliberation, and said at them, 'I . . . I tried to get here earlier. I . . . I just had to speak to you. There was a traffic hold-up. A . . . a fire in Nathan Road, I believe.'

'I missed that,' I said.

We sat in a stricken silence and I fought my growing hostility. This was Jan's mother. Soon she would be my mother-in-law and

255

I would bow to her. Now I must show her respect; Jan would demand it. I said with an effort. 'You wanted to speak to me?'

A pulse in her temple was beating violently and the sight of it held my attention with rooted force. She was enduring a great emotion and I wanted to comfort her. Then panic seized me. I said, 'Jan's all right, isn't he?'

She nodded, smiling faintly, her bright eyes moving over mine.

'Jan was right. How beautiful you are.'

The public address bellowed between us, and in its pause she added, 'Oh God, I'm making a dreadful mess of this and it is so terribly important.'

I turned away. 'I think I know what you have come to say.'

For now I had realised the purpose of this meeting, and that she had planned it. And it was an approach so typical of a European. It had begun with flattery; soon would come her sincere understanding of my love for Jan and the predicament of that love, then an offer of friendship. Then there would be wonder at the wisdom of it, mention of the barriers between East and West, and blood, clan, custom. Social stigma if all else failed – the bright young European engineer and the Chinese concubine. All the old ghosts would be raised – ghosts that Jan and I had long since laid in the face of a love that was indestructible. Last would come talk of sacrifice, by Ming Pei Sha, then anger.

'How old are you?'

I said, 'I am twenty by your calendar, twenty-two by Chinese age.'

'And Jan is twenty-one – old enough for responsibility, but it is still very young, Pei Sha.'

I did not reply. I could have told her that I was older than she in the ways of men.

'You have known Jan for about two years?'

'I have known him all my life.'

She understood, nodding, smiling with a new sweetness, but I was determined not to like her, terrified by the possibility of weakening before her.

'Jan knew from the start that you were a concubine?'

'Almost from the start, but I am not a concubine now, Mrs Colingten.'

'Yes, I understand that you have left your husband.'

'I would have left him for Jan, but he was quicker. He left me.' I added, 'I deserved worse than this, but Lo is a gentleman.'

'You were a wife by Customary Marriage, I understand.'

'I was a legal wife. This is not a mistress,' I said. 'I was a wife in law. A concubine under Ching Law is not a mistress — she is not immoral.'

'My dear, I didn't suggest it. I have lived with the Chinese most of my life. I respect them, their laws, their culture. But does Jan also know that you have been a mother?'

I was beginning to dislike her. Somebody had been giving her information, and I was wondering who it might be. Lo? I doubted it. He would be far too active with Anna Toi to bother with such intrigue. Lo Tai? This was possible, but I could not rid my mind of visions of First Brother. Certainly he hated me enough. I was astonished that Mrs Colingten had stooped to listen to such gossip. She said:

'It is true that you have just had a child, isn't it?'

'Yes, it is true.'

'Was it Jan's child?'

I faced her instantly. 'It was not Jan's child. I was married to Lo Hin Tan.'

She said blandly, 'This may be so, Pei Sha, but who knows what can happen when people fall in love?'

I did not reply. She was not having me so easily. If I had shouted into her face that the child was Jan's it would have made her task supremely easy, and however much she disliked it she could snatch at it on moral grounds. Against the backcloth of duty and good manners, Jan, who had made his bed, must lie on it: the father must now come into it. The girl must not be abandoned, whatever the cost to the family honour, and I was having none of such damnable stupidity. I was very close to tears, and it infuriated me. I bit the inside of my mouth and tasted the sweet saltness of the blood, concentrating on the pain, and fighting back the tears. I was wishing her to the devil. At the very last moment, after weeks of waiting and pain, she had come to sully the hallowed moments of our reunion. It is terrible to me how the middle-aged forget the pangs and acute joys of their youth so soon.

'It was not Jan's baby?'

'It was not,' I said.

'I am glad, Pei Sha. I am also very sorry that your baby died.'

She did not believe me, of course. She knew the child was Jan's. She was a woman. In order to enforce the lie I should have been appalled at her suggestion, but I could not act the lie. It was effort enough, with Jan moments away from me, to just sit and lie, not really caring whether she believed it or not. Officially she had accepted it. Relieved of obligation, she was now free to bargain. Any moment now, I thought. Without doubt it would end as it always ended when the rich bargained with the poor. Money. I was ready for her.

'Strange that Jan never mentioned the baby in his letters home.'

I glanced at her. 'Why should he?'

'He told us everything else about you, but not this. He surely must have known.'

'Well, he did not know.'

'Why didn't you tell him?'

'Because he wasn't in the least concerned.'

'The girl he intends to marry and he wasn't the least concerned? You underestimate him, Pei Sha. Jan's no fool, and neither am I. Lo Hin Tan's seventy if he's a day. Listen, girl, my son is as normal as any other young man. If this child was his then his father should know about it.'

No fool this one. I did not reply immediately. In the vibrant air about me I felt, rather than heard, the growing jet-roar of a big plane. The sound seemed to consume me. I glanced at the clock. It was eight minutes past ten. Simultaneously, the public address announced crisply that Flight 307 BOAC was about to land from London and Singapore.

Mrs Colingten put down her coffee cup. 'You will probably have noticed that my husband isn't here tonight.'

It was stupid of me, but I had not noticed his absence. Strangely, I imagined he was lurking in his six feet height in some dark place, ready to pounce and devour me at the first moment of pause, when his wife was failing. I said, 'Why . . . why hasn't he come to meet Jan? He will be terribly disappointed, he adores his father.'

'His father loves him, but my husband has a will of his own. He has written to Jan telling him of his rooted objection to his marriage. The very fact that he has been seeing you has caused repeated quarrels in the house.'

I stared at her. It was like the last act of a fantastic play. Jan had never given me a hint of any trouble at home – he had even said that his father would approve of our marriage – as long as we left Hong Kong and started afresh elsewhere. Mrs Colingten said:

'Did you know anything of this?'

'I didn't think you even knew we were meeting.'

'That was optimistic of you. This is Hong Kong.' Quoting Confucius, she added, ' "All calamity comes by means of the mouth." The scandalmongers are as bright here as any other place.'

She spoke again but her words drifted over me, then I heard her say, 'Pei Sha – see the sense of it. How could we possibly approve of such an early marriage for Jan? He has had a wonderful education and his father has great plans for him. In anticipation of him getting through his exams he paid out big money to give him experience with a London consultant. He has even bought him a junior partnership in a firm here. My husband has tremendous influence in the Colony – everything at his fingertips, all the contacts necessary to the young engineer. In Manila he would be one of hundreds – sinking into some mediocre job for the rest of his life.'

'You are really saying that I would pull him down.'

'I am saying that it just won't work. You know people as well as I do. If it once leaked out who you were and what you had been Jan wouldn't last five minutes with the Europeans – here, in Manila, or anywhere else.'

I glared at her. 'This is all business, business! Where does love come into it?'

Instantly, 'That is what I am asking you, Pei Sha.'

I got down from the stool, suddenly lost. She was still speaking and I fought to obliterate her voice. For it was now an impassioned plea from the heart of a mother and I found it of little interest; certainly it stirred in me little emotion.

I would have preferred her angry.

For I could oppose the authority and pleas of this woman without conscience if needs be – blinding my sense of duty to an elder in my love for Jan.

But I could not forget Jan's father. To me it was terrible that I had come between them, and the authority of a father was too great to be challenged in the face of all I had been taught. The thought that I had divided father and son was terrifying. I deserved no pity in my loss, no sympathy for the crime. For it was not only against the laws of the Taoists and the great Confucius, it was against the law of life.

Mrs Colingten said, 'Jan should have told you the truth, Pei Sha. You were bound to know it in the end – just one letter telling the truth. It would have been kinder.'

The plane bringing Jan now rushed overhead and in the crescendo of its roar the public address was announcing it metallicly. Through the window I saw its torrent of darkness and crimson, flashing lights. I watched it until it was a speck of red light over Lyemun; saw it turn for the runway. Its headlights blazed and the finger of tarmac was a blade of light.

'What are you going to do, Pei Sha?'

I said, with an effort, 'I am going to meet Jan.'

'It is against all your laws, you know. And you will be the only one to meet him, for I am going home. I am in a terrible position. I stand between my husband and my son. In many things in our life together my husband has been wrong, but in this he is right. To join with you in greeting Jan is to condone your affair with him – yes, it was an affair, nothing more, for while you were in love with my son you were the wife of Lo Hin Tan.'

Mrs Colingten knew her Chinese. No better ambassador against our love than Mrs Colingten.

The plane had landed and was racing towards us. I was hypnotised by its very enormity and sounds. Slowly, gripping my hands, I moved away from the counter.

'God help you both,' she said.

Beyond the barrier, in the crush of people, I waited. The passengers, blocked by the Customs, were arriving in little groups or one by one. On the fringe of the friends and relatives I sought the oblivion of a crowd, seeking to lose myself in their private conversations, the brittle joy of their anticipation. But I could not forget Jan's father. His absence was terrifying proof of the rift between him and Jan, a chasm which to me was the death of love in its greatest purity. By Chinese standards, any interference with the spiritual union between father and son was a thought too outrageous to contemplate. Under the old laws of China only a pig-basket drowning death could absolve such a sin. And I stood there amid the chattering people, trying desperately to bridge the gap that I had blown between them. But there was no way save one. This is the extremity of loneliness – the unsolvable problem amid the laughter of the crowd. I heard Jan's voice, not in the maelstrom of that place, but in the secret places of our love. Now surrounded by new arrivals, I lowered my head and gripped my hands in a frantic evocation of the sound of him, the sight of him running on Yim Tin Tsai. In an effort to snatch the courage that would keep me in his path, I conjured up the most intimate moments of our love, the most joyful and abandoned, aye, and the saddest, in farewell. Yet nothing removed the terror of a tainted filial piety. When all attempts to revive reasons of justice and raise the banners of the right to love failed, this sin against parenthood remained violent, tangible, and its horror was growing within me; there was no release from its consuming sense of shame. I looked around. Yet another plane roared in, still more people crowded in to greet the travellers. There was a strange security standing there on tiptoe with the black shoulders of men about me, and I moved to an even denser part of the waiting crowd. And then I saw Jan. I saw his bright hair first, lost it, then got another glimpse of him at the head of the crowd. He was looking about him, disappointment on his face. He looked thinner, almost ill, and a new panic gripped me. The people moved. When I looked again Jan had gone and I fought myself through men and women, ill-mannered, elbowing for room, until I reached freedom. I saw Jan again, but this time I saw his back. Obviously believing that I was waiting outside, he was striding towards the exit. Nothing was between us. I could have called once and it would have halted him – one short cry of greeting and raised one hand, and he would have stopped: stopped, lowered his suitcase, and run back to me.

'*Pei Sha!*'

But I did not call to him. With my bundle held against me I watched his tall figure reach the exit, and turn from sight.

Following him slowly, I reached the door. As I had expected, his mother had not gone and Jan was talking to her urgently. With fifty yards between us I almost heard her calm, consoling replies. Pei Sha had not come. She could not understand it. No, she had not seen her. It was inexplicable. She was Chinese, he must remember: to set against their many attributes the Chinese had little sense of time. Had she said she would come to meet him?

A taxi drew up. Jan, with a last look about him, opened its door. And his mother, in the moment before she got in, turned and looked deliberately in my direction. I drew into the shadows. She could not see me but she knew I was watching from the airport building.

To my astonishment Jan actually called:

'*Pei Sha!*'

I did not move. Leaving the taxi he walked to a raised plinth nearby and upon this he stood for greater height. The window of the taxi went down. His mother called. With the relaxed air of a man defeated he went back to her, got into the taxi, and slammed the door. It drove away. I watched it until it reached the junction of the Olympic Avenue, saw the red blaze of its brake lights as it reached the traffic.

'Goodbye, my sweet,' I said.

30

I HAD TO see Suelen. Nothing but her presence could remit this violent sense of loss.

Crossing the road to Kowloon City I caught the New Territories bus to Ho Chung village, remembering with a little surge of relief that I was going towards the sea. In a sort of clenched despair I stared through the flying window at the incredible, incandescent glare of Prince Edward Road. It was more than just illumination, it was a configuration of beams and flashes, a new world of radiance, blinding in intensity. And this rape of light slowly dimmed as we rocked and swayed past the Tung Tau Tsuen Resettlement, great concrete land-locked ships of winking windows overlooking the sheet-calm harbour of Kowloon. Now the quiet countryside, serene under the hand of night, the land of the Hakka and tiny homesteads. Calmer now, I saw far below me the water of Pak Sha Wan, the clustered play-boats of the rich: the distant Marina was a diamond of light in the darkness. The bus whined along, myself and a little bald-headed gnome of a man in the front seat its only passengers. In a smell of burned electricity and diesel we went, rocketed into insensibility, lured towards sleep by tyre-whine and the world of flying darkness beyond the windows. But at the great height above Hirons Highway I saw the sea beyond the Ninepins in a sudden and glorious sheet of moonlight, and *more* – I saw on the sea the fleet of Sai Kung in line for the northern fishing grounds, sails full set. It was a barbaric sight of age and power – the batwinged sails, unchanged for a thousand years of sea-going: a panorama of marvellous purity after the artificial neon flashes and traffic roars of Kowloon. On the edge of the seat I stared down at the sea. Right across the horizon they were spread, the three-masted big boys, a small army of thumping diesels and wind-lash, rolling, spitting, flinging their prows up to the crested rollers, swilling their bilges full length with foam. The little gnome in front saw, and turned from the phenomenon.

Speechless, he pointed down at the sea and the scouring Ninepins.

'*Ah!*' I said.

The bus swung round the hairpin at Hirons and we clung on, still staring, but the wonderful vision of power and freedom was gone.

And in going, it had taken me.

'*Do not go, Pei Sha,*' said Jan. '*If you go to Sai Kung I will come to Sai Kung – wait there for me.*'

I rose and went unsteadily to the back of the bus, staring at the clouded hills all tinted silver to a sudden blaze of moon. And reaching into me, thrusting aside the despair, greater even in intensity than my love for Jan there came a sea-call of a violence I had never known before. And the call grew into a clarion cry that dominated my spirit, banishing every emotion of sadness. It was a wild call, untamed and free: it was all wave-crash and spume and wind. It came up from the lonely wastes where men feared to go, and it possessed me. It reeked of timber and tar, and tang of new hempen ropes; and it had sound as well as smell and form. The bus stopped. 'Ho Chung,' said the driver.

I did not move to face Ho Chung village and my sister Suelen, for this was not to be.

'Sai Kung,' I said, and gave my last dollar. The bus ground its gears, and blundered on.

It had gentleness as well as violence, this cry of the sea. It had love and hate, and the threat of death in bubbling, distended torture: it had the joy of life in full when you swung the prow two points starboard and ran her goose-winged for the homing run – down the hissing, roaring sea-lanes of the Shamshuipo tugs and the New China barges with their starred pennants flying. Along the coast of Kwangtung it went, as it had gone for generations of seafarers, calling, commanding as it now commanded me.

Only in the sea could I wash myself free of this lost love.

I ranged the length of the rumbling bus, my samfoo bundle in one hand, the Ming mirror in the other, seeking yet another glimpse of the Sai Kung fleet by moonlight, but the contorting rocks of Hebe Haven, where Jan and I made love, barred the way. Past the little fish restaurant we went, and I remembered with a new joy the little white junk with its white and scarlet sail, and the way we ploughed her through the Narrows; past the Stranger's Grave and the brilliant houses of Clearwater Bay, there to watch the dawn come raging over the hills of China. The bus stopped. Lost, clasping my memories within me with such intensity, the sudden calm surprised me, but then I saw Sai Kung, and leaped down from the footboard.

The village was quiet. Slowly I walked down Tak Long Middle Street, reliving the memories of that same walk five years ago, after the typhoon. The little stores selling kerosene were still open, the food shops and stalls doing a brisk trade. Outside the Tea-house of Exalted Virtue sat the bald elders, their expressions inscrutable behind the great bamboo pipes. Mothers were on their haunches along the sea-wall, feeding their babies; urchins and girl-mothers were prancing hop-scotch along the uneven flagstones. It was the same, changeless Sai Kung that I had always loved, and the sight of it, the smell of it brought me to joy, and more than joy. It was consoling, a balm to my very weariness, and it welcomed me as Sai Kung welcomed everybody – friend, stranger, with its smiles and nods;

knowing, safe in its heroism and legends, that it could afford such generosity.

Now I saw the sea, again. It was astonishing in brilliance. Under the full summer moon it possessed a quicksilver beauty I had never seen before. And more – the fishing fleet was still leaving. At the end of the quay the last great junks were moored, savaging their cables with the lust for action, and from them came the old beloved music; the hoarse cries of the Old Men, the shrieks of wives and children. Dogs barked, hens crowed and scratched in their aft pens. The last stores were going aboard, their decks were swarming with women and old men net-mending and baling storm canvas, for the sky that morning was bronze, some were saying, and there was a sea-bitch moving in at eight knots east from the coast of Luzon.

I was trembling. With my eyes fixed on the junks I ran, found a dark corner of the sea-wall, and there squatted. I untied my blue labouring samfoo and clog sandals and rolled them on the cobbles. I stood up and pulled the sleek, green cheongsam over my head and rolled it into a bundle around my high-heeled shoes. Swiftly, in gasping haste, I fought my way into the sam-foo, and kneeling, drew on the clogs. I pulled down my hair and plaited it. Grabbing the Ming mirror I ran round the end of the sea-wall to the jetty and joined the thronged activity of the departing junks.

And I saw him immediately. He was old and grizzled, he was a sea-dog, and I knew him on sight.

'Fan Lu!'

It was Po Shan's mutilated friend of the sampan, and his missus: old enough for dead crows, the pair of them; once sampan, now junk people, going up in the world.

On his knees at the prow, knotting up an anchor cable, he did not hear me at once.

'Fan Lu!'

My shriek turned him and the companion canvas went back and the head of his old wife came out.

'Missus!' I cried, delighted.

'Ming Pei Sha!'

His wife cried, waving a dish-cloth, 'Old Man – look, Pei Sha – Chu Po Shan's child! The sister of the big Hakka!'

'And Hui, and Tuk Un. *Ai-yah!*' Rising, he stared at me.

'You come aboard? Us just leaving,' yelled his wife.

'Where for you leaving?'

'Big snapper moving up Kwangtung – everybody going out.'

'And just you two?' I asked. 'You got no crew?'

'I got man sons.'

'Got room for girl daughter, Fan Lu? I cook good, I feed you proud. And I fish the best of them like a man – you heard Po Shan say, eh?'

'She fish with men,' said his missus.

'Where you been, child?' Fan Lu peered, his red eye blinking from his scalded face.

'Never mind where I been – you take me Kwangtung?'

He turned his back and cried hoarsely, 'Ah, you Po Shan's child, you come aboard.'

I leaped the six feet into the heaving junk. His sons were nudging and whispering as I crawled into the aft cabin; boy-sons, eighteen and twenty, if I remembered right: children, and I was old. They would not pester me.

Within minutes we sailed, under the summer moon of Tin Hau, who ordains and governs all things.

Eyes closed, standing on the stern amid the fumes and booming of the diesel, I watched Sai Kung fade into moonlight. Past the Stranger's Cave we went, and before us the fleet was a string of black pearls tossing on the threatening sea, for the moon had dropped skirts over her brightness.

I watched Hong Kong gather light-shape in the blackness; an orgy of brilliance, the mantle of her suffering; a cement wilderness of ambition, without history, without future, the vast clearing-house of the East where capital gains are bought with human dignity and blood. Land of sacrifice, of warm generosity, of greed at its fantastic worst and courage at its proud best. Possession Point, Aberdeen and Repulse Bay! Kennedy Town and Causeway Bay, the Peaks of riches and poverty, the houses of greed, the homes of the saints. *Hong Kong!*

I took aim into the wind and flung the cheongsam high, and the wind took it gladly, floating it down on to the sea. It sank almost instantly, shimmering and waving in phosphorescent shapes of green until the wake got it, churning it high and drowning it in foam.

'Goodbye, my darling,' I said.

But I knew no sadness standing there watching the island mounding the world with light, for behind me, in the grey wastes roaring along the coast of Amoy my beloved Hui and Tuk Un would be sailing – Tai Tai and her adopted son Yin Yin – even Chen Fu Wei, her baby, and the primitive Chu Po Shan.

And his very savagery called me. . . .

'Pei Sha!'

I heard the command of the Old Man, but did not answer. Jan, I thought, might be sleeping now; soon another, a bright-eyed English girl, would lie beside him, and I would no longer be a part of his dreams. Suelen would be hand in hand with her beloved Kwai, their son between them. Orla would be obliging, with honeying kisses, all her lonely men; Lily Ting clutched in the terror of her childhood.

'*Ming Pei Sha!*' It was Fan Lu again, his voice sharper. But I dreamed at the sea, lost in my love for Jan, disobedient to commands. The long, lazy afternoons of Lo's house, the pampered years had softened me and thieved my birthright. Fan Lu again, up on his pins, furious, his stumpy arm waving.

'*Tan-gar!* I called you twice! *Mooning bitch!* If I call again you'll go back ashore first landfall. You hear me? *Tan-gar!*'

I leapt to face him, joyful. I was safe, I was whole again.

'*Ah! Coming!*' I cried.

Race of the Tiger

Alexander Cordell

He left the grinding poverty of the Old World for the jungle-law life of the New

Born to the riveting penury of nineteenth-century Ireland, Jess O'Hara and his high-spirited sister, Karen, flee their wretched homeland for a new life in America.

Exhausted after a nine-week crossing in an overcrowded, disease-ridden "coffin ship", they arrive in Pittsburgh— the thrusting, turbulent steel capital of the United States. Surrounded by smoke and fire-belching chimneys, deafened by the beat of giant hammers, they struggle to adapt to this alien world.

At first resisting the tug of easy wealth, Jess forsakes his fellow immigrants and bulldozes his way to fame and fortune, exploiting the love of two women to become a financial tiger in a city where mere jungle-law prevails.

"The most compelling book I have read for a long time . . . dramatic on a breathtaking scale"—*Manchester Evening News*

"Vastly entertaining, fast-moving, full of splendidly full-blooded characters"—*Books and Bookmen*

"A great Technicolour epic of a book, full of heart"
—*Sunday Times*

Richard "Crouchback" they called him, the last of the
Plantagenets, the vilest king that ever sat on the throne of
England, with the vilest emblem of any English king.
The emblem of

The White Boar

Marian Palmer

"The Rat, the Cat, and Lovell our Dog,
Ruleth all England under an Hog"

Here is a superb historical novel of the life and times of
Richard III, branded for centuries as one of the most
infamous princes ever to wear the English crown.

Richard—seen in this novel through the eyes of
Francis and Phillip Lovell—emerges as a complex
character, full of violent contrasts and red-blooded
emotions.

The battles, the duels, the love-affairs, the pomp and
pageantry of the royal court, the treason and intrigue that
brought death to the Plantagenet dynasty, the bloody
Wars of the Roses—all are here, vividly recaptured and
energetically portrayed.

Robert the Bruce:
The Steps to the Empty Throne

The first of three superb novels about
Scotland's greatest hero

The heroic story of Robert the Bruce
and the turbulent struggle for an
Independent Scotland

The year is 1296 and Edward Plantagenet, King of England,
is determined to hammer the rebellious Scots into
submission. Bruce, despite internal clashes with that
headstrong figure, William Wallace, and his fierce love for
his antagonist's god-daughter, gives himself the task of
uniting the Scots against the invaders from the South.

And so begins this deadly game for national survival—with
battle-scarred Scotland as the prize.

"Very readable . . . the author weaves his way authoritatively
through the highways and byways of this bloodthirsty
period, and paints some life-like portraits of top people of
the time."—*Daily Telegraph*

"Mr Tranter writes with knowledge and feeling."
—*The Scotsman*

"Nigel Tranter's gift of storytelling is aided in this superb
tale by a wealth of historical incident and colour."
—*Darlington Evening News*

Russell H. Greenan

In the tradition of *Rosemary's Baby*—a spellbinding
novel of murder and the Supernatural.

It happened in Boston?

"Lately I have come to feel that the
pigeons are spying on me . . .

Thus reads the first line in this fascinating tale of a genius.
A man endowed with a talent as glorious as Leonardo's
and an imagination which transcends the Fourth Dimension.
But his genius is no match for the hazards of modern life—
the stupidity, the greed and the treachery he finds all
around him.

   He decides to communicate with God. Not through the
usual channels but person-to-person, face-to-face. Why,
how and when he succeeds is the theme of this extraordinary
novel.

   And it all happened in Boston. Boston is anywhere,
yesterday, today and tomorrow.

"A superbly macabre and satisfying novel. The details are
grisly, the people lunatic but the results are magnetic"
—*New York Times*

"It is a book of many parts—all of them delightful—but
mostly, it is very funny, a book of exhuberant comedy"
—*Look Magazine*

"This fantastical and compelling first novel"
—*Time Magazine*

GREAT READING FROM THE BEST AUTHORS
IN CORONET BOOKS

		Alexander Cordell	
☐	15383 0	RACE OF THE TIGER	40p
☐	15814 x	Marian Palmer THE WHITE BOAR	40p
☐	15098 x	Nigel Tranter ROBERT THE BRUCE: The Steps To The Empty Throne	40p
☐	15885 9	Alison MacLeod THE TRUSTED SERVANT	30p
☐	15807 7	NO NEED OF THE SUN	35p
☐	15111 0	Norah Lofts THE KING'S PLEASURE	35p
☐	12360 5	Ellis K. Meacham THE EAST INDIAMAN	35p
☐	15021 1	D'Arcy Niland DEAD MEN RUNNING	35p
☐	15074 2	Russell H. Greenan IT HAPPENED IN BOSTON?	35p
☐	15100 5	H. Rider Haggard SHE	30p
☐	12504 7	John O'Hara BUTTERFIELD 8	30p
☐	16071 3	Henry Sutton VECTOR	40p

All these books are available at your bookshop or newsagent, or can be ordered direct from the publisher. Just tick the titles you want and fill in the form below.

....

CORONET BOOKS, Cash Sales Department, Kernick
Industrial Estate, Penryn, Cornwall.

Please send cheque or postal order. No currency, and allow 7p
per book (6p per book on orders of five copies and over) to cover
the cost of postage and packing in U.K., 7p per copy overseas.

Name...

Address..

....